THE HISTORY OF NOW

THE HISTORY OF NOW

DANIEL KLEIN

The Permanent Press
Sag Harbor, NY 11963

For information, address:
   The Permanent Press
   4170 Noyac Road
   Sag Harbor, NY 11963
   www.thepermanentpress.com

Library of Congress Cataloging-in-Publication Data

   Klein, Daniel M.
      The history of now / Daniel Klein.
          p. cm.
      ISBN-13: 978-1-57962-181-0 (alk. paper)
      ISBN-10: 1-57962-181-3 (alk. paper)
          1. City and town life—Fiction. 2. Intergenerational relations—Fiction. 3. Life change events—Fiction. 4. Colombians—United States—Fiction. 5. Massachusetts—Fiction. I. Title.

   PS3561.L344H57 2009
   813'.54—dc22   2008039875

Printed in the United States of America.

For Freke

ACKNOWLEDGEMENTS

The characters in this novel are entirely a product of my imagination, but the town of Grandville itself—its geography, demography and, to a lesser extent, its history—are patterned after the town I call home: Great Barrington, Massachusetts. For some information I used about the town of Grandville/ Great Barrington, especially its old theater, I am indebted to our diligent local historian, Bernard Drew.

I am also indebted to my friend, Pato Fornou, for telling me in dramatic detail about the lives and personal histories of Latinos living in New England towns.

A number of friends and family members read various drafts of this book: Tom Cathcart, Liz Socolow, Hester Velmans, Denis Clifford, and Lee Kalcheim; my wife, Freke, and my daughter, Samara. They are patient, acute, and generous readers all, and I hope they know how much I appreciate their help.

My agent and friend, Julia Lord, has once again gone far beyond professional duty in helping me with this book, knowing how important it is to me.

As always, I am deeply appreciative of Beverly and Kim Kimball, known to us on the Third Floor of 292 Main Street as the Medicis of Main Street. Generously, if unwittingly, they have supported a fertile art colony in their old building here.

Finally, I wish to thank Marty and Judy Shepard, co-publishers of The Permanent Press, for taking the risk of publishing a philosophically inclined novel in the early 21st century.

—DMK

"If we take eternity to mean not infinite temporal duration but *timelessness,* then eternal life belongs to those who live in the present."

—LUDWIG WITTGENSTEIN

PROLOGUE

Although at the time there were no laws shielding the identities of juvenile offenders, the name of the teenager who set the Melville Block ablaze in 1892 is unrecorded and long forgotten. What is known is that the boy subsequently torched the McCauley Cigar Company on Railroad Street and a stable in Housatonic before finally being caught and sent off to reform school in Boston. Still, like the unknown soldier entombed in Arlington Cemetery, the unknown pyromaniac of Grandville, Massachusetts is invoked here with something akin to honor—a sort of nefarious patron saint, the boy who single-handedly ignited Grandville's glorious renaissance.

The names of the four men comprising the business syndicate that resurrected the Melville Block are known to anyone who inspects the granite cornerstone on the corner of Melville and Main streets today: Jay M. Cosgrove, a New York City industrialist who summered in his family's 'cottage' in nearby Lenox; Isaiah Smith, a Yale friend of Cosgrove who was in banking; William W. Watts, an English-born land speculator; and Hans Quirinus deVries, the sole Grandville native in the mix and the former owner of DeVries Clothiers, which went up in flames with the rest of the original wooden building.

The four met every Sunday afternoon (except Easter) from March through November of 1893 to discuss their vision for the new structure. Usually these meetings took place in Cosgrove's stove-heated study in his twenty-room cottage known as 'Sway Lodge,' but at least three times they convened at deVries's far more modest digs, his six-room Dutch colonial on Upper Mountain Road in Grandville. If that setting was less grand than Sway Lodge, the refreshments surpassed anything Cosgrove's cook ever offered, with the possible exception of Cosgrove's imported brandy. That is because Hans deVries's wife, Françoise, set the table.

French Canadian by birth and mother tongue, Françoise was a supremely talented and painstaking cook. The Melville group was welcomed with a tub of raw oysters, followed by a dish of fried smelts dabbed with *aioli*; next, sweetbread pâtés and rice croquettes. At their second meeting in the deVries home, although it took place in the middle of a winter afternoon hours before suppertime, Françoise presented the assembled planners with a half dozen quail with truffles.

As it turned out, the petite, dark-eyed Françoise was a hostess with an agenda. She fervently wanted the new, fire-resistant, Pennsylvania pressed Roman brick and white marble building to include a theater. Not merely some social hall-cum-proscenium, but a grand theater, one that would rival Le Monument National on the rue Saint-Laurent in Quebec, a theater she had only been inside once, but which had made an indelible impression on her. Of course, Françoise left it to her husband to offer this proposal, yet each time he brought it up, she would miraculously appear from the kitchen hoisting a plate of mouth-watering delicacies.

At first, Cosgrove, Smith, and Watts would hear none of it; a theater was an investment sink hole. Grandville had fewer than six thousand citizens, at least half of whom could not afford a plate of oysters, let alone a theater ticket. Perhaps an especially popular theatrical could draw an audience from Stockbridge and Lenox, maybe even from Albany, but how often might that happen? Once a year? Twice? Shops, offices, taverns, a small hotel—cubic foot by cubic foot, *that's* where the profit on our two hundred thousand dollar investment lies!

Enter Françoise deVries with a plate of steaming asparagus blanketed with nutmeg-scented hollandaise. She is singing. No, not chanting some cheerful, housewifey ditty as she scoops the stalks onto the men's plates, but singing full out, "La Pute Protestante," from the operetta *Nell Gwynne*. She is a contralto with a silverware-jangling vibrato modeled after Lillian Russell. Not even Hans has ever heard her vocalize with such passion, and certainly not at such volume. She concludes on a thrilling high C (optional in the original score). Stunned silence follows, then a full minute of applause. Jay Cosgrove knocks his asparagus fork against his ale mug, calling for order. "I suggest we name the theater, the Phoenix," he says.

This is but one of several variations on the story. Another has Françoise entering the deVries salon warbling, "Master, master, do not leave me! Hear me, ere you go!" from *The*

Pirates of Penzance, and Cosgrove (as Fredrick), crooning back, "Faithless woman, to deceive me, I who trusted so!" An unlikely scenario, considering how racy the Gilbert lyric was regarded at the time, especially as sung on a Sunday afternoon in a family salon in New England. But, singing or no, from the minutes of that meeting preserved at the Grandville Historical Society, it is clear that on that November Sunday a motion was passed to construct a theater at the high end of the Melville Block, contiguous with but separate from the main edifice. Further, for obvious reasons but without comment, this theater would be known as the Phoenix—a roundabout tip of the hat to the anonymous arsonist.

For the project, Cosgrove selected a Pittsfield architect who previously had designed a cavernous bank in that city and a birdcage-like conservatory for Sway Lodge. His name was Karl Klopp and, much to the deVries's dismay, he had never designed a theater in his life. Upon meeting Klopp, Françoise deVries even had her doubts that the clean-shaven young architect had ever been inside one. Surely, the deVrieses were in no position to protest Cosgrove's choice. They had won Françoise's major goal and would not have been about to risk that by objecting to the designated architect. Furthermore, though Hans deVries constituted one fourth of the Melville project's board of directors, his actual monetary investment was one quarter of that quarter—just his $6,000 settlement from his Hartford Fire Insurance policy. Hans's fellow directors were all gentlemen, so the relative size of his share was never mentioned—at least in his presence—but it must have put an unspoken limit on Hans's options for disagreement.

Hark! Once again, Françoise deVries flies in from the wings, but this time in lieu of tender morsels and treble warbles, she comes bearing train tickets. With money she had been saving scrupulously for a theater trip to New York City, she has purchased a roundtrip ticket from Bennington to Quebec on the Central Vermont and Canada Railroad. Her first thought was to accompany Klopp on the excursion, but even this free-thinking woman recognizes the inappropriateness of that idea. Instead, she arranges for her maiden cousin, Camilla, of

Quebec City, to serve as Mr. Klopp's guide and translator on his tour of Le Monument National.

Françoise's scheme was exceeded by reality. Not only did young Karl Klopp create detailed drawings—many embellished with egg tempura wash—of the elegant French Renaissance theater, but on the spot he sketched a modestly scaled-down version of that theater that would serve as a template for the Phoenix of Grandville. Everyone—even Cosgrove—was impressed by Klopp's diligence and surprised by the passion with which he undertook the project. That is, everyone but Françoise who, a few days after Klopp's return, received a letter from Cousin Camilla describing in breathless, Gallic prose, her *liaison erotique* with the smooth-cheeked American architect at the newly-erected Château Frontenac.

Cubic foot by cubic foot, the Phoenix cost more than twice the rest of the new building complex, but it was vividly clear to even the humblest Grandville farmer that the theatre was the jewel in the new Melville Block's crown. The December 30th, 1899, *Grandville Chronicle* deemed it "as up-to-date as any playhouse in the country. In size, it ranks with many a so-called metropolitan theatre, while in equipment and decorative features, the structure has no superiors." Opening its doors for public inspection eight years after the infamous blaze, the Phoenix was as much celebrated for its fire safety features—asbestos curtains, automatic fire extinguishers, exits galore—as for its Nile green, rococo appointments.

Yet a melancholy shadow flickered across those asbestos curtains on opening night. Hans deVries had succumbed to pneumonia just weeks before that curtain—the final touch—was hung. After the orchestra had tuned up, but before the overture to the comic opera, *Happyland*, began, Jay Cosgrove took to center stage and asked for a minute of silence in honor of his beloved colleague. But the show, of course, went on. And Françoise deVries, in ink-black, crape cloth widow's weeds patterned after Queen Victoria's, sat front and center, flanked by Cousin Camilla and Karl Klopp.

Every seat, numbered in brass plates from 1 to 1000, was occupied that evening, just two months into the exhilarating new century. Indeed, the audience came not only from Stockbridge, Lenox, and Albany, but from Boston, New York City, and, in the person of Camilla Carriere, from Quebec City. Featuring the flamboyant De Wolfe Hopper and a cast of one hundred—*count them!*—players, *Happyland* elicited more laughs, tears, and standing ovations than at any of its New York performances. It played to packed houses in the Phoenix for six consecutive days.

Filling the office and shop spaces of the new Melville Block proved more difficult. The three-story structure, imposing and sun-filled as it was, remained at only one-third occupancy through *Happyland* and the *All Star Vaudeville* bill that followed one month later. But the latter show—again featuring Mr. Hopper, this time reciting "Casey at the Bat" (a *tour de force* that kept Hopper in work well into his sixties), plus the conjurer, J. Warren Keane; Pierce and Roslyn singing the one-act operetta, *The Toreador*; and the dancing comediennes, Misses Ranier and Gaudier—marked a turning point for the Melville investors.

Sitting in the balcony of the *All Star*'s second-night audience was one Billy Cannon from Cork, Ireland, by way of Boston. A rosy-faced man with a handlebar moustache, Billy had risen from rag picker to barkeep to South Boston pub owner in his ten years on this side of the Atlantic. He had journeyed to Grandville by train and coach expressly to hear De Wolfe Hopper declaim the mighty Casey's exploits. He was not disappointed. During the intermission, when Billy Cannon stepped out onto Melville Street to light up a cigar on that frigid March 1900 evening, he made a remarkable observation: there was nary a pub in sight. Yes, around the corner on Railroad Street there were pubs aplenty, pubs not unlike his own Bottle and Corker in South Boston—loud, dirty, awash in ale and stinking from it, and crowded with men in overalls whose ejected wads of tobacco failed, nine times out of ten, to reach the cuspidors. But, Cannon noted, the Phoenix crowd was a wholly different sort, more likely to sip port than swill ale, and entirely willing and able to fork over one half of a silver dollar apiece to dine on sweetbreads and lake trout. The following week, using the Bottle and Corker as collateral, Cannon borrowed a mid-three-figure sum from Boston's First National Bank, and initiated plans for the Phoenix Café. It was up and running for opening night of George M. Cohan's *So This Is London!* So overwhelming was his patrons' response that first evening that Cannon ran out of trout by ten o'clock.

An intimate and stately transit hotel followed only months after the café opened, then a dressmaker's shop, a tobacconist, and a wine and spirits emporium, filling the remainder of the Melville Block's street-level spaces. The upper floor offices, heretofore only occupied by a dentist, a doctor, two attorneys, and a real estate entrepreneur, quickly added a print shop, a barbershop, a telegraph office, and a good dozen other enterprises, some, like Fitzsimmons Iron Garments, of a mysterious and questionable nature. By January first, 1901, the Melville Block was at full capacity and turning an excellent profit for Messrs. Cosgrove, Smith, Watts, and the Widow deVries. No one doubted that the extraordinary success of the Phoenix Theatre was the font of their good fortune.

We shall speed ahead here as one theatrical after another rolls into town and onto the Phoenix's spacious stage—the operatic extravaganza, *Sunny Italy*; John Philip Sousa and his clamorous band; Eddie Foy in *The Earl and the Girl*; The Ed. Wynn Carnival, "A Frisky, Frivolous, Jazzy and Joyous Festival of Gaiety, Girls, Music, Scenery, Costumes, Dancing, and Mr. Ed. Wynn Himself!" As it dances by, we also observe that Primrose's Minstrels, a black-face variety show, comes and goes without public comment by Grandville's small Negro community which, at the time, includes a bright young woman descended from travelers on the Underground Railroad whose son will later become a dedicated educator and lifetime member of the NAACP.

In time, the traveling theatricals become more expensive to produce, ticket costs soar, and the audience dwindles. A decade flies by, and then another. Like spectators in a dusky balcony, we watch as in fast motion the Widow deVries is courted and wed by Billy Cannon, then bears him a son, named Phillip, a half-brother to her son with Hans, Emile deVries. We applaud as, after his father dies, Phillip takes over the Phoenix Café, adding oysters and champagne, New York steak and fried onions to the menu. And we sigh wistfully as Emile closes and locks the six, capacious dressing rooms that flank the Phoenix stage before he dejectedly lugs a brand new Edison Vitascope up to a three-sided canvas tent he has erected at the front of the theater's balcony.

Ah, but how quickly those sighs abate as the Vitascope's powerful lamp erupts in a blaze of light, the sprockets catch, the gears turn, and on the eggshell linen bedcover Emile has suspended from the flyloft, a small-framed, mustachioed young man appears in a mourning coat and bowler hat, at once dignified and absurd as he casually trips ice skaters with the crook of his cane. Doubled over with laughter, we have all but forgotten the hundred-man operetta casts in full period costume, the fanciful, New York sets that required two horse-drawn lorries to transport, and the pit orchestras comprised of New York violinists and local brass and drum players. And when, after a brief pause while Emile changes reels, there appears on the screen a pair of granite-faced horsemen astride white stallions that are galloping directly at us, we slink down in our seats, thrilled and astonished. This magic surpasses anything we have seen on this stage before. Karl Klopp's meticulously hand-painted, Nile green curlicues spanning the Phoenix proscenium recede into the dark, vanishing like Karl himself, who left the area a decade earlier to take up a lonely residence in Montpelier, Vermont, halfway between Pittsfield and Quebec City—the home of a memory that only barely sustains him.

Under Emile deVries's stewardship, the Phoenix Motion Picture House, as it was renamed on the marquee constructed in 1926, once again became an entertainment Mecca, attracting patrons from as far as Schenectady and Springfield. They came to see *The Thief of Bagdad*, *The Birth of a Nation*, Buster Keaton in *Sherlock, Jr.*, Chaplin in *The Gold Rush*. For those who had only heard or read stories about the trench war 'over there,' the Phoenix brought it home with their sold-out screenings of John Gilbert in *The Big Parade*.

Emile married Sally Burton, one of the Burton twins from New Marlborough. He prospered. He and Sally bought twenty acres of farmland on the outskirts of Grandville and there built a fifteen-room, Greek revival estate that they proceeded to fill with children, nine in all, five girls and four boys. All of the girls married and remained in the county. Boys One through

Three went to college at the University of Massachusetts in Worcester, became lawyers, and went on to live in either Boston or New York. But the fourth son and youngest of the entire brood, a big-boned, barrel-chested boy named Wendell, never left Grandville. He never wanted to.

Wendell started helping out his father at the Phoenix when he was seven, selling tickets and handing out Vitagraph give-away cards with likenesses of motion picture stars like Helen Gardner or Leo Delaney on one side, and on the other, "Ode to Grandville," a trio of iambic couplets composed by his grandmother, Françoise. By the time he was thirteen, he could thread the theater's new, streamlined Brenkert BX-80 projector with one hand while rolling a cigarette with the other.

Wendell reveled in it all: threading and projecting motion picture film, spotting the watermark-like circle in the upper-right-hand corner of the screen that signaled a reel change and then doing so with undetectable precision, squinting through the six-inch window of the projection booth at the images on the glass-flecked screen below. He felt like a magician. A flick of the hand and he conjured up MacMurray and Stanwyck in *Double Indemnity* or Bogart and Bergman in *Casablanca*. His was the last commission in a process that had begun on a sound stage in Hollywood, and no less crucial than anything that had been done in California. Not that Wendell had any illusions about the artistry of his contribution—although there *were* times after, say, watching *Casablanca* eighteen times in a row, and mouthing every Bogart word and miming every Bogart gesture to perfection, when Wendell wondered just how much artistry it took to be a movie actor.

There was no reason for Wendell to go off to college, no reason for him to leave Grandville. He knew his vocation and it was right here. And so was the girl he intended to marry.

Her name was Beatrice Cosgrove. Yes, from the selfsame family as Jay M. Cosgrove, one of the original investors in the Melville Block along with Wendell's grandfather, Hans—although this congruence would mean little to them and even less to their families, especially hers. Beatrice was Jay M's grandniece, as well born by local standards as Jay Cosgrove's direct line of descendents, and far prettier by any standards. She was raised in a house adjacent to and only slightly smaller than Sway Lodge. Unlike Wendell, who coasted through Grandville's public schools, only distinguishing himself as a tackle on the high school football team, Beatrice attended Berkshire Normal School, and was then sent off to Abbot Academy in Andover. Like her mother and grandmother, she was destined for Wellesley College and undoubtedly would have gone there had not she sat in the next-to-last row of the Phoenix balcony for a Christmas Eve screening of *An Affair to Remember*.

It is 1957. Beatrice is seated next to Gwendolyn Fayette, an Abbot friend from Palm Beach who is spending the winter holidays with the Cosgroves. Both young women sport the popular French pleat hairdos of the day, wear plaid kilts fastened with oversize, brass safety pins, and collarless, pleated blouses with gold circle pins fixed daringly close to the spot where the pleats begin to separate to accommodate their burgeoning breasts. Both believe that Cary Grant is absolutely dreamy.

Directly behind them in the projection booth, Wendell deVries is smoking a Lucky Strike cigarette and reading a collection of sonnets by Edna St. Vincent Millay. The volume is his Christmas gift for his sister, Marie; he grabbed it, prewrapped, on his way out of the house, having already seen *An Affair to Remember* eleven times. To pass the time between reel changes, Wendell will read just about anything that is handy, including the copies of *Silver Screen* magazine that arrive, gratis, with every case of film, but also including the poetry books his sister lends him. Although he is, relatively speaking, uneducated, Wendell has a connoisseur's ear for verse. He is reading the lines, "If I should learn, in some quite casual way/ That you were gone, not to return again—" when he hears a plaintive cry just outside the booth. Looking down at the movie screen, he sees that Deborah Kerr has just been hit by a car on her way to meet Cary Grant atop the Empire State Building.

Wendell has heard such cries—invariably from women—eleven times before when the film reached this maudlin moment. So perhaps it is the confluence of the nearby whimper with those anguished Millay lines that compel him to rise from his padded chair, step to the projection booth door, open it, and search for the whimperer. He finds Beatrice immediately, for she is sobbing in earnest now, and embarrassedly has turned her head away from her friend to dab her eyes on her sleeve. Again, it may have been the Millay, but Wendell is overwhelmingly moved by the sight of this weeping girl, so much so that he descends to the row just behind her, leans down, and whispers, "It all works out in the end."

Beatrice is startled and now doubly embarrassed. For a mere fraction of a second, she looks angrily into Wendell's eyes and then turns back to the screen. Wendell returns to the booth just in time to launch the final reel. He closes the book of sonnets. He feels like a blockhead. But only a half hour later, after the final credits have concluded and Wendell is lining up the reels to be rewound, there is a soft rap on the projection booth door. It is Beatrice. Her eyes are cast down at the small purse she is clutching in both hands in front of her.

"That was kind of you," she says softly. "I'm sorry if . . ."

"I didn't mean to ruin it for you," Wendell replies. "It's just that you seemed so—well—distraught."

"I was."

"I'm sorry."

"Thank you," Beatrice says, now pulling on her camel hair coat and turning to join her friend.

Wendell desperately wants to delay her. Without thinking, he calls out to her, "Really! It *does* work out in the end!" and she smiles beautifully, then leaves.

Three nights later, the feature is *Peyton Place,* a racy exposé of the craven lives that lurk behind the gingham curtains of small-town New England. The press release accompanying the crate of reels states that the movie is thoroughly modern, an unflinchingly honest portrayal of real people. It even quotes a New York critic who declared that the film is "a rebuke of the Capra-esque romanticism that plagued Hollywood films of the previous decade." Wendell thinks they are all full of baloney. He regards *Peyton Place* as a laughable soap opera, less honest in its own way than *It's a Wonderful Life*, and far less entertaining. Tonight, after only one ungratifying viewing of the film, he is reading again, this time his Christmas gift from his brother, Seth, the bestseller, *Kids Say The Darndest Things!* by Art Linkletter. So far, Wendell finds the book only marginally more interesting than *Peyton Place* and he is wishing he still had the Millay sonnets with him for consolation. Below, Peyton Place doctor, Michael Rossi is intoning "I kissed you. You kissed me. That's affection, not carnality. That's affection, not lust. You ought to know the difference."

Wendell hears a derisive snicker just outside his window and recognizes its pitch and timbre instantly. It is Beatrice, again sitting in the next-to-last row of the Phoenix balcony, but this time alone. In a flash, Wendell is out of the booth and behind her.

"It only gets worse," he whispers.

She turns and smiles.

They fall in love.

Her parents object for the traditional reasons, so they elope. Beatrice's Wellesley career is forsaken. They rent a two-room apartment on Board Street to which, five years later, they take home their newborn daughter, Francis. *Irma La Douce*, blaring from newly-installed stereo speakers, is playing at the Phoenix.

Wendell and Beatrice are a doomed match. Less than a decade passes before Beatrice declares to her husband that she has "finally come to her senses." By this she means that being married to a film projectionist whose only ambition is to one day manage the local movie house is not fulfilling her. While raising Francis—first in the Board Street Apartment, then in half of a converted, two-family house on Mahaiwe Street—Beatrice has been reading hundreds of books, often one a day. In the year leading up to her devastating declaration to Wendell, most of those books were on the subject of the plight of women, including one volume that she bought through the mail and hid at night in her dressing table, entitled, *The Second Sex*. Beatrice moves back to her parents' grand cottage in Lenox, taking Francis with her, but the child will take every opportunity she can to be with her father.

It is the spring of 1968. After ballet class at Mrs. Hampton's studio, six-year-old Francis Cosgrove deVries walks down Main Street in her gauzy pink tutu and Keds. She waits for the light at Main and Melville, then crosses and makes her way to the Phoenix. Inside, she yells up to the projection booth, "I'm home, Dad," and Wendell calls back, "Hey, Sweet Patootie, be right with you." She skips down the center aisle of the theater and hoists herself up onto the stage. There, she balances on one leg, her beaming face turned toward the orchestra seats as she executes a wobbly arabesque. *Here I am! Look at me!*

I

~ *The Little World* ~

CHAPTER ONE

Next to the Phoenix Theater on the century-old, brick-and-marble Melville Block, is a shop where no fewer than thirty-two tradesmen have run and subsequently closed their businesses since 1901. The store, Write Now, sells newspapers, magazines, greeting cards, cigarettes, cigars, and candy, and is owned and operated by one of Grandville's most attractive natives, thirty-seven-year-old Francis deVries. Easily half of Franny's patrons drop by the shop just to chat with her and each other, buying a pack of Wrigley's gum or a cardboard cup of coffee by way of rent for their brief daily occupancy. And virtually every one of these visitors walks in the door telling Franny how lovely she looks today.

As anyone in Grandville will tell you, the town has been blessed with a disproportionate number of good-looking women. A visiting Los Angeles film executive is rumored to have quipped that he spotted more knockouts passing by the corner of Melville and Main than on the corner of Hollywood and Vine. Some attribute this phenomenon to the recently-arrived colony of Rudolf Steiner devotees whose macrobiotic diet and eurhythmic exercises appear to promote glowing, unblemished cheeks. A better bet is the even *more* recently arrived group of blue-eyed, blonde Ukrainian girls who waitress in the new, toney restaurants that dot Main Street. But the older folks in town insist that the top beauties are home-grown, the result of the blend of old Berkshire people and the immigrants, by which they mean the cross-pollination of the original, moneyed, cream-skinned, Anglo-Saxon families with succeeding waves of strong-featured Polish, Irish, and Italian mill workers. Yet this genetic concoction hardly distinguishes Grandville from most towns in the Northeast, plus, in most cases, it is out of date by at least two generations—the local mixes have mixed and mixed again with all manner of stock.

The theory both Franny and her dad jokingly subscribe to is that it is something in the water—all this Grandville pulchritude is generated by a rare, unidentified mineral that percolates into Great Pond Reservoir. "If either of us had a head for business, we'd bottle the stuff and sell it to all those New York harpies that come up here," Wendell deVries likes to say.

But even in this context, Franny deVries looks good—*damned* good, and not just for her age. She is long-limbed, smooth-skinned, and shapely, with wide-set, Delft-blue eyes from the deVries side, and pronounced, high-angled cheekbones from the Cosgrove line. Her face has always been lively and expressive, and became even more so after her three years studying drama at Ithaca College. Those years also contribute to Franny's theatrical flair for dress. Often she selects the day's outfit, hairdo, and make-up with an eye on a role, an aspect of her personality that she wants to bring to the fore for the day, usually just for her own amusement, though sometimes she has a few half-rehearsed lines in mind to go with her costume.

On this cool, September morning, Franny is standing at the window of Write Now in a pair of snug-fitting, Calvin Klein jeans and a tie-dyed, '60s vintage T-shirt that features the peace symbol. The prongs of the inverted 'Y' of the symbol seem to point straight to the tips of her breasts and Franny is well aware of that. It is just such touches that sell unorthodox ideas. Today, Franny is selling an end to the war in Iraq.

She smiles as two early-morning regulars approach the shop door: Archie Morris, the soon-to-retire fire chief, and Michael Dowd, one of the half-dozen second-homers who moved up to Grandville to live full time after 9/11.

"You're too sexy for your shirt," Morris says to her, holding the door open for Dowd. Although Morris is the same age as Franny's father—they graduated together in Grandville High's class of '56—he likes to keep up with what he believes is current lingo, and no one, least of all Franny, would think of telling him that his 'too sexy for your shirt' line is a good ten years out of date.

"Looks good to me," Dowd says, flashing Franny a peace sign. Like most New York transplants, Dowd arrived here with a preconceived portrait of small town life and his role in it. Certainly some of this picture comes from his summer vacations and winter ski weekends in Grandville, but much of it is an amalgam of books he has read (*Spoon River Anthology* was a favorite of his in prep school) and films he has seen (he owns the DVD of *It's A Wonderful Life*), plus a kaleidoscope of images torn from L.L.Bean catalogues. *Spoon River* accounts for the sepia-toned naiveté with which he imbues even the most wily Grandville natives, Bean for the red, clip-on suspenders that hold up his corduroy trousers this morning.

"Car bomb in Baghdad," Franny says, handing Dowd his reserved *New York Times* and *Wall Street Journal*. "Seven dead."

"How's the coffee today?" Morris asks.

"About the same as yesterday's, only a day older," Franny replies, sliding behind the counter to pour him a cup.

"How many of them were American?" Michael Dowd asks.

"None."

"Thank God for that," Morris says.

"Unless you happen to be Iraqi," Franny says, handing the fire chief his coffee.

Morris grins. "Too early in the day for politics, Franny," he says.

"It's the middle of the afternoon in Baghdad," Dowd says. Although Michael Dowd is in his mid-forties, he has never completely shed his earnest, smartest-boy-in-the-class manner.

"Didn't say it was too early in the day for *them* to talk politics," Morris retorts.

Franny cannot help but appreciate Archie Morris's effortless one-upmanship, the wisest wise guy in the class. Still, she wishes he would consider this awfulness in Iraq more seriously. "I just hate to see innocent people die for no good reason," she says.

Morris sips his coffee, says nothing for a moment, then, "Wendell going to get that new Angelina Jolie movie?"

"Hope not," Franny says. "I hear it stinks."

"Not if it's got close-ups of her lips," Dowd pipes up. "Pillows. They look like silk pillows." Dowd is clearly trying to regain some traction in the conversation with some man talk, and indeed, Archie Morris favors him with a knowing smirk. So much for the mayhem in Baghdad.

Dowd selects a Triple Threat Caramel Peanut Fusion PowerBar, pays up, and heads back for the door. "Babs is really looking forward to tonight," he calls to Franny before he leaves.

Michael Dowd will now make his way to the third floor of the Melville Block, then down the corridor to his three-room office containing eight computers, two fax machines, and a specially-wired phone system with five separate numbers, including two with a Manhattan prefix that relays to Grandville via 'call forwarding.' Here, with the assistance of two locally born young women, he manages the mutual fund he founded in New York, but with an overhead of less than twenty percent of his former office there. For this reason alone, Dowd blesses the day that he and Babs decided to leave Manhattan's Upper East Side for Grandville.

Archie Morris leaves the shop moments after him, taking a second cup of Franny's coffee with him. He will stroll past the Phoenix to the firehouse on its other side, the consequence of some curious, 1910 town planning that has pitted sirens and bells against singers and soundtracks for close to a century. There, as the only paid member of Grandville's volunteer fire department, he will sit beside the phone watching soap operas and talk shows on teevee for the next nine hours.

Only minutes later, a second pair enters Write Now: Franny's father and his dog, Binx, a mongrel terrier who has been Wendell's faithful sidekick for nine years. Wendell deVries is a big man, both in height and around the middle. His face is large and ruddy, capped with a full head of unruly white hair. That and the incipient grin that perpetually plays on his lips give him the appearance of an overgrown boy—say, a scruffy farm kid who is well known to the truant officer.

Last night, Wendell did not return to the half of the two-family house on Mahaiwe Street that he shares with Franny and her daughter, his granddaughter, Lila. This is not an unusual occurrence. Two or three times a week, after the evening's last screening and after he has perfunctorily cleaned up the theatre, shut off the popcorn machine, and locked the Phoenix's doors, Wendell stops at the Railroad Car, the last of the original taverns on Railroad Street and the bar of choice for native-born Grandvillians. There, he downs two or three double Scotches before stumbling back to the Phoenix to sleep in a brass bed in the largest of the old dressing rooms. On some of those nights, Wendell's lady friend, Maggie Bello, may join him. On those occasions, Binx sleeps fitfully in the theater wings, stage right. From the look of both Franny's father and his dog, last night was not one of those occasions—Binx looks rested and Wendell has clearly slept in his clothes.

"Hey, Monkey," Wendell says as he comes in. "You're the prettiest thing in the world."

"Runs in the family," Franny replies.

Wendell kisses her in the middle of her forehead, then scoots behind her to pour himself a cup of coffee.

"There was another car bomb in Baghdad," Franny says, pointing at the headline in the *Boston Globe*.

"This country is run by a bunch of assholes."

"I'm glad somebody notices," Franny says. She hands Binx half a bagel-with-peanut-butter sandwich left over from yesterday's lunch.

"Oh, people are starting to notice," her father says. "It just takes time to sink in."

"And how time flies while bodies are being dismembered."

Wendell offers his daughter a smile touched with both pride and reproach. He has always thought Franny over-dramatized things—a trait of her mother's exacerbated by her Ithaca theater training. But he also admires that pungent mouth on her; she is what his father used to call, "a firecracker."

Franny scribbles a few grocery items on a note pad, then rips off the page and hands it to her father.

"Jesus, tofu again?" Wendell says.

"She's got to get *some* protein in her," Franny replies. Last spring, when she turned sixteen, Lila declared that she was becoming a vegetarian, and although Franny approves in principle, she is worried sick that it is the first sign of anorexia, a condition that is currently sweeping Grandville High School.

"That stuff puts my bowels in an uproar," Wendell says.

"So get yourself a steak."

Wendell shrugs and stuffs the list into his back pocket. Both of them know that he will not buy himself a steak, and not because of the annoying complication of cooking two separate dinners. Rather, Wendell will not buy himself any red meat because of the sickened expression in Lila's eyes it would elicit. It does not really matter to him anyhow. He looks forward to his once-a-week dinners alone with Lila, even if lately she does not have much to say to him. Wendell is more than content simply to look across the kitchen table at his granddaughter. That act alone suffuses him with gratefulness.

After he leaves, Franny—honoring the new town ordinance—steps outside her shop for the first of her self-allotted, six cigarettes of the day. A few leaves have turned yellow on the tops of the poplars that line Melville Street. That, and the sudden absence of vacationers, put her in an inward mood. Franny is devoted to the change of seasons and to the changes of temperament that accompany each of them. She believes that people who live in single season climes, like the tropics, must lack a living sense of history. True enough, but then September is here again so quickly that it feels like last fall's melancholy never completely vanished. Franny smiles at the distinctly autumnal cast of her thought.

CHAPTER TWO

For the twenty-six years since Sally deVries passed away and Emile retired, subsequently selling the family home and moving to Arizona, Wendell deVries has been the projectionist and sole manager of the Phoenix Theater. But the tasks and routines that thrilled him as a boy and young man no longer do so. One reason is that in 1987, the heirs of Jay Cosgrove, Isaiah Smith, and William Watts, along with Emile himself, sold the theater to a chain headquartered in London. In itself, that would not have troubled Wendell—unlike his forebears, he never had an appetite for ownership. But along with the deed, the London group also took remote control of the basic operation of the theater: what films it would run, when, and for how long.

Yet Wendell still cherishes the place. He has a dog-like dedication to familiarity. The walls of the projection booth are his personal museum: a framed, hand-colored photograph of the original Melville Block investors; posters for All About Eve, The Court Jester, *and* Flame Over India; *the instruction manual for his first projector, the Brenkert BX-80; several Vitagraph cards; a good twenty out-of-date calendars; half a dozen pictures of Franny growing up, plus a half-dozen more of Lila. Layers. If at times, idly peering out of the booth's six-inch window, Wendell glimpses a patch of paint hanging from the Phoenix's vaulted ceiling or a tear in the back of a velour-covered seat, he sees it as natural history—maturation, not deterioration.*

Without informing the Phoenix's overseas owners, Wendell does not show films on Tuesday nights—which, in any event, are slow nights at best. He simply subtracts a few ticket sales from Saturday and plugs them in on Tuesday on his weekly receipt report. On Tuesdays, the Grandville Players take possession of the theater while Wendell feeds and, if she is in the mood, talks with his granddaughter. Later, Wendell is likely to pull a book from the shelf in the living room, there to read and smoke until Franny comes home.

* * *

After buttoning a denim work shirt over her T-shirt, Franny sets up ten folding chairs in a circle on the stage. The few foot-lights still operable are on, as are the cyclorama floods illu-minating the stage's brick rear wall. The lighting secludes the stage from the rest of the theater transforming it into an inti-mate space, although obviously anyone lurking about in the dark could plainly see what is happening onstage. Live drama depends on this pretense—intensely private moments shame-lessly exposed to public view—and Franny often wonders if this fundamental deception is theater's main allure for her. God knows, she is packed with hidden thoughts and feelings she yearns to expose.

Franny is sitting in the chair nearest the back wall munching on a Milky Way when the newest member of the Grandville Players arrives, Babs Dowd. She is an angular woman with straight, shoulder-length, auburn hair who wears wool sweaters and tweed skirts undoubtedly bought at the same Lenox dress shop Franny's mother fancies. As Babs men-tions at virtually every meeting, she joined the Players the very day she and Michael moved up permanently to Grandville. She says that she always dreamed of being a part of what she calls "a small regional theater" because it has so many more possi-bilities than the money-driven theaters of Manhattan. Franny is fairly sure that this is just another way for Babs to say that the theaters of Manhattan never expressed any interest in her, but Franny is not bothered by that. She likes Babs's verve. Most of the other members of the troupe are long past verve.

"How's Lila?" Babs asks, striding down the center aisle with a calfskin attaché case swinging at her side. Babs mem-orized the names of every family member of the Grandville Players on her first day.

"Good. Last time I saw her," Franny replies. She knows that Babs has two children of her own, young teens boarding at the Hotchkiss School in Connecticut, but she can never remember their names so she is unable to reciprocate the pleasantry.

"I guess I'm early," Babs says, seating herself directly across from Franny.

"Right on time. The others are late."

"But it does give me a chance to ask you something," Babs goes on. "A favor, actually."

"Shoot."

"Well, I know we're kind of casting about for our next production."

"That we are," Franny says. In truth, Franny has a play very much in mind for the next production—Arthur Miller's *The Crucible*. Although it requires a large cast, Franny is sure they could pull it off. She is drawn to the play by its pertinence to the current political climate, now even more relevant than to the McCarthyism that was gripping the country when the play was originally produced. But choosing productions is a democratic process, even if in the past Franny's choices have always prevailed.

"There's a new play I was hoping we could consider," Babs is saying as she snaps open her attaché and withdraws a bound manuscript. She stands and delivers it to Franny.

The title is *How's Never?* and the author is one Barbara Perkins. This playwright is new to Franny, but before she can inquire about her, Babs says, "I cannot tell a lie. It's my maiden name, the name I write under."

Franny smiles. "I didn't know you were a playwright."

"Only for about twenty years. It was my major at Brown."

"That's terrific." Franny knows better than to ask what other plays Barbara Perkins has written and where they were produced. She opens the manuscript to the second page, the settings and cast of characters. The entire story takes place in a bunker deep below the White House, and there are six characters—the President, the Vice President, each of their wives, a Southern evangelical preacher, and someone identified as "Clown/Angel." It is this Clown/Angel that distresses Franny right off the bat; it strikes her as both avant-guard *and* derivative, a perilous combination. But she cautions herself not to prejudge the play. "Maybe we could give it a reading some evening."

"That would be wonderful," Babs says. "I've never heard it read out loud."

"How about tonight?" a voice in the dark calls out. It is the operatic voice of Sally Rule, a Stockbridge matron who was one of the original Grandville Players. Sally is a popular amateur actress in town, even if her range is limited to uppity ladies of a certain age. People still stop her in the street to rave about her portrayal of Lady Britomart in *Major Barbara* four years back. Sally Rule and Franny's mother, Beatrice Cosgrove deVries Hammond, both belong to the Lenox Garden Club.

"Actually, I have something else planned for tonight," Franny says as Sally approaches the stage. "But let's read it next week for sure."

"Oh dear, why do I get the feeling you've got something grim and politically correct in store for us?" Sally says to Franny, smiling grandly as she seats herself next to Babs Dowd.

"*The Crucible*," Franny says. "Arthur Miller."

"As I said," Sally says, winking broadly at Babs.

But Babs, as earnest and well-mannered as her husband, counters with, "I'm afraid mine's political too."

"*And* grim?" Sally asks.

"Well, it's supposed to be funny," Babs replies ingenuously.

"Thank God for that," says Sally. "Three cheers for funny!"

Franny already can feel the evening slipping away from her.

* * *

That morning, Wendell spent an entire half-hour in the food co-op garnering tips on palatable ways to prepare—and disguise—tofu. Wendell has been intrigued by the co-op from the day it opened across the street from the old, abandoned grammar school. He likes the retro feel of the place, especially the barn board corner that displays rice, dried beans, and nuts in wooden barrels. And he particularly likes the women who work there, open-faced, unmade-up women in their thirties and forties who favor flannel shirts with the top three or four buttons unfastened. Even if many of these women are relocated urbanites, for Wendell they exude a rustic sexuality that he finds lacking in Grandville women today, even in those who are pretty. That includes his sometime bedmate, Maggie Bello. Maggie definitely turns Wendell on, but she hardly ever inspires affection, and never poetry.

A forty-something redhead in produce enthusiastically recommended smoked tofu in sesame marinade stirred into

Bangkok Temple Instant Pad Thai Noodle Mix. "My kids love it," she told Wendell. "And it feels so good in the mouth. Slurpy."

Slurpy? For reasons he could not account for, that word—and the delight with which the sexy, middle-aged redhead uttered it—made Wendell, a man approaching his sixty-fifth birthday, feel whimsical. Following her to the Asian packaged goods shelf, he asked her name.

"Esther."

"I'm Wendell deVries." Here, Wendell executed a modest bow while holding his container of smoked tofu above his head in both hands, a maneuver he had seen Keanu Reeves execute in *Little Buddha.*

Esther laughed. "I've seen you at the Phoenix. I'm a movie nut. Now that my kids are old enough to stay home alone, I sneak over whenever there's a new film."

As he made his way up the hill to Mahaiwe Street with Binx jogging at his side, Wendell replayed the little encounter in his mind several times, including the hints that there was no husband in Esther's home. It was unlike Wendell to muse in this way. Decades ago, he had stopped thinking of women as candidates for anything more than casual friendship or dispassionate sex. And indeed, by the time he reached home, he had completely stopped thinking about the redhead in produce.

His Thai tofu extravaganza was a big hit with Lila. "Far better than anything Mom makes," she declared. Wendell is dishing out her second helping, when Lila says, "Who are the deVrieses anyhow? I mean, way back."

Not only does the question come from out of the blue, but it is posed with more animation than Lila has exhibited in weeks. Like her mother, Lila is tall and slender, with fair skin and luminous blue eyes, a pretty girl in the estimation of everyone in Grandville, but particularly the boys of Grandville High School. Yet in contrast to Franny, Lila's facial expressions rarely vary. Her countenance is generally blank, almost stony. Not surprisingly, she has never evinced any interest in the dramatic arts.

"How far back?" Wendell replies. "Before the Phoenix?"

"Way before that," Lila says. As if she has caught herself being overly spirited, she delivers these words in a monotone, looking down at her bowl of noodles.

"Well, they're Dutch, for starters. Came over in sixteen hundred-something and settled in Rensselaer. Indentured servants."

"That's like slavery, isn't it?"

"They certainly had a thing or two in common. Like you couldn't run away or they'd go after you. And their masters—Patroons, they were called—weren't above giving them a few lashes if they didn't hoe the line."

Lila seems pleased with this answer, so much so that the corners of her bow-shaped lips rise ever so slightly. "Any blacks?"

"How do you mean?"

"In the family. The deVrieses."

"Not that I know of," Wendell says. He grins, then immediately regrets it when he sees Lila's eyes narrow. "But it would probably be a good thing if we did. Mongrels have more spunk."

"We're doing a black history unit in social studies," Lila says seriously. "Some guy from UMass came in and gave a talk about Berkshire blacks. There was a black family named deVries in Grandville."

Wendell is amazed. His father never mentioned this, nor had any of his college-educated siblings. "Could be that deVries was a common name back then," he says.

"It's a slave name," Lila says. "Slaves took their owners' names because they didn't have any of their own."

Wendell nods, still astonished. "Could be even closer than that, I suppose. Slave owners were known to father children with slave women. Maybe we *are* related."

There is nothing subtle about Lila's smile this time. Obviously this is what she was hoping to hear—that there could be African blood coursing in the pale blue veins that are visible on the undersides of her long white arms. Wendell wonders why this intrigues her more than her connection to her father, a man from Paris whom she never met, nor ever showed any interest in knowing.

"Why don't I try to look it up?" Wendell says to his granddaughter.

Without responding, Lila takes their plates to the sink and rinses them. Then she heads for the stairs and her bedroom, her thin shoulders hunched forward.

* * *

Around the corner from the Phoenix, where the Grandville Players are now venturing into a cold reading of the new Barbara Perkins play, *How's Never?*, Michael Dowd is sitting at a window table in Santorini's, having a drink with Terry Cyzinski, tennis coach and guidance counselor at Grandville High School.

Michael went to Harvard and, like many of that college's graduates, has incorporated those four years in his late teens and early twenties deep into the core of his middle-age identity. This, in spite of the fact that at Harvard he had been a middling student who might very well have learned as much or more at a state college, and the fact that he was far from a social success in Cambridge. Although he possesses a British surname and lineage, Dowd comes from a long line of undistinguished petite bourgeoisie, so Harvard, Fair Harvard, feels to him like the pedigree that was otherwise denied him.

In Manhattan, Dowd joined the Harvard Club of New York City where he became a member of the Speaker's Committee and signed on as an alumni interviewer of Manhattan applicants. The latter responsibility was particularly gratifying. He would interview nervous prep school and high school seniors in an alcove off the club library, waiting patiently as they formulated answers to his questions—answers that they desperately hoped would set them apart from the others. The process brought out something warm and paternal in Michael. He felt magnanimous, even wise. When fellow interviewers compared notes in the club dining room, they would marvel at how smart and accomplished the new crop of applicants was, and invariably someone would say, "Lucky I'm not applying today, I'd never get in." Michael would join in the laughter that followed, but the observation always made him feel more lacking than lucky.

When the Dowds decided to move to Grandville, Michael made inquiries at the club about Harvard's presence in western Massachusetts. He was told that there was a Harvard club in Springfield, but no building, so it met—twice a year—in a banquet room at a Marriott hotel. But, as luck would have it, the college's admissions committee was just now actively seeking alumni interviewers in the area, except they were not calling them 'interviewers,' they were calling them 'recruiters,' a designation that Michael found inspiring.

It is this inspiration that has paired Michael Dowd with Terry Cyzinski this evening. Michael phoned Cyzinski at Grandville High just yesterday, identifying himself as the new Harvard recruiter for the area. Cyzinski had laughed and said, "You got to be kidding—since when does Harvard need to recruit anybody?" A perfect response, Michael thought.

In person, Cyzinski looks more like a linebacker than a tennis coach. He is at least six-foot three, and broad of chest and shoulders with a double hump of belly ranging just above his belt line. He has a large, open face and a hail-fellow manner that is not quite offset by a hint of wariness in his eyes. For the meeting, Cyzinski is wearing a blue, button-down Oxford-cloth shirt, a navy blue tie embroidered with pheasant and quail, a brass-buttoned blazer, and gray flannel slacks. Michael Dowd, on the other hand, is wearing corduroys and a sweatshirt he picked up at his twentieth reunion. The sweatshirt's only ornament is a single, crimson, capital 'H' over the left breast, a touch that Michael treasures—Harvardian understatement.

The waitress is taking their drink orders. She is one of the Ukrainian belles who seem to work in every bar and restaurant in town to pay their way through the local two-year college. Dowd recently heard that a dean at that college, Grandville Community, discovered this source of full tuition-paying students through a cousin of his in the foreign service. These Ukrainian kids just wanted to get *anywhere* in the USA for a year or two; Grandville Community College was running at a substantial loss, but had an underused quota of student visas at their disposal. Zip, zip, the connection was made and everyone seemed delighted, including the restaurant owners and patrons of Grandville. The tall, young blonde hovering at the side of their table is certainly delightful to behold.

Michael casts a quick glance up at her, then flashes a look of mock incredulity—*Can you believe how gorgeous this girl is?*—to his table mate. Up here in the country, Michael feels this kind of man-to-man exchange is not only permissible, but an expedient social leveler. But Terry Cyzinski does not respond; he suspects Dowd may be testing his political correctness.

After their orders are taken, Cyzinski says, "I'll tell you the truth, Dowd. We never sent anybody to Harvard. Or Yale or Princeton for that matter. At least since I've been around."

"Why's that?"

Cyzinski shrugs. "Just hasn't been on our radar."

"Does it seem like too much of a reach for your kids?"

Cyzinski nods. "Plus, it's not in most of their families' budgets."

"Harvard is need blind," Michael says earnestly.

"What's that?"

"They decide who gets in first. And only afterwards do they open the financial aid envelope."

Cyzinski looks deeply impressed. Michael likes that the man does not even attempt to hide his awe.

"So what are they looking for?" Cyzinski asks.

"Good question," Michael answers. The girl arrives with their drinks and he takes his—his first bloody Mary of the season—without looking at her this time. "Actually I have a pretty good answer to it. They aren't looking for one kind of kid, they're looking for a whole bunch of very different, but very particular kids."

No one at Harvard or the Harvard Club ever explained this calculus to Michael; he figured it out on his own. The college is a community of eight thousand—a little larger than Grandville—and that community is loaded with almost one hundred student associations: drama groups; singing groups; two different orchestras; a fencing team; a cross-country skiing team; even a water polo team. The list goes on. Well, every one of those clubs and teams needs members to operate—very specific members. Say, the wrestling team's 197-pounder just graduated and there is nobody to fill his spot. The wrestling coach takes a stroll over to University Hall and informs the dean of admissions he needs a 197-pounder in the incoming class.

The same was true in the academic departments. Harvard has five tenured professors who teach Latin and Greek. So what happens when there is a precipitous drop in classics majors? The head of the department strolls over to University Hall. On top of that, Harvard is committed to taking at least one kid from every state in the union.

"For us, that means niche marketing," Michael says in conclusion. "I always say that the best way to get into Harvard is to move to Mississippi, take up the bassoon, and perfect your game of water polo."

Cyzinski is smiling. "So how do you know what they need? What's missing in their mix for the coming year?"

"Research. Straight from the source," Michael replies, smiling back. "But why don't we start with what you've got? What your top kids have to offer."

"How top?"

"1350 SATs. That's minimum. And class rank no lower than number five."

Cyzinski leans back in his chair. He hasn't touched his drink, a Heineken's light. Several seconds pass before he says, "How about tennis? Girls' tennis."

"Good. I'll check the job market for girl tennis players and let you know soon, Terry," Michael says. He turns to the café window and gazes down Railroad Street. He feels a swell of well-being in his chest and shoulders. It is the feeling of having found his place here in Grandville.

It is just past nine o'clock on a weeknight after the summer people have gone, so there are few pedestrians on the sidewalks. Local restaurant patrons eat an hour or two earlier than the tourists do. The only noticeable movement is the shimmering shadows of poplar leaves cast by the streetlights on Railroad Street's old brick buildings.

Unlike New York City where Dowd lived for most of his life, Grandville can almost be taken in at a glance. It has a comprehensibility that springs from limited variables. If one sees Mrs. Carpolino at the post office in the morning, it is not in the least surprising to see her again at the Grand Union supermarket in the late afternoon, and even again that evening as she makes her way with her new aluminum walker down Main Street, heading for the quilt sewing circle at the Congregational Church. A remarkable coincidence in Manhattan is a natural beat in the rhythm of daily life here. Although Michael Dowd has now lived full-time in Grandville for almost a year, he does not completely grasp this phenomenon; he may notice it now and then, but it is not yet part of his nervous system's expectations. That is why Michael is startled when he sees his wife, Babs, round the corner of Main and Railroad at the center of a small group of men and women.

Without thinking, Michael waves at her through the café window but, of course, she does not see him. Again without forethought, Michael raps sharply on the windowpane, hoping to get her attention, but Babs is more than a hundred feet away on the other side of the glass and her companions are noisy. Several patrons at Santorini's, however, turn from their drinks and each other to see what Dowd is up to. Terry Cyzinski is bewildered too. He follows Dowd's gaze down Railroad Street where he sees an attractive, auburn-haired woman suddenly wrap her arms around Ned Shields, the drama teacher at Berkshire Community College. The woman looks enchanted.

* * *

Franny opted out of the regular, after-meeting drinks at the Railroad Car, saying that she had promised to help Lila with her homework. If some of the Grandville Players guessed her real reason for not joining them—and Franny was certain some did—they covered it well with solicitous comments about all the homework teachers gave kids these days. But Franny is pretty sure that Babs Dowd does not have an inkling of her state of mind, and for that she feels relieved.

Franny detests Babs's play. It makes her angrier than she would have guessed any amateur play could. It is not its cartoonishness that gets to her; hell, Franny directed the Players' production of *Little Murders*. Nor its obviousness or its catchy, TV commercial-like dialogue. She could even tolerate Babs Dowd's grand larceny from *Angels In America* in the form of her Angel/Clown who descends into the White House bunker in a beribboned bassinet to enlighten the dim-witted evangelist preacher; certainly it posed no threat to Tony Kushner's masterpiece.

But, oh, the *smugness* of that woman's play! Its self-satisfied certitude that *we* are so smart and *they*—the Christian right-wingers—are so moronic. That we, the cognoscenti, have to dumb-down our arguments to reach their feeble minds and save them from themselves. God knows, Franny is every bit as upset by the ultraconservatives as Babs is. That is exactly why she wanted to put on *The Crucible. But dammit, Mrs. Dowd, you need to get inside these people's minds and hearts before you ridicule them!*

Climbing the hill to Mahaiwe Street, Franny curses Babs Dowd out loud without intending to. She is startled by her own voice. The street is empty so no one has heard her, but nonetheless she decides she needs to get a grip on herself. *Come on, girl, it's only a play!*

Franny has always thought of herself as easygoing like her father, but lately malicious moods have been sneaking up on her. One moment she is merrily singing along with 'N Sync' on the shop radio and the next she is fuming about some port in Florida that refuses to allow a Greenpeace ship to dock. Everything in the world suddenly feels personal—the refused ship, a batch of tasteless birthday cards Hallmark just sent to her shop, a suicide bombing in Kashmir, Babs's inane play, the war in Iraq.

Damn it, that is the problem right there: *there is no scale to her anger!* All the indignities and stupidities of the world— small or large, local or global—enrage her equally. *Ah, so the fault must lie in her self, for she has hormones.* Franny's mother went into a temperamental menopause when she was only thirty-eight, reason enough to suspect the same was happening to Franny—even if the idea of being similar to her mother in *any* way was abhorrent. Franny stands motionless under Mahaiwe Street's lone streetlight, calming herself by letting her imagination parody Mrs. Dowd's ridiculous parody of a play:

Enter Clown/Angel from above under single spotlight: Hormones, schmormones! The world *is* a mess, Franny-girl! And if your hormones have anything to do with it, they've only made you more sensitive to the ugliness you've been blind to until now. They've opened your eyes!

Franny: Just as I thought, you are as insipid as you look! Let me guess, Clowny, you're crying on the inside, right?

Clown/Angel: Actually, I'm praying on the inside.

Franny: God save us!

Clown/Angel: You said it.

Franny: I suppose in your world of infinite treacle all tragedies *are* equal—a stubbed toe, genocide in Rwanda, bad hair.

Clown/Angel: That's true, Missy deVries. It's all relative. Human agony is human agony whatever the cause.

Franny: That's amoral!

Clown/Angel: No, that's amore!

Franny laughs out loud as she continues up the street, and she is still smiling when she lets herself in her front door. Wendell looks up from his book and says, "Hey, pal, you're early tonight."

"I was feeling anti-social, so I had a good talk with myself instead."

"You meet a better class of people that way."

"How's Lila?"

"Good," Wendell replies. He is not ready to talk about Lila's newfound interest in deVries genealogy, so he does not. He and Franny are so effortlessly connected they can hold things back from one another in good faith.

"I see our neighbors moved out already," Franny says. The other half of their house has had a rapid turnover of occupants in the past few years.

"Can't be anything I said, because I never got a chance to speak to them," Wendell says, smiling.

"I'm bushed. Think I'll turn in," Franny says.

"Goodnight, Franny." Wendell watches his daughter disappear up the stairway, then turns back to the poetry book he selected for this evening, his Langston Hughes anthology.

CHAPTER THREE

*O*f all the discussion topics that come and go inside Franny's shop—the new dentist who is taking over Dr. Schuster's practice; the state highway crew that is taking forever to paint the Main Street Bridge; the whooping cough outbreak at the Rudolf Steiner School where they refuse to inoculate their kids—the topic with the most staying power is, The Day Grandville Changed Forever.

By this, the discussers mean that tipping point when Grandville no longer was a town unto itself but became a mere adjunct to something larger. As Write Now topics go, this one is fairly abstract, touching on the culture of place, on manners, even on what many call the "new feeling in the air," as well as on more concrete conditions like the price of real estate and the flow of traffic. Franny, who finds these debates more interesting than most, especially likes the commonly-held assumption that a single event marked the change. What precise straw broke Grandville's back? For Franny, there is a literary feel to this question; it reminds her of the defining moment—the rupture of the violin string—in 'The Cherry Orchard.' In fact, these discussions often rouse memories of debates in her college Russian drama class, although here—thank God—the word 'symbolism' is never uttered.

For a while, the final closing of the Grandville Fairgrounds was the winner of the tipping-point sweepstakes. The Grandville Fair had been the longest-running country fair in the entire country—one hundred and fifty-five nonstop years—until 1999 when it remained as dormant and desolate through the summer as it was throughout the rest of the year. It never reopened. Some blamed the end of the fair on the tornado that touched down on the fairgrounds in '98, destroying most of its wooden stables, but others insisted that the fair had been doomed for years before that. To start with, there had not been a chapter of the 4-H Club in town for almost two decades, so gone were the sheep-shearing demonstrations, the giant zucchini contest, and everybody's favorite, the hog obstacle course competition.

All that remained of the Grandville Fair's farmland past was the Lenox Garden Club's cut flower exhibit and, most of Franny's patrons agreed, that smacked more of suburbia than of agriculture.

For years before the tornado, the fair had become nothing more than an annual excuse for legalized gambling, a Mardi Gras-like furlough from sensible New England thrift. A caravan of second-rate racehorses and third-rate jockeys would amble onto the fairgrounds like the troops of faded, has-been actors that appeared at the Phoenix in the final years of live performances there. Grandvillians wagered up to fifty dollars per race although they all knew the races were fixed, that the winners at the Grandville Fair were chosen at the previous fair the caravan had worked somewhere in western Pennsylvania. No mind. Guessing which horse the fix was on was just as reliable as picking a winner by studying the horses' rickety flanks as they paraded by in the fairground's paddock.

Recently, however, the demise of the Grandville Fair has lost popularity as Grandville's official swan song. For that honor, Franny's rotating discussion group now focuses on the town's new restaurants. Franny can remember when there were only three places to eat out in Grandville: the Phoenix Café and the Railroad Car in town, and Friendly's out on Route 7. Now there were a total of thirty-three of them, including two Italian restaurants, two Chinese, an Indian, a Greek, and a Japanese, as well as a good dozen gourmet establishments with prices that few year-rounders can afford. As Archie Morris pointed out just the other day, one of these chichi joints recently dropped both potatoes and pasta from its menu in deference to that low-carb diet all the second-home people were on.

"That's got to be it," Archie said. "When you don't serve potatoes in Grandville, it ain't Grandville anymore."

Franny is always charmed by the freshness of Archie Morris's perceptions. In large part, Archie's originality stems from his basic illiteracy; he has little idea what others have said or written before him, so most of his notions are original. Franny believes this constitutes the most undervalued quality of ignorance.

But today's nod goes to Nakota out on the highway, and not simply because the pricey Japanese restaurant serves raw fish, but because it replaced Friendly's. Two and three generations of Grandville families have gone out for an early Sunday dinner at Friendly's, consuming Awful Awfuls, deep-fried cod, and burgers on toast with a side of creamy cole slaw, all the while joking with the waitresses, every one of them Grandville High girls. This treat was both predictable and affordable. Even if Friendly's was part of a restaurant chain, it was a Massachusetts chain, and it felt homey.

From a strictly economic viewpoint, it was probably the McDonald's out by Grand Union that did Friendly's in. But it is the way some architect reconfigured Friendly's basic, farmhouse-like structure into an ersatz pagoda—even transforming the restaurant's signature crowning cupola into an oriental spire—that rankles Franny's patrons. Now that marked the end of Grandville as a town of one's own.

* * *

Lila deVries sees Nakota as an island of rescue. She works there six afternoons and nights a week in the summer, and Friday and Saturday nights during the school year. Among other things, it rescues her from dating. The boys of Grandville High know her work schedule and no longer bother to ask her out anymore, which is nothing but a relief to her. The idea of cruising in a car or going to the movies with any one of those boys feels like emotional suicide, one more deadening experience in a daily assault of deadening experiences. What other people in town find comforting in the ring of mountains that surrounds Grandville, Lila finds imprisoning.

She comes to life at Nakota. Actually, she enters an alternate life there. As one of only two Caucasians on the staff—the other is a fiftyish bartender who commutes from Westfield—Lila feels exotic, foreign, a stranger. She savors the otherness she feels, seeing faces and hearing words that exist so completely apart from her. Sometimes, it all feels like a hallucination.

Yet Lila also feels a pull to be one of them, both the Japanese women with whom she works in the dining room and the Latino young men in the kitchen. With the help of Takaaki, a waitress of twenty who looks much younger, Lila has learned to properly pronounce every item on the menu, from the colliding 'ch's and 'sh's of *chirashi-zushi* to the sputtering consonants of *teppanyaki*. Sometimes, in a quiet, authoritative voice, she will even correct the pronunciation of her customers. And although there is nothing particularly Asian about the white blouses and black skirts required of the wait staff, Lila took a bus all the way to Pittsfield just to find a short-collared, Pima cotton blouse that matched those of the Japanese girls.

She is also picking up Mexican and Colombian slang from the boys in the kitchen. They adore her, of course. Her blonde hair alone would be sufficient for that adoration, but Lila's grace with them, her interest in their lives, especially endears her to them. Most of them come from inner-city slums and shantytowns on the periphery of overcrowded South American cities. When Lila told her grandfather that some of these boys had already learned how to slice slabs of raw fish with a razor-sharp knife into delicate sushi portions, he burst out laughing. "Adaptability!" he had roared. "Man's greatest gift!"

Between seven-thirty and eight, there is usually a lull at the restaurant, so that is when the staff takes staggered, ten-minute breaks. Early on, Lila realized that during these breaks the Japanese women like to chatter in their own language just outside the kitchen door, so she usually has a cigarette with one or two of the Latino boys out by the dumpster. The boys are afraid to flirt with her and that is not what she wants anyhow, so they just joke around the best they can in the limited vocabulary they have in common.

During one of those dumpster breaks, a new boy named Pato reached into his jeans pocket and pulled out a brownish pellet that he proceeded to stuff into the end of his unfiltered Camel. Another of the boys, a favorite of Lila's named Alarico, spoke to him angrily, gesturing with his head toward Lila, but Pato just shrugged and lit up. Lila recognized the aroma of marijuana. One of her classmates regularly sucks on a joint she keeps hidden under a rock in the copse of spruce trees across the street from the high school. Lila joined her once, but the drug seemed to make the rest of that school day even more agonizing than usual. So when Pato offered the burning cigarette to her, she politely declined.

But Pato's weed was potent, and when he teasingly blew a dense cloud of its smoke in her face, Lila sniffed at it playfully. She was back inside, waiting on an elderly Boston couple, when she suddenly became exhilarated by the fragrance of the seaweed in the miso soup she was setting on the table. She had never before grasped that saltiness could be a smell as well as a taste. Even more than the exotic faces and languages and décor of Nakota, this smell transported her.

It took Lila only a moment to realize she was stoned and that thought terrified her. Not because she believed it was morally wrong, and definitely not because of the way it made her feel—unlike that time at school, this high was light and delicious like, well, like miso soup. No, what terrified Lila was that the drug could make her screw up her job; and if Lila lost her job, she was sure she would fall into a deep and inescapable depression. There was nothing to do but force herself to stay sharply focused on her tasks, and that Lila did far more effortlessly than she had expected. In less than an hour, she felt so confident in her self-control that now and then she would indulge that light, delicious feeling, inhaling the scented steam that rose off a plate of *ohitashi* and joking with a table of college boys who wanted to know her name. That night was even more transcendental than her usual Nakota hallucination. What is more, at the end of the night, Lila could tell just by the weight of her pocket that her tips were much bigger than usual.

She took a puff with Pato the next time. Just a single puff, and a slight one at that. She wanted to float, not to soar, and one little puff was just enough to put her where she wanted to be. Those nights at Nakota are the only times Lila ever smokes pot. They are the only times she ever wants to.

It is the second Saturday after Labor Day, so business at Nakota is sluggish, as it will remain until mid-October when the leaf-peepers come to town. On slow nights, Lila tries especially hard to make herself useful in the kitchen, stripping soy beans, rinsing trays, hauling garbage bags to the dumpster. Although her boss, Ichiro, has never hinted that he might lay her off during these fallow periods, she does not want the idea to even occur to him. After a quick dumpster break, she is tamping down garbage in a plastic bag when Takaaki comes through the kitchen's swinging door and tells Lila that she has customers at Table Five.

So Lila is freshly high as she steps into the dining room and, menus in hand, saunters toward Table Five. It is occupied by regular patrons, Mr. and Mrs. Dowd, but this time they have two kids with them, a teenage boy and girl, presumably their children. The man has an office in the Melville Block above her mom's store where he does some kind of stock trading that Grandpa disapproves of; Wendell says there is something basically corrupt about making money with money. And the woman belongs to mom's drama club. But Lila does not know anything about the boy and girl except that neither goes to Grandville High. The boy, who looks to be fifteen or sixteen, has a sour expression on his baby-fat face that makes Lila guess he goes to private school. The girl looks a year or so younger. She is freckled and pretty and both impudent and nervous-looking. Lila smiles at her.

"Oh, good," Mrs. Dowd says. "We hoped we'd get you, Lila."

"Hello," Lila says cheerfully, handing out the menus. "We've got a couple of specials tonight. For *donburi*, we have *unagi don*—that's broiled eel on rice. And for an entrée we have beef *negimaki*—that's basically a *teriyaki* dish with scallions."

Customers always give Lila their full attention when she makes these recitations. In her first months at Nakota, Lila's self-consciousness made this the most trying part of the job. For the life of her, Lila cannot imagine what possible pleasure her mother and the rest of the Grandville Players take in being under a spotlight in front of an audience. People's expectant gazes obliterate any feelings Lila has of her own. But in time, Lila found that conscientiously pronouncing the Japanese food names helps divert her self-consciousness. And later, the puffs with Pato have made these performances even easier. Franny sometimes says that acting in a play gives her a high; for her daughter, cause and effect are reversed—getting high gives her the talent to perform.

Lila notices that the Dowd boy smirks when she intones, 'unagi don,' as if he is a critic who finds her presentation lacking. Lila knows that people from New York City pride themselves on their biting critiques of just about everything. Wendell says it comes from living in a crowded environment; they are always trying to tear things down to get some breathing room. Nonetheless, the boy's sneer gets to her. She imagines tipping a bowl of *unagi don* onto his fat face.

"You sure do look a lot like your mother," Mr. Dowd is saying. His eyes have lingered on her face longer than the others and there is an adolescent eagerness in his expression that makes Lila doubly irritated.

"That's weird," Lila replies. "Because I'm adopted."

All four occupants of Table Five look embarrassed, which is exactly the reaction Lila was hoping for, albeit unconsciously. Of course, one thing about being high on Pato's pot is that the barrier between the conscious and the unconscious is porous at best, and that instantly alarms Lila. Did she get too high this time? Go too far? Could the Dowds tell she was stoned?

Everybody in Grandville knows that Lila is not adopted, even if her father—a man her mother fell in love with in college—has never made an appearance here. Occasionally, Lila likes to think this makes her *half* adopted, but there is no doubt that she is Franny's daughter, and Lila does, indeed, look very much like her mother.

The Dowd girl looks disdainfully at her father, then apprehensively at Lila. There is a fierceness in the girl's eyes, yet there is something almost maternal there too, like a creature that would kill to protect its young. She starts to stammer, "You . . . people say . . . you know, that when you live together, you . . . you start to look alike."

As the girl stumbles through her little piece, her brother simpers. He seems about to add some choice words of his own—possibly about how dogs come to resemble their masters—when his sister's face suddenly clenches. The girl is livid, embarrassed, on the brink of tears, and Lila wants to save her. She knows the best way to do this would be to confess she was just joking about being adopted, but she cannot bring herself to do that. She could not bear to give the boy even an ounce more satisfaction to add to his overflowing well of self-satisfaction. So instead Lila leans forward and very quickly plants a kiss on the top of the girl's head, then straightens up and says, "I'll give you all a few minutes to make up your minds."

Gliding back into the kitchen, Lila feels glorious. Although she never thinks in such terms, she feels the way an actress does when she pulls off a difficult scene with total mastery. She has left her audience stunned, breathless, completely in the thrall of her fantasy. When she returns in a few minutes to take their orders, and later to serve them, the Dowds are subdued and awkward. They seem defeated. Mr. Dowd leaves Lila a twenty-five percent tip.

* * *

Tonight, Wendell projected *Monsoon Wedding* for the third and fourth times, rarely taking his eyes off the screen below. He never even cracked the book he brought with him. The colors in the film bewitched him—saffron saris and lime-green scarves, a gilded carpet, a rainbow of spice mounds in a street stall. This is the way he tours the world and it is sufficient for him.

He was surprised when the programmer in London complied with his request for this film. Wendell does not make such requests often for fear of being too visible to his overseas employers, but now and then when he sends in his monthly balance sheet, he attaches a note pointing out that the audience at the Phoenix is changing, that the occasional foreign or independent film brings in as much revenue as the Hollywood blockbusters. He was right about *Monsoon Wedding*; tonight he filled a decent amount of seats for both showings.

The part of the film's story that most interests Wendell is the way an arranged marriage works out so well for the sophisticated Indian couple. He finds something consoling in the idea of a calculated match of a man and a woman. Even though it is over thirty years since Beatrice left him, Wendell still harbors a deep distrust of the heart's reliability.

After locking up the projection booth and retrieving empty boxes of Junior Mints, Milk Duds, and Gummi Worms from the balcony floor, he heads downstairs to police the floor of the mezzanine, Binx trotting beside him. It is down here where he sees Esther, the hazel-eyed redhead from the food co-op, lingering at the lobby door.

"I don't want to go outside," she says, smiling at him. "I'm afraid of losing the colors."

Wendell nods. "Saffron," he says. "My kingdom for a saffron robe."

They look at each other silently, both of them relishing the unhurriedness of this act and the ease with which they understand one another that made it possible.

"Well," Esther says finally. "I guess I'll just squint all the way home."

"Do you live nearby?"

"On Board Street. We have a two-room apartment."

Wendell is just about to offer to walk Esther back to her apartment when he remembers that Lila is waiting for him to pick her up at the Nakota. Again, he and Esther simply smile at each other.

"Is that what you do up there? Read?" Esther asks after a moment, gesturing with her head to the book in Wendell's hand. It is the copy of *New England's African-American Heritage* that he got through inter-library loan after he could not turn up anything about a black family named deVries on the Grandville Historical Society's bookshelf.

"Sometimes, but not tonight," Wendell answers. Binx has dashed down and back a side aisle, reminding Wendell that he has not finished his clean-up job. "The colors were too distracting."

"Goodnight."

"Yes, goodnight."

Wendell is late picking up Lila tonight. As he turns his red pickup truck into Nakota's parking lot, he sees his granddaughter bent down to the open window of a Grandville police cruiser at the rear of the restaurant. The driver is Flip Morris. He is easy to identify from any angle because of his spiky crew cut and horseshoe moustache. He is Archie Morris's son, which can be the only possible reason he got a job in the police department. Wendell applies his brakes slowly, then lets the engine idle as, still unseen by the two, he watches them. Lila is so long-legged that leaning over to talk face-to-face with Flip, her buttocks are higher than her head. That is clearly why Flip keeps cocking his head from one side to the other; he is looking past Lila's face at the animated shifts and sways of her hips. Wendell hits his horn. Lila glances back at him, then says a few more words to Flip before strolling leisurely to the truck.

"Just in time," she says, leaning back in her seat.

"Sorry I'm late."

"Flip was going to give me a lift."

"Then I'm *real* glad I made it." Wendell peers at the cruiser. Flip Morris is examining himself in his side-view mirror while lighting up a cigarette. By God, the idiot even leers at his own reflection. Wendell presses down on the accelerator and lets out the clutch too quickly, making his truck lurch onto the highway.

"He's perfectly harmless, Pops," Lila says, looking at her grandfather.

"For an asshole," Wendell replies.

Usually on Saturday nights, Wendell drops off Lila at home and then heads back into town where he ties Binx to a tree in front of the Railroad Car. Inside, Maggie Bello will be sitting at the far end of the bar, pacing her bourbon and water intake until his arrival. But this Saturday night Wendell decides that he would rather read a bit and then turn in early with only his dog.

Chapter Four

There are close to half a million towns and villages in the world that are the size of Grandville, and surely it is an accident of the highest order to happen to be living in one of these towns at one particular interval of history. It is as random a conjunction of time and space as, say, the sudden bolt of lightning that split the cross atop the onion tower of St. Joseph's Parish Church in Triesenberg, Liechtenstein, in the summer of 1937; or the poppy seed that germinated from a four-hour-old pile of donkey dung early this morning on the Pondicherry Road in Krishnagiri, India. Or, say, the swaying palm tree that will fail to deflect a bullet's trajectory when it spirals toward the forehead of a young Hispanic recruit from Grandville, Massachusetts, the winter after next in Samarra, Iraq; or the rock that at this moment shields a child from a bullet in Puerto Alvira, Colombia.

Yet the citizens of each one of these towns feel an inherent belongingness, as if we absolutely fit in this place at this time. To us, it seems as basic to who we are as the genetic blueprint that has molded our bodies and faces.

* * *

Marcella Mondragon recognized the boy who beat her husband, Nicomedes, to death outside their home in the town of Puerto Alvira, Colombia. His name was Pedro and he once had been a classmate of her son, Hector, at the village school. In fact, Pedro had come home with Hector several times, and the two boys had played kickball in the sugarcane field where Hector's father worked across from their house. That, of course, was before Pedro joined the Revolutionary Armed Forces of Colombia. It was as a revolutionary guerrilla that he murdered Hector's father.

After the murder, one of Pedro's comrades declared that the rest of the family had one day to get out of Puerto Alvira or they would suffer the same fate as Nicomedes. Marcella worked fast. She packed only possessions she thought she could sell—her confirmation necklace and Nicomedes's musical instruments—two *tiples* and a *cuatro*, both of them guitar-like instruments with which her husband had accompanied himself when he sang after supper. Marcella and Hector assembled the family—Nicomedes's and Marcella's parents, and Marcella's three young daughters—and the nine of them set off by foot to Mapiripan. Toward the end of their trek, Hector was carrying his paternal grandfather on his back while Marcella alternated between carrying her youngest daughter, Maria, and her next youngest, Tati.

In Mapiripán, Marcella could not find any buyers for her necklace—a jeweler informed her that the crucifix was made of brass, not gold—but at a music shop near the bus station she was able to sell Nicomedes's instruments, eight thousand pesos apiece for the *tiples*, and five thousand for the *cuatro*—a total of a little less than six American dollars, enough to buy only seven one-way bus tickets to Bogotá, where there were no insurgents and it was said there was work for everyone. As the eldest—sixty-one and sixty-two—Nicomedes's mother and father volunteered to be the two who stayed behind, and they did. It was not until the midnight bus rumbled out of the bus station and onto the streets of Mapiripán that Marcella cried, as much for what faced them as for what they had left behind.

On the bus trip, Hector fell into conversation with an old woman from the south who had relocated to Bogotá two years earlier. She told him there were only two sections of the city where he and his family could find a place to live, Ciudad Bolivar, in the inner city, or Soacha, a shantytown on the edge of the city. Both were for *desechables*, she said, using Bogotá slang for 'disposables.' She, herself, preferred Soacha because there were fewer prostitutes there.

This, then, was the full extent of Marcella and Hector's knowledge about housing in Bogotá when they arrived in that city late in the morning with eight hundred pesos in their possession.

The seven of them went house hunting. Allowing for a short stop at a street stand to buy and share a loaf of bread (three hundred pesos), it took a full hour to walk to Ciudad Bolivar, the closer of their two options. Marcella was a farmer's daughter and a farmer's widow who had only visited one city in her life, Mapiripan. She had seen photographs of Bogotá, even of foreign cities like Buenos Aires, Rio, and New York City, but she had never smelled a city before. After a lifetime of inhaling the cane-scented mountain air of Puerto Alvira, the stench of Ciudad Bolivar filled her with a despair deeper than any she had felt since their journey began.

It took three hours to find their way from Ciudad Bolivar to Soacha. At first sight, it looked like a garbage fill—empty cans, upended broken chairs and tables, banana peels and granadilla husks, piles of excrement feeding swarms of flies and mosquitoes. But as the family came closer, they saw the corrugated tin roofs of mud-brick shacks that joined one another wall to wall, zigzagging along one side of a hill. At the moment they approached Soacha, the wind current was blowing north to south, bringing with it notes of cherrywood and lemon from the Loaya Herrera. That current shifted in less than an hour, the new wind carrying the full fetor of the shantytown, but by that time Marcella and her son had claimed a nine-foot square of land at the end of the bottom-most row of shacks.

Like any isolated village or neighborhood, Soacha had developed a social system of its own, complete with chiefs and rules of conduct. No one from the city government, police or military, ventured out to Soacha, so there was no limit on the self-appointed rulers' authority. Yet the scarcity of basic goods—water, food, and building materials—was so great that in itself it restricted these overlords' power. There was little to seize except labor and flesh.

One of the chiefs was named Rico. He was also from the South and only a couple of years older than Hector. The scars on his powerful neck and face, proof that he had escaped from a Revolutionary Army assault, were his insignia. He approached the family as they stood in a loose circle around their newly-claimed plot.

Rico stands, his muscular arms folded across his substantial chest, inspecting the family members one at a time. His eyes linger on Fernanda, the eldest of the Mondragon daughters at fifteen. Her moon face is distorted by welts from crying, making it look even more cow-like than usual, and her late-arriving breasts are all but invisible under one of Hector's alpaca shirts. Marcella experiences an emotion that just a day before would have been unimaginable: consolation in her daughter's unattractiveness. Rico's eyes move to Hector.

At seventeen, Hector is still growing, but he is already taller than any man in his home village and appears to be taller than any man in Soacha too. There was a rumor of a lanky Brazilian landlord on his father's side, although Nicomedes, himself, was only five feet tall, as was his father before him. Without being conscious of it, Hector has the posture of a man who is at ease with his stature. He holds his shoulders back and his head erect, habitually looking down at the people he talks to. This last does not please Rico at all.

"Your name!" Rico barks.

"Hector."

"A farmer, I bet."

"I was." Hector hesitates a moment, then adds, "Sir."

Rico squints, studying Hector's face for signs of sarcasm, but Hector answers this scrutiny by casting his gaze even lower, to Rico's feet. Hector understands that, real or feigned, this gesture signifies submissiveness—even the dogs of Puerto Alvira can read its meaning. Hector also knows that he values his family far more than his pride.

"I'll give you a chance," Rico says. "You can sell cigarettes for me. At least they'll be able to see you." He gestures for Hector to follow him up the hill.

"Now?" Hector asks.

Rico glares and Hector follows.

The rear half of Rico's hovel is shrouded in a blue plastic tarpaulin. From beneath it, he withdraws three cartons of American cigarettes, Camel and Camel Filters, and shoves them at Hector.

"Twenty thousand a pack," Rico says. "You take that Number 2 bus over there and get off at Sagrado. Carrera Seven. You'll see other boys there too. The brave ones stand right in the middle of the road. They sell twice what the others do."

"Then that is what I will do," Hector says. Before leaving for the bus, he again stares compliantly at Rico's feet and asks, "Can someone help my family?"

"Let's see how you do," Rico answers.

If we were visitors from Rio or Buenos Aires or even the United States, touring Bogotá in our rented BMW, and on our way to dinner at, say, Andres Carne de Res out on the Autopista Norte, we would pass the American Embassy on our left at Sagrado and then brake to a stop at the traffic light at Carrera Seven. There we would encounter ten or twelve boys, most of them teenage, but some younger, and every one of them seedy and foul looking. Some look threatening, conveyed as much by the need in their eyes as by the seemingly menacing way they dart from car to car, brandishing their wares, contraband foreign cigarettes and domestic flowers. On this particular evening, however, one of the boys appears neither seedy nor menacing. To be sure, he looks indigent; his unwashed face and hair and his stained shirt attest to that. He is taller than the others, yet this alone does not account for the difference in the impression he makes. There is in his bearing a confidence that the other boys lack, a sense that while he knows he is better than this job, he will nonetheless perform it with dignity.

He appears to walk more slowly than the others as he approaches our car, but we quickly realize that this is an illusion—his stride is twice the length of theirs so he is at our window before them. We now see his face and it, too, seems out of place—too sympathetic, too refined-looking. We wonder if he is one of the 'fallen ones' we have heard about, a son of a government functionary who fell out of favor and lost his job and then his property. Smiling, he holds his cigarettes in front of his thin chest. Although none of us smoke, we feel compelled to buy a pack from him as an act of charity. We also think of the twenty thousand pesos we hand to him as encouragement—we do not want this young man to give up hope. Of course, our compassion is made easier by the fact that twenty thousand Colombian pesos will in no way affect which items we will choose from the menu at Andres Carne de Res.

Hector surprises himself with his ease and proficiency at this job. It is little more than forty-eight hours since his father was murdered and they fled Puerto Alvira, although he does not reflect on any of this as he stands in the middle of Carrera Seven. He only thinks about his prospective customers, evaluating their faces through their windshields and calibrating his facial expression and gait accordingly.

Within two hours, he has sold out the three cartons Rico gave him. It is dusk in Bogotá and the traffic doubles as well-to-do natives and tourists set out for their evening's entertainment. It would be a pity to forgo this opportunity to sell even more cigarettes, so Hector strikes a deal with one of the younger salesmen, a boy of no more than twelve from Ciudad Bolivar. Hector buys this boy's remaining stock—two cartons of Winstons—for half the street mark-up and sells them out by eleven p.m. In this way, he will be able to keep fifty thousand pesos for himself while giving Rico full payment for the three original cartons.

It is when Hector is down to his last two packs of Winstons that a BMW sport convertible containing two laughing middle-aged women slows in front of him. Hector can tell just from the timbre of their laughter that they are foreign, and indeed, they are German tourists doing the grand tour of Brazil, Argentina, and Colombia. They buy both packs of cigarettes, handing him a fifty-thousand note and waving off the change. The driver, a dyed blonde with thin lips, asks his name and he gives it, bowing slightly when he does so. Then the woman tells Hector that she and her friend are looking for a guide for the night, a personal guide who can show them the *real* Bogotá. The light has changed and behind the BMW other cars start to blare their horns, but the German visitors pay them no mind, waiting for Hector's reply.

The only parts of Bogotá that Hector knows at all are Soacha and Ciudad Bolivar, and although these are, indeed, the real Bogotá, they are not what these two women have in mind. It should be said here that at this point in his life Hector has never had a sexual experience with anyone but himself, but he is both a farm boy and a reader, and between these he has a comprehensive knowledge of sexual acts and behavior. He knows what these women want and he knows how profitable it could be for him, but he passes up the opportunity this time, mostly because he wants to get back to Soacha to be with his family on their first night in Bogotá.

A mud brick hut was built and inside it a wooden platform on which the seven family members slept in clumps. Going door to door in the residential quarter of La Merced, Marcella found herself and Fernanda housecleaning jobs at five hundred pesos per twelve-hour day. But it was Hector who kept the family from sliding off the embankment into the trench that was known in Soacha as 'the pit of the homeless.' For fourteen hours each day, he sold both Rico's cigarettes and the contraband he began buying himself from a dealer in Ciudad Bolivar. And there were times now and then when Hector accepted the propositions of middle-aged female tourists along with their money. From these women he acquired what might be called a working knowledge of feminine desires along with a vocabulary of basic English.

A year passes, then most of another. Unknown even to his mother, Hector is saving money, hiding it in a small tin box he buries under their hut's mud floor. He has a plan that will bring his family sanctuary.

One night, an Australian woman brought Hector back to her room at the Melia Santafe. After he had completed his chore with her, Hector stopped at a beer stand across the street from the hotel where he found three boys about his own age having an animated discussion about the best way to get to the United States. If you went to Mexico, made your way north, and then swam across the Rio Grande at night, you could get there without encountering a single immigration policeman. But one of the boys had a cousin who had tried that route and was captured and beaten to a pulp—not by police, but by Texas vigilantes. No, the best way was to fly directly to Miami with a counterfeit visa and take your chances. The worst that could happen is they sent you back.

But if you made it—if you got there home free, my friend— your life will be made of gold! And so will the lives of everyone you love.

The cost of a counterfeit visa bought directly from an officer at the American Embassy, Hector was told, was five million pesos.

CHAPTER FIVE

Every Christmas Eve after dinner, Franny deVries slips her DVD of Fanny and Alexander *into her player, and she and Wendell and Lila watch the movie to its end when, back together after some terrible trials, the extended Ekdahl family gathers in Uppsala for a grand christening supper. Franny calls the Bergman film their very own midnight mass.*

Franny can live inside this movie, burrowing under a fur comforter with the rest of the Ekdahls as they set off in a horse-drawn sleigh on the snow-covered streets of Uppsala. A small family theater binds this Swedish family together. There, speaking lines written by Strindberg and Shakespeare, they are able to connect with one another more intimately than they can anywhere else. At the christening supper, Carl Ekdahl raises his glass of aquavit, calling for a blessing on their family and their theater:

"The world is a den of thieves and night is falling. Evil breaks its chains and runs through the world like a mad dog. The poison affects us all. No one escapes. Therefore let us be happy while *we are happy. Let us be kind, generous, affectionate and good. It is necessary and not at all shameful to take pleasure in the little world."*

"The little world," Franny echoes in a whisper, and she weeps.

* * *

It is mid-October in Grandville with a premature winter chill in the evening air. Franny has heated a Lipton chicken Cup-a-Soup on her hot plate. She locks up her shop and, Cup-a-Soup in one hand and sketchbook in the other, walks briskly to the Phoenix, lets herself in, turns on the stage lights, then heads back to the stairs where she climbs to the balcony. There, she sits in the front row, sipping her soup and gazing at the stage.

She does not know if it was duty or guilt that compelled her to volunteer to design the set for *How's Never?* She does know that this allowed her to gracefully withdraw from either appearing in the play or directing it, as Babs Dowd had asked her to do. Franny told Babs that she had not had a chance to design a set in years and only now, with all this wonderful new talent around, could she get back to her first love in theater. There was some truth in this, more of it as Franny immersed herself in the project, sketching late into the autumn nights. Her personal challenge was to see how much she could alter the play itself, rescue it from its inherent self-parody, by placing it in an ingenious environment. Her first attempts were to pattern the presidential bunker after the hovel Jean-Marc had designed for their college production of *Lower Depths*— dark, oppressive, damp. But just watching a single rehearsal of *How's Never?* with such a set in mind, Franny knew it was a very bad idea; it would only exaggerate the play's unreality, tear at its already threadbare substance.

The trick would be to push the design in the opposite direction, toward the fantastic. Franny's first attempts at this were Disneyesque—broad, rounded oblongs in primary colors bordered in black stripes. Put a cartoon in a cartoon box. But again, Franny realized this would just cheapen Babs's play even more than it already was. Of course, that had a certain appeal—calling a spade a spade; at least the audience would know *Franny* knew exactly what they were getting. But she could not permit herself to be that devious.

"Don't design a set—invent a language!" Jean-Marc always said. It was just such pronouncements, delivered in a lilting Parisian baritone as if each time he had just invented the idea, that made Franny fall in love with Jean-Marc when he arrived on the Ithaca College campus in the spring term of her junior year. After not thinking about Jean-Marc for years—maybe even a full decade—he had been creeping into Franny's mind regularly since she began working on the set for *How's Never?*

A perfect language for the set popped into Franny's mind when she awoke this morning—*Biblical!* Yes, obviously, a biblical language. Take all of that glib, *faux*-theological dialogue in *How's Never?* and surround it with New Testament images. That could put the entire play in winking quotation marks without compromising it. Franny had immediately grabbed Jansen's *History of Art* from her bed table and begun searching for prototypes. A Renaissance Madonna—say

Bellini or Raphael? No, that could too easily veer from a wink to a supercilious put-down. She flipped the pages to William Blake's surreal illuminations for *All Religions Are One*. Jesus, they were gorgeous, and heaven knows they were biblically inspired, but they were *genuinely* spiritual, and any audience member who tuned into that spirituality would be lost from the get-go. But as she looked at Blake's painting of God contemplating the world He just created, Franny had an inspiration.

After Lila left for school, Franny went into her daughter's bedroom and scanned the bookshelf. There, on the bottom shelf, dusty and long-unopened, was the children's illustrated Bible that Beatrice had given her granddaughter on her sixth birthday. Sitting cross-legged on the cold floor, Franny studied the pictures: Adam and Eve gaping at the serpent, their nakedness camouflaged from young eyes in a peek-a-boo of hanging leaves and fruit; Moses hoisting the holy tablets above his head like an athlete displaying his trophy; Jesus astride a donkey, waving shyly at the villagers who line the streets as if he is a matinee idol embarrassed by his sudden notoriety. The pastel colors, the earnest expressions on the subject's faces, the artist's clumsy but touching attempt to give them a contemporary feel, as if these biblical folk could be living right next door—it was all just perfect for *How's Never?* Like the play, the illustrations were both sincere and naïve. Franny could have her wink and serve the play too.

Some of Franny's customers that morning were disappointed by her unwillingness to join the daily seminar, but Franny was drawing. And by the time she closed up her shop, she had filled an entire sketchbook.

Now Franny flicks her eyes from a page in her sketchbook to the stage and back again. She has patterned the presidential bunker after the holy manger in the children's Bible. Straw-covered dirt floor, stone foundation, raw wood roof beams, the gate of a horse stall deep on stage left, and flying overhead, like the canopy that hovers over the Blessed Infant's crib in the book, a silk banner displaying the presidential seal. Franny is thrilled; she has invented the perfect visual language for *How's Never?*

Down below, people are arriving for tonight's rehearsal, the first without scripts in hand. Franny recognizes Sally Rule's voice. Sally is playing the president's wife, playing her in much the same manner as she portrayed Lady Britomart—vaguely British, haughty, and snippy. It is what Sally does, but actually her hauteur works quite well in *How's Never?* Franny can easily visualize Sally tossing her head imperiously as she kicks up some manger straw. Next, Franny makes out Babs Dowd's voice. Babs is directing her own play; despite her request to have Franny direct, Babs is obviously delighted with the way things have worked out. She has developed a little routine that she uses at every rehearsal; she will start a note to an actor by saying, "I'm not sure what the author had in mind here, but . . ." The actors love it.

It takes Franny a fraction of a second longer to recognize the third voice, possibly because it does not belong to a member of the company. It belongs to Franny's mother, Beatrice. Franny automatically shuts her sketchbook. If she timed it just right and walked very softly, Franny could be down from the balcony and out the theater door with no one noticing. And there is a good chance this is what Franny would have done if she had not heard footsteps ascending the balcony stairs. She recognizes her mother's tread more quickly than she recognized her voice. Franny also recognizes the anxiety the sound of that tread still calls up in her.

For most of her childhood, Franny felt like a sneak. Not because she was particularly deceitful or naughty, but because of her mother 's relentless scrutiny of her. In the mornings, her mother would examine her hands and nails, her hair and face and, on occasion, she would lift the hem of Franny's skirt to check her underpants. This last Mother did sterilely, her arm extended straight out, grasping the hem between her thumb and forefinger, and peering at Franny's underpants through her reading glasses as if they were a research specimen. But even more humiliating were Beatrice's evening invasions of Franny's bedroom when she would snap on the overhead light, and say, "I was so worried about you, Darling!" Years later, when Franny confronted her mother about this practice, Beatrice insisted that she was simply concerned about her only child's health, but by then Franny knew better. It was not germs that terrified her mother, it was vulgarity. The contamination she probed was not viral, but social. Beatrice's obsessive fear was that her child would turn out like Wendell—fatuous, uncultivated, and ambitionless. And that is why Franny, who adored absolutely everything about her father and yearned to be like him, felt like a sneak.

She feels this now as her mother appears at the top of the balcony stairs and peers around. Franny is fully aware that if anyone in this diagram is sneaky, it is her mother, just as it was her mother who was the sneak when she barged into her bedroom as she lay on her back, staring at the ceiling and dreaming of escape. But even though Franny is now thirty-seven years old, this awareness is no match for the guilt her mother's footsteps reflexively inspire in her.

"Sally said I might find you here," Beatrice is saying as she strides down the aisle.

For a woman of sixty-one, Beatrice looks fabulous, in part because of the care she bestows upon herself—her weekly facials at Canyon Ranch, her biweekly trims and dye-jobs at the Hermes Salon, her daily workout at home—but also as a result of the 'little tuck' in Costa Rica that her new husband treated her to as a sixtieth birthday gift. Beatrice's vanity came late in her life—about the same time Lila started needing a bra, as Wendell once pointed out.

"Well, you found me," Franny replies.

"I hear you're doing the sets. I'm so glad. I always thought that was your special talent."

Beatrice's implication—that her daughter's acting, directing, and producing are *not* her special talents—is obvious to Franny, just as it is obvious to her that if she brought this implication to her mother's attention, Beatrice would deny it and then proceed to lecture Franny about her unbecoming childishness.

"I'm still working on the drawings," Franny says. Beatrice has taken the seat just behind Franny, and Franny has to swivel around uncomfortably to look at her.

"Any peeks allowed?" Beatrice has added a trilling, youthful laugh to accompany her renovated face.

"No," Franny retorts—a little too vehemently, she decides, so she adds, "I haven't even shown the director yet."

"Mrs. Dowd."

"You know her?"

"Sally introduced us. She's trying to bring her into the garden club, but Babs says she's too busy just now with her play."

From the corner of her eye, Franny sees Babs Dowd at the side of the stage, speaking intently with Sally Rule and Ned Shields, who is playing the President. Franny has the sudden urge to spring to her feet and scream at the stage, *"She's a fucking fraud! Doesn't anybody see that?"*

She does not scream anything, of course.

"Her husband is the recruiter for Harvard in this area," Beatrice is saying. "Has Lila started thinking about college?"

Franny roars with laughter, filling it with the unexpended force of her stifled scream. Babs and her actors look up at the balcony, then return to their conference.

"Is that so funny?" Beatrice asks.

"I don't think Lila will be applying to Harvard, Mother," Franny says, rising from her seat. "But I did promise to help her with her homework tonight."

Franny had been planning to sit through the entire rehearsal and then latch onto Babs Dowd at the end to show her drawings, but sitting with her mother even a few minutes longer is unthinkable. Also, the idea of showing Babs her sketches of the bunker-cum-manger now makes her feel unaccountably insecure. At the bottom of the stairs, Franny casts a last look at the stage and there sees Babs administering a shoulder rub to her star, Ned Shields. She is a busy one, that Babs.

Franny had been saving her sixth and final cigarette of the day for home, but she lights it up as soon as she steps out onto Melville Street. Heaven knows her mother's worst fear has certainly come true: she *has* become like her father. She is a single parent who never finished college and runs a shop on the Melville Block. And the only place where her dreams ever soar is inside the Phoenix. But not tonight. No, tonight there is a new show in town.

Instead of walking up Melville Street toward home, she heads down toward Main. She needs to calm herself. The air is nippy and all she is wearing on top is her old Ithaca sweatshirt, selected from her wardrobe this morning in celebration of her rekindled collegiate enthusiasm for set designing. But that enthusiasm has withered and the sweatshirt lets the cold air in.

At Main Street, a single car idles at the stoplight. On its side, 'Grandville Driving School' is painted in large block letters. Peering through the passenger window, Franny sees Mel Gustal sitting next to the driver, a beefy teenage boy who is apparently learning the fine art of night driving. One morning, Archie Morris declared that the day Mel opened his driving school was the definitive day that Grandville started going downhill. "When your dad isn't good enough to teach you how to drive, the whole family thing is shot to hell," he said.

On the other side of the street in front of the town hall, four figures are standing at the curb, one of them holding a cardboard placard that faces oncoming traffic that, at this moment, is comprised only of Mel Gustal's driver's ed automobile. Franny has to wait until the light changes and the car jerks forward, casting its beams on the placard, to make out the message written on it: '138 Soldiers Dead in Iraq.' She has never seen this group or this sign before. She crosses toward them.

"Hi, Franny." Marta Newman, the pastor of the Unitarian Universalist Church, smiles at Franny as she approaches. They only know one another from Franny's shop, where Marta buys more birthday and bereavement cards than anyone else in town.

"Hello, Marta," Franny says. "Is this your group?"

"Nobody's really. Just some like-minded friends."

The others smile at Franny, clearly eager to make her one of their number, but Franny hangs back. She has a longstanding distrust of organized do-gooders. She suspects them of a moral vanity that equals that of any Christian evangelist; they just adore the drama of being right. But neither does Franny move on. She recognizes another protestor, a philosophy teacher at the community college named Herbert Something. He wears a full beard and ties his kinky hair back in a ponytail with a red rubber band. He looks Jewish or Italian and is either stoned or slightly daft, yet his smile is engaging. Doing a passable imitation of President Bush, he says to Franny, "You're either with us or against us." Then he laughs.

"How about the number of Iraqis who've been killed?" Franny asks.

"Good question," Herbert replies. "Somebody needs to make a sign with that too."

The young woman holding the placard turns around and Franny recognizes her, too. She is a girl in Lila's class at Grandville High, the daughter of the guidance counselor, Terry Cyzinski. Franny has frequently seen her photograph in the *Grandville Chronicle* for one achievement or another—elected president of the Honor Society, winning the countywide girls' tennis tournament, named captain of the math team. Stephanie—yes, that is her name—is everything that Lila is not: dedicated, ambitious, cheerful. And Franny cannot help wishing that Lila were just a little bit more like Stephanie, if only for her own sake.

"I could make that sign," Stephanie is saying to Herbert. "I'll get the number off the Net."

Franny is surprised to see Stephanie Cyzinski here. In Franny's day, peppy tennis players and political protestors rarely mixed, especially not in one person.

"It's okay. It's my idea, so I ought to do it," Franny says.

Without giving it any thought, Franny has just made a commitment of sorts: she will make a poster and she will stand with this little crew at their next vigil. Once she realizes what she has done, she panics. As it is, she spends too little time at home with Lila, what with the shop and the Grandville Players. But she could hardly just take back her offer and march away. She decides she will come back just one time, hand over her placard of the Iraqi death toll, then make her apologies. That helping-Lila-with-her-homework line has been working well lately.

So now on this crisp October night, Franny stands at the curb on Main Street, waving with the others at passing cars and cheering when one toots its horn in approval. After a while, she sets her sketchbook against the base of a poplar tree so she can wave with both hands. The bearded professor smokes, so Franny allows herself a seventh and eighth cigarette tonight; she will subtract it from tomorrow's allotment. If she were to think about it, Franny would doubt that anything this earnest group did could possibly make a particle of difference in the grand scheme of world politics. But Franny does not think about that. In fact, she does not think about much of anything except how exhilarating the chilled air feels in her lungs.

CHAPTER SIX

It takes a lot to get Wendell deVries to leave Grandville, even for just a day. He certainly is not intimidated by new places. And it is not as if he has an oldtimer's prejudice against anything different from what he is used to; Wendell rejoices in the wider world's variety when he sees it in movies or reads about it in books. No, Wendell's inertia is born of his honestly-held belief that there is more than enough variation and complexity right in front of his eyes. He is a student of the here and now so he rarely sees a reason to go *there*, wherever it is.

But this morning is the exception. He is driving in his pickup all the way to Amherst, an hour and a half northeast of Grandville, because in this particular situation there is something in Amherst that he has been unable to find in Grandville: Howard Gnomes, Professor of African American Studies at the University of Massachusetts. Although Lila has not brought up the subject again, the black deVrieses of Grandville have settled in Wendell's imagination.

This bright autumn morning is exceptional in another way, too: the pickup is carrying a passenger in addition to Wendell and Binx, who stands in the truck bed with his ears flying and his nose cocked high, believing everything he smells. That passenger is Esther.

How this came about is a simple story: Wendell returned to the food co-op for what had become his regular Tuesday tofu tutorial and Esther was prepared with her personal recipe for tofu manicotti printed by hand on a 3-by-5 card. As Esther led Wendell around the store to pick up the ingredients, she asked him why he had been reading about New England African-Americans in his projection booth, and he told her.

"There's a professor up at UMass who knows more about local blacks than anybody I've ever heard of," Esther said.

"Maybe the same guy who came to my granddaughter's class," Wendell said. "How do you know about him?"

"I went to college up there a million years ago."

"You studied about blacks?"

"Among other things. I was something called an American Studies major which basically meant I couldn't make up my mind what I wanted to study. It's the major for people with Attention Deficit Disorder."

Wendell laughed, as he often did when chatting with Esther. "Maybe I'll give him a call," he said.

"I could call him if you want," Esther said. "We've kept up a bit, mostly because his wife and I became friends. We were two of the five members of the Lebanese Club."

"Are you Lebanese?"

"Half. My mother is." Esther selected a package of Celentano whole wheat manicotti shells from the shelf and deposited it in Wendell's basket. "I've been meaning to call them anyhow."

And that was pretty much it. That evening Esther called her friends in Amherst who suggested a lunch date for all four of them. Then Esther walked down to the Phoenix where she climbed the balcony stairs and knocked on the projection booth door during a screening of *Seabiscuit*. She asked Wendell what he thought of the lunch idea. He thought it was splendid.

"This is a treat," Esther is saying. Her window is open and she faces it, letting the wind swoop up her red hair much the way it swoops up Binx's ears.

"It definitely is."

"Did you tell your granddaughter about your research?"

"Lila? Yep. But I think her mind has moved on to more pressing matters, whatever those might be."

"She's sixteen, right?"

Wendell nods.

"It's a whimsical age," Esther says, smiling. "There's something to be said for being able to take every new thought more seriously than the last."

Wendell looks at Esther, then back at the road. "But the strange part is, she wanted to know about some distant relatives on my side, but she never asks anything about her own father. Never has."

"I take it he's not around."

"Nope. She never met him. Neither have I, for that matter. He was a teacher of her mother's in college. A set designer from France. They had a thing—an affair." Wendell purses his lips. This is a subject he never talks about with anyone, not even with Franny in the last ten years, so he cannot understand why he is talking about it now, and with a woman he barely knows.

"I had an affair with one of my professors too, an anthropologist," Esther says. "It was considered the liberated thing to do back then. You know, breaking down old-fashioned sexual barriers. Of course, it wasn't liberating at all. It was just the same old, same old. I was young and he was impressive, mostly because he was my professor. So he had his way with me, as the old-fashioned types used to say."

Wendell is shocked by Esther's candor. He is not accustomed to hearing women talk about their sexual experiences, even if such talk is staple dialogue in many of the Hollywood films he now shows. He wonders if he is just an old prig, stuck in a generation of men who want to believe that a decent woman does not even think about sex, let alone speak of it in mixed company. But for heaven's sake, did that include a forty-something woman with an apartment full of her own children?

"Why are you laughing?" Esther asks.

"Because I'm an old fart," Wendell answers, grinning at her.

Howard Gnomes has reserved a table in the dining room of the University of Massachusetts Faculty Club. Not only is this the first time Wendell deVries has ever been inside a university building other than Grandville Community College's single structure that once housed Foster's Printing Company, but it is the first time he has had lunch anywhere with a black man. There were no blacks in Grandville High School when Wendell went there; he was never in the army; and the fact is he has not gone out for a meal with anybody other than Franny or Lila in thirty years. Both the austere, colonial dining room and Professor Gnomes's blackness make Wendell feel awkward.

Fortunately, Esther and Zeina Gnomes immediately launch into a discussion about their children. In this discussion Wendell learns that Esther has two children, not three as he had somehow imagined. Gnomes periodically smiles at Wendell, but mostly busies himself studying the menu. Finally Gnomes says, "I recommend the pot roast. Actually, it's the *only* thing I recommend."

Wendell is surprised by Gnomes's voice. It is certainly a black voice—deep and resonant, like the voice Wendell hears in his mind when he reads Langston Hughes poems. There is even something of Hughes's black diction in the way Gnomes stresses the middle syllable in 'recommend.' But it is also a voice of authority—consummate, literate authority. Wendell is well aware that there is not a reason in the world to think that a black voice cannot also be professorial, but nonetheless Wendell has never heard this combination before in his life, so it puzzles him.

After their orders are taken—pot roast all around—Gnome turns to Wendell and says, "Esther tells me that you are wondering if you are related to a black family with your surname that once lived in Grandville."

"That's right. My name is deVries."

"Yes, she told me. Are your people from the Netherlands by way of Rensselaer?"

"Yes."

"Then you *are* related. The only question is how closely." Gnomes delivers this information with a wry smile.

Wendell smiles back at him. "Well, that was easy," he says.

"Of course, however close, it is very unlikely that you have any African-American antecedents yourself," Gnomes goes on. "Your black relatives may have white blood in their veins, but I'm certain you don't have any black blood in yours. I'm afraid that's one club you cannot belong to."

Esther winces when Gnomes says this last and Wendell touches her arm to reassure her that he is not offended. Wendell knows very well what clubs Gnomes is referring to, although in truth there are many of them that would not welcome Wendell as a member either; his ex-wife, the former Miss Cosgrove, could testify to that.

"But you think it's a relative, not just a slave name," Wendell says to the professor.

"I looked it up and I'm almost certain," Gnomes says. "The deVries of Grandville were light skinned. That's a clue right there, especially for the 1810s and '20s which is when they settled there. The older Dutch families were pretty strict about sex with *anyone*, let alone with their slaves. So that suggests they were a first generation mix."

Wendell nods. He is fascinated.

"There was a man named Henk deVries who served out his seven-year indenture in 1771 and immediately bought himself two slaves and started a dairy over the border in West Stockbridge, Massachusetts. One of these slaves was a woman named Agnes. Henk had two children with her. He actually helped raise them although he never formally recognized them except by giving them his surname. Of course, that didn't mean anything because a white man gave his name to his slaves and their children anyhow. My guess is that the deVrieses of Grandville—the *black* deVrieses of Grandville—are one or the other of those children."

Wendell smiles at Gnomes. He automatically latches onto the part about Henk deVries helping to raise his half-breed children; it is a detail he thinks will gratify Lila.

"I can't thank you enough, Professor," Wendell says.

"How did you hear about your namesake?" Professor Gnomes asks.

"From my granddaughter. She's taking a course about local black history in high school and a professor from UMass gave a talk in her class. He mentioned the name deVries. Was that you, by the way?"

"No, one of my graduate students." Gnomes studies Wendell's face. "Was she upset by this news?"

"Actually, she was delighted by it," Wendell says. "She was hoping she's directly related. That we have black relatives."

Gnomes's laugh is cynical and again Esther looks apprehensive.

"I imagine she likes hip-hop, Ice-T and MC Rule," the professor says coolly.

"Not that I know of," Wendell answers. "You know what I think it is? We live in a town that's ninety-five percent white and she's not a very happy child. It gives her an out. Some dreaming room."

"White fatigue," Gnomes says.

"Well, some kind of fatigue anyhow." Wendell smiles. "Tired of being who she is. I've got a little case of that myself. Must run in the family."

Gnomes regards Wendell for what feels like a full minute, then reaches out his large right hand and clasps Wendell's shoulder. "Trying to burst out of your skin—whatever its color—is a common human problem," he says. "Unfortunately the universal problems of mankind are outside my field of expertise."

Both men laugh, joined quickly by the women.

Later, when they all are saying goodbye in front of the old university building, Esther and Zeina hugging one another, Gnomes and Wendell shake hands.

"There's a black church in Grandville," Gnomes says.

"The Zion on Pleasant Street."

"It's been there a long time. I understand they've kept pretty good records of their past members."

"Thanks. I'll check it out."

Binx has been fed some leftover pot roast—"Probably the first time a doggie bag from that place ever went to a real doggie," Wendell joked—and is sleeping in the truck bed for the trip back to Grandville. Both Wendell and Esther seem content to remain silent for a long while.

When Wendell turns onto the turnpike, Esther says, "I asked Zeina to come down for dinner some Sunday. Howard too, of course."

"Nice," Wendell says.

"Maybe you could bring Lila. She might find him interesting."

Wendell does not reply. He does not know what to say. He feels very comfortable riding in his pickup with this sweet and lovely woman at his side, but her casual invitation distresses him, makes him want to slow things down.

"Just a thought," Esther says after a moment.

Wendell looks over at her. She does not look offended in the least. He does not believe that she is hiding hurt feelings, or even that she has girded herself against them. It strikes Wendell that Esther has simply forsaken all disappointments as an act of will, that she simply cannot be bothered with them.

"I'm older than I want to be, Esther," he says softly.

"If that's an apology, I don't accept it," Esther answers, smiling at him. "I thought you could tell by now that I don't want anything that doesn't come naturally."

"I'm just starting to realize that," Wendell says. He is also just starting to realize that he likes this woman a great deal and that feeling is not altogether disagreeable. Just unsettling. He smiles at her. "What are you serving?" he asks.

"Pot roast."

Esther turns on the radio and tunes in the Five Colleges station that is playing folk music, both old and new. She sings along with some of the older ones, laughing when she slides off tune. And now they are back on Route 7 on the outskirts of Stockbridge heading for the Grandville town line. Wendell senses something in himself that he does not remember feeling since he was a child—melancholy that the day is coming to an end.

Chapter Seven

After school on Friday afternoons, Lila hangs around Grandville High for a while, then makes her way along the highway
to the Nakota for the evening shift. This makes more sense
than taking the school bus home and killing an hour there
before walking into town and taking the four o'clock Loop Bus
back to the highway.

Usually, she cannot get away from the high school fast
enough. Every minute there feels like house arrest. She
believes that high school basically serves the same function
as nursery school—*in loco* surveillance. The courses in geometry, French, and history are all a cover for the real purpose of
the institution—keeping an eye on teenagers so they can do
no harm.

Lila has few friends at school. Most of the students she
talks to are smokers like herself, the kids who sneak out of
lunchroom or study hall to dash across the highway and grab
a cigarette behind the trunk of a spruce tree. All of these kids
are in the vocational program—car repair, building trades, or
computer technology, which used to be called stenography—
so Lila does not see them in her classes. She is in the college
preparation program, even though going to college is something she never thinks about.

The other college prep students think Lila is a snob because
she does not talk to them, but mostly because she is so *pretty*
and does not talk to them. Lila thinks they are all deluded, that
they have never even tried to discover what they really want
or feel, so they go through their day playing the role of High
School Student and get so immersed in this role—the dating,
the gossip, the grade warfare—that they forget what it is to be
a real person.

On these Friday afternoons, Lila roams around the high
school building and grounds feeling like a spy, or maybe an anthropologist on a field trip to a remote, hither-to-undiscovered
society, trying to make sense of its patterns of behavior.
She peers through the window in the door to Study Hall B
where the French Club is watching a video of *Au Revoir Les*

Enfants with English subtitles. She wonders how many of them—the teacher, Mlle. Glass, included—have convinced themselves they actually understand what the actors are saying without the aid of the white letters at the bottom of the screen.

Through the door window to Study Hall C, she sees several of her secret smokers and realizes immediately that they must be in Detention, the prison within the prison. She catches Amanda's eye—she of the roach hidden under a rock—and waves, then scurries down the corridor to the outside door.

Mr. Cyzinski's voice carries up to her from the tennis courts. It is loud and boisterous like a sportscaster's, but Lila easily recognizes its testy bass notes. Personally, Lila has reached an understanding of sorts with the guidance counselor. The few times she was required to attend 'college readiness' sessions with Mr. Cyzinski, he informed her that she was not only wasting the school's time, but her own, and Lila could not have agreed with him more. Like most sports coaches, Cyzinski views the entire world as made up of either winners or losers, and Lila takes a perverse pleasure in willingly volunteering for the latter category. So it is not Mr. Cyzinki's winning voice that captures her attention, it is the distraught sound of his daughter, Stephanie's, faint reply. That is what draws Lila to the stand of scotch pines that protect the tennis courts from the wind.

Lila is now standing behind a low-hanging bough of one of these trees, furtively eyeing the courts. Cyzinski and Stephanie are there, facing one another across the net. No one else is around.

"I don't think you realize how lucky we just got, Sweetheart," the father is explaining to his daughter.

"But . . . I like regular tennis, Dad. I'm . . . I'm pretty good at it," Stephanie stammers back, looking down at her racket.

"Sure you are, Steph. Just like you'll be terrific at royal tennis too. If you work at it, you'll be fantastic. I guarantee it, pal."

"I don't know about that. I don't even know what the heck it is."

Everybody in school knows Stephanie Cyzinski. She is well liked by both her classmates and teachers for her good cheer and hard work. Even Lila has less disdain for her than for most of the others. Lila senses a struggle going on inside Stephanie. More than once she has spotted Stephanie peering out the window of their social studies class with a look of rueful longing on her face. Still, Lila would never consider talking to her.

"Let's just give it the old college try," Mr. Cyzinski is now saying, the laugh in his voice suggesting that he thinks he has said something witty.

"Actually, I don't even know if I want to go to Harvard," Stephanie answers quietly.

"*Want* to go to Harvard?" Cyzinski bellows. "Are you crazy?"

Stephanie bursts into tears, and Cyzinski reaches across the net and wraps an arm around his daughter's shoulders. "Aw, Steph, I'm sorry. Just think about it, okay, kiddo? Just give it a chance."

Lila takes this opportunity to sneak back from the trees toward the highway. She rarely thinks about what it would have been like to have a father, largely because Wendell feels like a father to her, only milder and less judgmental. Mr. Cyzinski's attitude does not surprise her. Back in middle school when she still hung out with her grade school friends, she would occasionally attend intermural basketball games and she never forgot the time Sandra Hurp's father screamed at his daughter in the middle of a game, calling her 'spastic.' When Lila told Wendell about this, he said that most girls' competitive sports are a result of the women's liberation movement; then he added his favorite saying, "Beware of what you desire, for you will surely get it."

Lila is walking along the shoulder of the highway, leaning forward to counterbalance the weight of her backpack. It is loaded with books and notebooks that she will not open over the weekend. She thinks of it as a disguise. Sometimes, she will encounter Appalachian Trail hikers along this stretch, off the trail to get a cup of coffee or shop for groceries. For the most part, they are a grim bunch, preoccupied with how many miles they have walked or how many are left to go. Nonetheless, Lila likes to think that with her long gait and bulging backpack, a passing out-of-town motorist will assume she is one of them, a traveler from afar.

As Lila sees Nakota's gold spire appear over the crest of the hill, she starts looking forward to her first dumpster break with Pato. Suddenly, she hears tires crunch against pebbles behind her and she jumps to her right, landing in the gutter. She twirls around and sees a Grandville Police car inching toward her, then come to a full stop just a couple feet away from her. The cruiser's cherry light is on and spinning. Flip Morris is leaning over the passenger seat, his face in the open window.

"You're a hazard, Lila," he calls to her. "A crash just waiting to happen."

"You'd have to be blind not to see me," Lila answers.

"That's for damned sure," Flip says, pumping his eyebrows a couple of times in a gesture that he probably thinks is macho. "Get in the car. I'll drive you the rest of the way."

Lila hesitates. She would rather walk and certainly would rather remain by herself until she joins her co-workers at Nakota, but the idea of a drawn-out argument with Flip Morris is even less appealing. She slips off her backpack one shoulder at a time, while Flip watches her. She gets in the cruiser, placing the backpack between them.

Flip snaps off the cherry light, slips the car into gear, and peels onto the highway. He reaches into his shirt pocket, pulls out a pack of Camels, and expertly shakes a single cigarette up from its opening. He offers it to Lila.

"No thanks," Lila says. "I'm underage."

Flip laughs. "That's a matter of opinion. Some people just grow up faster than others," he says.

Lila definitely agrees with that. For starters, she feels a lot more mature than Flip Morris. "But I wouldn't want to break the law, especially in the presence of a police officer," she says with deadpan coyness.

Flip laughs far harder and longer than Lila's comment merits, possibly thinking his appreciation will win points with her, but it only confirms her assessment of his maturity.

"What time do you have to be at work?" Flip says. He has placed the cigarette between his lips and now lights it with his Harley-Davidson Zippo.

"Four," she lies.

"Why the hell so early?"

"Prep work. I need to do some stripping—bean stripping." Lila realizes immediately that the word 'stripping' was poorly chosen. Does she say things like this on purpose just to provoke assholes like Flip Morris?

Indeed, Flip's eyes glint as he looks over at her. "Do you have any idea how hot you are, girl?" he says with a swaggering smile.

Lila quickly turns away from him and stares out the windshield. She can feel her pulse accelerate, her face flush. Thank God the Nakota is only a couple hundred feet ahead. "You can let me out on this side," she says evenly. "It's easier."

Flip does not slow the car. He drives past the Japanese restaurant without saying a word. Lila swallows hard, folds her arms across her chest. "Just drop me off here, Flip. Here is fine," she says, still staring straight ahead.

Flip presses down on the accelerator. They fly by the Getty station, the new motel, the pottery outlet. Lila takes a deep breath, feeding her panic some oxygen. She knows instinctively that begging is not the way to go; it only arouses assholes. She turns and looks him straight in the face. "Don't embarrass yourself, Flip," she says coolly.

Lila does not know where these words come from, probably a movie she once saw, but they feel right and strong coming out of her mouth. They work too. Flip abruptly applies the brakes. Before the cruiser comes to a full stop, Lila opens the door and jumps out. She stumbles, but does not fall. Her backpack is still on the car seat. She leaves it there.

"Fuckin' tease!" Flip snarls. He guns the motor, pops the clutch, and his car lurches forward. Seconds later, he heaves Lila's backpack out his window and it lands in the middle of the highway.

Lila waits until the cruiser is out of sight before stepping out onto the road to pick up her backpack. The top flap is torn and her history and geometry texts have bounced out, their pages turning swiftly one by one, as if the wind were a speed reader. She gathers them up, then sprints to the other side of the highway. She feels heroic.

CHAPTER EIGHT

*W*GVS-AM broadcasts at fify watts, which is just about as low-powered as a radio signal can get and still have listeners. But because its transmission tower stands in the valley at the center of the Grandville mountain range, those fifty watts are enough to get the job done. Most locals switch on the station first thing in the morning, especially in the winter months when snow day school closings are announced starting at 6:30 a.m.; at those times, WGVS has more juvenile listeners than at any other.

The dial stays on the station after the kids leave for school or, better yet as far as they are concerned, go back to bed for a delicious mid-winter sleep. Nick Palmer, the morning deejay, plays golden oldies and light pop, like Martina McBride's In My Daughter's Eyes or Billy Mure singing April in Portugal. In between songs, Palmer sprinkles regular features like Lost and Found (mostly cats and dogs, although some people still chuckle about the time Ted Barrett posted the loss of a wood bridge that broke free of its moorings during the big hurricane and sailed down Mahaiwe Brook to points unknown) and The Trading Post, where on the air you can buy and sell such items as used vacuum cleaners and exercise bicycles, and during hunting season, fresh venison. There are also birth and death notices, along with the occasional 'Happy Birthday!' sent out by request of a loved one or, at times, just as one of Nick Palmer's pranks.

At noon, the AP comes on for a three-minute wrap-up of world and national events, followed by a five-minute wrap-up of local news. Then Bob Balducci takes over for Nick with only oldies, some going as far back as Johnny Ray. Bob often has a guest he interviews live, like a town selectman or the high school principal, although lately he also has been getting people like Andrew Fellows, who runs the chamber concert series at the Congregational Church, or Babs Dowd, a newcomer to town who wrote and is directing the new Grandville Players production coming up next month.

As one leaves the house to go shopping or get a haircut or buy stamps, the car radio picks up where the kitchen radio *left off. And stepping into Artorian's Package Goods or Bob's Barber Shop or the post office, only a line or two of a familiar song is missed before it continues on the radios playing inside these destinations.*

Franny sets the tuner in Write Now to WGVS when she opens at seven o'clock. In part, this is in deference to her customers, but Franny would not deny she finds the station comforting too. She likes the idea that it cannot be picked up even as nearby as Lenox; it is Grandville's secret signal. But at five, she switches over to the NPR FM station out of Albany for the news show, *All Things Considered*. At this hour, most of her customers are either school kids or day workers like herself who have had their fill of WGVS for the day.

Patricia Neighmond, *All Things Considered*'s chief science editor and one of Franny's favorites, is reporting on a new study published in the *Journal of the American Medical Association* that says a diet high in phytoestrogens reduces the risk of lung cancer by forty-six percent, even in smokers. Further, Ms. Neighmond says, there is no better source of phytoestrogens than soybean products, like tofu. This is cheering news for Franny. Although Lila never smokes at home, Franny knows her daughter is a smoker, so those tofu dinners are serving a double purpose. Franny is heartened by any sign that she is a good mother.

It is a Wednesday evening in late October and the leaves are long gone from the poplars outside her store's windows. Even on the hills on the edge of town, there are few leaves left on the trees except for the willows that can hold onto their foliage until past Thanksgiving. Last night, Franny finally got up the nerve to hand over her bunker/manger set design to Babs Dowd. She put her drawings in a manila envelope and sealed it before she charged up to Babs outside the Phoenix a few minutes before that night's rehearsal began. Then Franny headed down to Main Street to wait for her fellow 'vigil-istas,' as Herbert-the-professor calls their little crew.

Tonight, she is thinking of locking up a few minutes early so she can pick up a bottle of wine at Artorian's before it closes, then go home for an early supper with Lila. She has only one customer left in the shop, a woman who has been studying the rack of Thanksgiving greeting cards for the past ten minutes. Franny does not know her name or recall ever having seen her in the shop before, but the woman's long face is definitely familiar. On weekdays at this time of the year, virtually every face Franny sees is somewhat familiar. She would like the woman to hurry up with her decision and leave.

"Need any help?" Franny asks.

The woman offers a reticent smile and shrugs.

"I like the one with the turkey holding a shotgun," Franny says, walking over to her.

The woman remains looking at the rack of Thanksgiving cards as she starts to speak. "You're Franny deVries, aren't you? Lila's mother."

"Yes," Franny answers. "And you look very familiar too, but I'm afraid I don't know your name."

The woman finally turns around to face Franny. She appears to be about Franny's age, but looks much more worn. Her face is rutted and gray, her shoulders slumped. Franny guesses that she is poor, possibly from Housatonic or Frowell River, although heaven knows there are still poor people living right here in Grandville.

"Tiffany. Tiffany Korand," the woman says. She starts to extend her hand, but stops herself, apparently flustered.

"Do you know Lila?"

"Not really. But my son's been in school with her since second grade. He's a class ahead of her."

Franny nods. She wonders if Lila is involved with this boy and that is why his mother has come to the shop—she wants to discuss their suitability for one another or some such. That sort of thing might still be done in hamlets like Frowell River.

"What's his name?" Franny asks.

"Bret. Bret Stephenson." A surname different from Tiffany's own, Franny notes; certainly not unusual these days. "Listen, I drove past you last night," Tiffany goes on. "You know, in front of the Town Hall."

"The vigil," Franny says. "For the war dead."

"Yes. You were the only one I recognized."

The woman looks deeply distressed, and Franny reflexively steps back from her. Could this woman be some kind of zealot who is about to harangue Franny about her politics? She *did* wait until the store had emptied, obviously so no one would see her. Franny remains a few feet away from her, eyeing her closely, saying nothing.

"How . . . how do you know those numbers are right?" Tiffany asks.

"The number of soldiers killed?"

Tiffany nods.

"We get them off the Web. GlobalSecurity dot org. It's a non-partisan site," Franny says.

"On a computer," Tiffany says.

"Yes. It's just like a newspaper, really." Franny slowly backs toward the door, keeping her eyes on the woman.

"You never hear that on the radio," Tiffany says.

"On GVS?"

"Uh-huh, not on the news."

Franny considers explaining the reason for this to Tiffany: that the government does not want its citizens to become unduly preoccupied with the war dead, and the corporate media, like WGVS's A.P. news, is more than willing to cooperate in this act of patriotism. But Franny does not want to provoke this woman any more than she already is.

"So it's like a lie," Tiffany says. Her face is still creased with anxiety, but now seems more troubled than threatening.

"Pretty close to one," Franny answers.

"That doesn't seem right, does it?"

"Not to me," Franny says.

For a moment, Tiffany looks back at the Thanksgiving cards, then looks straight at Franny. "I never marched or protested or anything before," she says.

It takes Franny several seconds to grasp Tiffany Korand's meaning.

"Neither did I," Franny says, smiling with wonder.

"Aren't you afraid somebody will see you?"

Franny cannot help but laugh. "That's kind of the idea, Tiffany." She wants to hug this woman, and takes two long steps toward her, but now she is afraid of frightening *her* so she just touches Tiffany's shoulder lightly. "I was just going to close up and go over there now."

Tiffany shrugs. "I still can't make up my mind which card to get."

"I wouldn't get any if I were you. They make cards for every damned thing these days. They sent me a bunch for Groundhog Day last year—can you believe it? It's just another money-making business."

Tiffany laughs and for a moment Franny can see traces of what once must have been a fairly attractive face. "I can only do it for a few minutes," Tiffany says.

"Me too."

This time, Tiffany follows through with her handshake as she is introduced to Marta and Herb. Franny can tell her colleagues are overjoyed to have a new member of the group—especially one who looks so, well, average; they know how much that can count in Grandville. But fortunately both Marta and Herb control their enthusiasm and greet Tiffany with a kind of warm formality: "It's a great pleasure to meet you, Tiffany." Franny apologizes for not bringing her poster of Iraqi casualties this evening. They are waiting for Stephanie Cyzinski to arrive with the latest count of American soldiers killed.

The sun has dropped behind the mountains and the last refracted rays provide no warmth. An early evening breeze blows down Main Street and instinctively the vigil group huddles close together. For reasons she refuses to ponder, Franny feels content. Cars roll by, some honk and all four in the group wave back. Franny wants to ask Tiffany what brought her here tonight, but she does not want to break whatever spell the woman is under. No one talks; their silence is consoling.

"I guess I better go," Tiffany says after ten or so minutes.

"Me too," Franny says. "Got to get dinner going."

When they turn to leave, Franny sees Stephanie coming toward them with her poster under her arm: "412 American Soldiers Killed." Tiffany looks at the poster, then at Stephanie who is now walking directly up to her.

"Mrs. Korand!" Stephanie says. "I didn't know you'd be here."

"I didn't know myself," Mrs. Korand replies.

"But it . . . I mean, I can understand why," Stephanie says quietly.

Tiffany and Stephanie simply gaze at one another for a long moment while Franny stands beside them looking from one face to the other. Franny cannot guess what exact feelings are flowing between Tiffany and Stephanie, but she can tell these feelings are founded in compassion.

Finally Tiffany says, "I thought . . . you know, I thought the tennis . . . that it might lead to something. A scholarship . . ."

"I thought so, too," Stephanie says. "Bret's really super. My dad says he's a natural."

Tiffany shakes her head back and forth very slowly. Her eyes are tearing up. "He . . . he didn't even ask me. You know? Just came home and said he'd enlisted."

Tiffany looks like she might start to cry, and Stephanie wraps her arms around her and pats her mouse-brown hair. "We tried to get Bret to change his mind. Everybody did."

Tiffany whispers, "Thank you," pulls away from Stephanie, and starts to walk quickly across Main Street. Franny realizes that the woman is going to wait for the Loop Bus at the corner of Railroad Street. She does not want to leave Tiffany this way. She could go over to the Phoenix, borrow Wendell's truck, and drive Tiffany home, but at that moment Stephanie touches Franny's arm. This young woman, a high school girl, is signaling Franny to let the distraught mother be.

Franny sprints up Melville Street, past the theater and up the hill towards home. She urgently needs to see her daughter.

* * *

As Franny passes the theater, her father is inside, reading in the projection booth. Tonight, Wendell sold only seven tickets for the film *Radio*, and he considers this a testament to the town's good taste. He has only seen the film once and it pissed him off. Not because of its soppy life-affirming message, but because once again Hollywood had trotted out a retarded character to enlighten us with this message. The Forrest Gump factor. Wendell could not say who this contrivance insulted more, retarded people or the rest of us.

For a town its size, Grandville is home to a relatively high number of retarded people, the result of a Massachusetts law that gives full reimbursement to group residences for mentally-deficient people of all ages. Running these homes is a business, but it does seem to attract caring people, mostly semi-retired social workers from Springfield and Worcester who want to live out the rest of their lives in a rural area. The retarded, themselves, can be seen on Main Street just about any time during daylight. Their faces, stumbling gaits, and slow, loud voices are familiar to everyone who walks that street: the man with a large, round head and a hiccuppy laugh who calls himself 'Chief'; the pretty teenage girl with a look of perpetual bafflement on her fine-featured face; the one obvious Mongoloid, a man in his thirties who, for reasons only he may know, carries a backpack stuffed with thick books. One or another of them is often sitting at the counter of the Soup and Sandwich when Wendell drops in for his late-afternoon coffee and pie. He greets them the way he does everyone else in town: "How's it going?" Sometimes they even have a short conversation of sorts, about the weather or perhaps something that is on the shop's TV at that moment.

Wendell's father told colorful 'village idiot' stories from his childhood about a guy they called Pinky who spent his days standing in front of the Shays' Rebellion Monument next to Town Hall, playing with his yoyo and addressing every passerby by his full name. In the evenings, Pinky's father would pick him up in his truck and take him home. Wendell does not find anyone in the current population of simpletons particularly colorful. Like most people he encounters in town, they are simply familiar faces with private lives he will never know. But also as with the other people he sees on Main Street, Wendell is pretty sure they do not have any eye-opening lessons to teach him about what really counts in life. In his experience, he has never met an idiot who was a savant, although he has come across a fair number of savants who were idiots.

The buzz sheet accompanying *Radio* was freighted with quotes calling Cuba Gooding, Jr.'s portrayal of the retarded man "brave" and "daring." "Demeaning" is more like it. The Gooding character is a retarded *black* man for God's sake! To Wendell, the real message of the film is that only if a black man is retarded can you really love him for who he is.

Since meeting Professor Gnomes, Wendell decided to read up on African-American history. Over the years, it is in just this happenstance way that Wendell has pieced together his education, such as it is. He will, say, hear "Musetta's Waltz" on *Moonstruck's* soundtrack, and the next day he will stop by Digby's Music Shop and pick up a CD of *La Bohème* that he will proceed to play three or four times while reading the libretto in the accompanying pamphlet. Afterwards, he will put the CD on a shelf where it will remain untouched forever after. By that time, he may have overheard a conversation in Franny's shop about the old roller coaster in Coney Island, and off he goes to the community college library to take out a history or novel about Coney Island. He does not think of himself as an intrepid autodidact or even as a particularly curious man. Mostly, he thinks of himself as a man with a lot of time to spare in his projection booth. He is currently reading James Baldwin's *Go Tell It on the Mountain* and perhaps that is why he was so quick to spot the indignity at the heart of *Radio*.

With his feet stretched from his upholstered chair onto a pillow-topped box of old *Silver Screen* magazines, Wendell is reading the part of the book called, 'Gabriel's Prayer.' He knows some of the spirituals the characters sing in this section and hears their melodies in his head as he reads. Binx, as always, is lying on the projector stand next to the projector's motor, savoring the warm current that blows off it. Like his master, Binx is a creature of comfort.

There is a knock on the projection booth door, usually a sign that the film image has gone blurry or even disappeared altogether. Wendell gets to his feet and peers out the window slot at the screen: Cuba Gooding's demented smile is fully and vividly intact.

"Who's there?"

"Esther."

Wendell opens the door. "I didn't see you come in," he says.

"You caught me," Esther answers. "I didn't buy a ticket. But I promise not to look at the movie."

"That's a wise decision." Wendell gestures for her to come inside and when she does, he closes the door. He now sees that she is carrying a small wicker basket covered with a napkin.

"I made some *knafi*, but the kids were less than enthusiastic. They prefer Twinkies. The whole Lebanese connection doesn't mean much to them."

"Well, I don't think there are any in my bloodline," Wendell says. "But I am a good eater."

The projection booth is small to begin with, and Wendell's reluctance to dispose of anything that commemorates the Phoenix's past—including his beloved first projector, the stupendous Brenkert—has left so little space that Wendell and Esther stand just a foot away from one another. Esther removes the napkin cover, pulls out a pastry, and offers it to him. "It's a mid-Eastern cannoli," she says.

Wendell has to lean back at the waist in order to extend his hand without overshooting the proffered sweet. It would be an awkward maneuver for a smaller man; for Wendell it is a contortion. Esther laughs and positions the *knafi* in front of his mouth. He takes a good bite and chews slowly with a mock analytical expression on his face, as if he is a taste tester on one of those dueling chef TV shows.

"The hint of nutmeg is sumptuous," he announces solemnly.

They are both laughing now, and when Esther offers Wendell another bite, he leans past the delicacy and kisses her lips.

If, at this moment, we were able to peep in rather than out the six-inch window that commutes the projection booth with the rest of the theater, it would be hard for us not to giggle at what we saw: a tall, overweight, white-thatched man leaning down to kiss a small, middle-aged redhead who is arcing her right arm over their heads, suspending a flaky pastry as if it were some kind of ersatz mistletoe. But lingering longer, our eyes adjusting to the flickering rainbow of light reflected off the walls of this miniature stage, we would see there is more to this tableau than a simple sight gag. It is in their faces: They both look deeply relieved, as if for this moment they are released from a burden they have borne so long it felt like the burden of simply being human.

The kiss concluded, Esther looks around for a place to set down the half-eaten pastry. Binx has roused himself on the projector stand and sniffs in her direction. Esther looks at Wendell questioningly.

"He'd rather have a bagel, but I'm trying to expand his palate," Wendell says, grinning.

Binx hops down, takes the *knafi* from Esther's hand, and hops back onto the stand to eat it. Wendell leans down and kisses Esther again. He feels foolish and extraordinarily happy.

They keep kissing this way, holding each other softly, then tightly, then softly again. Every once in a while, they lean back from one another and look into each other's faces; they smile—sometimes laugh—but do not speak. Ten minutes pass. Down below, *Radio* is ratcheting up the mush for its three-hankie finale.

"I want to make love with you, Wendell, but I can't," Esther whispers.

"Okay," Wendell says.

"Aren't you going to ask why?"

"I figure you have your reasons."

"I do."

"Okay."

Esther leans back from him again, but this time she is not smiling. "I . . . I only have one breast," she says.

"Cancer?"

Esther nods. "Mastectomy."

"I'm sorry," Wendell says. This news does not much effect him. He feels neither shocked nor disappointed. He is so saturated with joy that it does not admit distraction. He touches the side of her face with his hand. "I may be behind the times, but I bet it's possible to make love without both breasts," he says, smiling.

Esther tries to smile back, but she cannot. "I guess I'm just not ready yet," she says.

"That's okay." He looks down at her. "The truth is, whatever we've just been doing, that's the sweetest lovemaking I know of."

* * *

When Franny returned home from the vigil, Lila was upstairs in her bedroom, and when Franny called up to her that dinner would be ready in a few minutes, Lila called back that she had eaten already. So Franny walked up and knocked on her daughter's door.

"I'm studying, Mom," Lila said.

Franny has a self-imposed rule against invading her daughter's room uninvited, so she said, "Can I to talk to you for just a minute?"

"Whatever," Lila replied.

Franny took this as at least a partial invitation and opened the door, but stopped at the threshold. Lila was lying in bed on her back, staring at the ceiling. Any mother but Franny's own would know that her child was busy dreaming she was somewhere else, *anywhere* else.

"I just had an amazing experience," Franny began. "And I knew you'd be interested. It's about people you know."

She then quickly told the story of Mrs. Korand, her son, Bret, who had enlisted, and Stephanie Cyzinski. But when she reached the part where Stephanie embraced Mrs. Korand, Lila interrupted her. "Stephanie probably does that shit so it will look good on her college transcript. Check off the box for 'citizenship.' She wants to go to Harvard, for crissake."

Franny was so stunned by her daughter's response that she immediately closed the door; she did not want Lila to see how wounded she felt. Reaching for the banister as she started down the stairs, Franny felt so weak and shaky she could not grasp the rail. She sat down on the topmost step and leaned against the wall. She took long deep breaths to counter her dizziness. Not for one second did she believe Stephanie Cyzinski had an ulterior motive for joining the vigil group. *How could Lila think that? What had made her so cynical? Was Franny to blame for that too?*

Franny waits until midnight for her father to come home. She wants to cry with him. She knows very well that she is beyond the normal age for a woman to still yearn for her father's embrace when she feels tears coming, but she does not begrudge herself this weakness. It is what it is, and she is grateful that she can find solace in her own home.

But not tonight. Wendell must be out drinking with Maggie Bello tonight. So Franny goes to bed and weeps alone.

* * *

After cleaning up and locking the theater, Wendell walks Esther home. She is carrying her basket of mid-Eastern pastries and

Wendell eats them one by one, relishing the sharp burnt surprise of toasted pine nuts inside the sweet cream filling. At the corner of Railroad Street, Wendell turns away his head lest Maggie Bello spot him through the window of the Railroad Car. He has only seen and bedded Maggie once since his trip to Amherst, and that was a dispiriting experience for him. Rather than introducing a thrust of life into his weary body, the act made him feel detached, a bored witness to a tired routine. He had hoped Maggie could tell they had come to the finale of their once-comforting alliance, but he realizes now that he will have to say something to her soon.

They pace slowly along Main Street, Esther's arm through his. It is mid-week at the tail end of foliage season and the streets are empty at this hour. Nonetheless, a number of stores have taken to illuminating their windows at night at this time of year, the way they only used to at Christmastime. Wendell and Esther stop to admire the window display in Cohen's Hardware and Plumbing; Syd Cohen has outdone himself this time with a diorama of leaf-gathering techniques ranging from an aluminum rake to a leaf blower the size of an industrial vacuum cleaner. A multicolor sprinkling of maple leaves adorns Syd's set.

"The man's an artist," Wendell says.

"But not a good businessman," Esther says. "One look at this and you'd feel guilty as hell buying anything but the rake."

They laugh and move on to Digby's Music Shop where the window display looks no different from the rest of the store—a muddle of CDs and sheet music with the occasional guitar pick thrown in.

"Now there's a merchandiser for you," Wendell says.

Usually, when Wendell passes the house on Board Street where he and Beatrice rented an apartment forty years ago, he quickens his pace so it cannot reach across the front lawn and touch him with memory, but tonight he lingers a moment in front of it and indeed, a memory does roll out to him: bringing newborn Franny home from the hospital.

At the three-story, Victorian house at the end of the block where Esther and her children rent an apartment, Wendell says, "I'm getting *Cold Mountain* on Saturday."

"Brrrr," Esther says. "I'll bring a sweater." She kisses him again.

Wendell feels dizzy with gladness as he returns to the Phoenix to pick up his truck and drive home and, when pulling into his Mahaiwe Street driveway he notices a 'For Rent' sign newly sunk into the lawn in front of the other half of their two-family dwelling, that gladness expands to a feeling of unlimited possibilities.

CHAPTER NINE

It had been another profitable night. Hector sold his allotment of Rico's Camels at the Sagrado stoplight in less than three hours, employing his new, musical sales pitch. Accompanying himself on a *cuatro* he bought from a street vendor in Ciudad Bolivar, Hector stood in the middle of Carrera Seven singing songs from Puerto Alvira—"Culebra," "Mis Flores Negras," "Por Un Besa de tu Boca." He wore a flowered linen shirt and a black Aztec cap, and under the band of this cap he displayed his wares of contraband cigarettes. It was a captivating sight even for downtown Bogotá: a towering boy with large liquid eyes and high-angled cheekbones in a hodge-podge theatrical get-up. To the tourists, he looks dashing and folkloric. And having learned to play the *cuatro* from his late father, Hector could produce flurries of staccato arpeggios that more than compensated for his tentative, thin voice. His tips exceeded his sales.

Cigarettes sold, Hector walks to the Casa Medina in the business district where he joins his friends, Mano and Sylvia. Mano is lounging in front of the hotel in his usual outfit of ragged jeans and side-slit T-shirt, his pan flute suspended from a brown cord around his neck. But nobody looks at Mano anyhow, not with Sylvia in sight. She is leaning against the trunk of a palm tree in a red-tasseled white skirt and embroidered, off-the-shoulder blouse, her waist-length hair flowing across one of those naked shoulders. Sylvia has more Indian in her than Hector and that is most evident in her narrow, tilted eyes, an angle she parallels in the luminous, Scarlet Macaw feathers fixed in her hair on the sides of her head. Sylvia is their star.

The three young people share a cigarette, then amble over to the square of pavement at the side of the Casa Medina where the hotel manager permits them to perform. Hector tunes up, Mano moistens the tips of his flute pipes, and Sylvia strikes a pose patterned after an American actress playing a Spanish dancer in a Hollywood film she once saw on television. It is a pose of total insolence. She sings.

Their first set is a mix of Jobim, Flamenco, and the Beatles. Sylvia has a forty-tone range that allows her to bounce up an octave when the spirit moves her, like in the last verse of "Michelle Ma Belle." For the most part, her voice is a flattish drone, but in the upper registers it is invaded by an involuntary catch that sounds like a desperate woman's plea. That is what tugs the audience around from the front of the Casa Medina.

Hector is adept at identifying the nationalities of their listeners and if, say, he picks out a French couple, he whispers to his companions and they break into "Auprès de Ma Blonde" or "Tes Yeux Sont Tout Fatigués." Sylvia's Spanish-accented Piaf impression can elicit a downpour of fifty-thousand notes into Hector's upturned cap.

Hector loves it all—the music, the performing, the money, and especially Sylvia herself. He adores the way she looks and the way she sings, but above all he adores her haughtiness and the self-confidence that underlies it. Sylvia treats Hector and Mano like brothers and comrades. She hugs and kisses them at the end of their performances, and she refuses to accept more than one-third of their take, even though she is clearly the main attraction. But when Hector looks at her with undisguised ardor, she merely laughs and nods and looks away.

Hector's feelings for Sylvia contributed to his decision to stop prostituting himself for lonely tourists, but certainly the money he takes home from their musical performances made that decision much easier. He has made another decision too: He is going to use his secret savings to pay for an apartment in La Sabana. He has already spoken with the landlord who will let them take possession of a two-room apartment if Hector produces a full year's rent in advance. Hector is now only three hundred thousand pesos away from that sum. The idea of emigrating to the United States is long gone from his mind.

It is past midnight when they call it quits. As usual, Hector is the last passenger aboard the Number 2 bus in its final night run to Soacha. As the driver approaches the last hill, he reflexively reaches for the shotgun leaning against his seat and cradles it across his lap in his left hand. To both the driver and Hector, this maneuver is no more than a routine gesture, like automatically crossing yourself when you pass the statue of the Virgin and Child at Santa Teresita Circle. Hector gets off at a pile of rubble that was once a street sign, saying goodnight to the driver. He slings his *cuatro* across his back.

He walks softly along the ridge of the Soacha basin to the back of Rico's shack where he takes the path down to Rico's front door. On the bus, Hector had separated his cigarette revenues from his tips, putting the former in a front pocket, the latter in a drawstring bag that hangs from his belt buckle to the inside of his undershorts. Rico sits just inside his open door, smoking a cocaine pipe. He looks up at Hector, then back at his pipe.

"A long night," he says.

"Yes. But I sold out everything." Hector reaches into his pocket and pulls out the wad of pesos.

"It must be that clown outfit," Rico says. He issues a graveley snigger and stands, but he does not reach for the money.

"I think it helps."

"And the *cuatro* too. I bet the foreign bitches love that. A boy and his *cuatro*."

"It helps me pass the time."

"Play for me, boy. Sing me a sad song."

"I do not sing very well."

"*Play!*"

Hector pulls his instrument around in front of him. He tunes it, then strums the opening chords of "Mis Flores Negras." He begins to sing.

> "Oye: bajo las ruinas de mis pasiones
> Y en el fondo de esta alma que ya no alegra,
> Entre polvos de ensueños y de ilusiones
> Yacen entumecidas mis flores negras."

Rico punches Hector on the side of his jaw and Hector falls backward, slamming his head against the doorpost. Hector slides to the ground. He can feel blood dripping from his scalp onto his neck.

"You are so pretty, aren't you?" Rico is standing over him. "How much do the cunts pay to squeeze your bony ass?"

Hector does not reply. His only movement is to breathe as deeply and regularly as possible. Above all, he does not want to lose consciousness. He orders his heart to slow down. He keeps his eyes open.

"Don't you know I always find out? You can't hide anything from Rico!" Rico punctuates this last with a vicious kick at Hector's ribcage.

Gasping for air, Hector blacks out, but only for a second; he seizes on his first dim glimpse of light and scrambles back to consciousness.

"You look like a woman to me," Rico is saying as he shoves his pipe into his pocket and begins to unbutton his fly. "Just like an Indian whore I used to fuck in Mitu. Because of this, I will not need to shut my eyes when you suck me."

His penis is out and rigid, a miniature replica of his own squat stature. *"Now, bitch boy!"* he growls.

Hector knows that if he screams, it will bring him no saviors, even if it might awaken scores of Soacha's inhabitants; relentless poverty does not inspire heroic acts. Hector considers surrendering to Rico's order. He has committed this deed before, although only once—with a British tourist—and for a great deal of money. It disgusts him, but he knows he can endure it; he has learned that there is little he cannot endure. And this is what Hector would have done had Rico not spoken again.

"Did you really think you could hide your money from me?" Rico snarls. "Do you think I am stupid?" He wags his penis with his hand as if it is a scolding finger.

So that is it. Rico found his buried box of savings.

Hector pulls himself up onto his knees, his *cuatro* still dangling from his neck. He opens his mouth wide. When Rico pushes his organ inside, Hector closes his lips around it in the same tender manner the British tourist instructed him to. Rico's sigh sounds like a child's. He pushes deeper. And that is when Hector savagely clenches his jaw together like a puma biting out the heart of a capybaras. The sound Hector's teeth make as they slice through skin and fat and blood vessels is no different from the sound they make when he chews down on a *chicharron*. Rico starts screaming. Blood gushes from his wound, and it is only when he looks down and sees this purple stream that he passes out.

Hector's fear has waited until now to seize him. He is quaking. Tears pour from his eyes, mucous from his nose. Dangling from his lips is a mix of spittle and clotting blood. Hector knows that if he is discovered by one of Rico's people now—even by just another cigarette boy—he, himself, will be beaten and killed. Blood is still pumping from Rico's ruptured member. Dazed, Hector scrambles to his feet, reflexively adjusting his *cuatro* between his shoulder blades.

Although unconscious, Rico emits a gagging sound from his open mouth. The sound stops, then starts again more loudly. Outside the hut, a flashlight scans back and forth, momentarily illuminating Rico's doorway. Hector picks up his cap from the floor, then squats behind Rico's head and stuffs the cap into the prone man's mouth. Now Hector pinches Rico's nostrils. It takes only a couple of minutes for the man to die. Hector pulls him by the feet to the back of the hovel where boxes of cigarettes reach to the ceiling. There, he covers the corpse by extending one of the blue tarpaulins and grounding it with a rock. This activity distracts Hector's fear, keeps it at bay.

He should leave quickly now, gather up his family and escape from Soacha, but he stands immobile at the back of the hut making a calculation of his terms of survival. It takes him only a moment to decide to risk his life to find his money.

Hector tries to imagine that he is Rico, pictures him standing just where Hector is now with a dirt-encrusted metal box in his hands. Hector stoops so he is the dead man's height, cocks his head back to approximate his dumb confidence. His eyes light on the pig haunch suspended by a rope slung over a beam at the ceiling. At times, when he was feeling magnanimous, Rico would haul that haunch down and pass it around for a gnaw apiece by his most loyal subjects. It is as large around as Hector's waist. Hector finds the free end of the rope wrapped around a table leg, unties it, and lets the fetid pig meat descend slowly. Flies and mosquitoes sail away, then immediately settle back to pick up where they left off. When the haunch smacks the ground, Hector's metal box tumbles out from a cavity of bone and muscle. Hector retrieves the box, looks inside; his earnings are still there.

Rather than continue down the slope to his home row of huts, Hector retraces his steps back to the perimeter, follows it to where it drops precipitously into the ravine, then edges down sideways to his house. He wakes his mother first.

"We have to go now, Mother. It is dangerous."

Marcella nods, leans over to wake the others on the platform, touching each of their lips to warn them to be silent. Without being conscious of it, she has been expecting this night; it does not shock her. She will not even ask her son the reason for their precipitous departure until they have walked through the night for over an hour, and when he tells her, she appears neither shocked nor scornful.

The first rays of equatorial sun are spreading down the Avenida Jimenez de Quesada when the family of seven arrives there. Hector waits until eight before walking alone to Calle 11 in search of Senor Garcia, the landlord he had spoken to. He finds him sitting at a table outside the Café con Pep Moso, sipping a *café con leche* and reading the sports section of *El Espectador*. Hector waits until he has finished before approaching him.

"Senor Garcia, I am Hector Mondragon."

"I remember you."

"I have eleven months rent in cash, right here." Hector holds out the metal box.

"I said a full year."

"I know this. I will have the rest in three weeks at the most."

"So you can come back then."

Hector does not reply. He bows his head.

"How tall are you, boy?"

"A bit under two meters."

"What is that on your back?"

"My *cuatro*."

"You know how to play it?"

Hector nods.

"What songs do you know?"

"Very many. Some from the South."

"Mis Flores Negras?"

Hector feels tears of panic gather in his eyes. "I was just singing that a little while ago," he says softly. *Just before I murdered a man.*

"Would you please me?"

"Of course, *Senor.*" He strums his instrument and begins to sing:

> *"Oye: bajo las ruinas de mis pasiones*
> *Y en el fondo de esta alma que ya no alegra"*

Hector's voice is stronger than it has ever been, the notes rounder, the timbre more complex and resonant. At the word, '*pasiones,*' there is a tormented catch in his throat just like Sylvia's. It is this that induces Senior Garcia to press a hand over his heart.

> *"Entre polvos de ensueños y de ilusiones*
> *Yacen entumecidas mis flores negras."*

The owner of the Con Pep Mosa comes to the door, wiping his hands on his apron. He stands and listens. He is followed by others from inside the café, then from the butcher shop next door to it. Even as Hector sings, he knows that he will not be able to duplicate this performance any time soon.

> *"Toma pues este triste débil manojo*
> *Que te ofrezco de aquellas flores sombrías*
> *Cógelas, nada temas, son los despojos*
> *Del jardín de mis hondas melancolías."*

Hector is singing for his life.

CHAPTER TEN

Wendell's mother, Sally Burton deVries, always found the very idea of playacting slightly disreputable and totally unnecessary. And although the Phoenix, first as a music hall and then as a movie house, provided her and Emile with an abundant income, she was perpetually embarrassed by her connection to the theater. She entered it no more than three times in her entire lifetime.

"Why in heaven's name does one need to dramatize life? Isn't it spectacular and stirring and ridiculous enough just as it is?" Sally would often say when Emile came home, raving about a new play mounted on the Phoenix's stage or a film that had just opened there.

Emile would shrug and laugh—he had ceased taking his wife seriously on most subjects early in their marriage—but Wendell's eldest sister, Marie, would always come to drama's defense.

"Life is so jumbled, Mamma, so muddled," Marie would reply. "Drama can break it down for us. Break it down and put it back together in a way we can understand."

"Put it together in a way that is not real, you mean. Sugar-coat it beyond recognition. Theater is simply a tool for deluding yourself, dear."

At this point, whilst pouring himself a snifter of brandy, Emile might not be able to resist chiming in, "Sort of like church in that way, isn't it, darling?"

Wendell, still a boy of eight or nine, adored these arguments. He would listen to every word from a corner of the kitchen or the bottom step of the stair. He kept waiting for his sister or father to say, "But the plays, the movies—they're fun! Isn't that enough?"

* * *

Babs Dowd knew her Halloween party would be a success a good week before it began. Starting then, several phone calls came each day asking her advice on what costume to wear, and when she told them she was decorating the interior of her Queen Anne home to look like a haunted house, they cheered like schoolchildren. That was just one more piece of her love affair with Grandville—everyone's un-self-conscious enthusiasm. It was such a relief after all that relentless posturing in Manhattan.

"Maybe I'll come as a skeleton."

"Well, actually, Ned has that one covered. How about a ghoul of some kind? Something Addams Family-ish."

"Morticia!"

"That would be just perfect."

What Babs did not tell her prospective guests is that by 'haunted house' she did not simply mean some indirect lighting and a few fake spiderwebs bought at Kmart and taped to her living room's corners. No, she was going whole hog with this one. It was going to be her surprise gift of appreciation to all the wonderful people in the Grandville Players and the Lenox Garden Club who had been so welcoming to her and Michael. She had plied the Off-Broadway designer, Gilbert Crespert, with a week in the country—plus "oodles of fun money"—in exchange for a haunted house *extraordinaire*.

"Not simply decorations, Gil—a *set*!"

"Tim Burton comes to the boonies."

"Oh, we are going to have fun, darling, you and me."

"What about Michael?"

"Michael doesn't know how to have fun, Gilly. I thought you knew that," Babs laughs.

* * *

No one told Franny about the party's macabre theme, so her decision to come as the Virgin Mary was innocently conceived. Her inspiration, of course, was her set for *How's Never?* That set had been so effusively received by Babs Dowd—"totally original and brilliant," Babs said—that Franny chose to further exploit her talent for biblical irony. Patterning her high-waisted, crimson gown and translucent black cloak after the Mother of God's ensemble in Raphael's *Marriage of the Virgin*, Franny designed and sewed the costume herself. But she took one liberty with Raphael's *couture*: in contrast to his high neckband, hers plunged. This Virgin was going to flaunt her cleavage.

Franny is smiling at her reflection in the full-length mirror attached to the inside of her closet door. With her hair loosely pulled back by an ochre silk scarf and the palest foundation she could find as her only make-up, she does, indeed, resemble a Renaissance image of a bride—a modest, dutiful, and diffident woman-child. But, oh that cleavage! Franny has given it extra definition with some artfully applied dark powder, and her bosom pops with provocative subtext: '*The* Seduction *By the Virgin.*' The Heavenly Father did not stand a chance once he got an eyeful of this!

Franny's *pièce de résistance* is the mask she is now fitting over her face. Years ago, she found it in a long-unopened wooden trunk deep in the bowels of the Phoenix's second basement. It may have been a castoff from the *Much Ado About Nothing* road show that came to town in 1916, or perhaps from Henry Ruprecht's Mardi Gras Spectacular, a 1918 extravaganza that closed ahead of schedule at the request of Grandville's Council of Clergy, an *ad hoc* group formed immediately after the Congregational Church's pastor, Ambroise Meechum, sitting in the Phoenix's front row, observed a sizeable gap between the top of a dancer's stocking and her garter belt.

The mask is fashioned from deep scarlet feathers that fan out from the eye slits, making its wearer look both ingenuously startled and sneaky, a combination Franny can relate to. Although she was thrilled that Babs loved her set design, Franny still thinks she has pulled one over on the woman, that at some level her set mocks Babs's play. Peering at herself through the mask, Franny feels wicked and sexy. *The Mysterious Woman in Red. The Virgin Slut.* For Franny, a masquerade is liberating. Masked and disguised, she can reveal a self that languishes in her day-to-day Grandville life—her uninhibited, insolent self. In this moment, she is convinced that is her true self.

She is wearing the mask as she drives her father's pickup to the Dowd home on Pickwick Road, near the Stockbridge border. Wendell's radio is always set to WGVS, but at this hour in the evening the station has already signed off with the Kate Smith recording of "God Bless America," and the same spot on the dial now picks up a French station from Montreal. Franny has no idea what the woman deejay is chattering on about, but she finds her voice comforting. Franny has French Canadian roots way back in the deVries line, and she wonders if somewhere in her genetic unconscious the language means something to her. She has had this thought before, including seventeen years ago when she was first mesmerized by Jean-Marc's voice. A song comes on, something about "fatigué" eyes; only the French could get away with that kind of treacle. Franny sings along with the chorus the second time around, *"Tes yeux sont tout fatigués . . ."*

She cannot remember the last time she went to a party other than the cast parties on the Phoenix's stage at the end of a Grandville Players run. The sort of men she has had relationships with over the last ten or so years were hardly party types, a good number of them for the simple reason that they were married and could not be seen with Franny at public gatherings. Early in motherhood, Franny's interest in the opposite sex narrowed to simple sexual utility, one more way she is like her father. She wonders if Lila will turn out to be another solitary deVries; for a beautiful sixteen-year-old, she certainly seems to go out of her way to avoid relationships.

Both sides of the Dowd driveway are packed with SUVs and foreign-made sedans with nary another pickup truck in sight. Maybe the day Grandville changed irrevocably was the day when BMWs began to outnumber pickups. Franny parks on the road and walks to the front door, holding the hem of her gown up to her knees. She rings the doorbell and Michael Dowd opens up. He is wearing a puffy white toga with a hood pulled back from his face. A ghost, Franny figures.

"My goodness, who can this be?" he says.

"Mary, Mother of God," Franny replies coyly, her mask still in place. She curtsies.

Dowd's eyes go immediately to the Holy Mother's cleavage. "The body is familiar, but I don't remember the face," he laughs.

"I've been away for a while," Franny says in a sultry voice. "This is my second coming." She is determined to play this role for all it is worth.

Franny walks past Dowd to the foyer and peers into what must have once been the living room. But the room has been transformed into a living painting and that painting is instantly recognizable to Franny: Hieronymus Bosch's *Hell*. It is absolutely fantastic—an ingeniously executed three-dimensional interpretation of the nightmarish masterpiece. It is as meticulously rendered as a Broadway set. Franny is spellbound.

A ghoul in a hook-nosed mask and bat-like wings approaches her. "Whoever you are, you are absolutely perfect," the ghoul says. Franny recognizes Babs Dowd's voice.

"I'm just visiting from The Garden of Earthly Delights," Franny replies.

"Why, you're Franny, aren't you?"

Franny nods. "This is fabulous, Babs. I've never seen anything like it."

"I can't take any credit for it. It's pure Gil Crespert. I asked him to give me a haunted house and he gave me hell. Literally!" Babs laughs and her bat wings flutter.

"*The* Gil Crespert from New York?"

"Yes, he's around here somewhere. Wearing a flesh-colored bodysuit with a fish in his hand. He says it's symbolic. Gil is a very naughty man." Babs gestures to the large bowl behind her. "Have some punch. Michael concocted it out of something syrupy—sloe gin, I think—but at least it matches the color scheme."

With this, Babs dances away to speak with another guest. It has been so long since Franny was at a party like this that she has all but forgotten that particular party maneuver—abbreviated conversations you quit with a laugh line.

"Dance Macabre" erupts from hidden speakers. At least thirty guests have already arrived and Franny remains just inside the room scanning them. Most of the costumes appear to be handmade or refashioned from antique dresses and theatrical costumes. Actually, most of the children who come trick-or-treating to her house on Mahaiwe Street still wear homemade costumes, just as Lila did growing up; but little by little these were being replaced by packaged Kmart and Brooks Drugs outfits that apparently resembled television characters with names like SpongeBob SquarePants and Pepper Ann.

The drink is indeed syrupy, tasting like what used to be called a Lime Rickey, but one sip is enough to alert Franny that the secret ingredient is vodka. She drains her glass and a nearby guest in a devil outfit immediately refills it.

"I was just talking about the apostrophe in Halloween," the devilish guest says. "Between the two e's. It's an abbreviation for 'evening,' you know—Hallowed Evening. What ever happened to that apostrophe?"

"It went the way of all underused attachments," Franny answers, making it sound as ironically lewd as possible, and walks away on her laugh line. Impeccable timing, she thinks. She should be this way all the time.

Sipping her punch, she makes her way to the far wall for a closer look at Gil Crespert's handiwork. The burst of hellfire at the ceiling is masterful.

"Darling? Is that you?"

Franny turns to see a figure in a black robe with gaping sleeves and a pointed hood. Its mask is a replica of *The Scream*, store-bought, but clearly from a high-end shop. It takes a moment for Franny to realize that it is her mother. Franny takes another, longer gulp of punch. Behind her mask, her mother is blinking rapidly, a sure sign that her contact lenses have become unmoored.

"I didn't realize you people up here had so much fun," Franny says, pitching her voice very low and hitting her consonants sharply, like a New Yorker.

Her mother issues her new, throaty laugh. "Oh. I thought you were my daughter," she says, flustered.

"Fascinating," Franny-as-Manhattanite replies airily. "Because you are the spitting image of my mother!"

Her mother laughs again, but more cautiously this time. She obviously senses that she is being mocked, but is not sure how. "That *is* you, isn't it Franny?" she says.

"Goldfarb," Franny replies in her deep phantom voice, extending her hand. "Madeleine Goldfarb."

Immediately after shaking hands, Beatrice takes her leave. As Franny watches her mother step toward the punch bowl, she feels wonderfully giddy. She giggles, then finishes off her drink and plants her glass between the horns of a Bosch-inspired gargoyle. But in only this interval Franny's giddiness is overcome by a familiar ache: How little misdirection it took for her own mother to fail to recognize her.

Franny has reached the point when a third drink would be superfluous, but that also happens to be the point when she thirsts for excess, so she again makes for the punch bowl.

"I was thinking of spiking it with a couple tabs of Ecstasy, but that doesn't seem necessary, does it?" a figure in a flesh-colored, head-to-foot bodysuit says, coming around a rock pedestal toward Franny. The lump in the suit's crotch leaves no doubt that it is a man, and the whole trout under his right arm confirms that it is Mr. Gil Crespert.

"Are you happy to see me or is that a fish in your armpit?" Franny says to him.

"Deliriously happy to see you," Crespert replies. "You're an oasis in the dunes. Or is it the boonies?"

"Neither, sir. I create my own space."

"Well, you certainly occupy it divinely," Crespert says, giving Franny a sultry once-over. "But I do believe you dressed for the wrong painting."

"What can I say? I'm a Raphael kind of gal." Franny ladles them each a glass of punch. She has not bantered like this since she was a college girl and it feels marvelous.

"I was thinking Rubens." Crespert says.

"In any event, here's to Hieronymus," Franny says, clicking his glass.

"To Hieronymus botch," Crespert responds and downs his glass. He makes a sweeping motion around the room with his arm. "I made it myself. You like?"

"Are you fishing for compliments?"

On cue, Crespert seizes his fish by the tail and swings it in front of Franny's décolletage. "Why it's the miracle of the fishes and the loaves!" he says through the mouth hole of his bodysuit.

"Watch where you dangle that thing, buster!"

"I think it likes you."

"My God, it's not alive, is it?"

"It's in the first stages of rigor mortis. Me too, actually."

Franny feels an all-but-forgotten sensation radiate from deep inside her: the sexual heat ignited by a match of wits. Well matched, too. It is erotic, every bit of it: the helter-skelter allusions, the provocative *double entendres,* and above all, the bait-and-switch tease of it. She has not yet seen Gil Crespert's face, but she wants to kiss it, to kiss his audacious mouth.

"Who are you, my dear? And what can I do for you?" Gil asks.

"I'm God's mother, but he's all grown up now and doesn't need me anymore, so I'm looking for a new line of work."

"I bet you're dying to know how I made the smoke," Crespert says, pointing at the ominous cloud hovering over Hell's mountaintop.

Franny replies with a husky sigh, knowing full well that sigh signals her assent to the next stage of their shorthand courtship.

Gil takes Franny's hand and leads her to the stairway in the foyer. As they start up the stairs, Franny's eyes light on two lone figures down the hallway smooching at the kitchen door. She stops, releases her hand from Gil's, and slips her mask above her eyes so she can see more clearly. That is a skeleton groping the bat-winged ghoul. By golly, Mrs. Barbara Dowd is a loose woman. Not that Franny needed it, but Babs has just given her permission to go wherever in Hell Gil Crespert is leading her.

That, of course, is his bedroom—the Dowds's guest bedroom under the eaves on the third floor.

"This is where you make the smoke?"

"Where there's fire."

They undress quickly. Gil takes both Franny's hands and looks at her. "Jesus, you're a beautiful woman. Really, who are you?"

"The Virgin Mary."

"No, honestly. Who?"

"I like it better this way," Franny says. "Okay?"

Gil shakes his head. Defrocked, he is a fine-looking man— lean, with a full head of curly black hair and glinting green eyes.

"What's the matter? Haven't you ever had a virgin before?" Franny says.

They fall into the unmade guest bed.

Franny deVries stopped rating her lovers years ago. One reason is that not only has she been blessed with a shapely, smooth-skinned body, but with one that is exceptionally responsive, so even the most crude and clumsy of her lovers— say, Bob Eberhart, the Grandville postmaster—gave her physical pleasure. But until this Hallowed Evening, she had fairly forgotten the pleasures of lovemaking that transcend the tickles and screams of quick and easy orgasms. She had forgotten the sensation of losing herself in a man.

"Night on Bald Mountain" wafts up to them from the party below. Moist and hot, Franny leans over the side of the bed and retrieves her feather mask from the tangle of her costume on the floor. She puts it on and straddles Gil Crespert's upturned body, her knees on either side of his hips.

"Hiding?" he asks. He reaches blindly for a pack of cigarettes on the bed table, finds it, retrieves a cigarette, and feels around for his lighter. Franny snatches it and lights him up.

"On the contrary," Franny says. "I feel totally exposed."

Gil laughs. He hands his cigarette up to her and she fits it through the mouth hole of her mask, takes a deep drag.

"You are glorious, Miss Mary," Gil says. "Would it be too much to ask where you live?"

"Here. In Grandville."

"Really?"

"Don't act so surprised. That's a sure sign of New York provincialism."

"I seem to have hit a touchy spot."

"Several of them, fella," Franny replies. She winks but, of course, it is hidden by her mask. She hands back the cigarette. Babs will undoubtedly tell Gil who she is, so she decides to spill it all and be done with it. "I'm a Grandville shopkeeper with an illegitimate child . . . Oh, and I live with my father. That 'boony' enough for you?"

"I don't need to be in New York for a couple more days. I'd like to see you again."

"How about right now?"

"Could you put out this cigarette for me?"

She does and they go at it again.

It is past three in the morning when Franny looks at the travel clock on the bed table. Neither music nor voices can be heard from below. It is a school night, so Lila stayed in, and

Wendell promised to come home immediately after closing up the theater. Nonetheless, Franny cannot spend the entire night here. Glorious as she feels, the idea of coming down for breakfast with Michael and Babs Dowd is definitely distasteful.

"Time to say goodbye," she says, swinging her legs over the side of the bed.

"I'll miss you." Gil remains lying on his back.

"You're very sweet, sir."

"Back at you," he says. "I hope we can do this again sometime, whatever your name is."

"What's in a name?"

"For one thing, a telephone listing."

"338-1727."

Gil repeats the number several times *sotto voce*, then says, "I'll ask for the lady of the house."

Franny laughs. "That's the nicest thing you've ever said to me."

She stands and begins to pull on her clothing. Gil, a connoisseur of beautiful objects, studies her body appreciatively. Dressed, Franny searches around for her shoes, red pumps from when she played Blanche DuBois on the Phoenix stage a full decade ago. It is while doing this that she spies a sheaf of sketches on a chair. They are her drawings for the *How's Never?* set. She picks them up. "Are these yours?" she asks, as casually as she can muster.

Gil laughs. "No," he says. "*Pu-lease*, no."

"That bad, eh?" Franny cannot stop herself.

"Oh, they're bad, but not as bad as the play they're for," Gil says, propping himself up against the bed's headboard and reaching for another cigarette. "Poor Babsy. She thinks if I tweak up the set, she'll come out smelling like a rose."

"So, you're tweaking it," Franny says. She feels dizzy and needs to sit down, which she does on the chair where the sketches had been lying.

"Are you okay?" Gil asks.

"I stood up too soon," Franny says. She does feel faint. She draws in a long breath to steady herself. "You didn't answer my question."

"Yes, I'm tweaking it for what it's worth. Why don't you come back to bed, darling?"

"No," she says softly. "I can't."

Franny takes a few more deep breaths, then stands again. The hell with her shoes. She walks out of the guest room and tiptoes barefoot down the stairs, a knot of hopelessness wrenching her insides. The line between playful pretender and rank fraud has evaporated, leaving her exposed as the worst kind of imposter she can think of—an amateur.

CHAPTER ELEVEN

With an oblong wooden racket, Stephanie Cyzinski is stroking hard felt-covered balls against the gymnasium wall. The balls feel leaden and so do her shoulders. Her hips are starting to ache too. That is good, she knows: No pain, no gain. Her father has identified her gluteus medius and hip adductors as her weak points; they are not muscles she needed to particularly develop for tennis, but for royal tennis, they are key for the 'chase.' And the chase is what royal tennis is all about.

She is weary, worn down as much by this grueling regime as by the pressure that drives her into the high school gymnasium every morning for an hour before classes, every afternoon from two-thirty to six, plus all day Saturday at the Boston Tennis and Racquet Club, the only royal tennis courts within a hundred miles. Her father's argument is compelling, although more for its relentlessness than its logic. He has what he calls 'inside poop' that in one-and-a-half years Harvard will be in desperate need of a topnotch girl player of royal tennis, an antique form of indoor tennis that neither her father nor she heard of until one month ago. It is a weird game that seems more like pinball than tennis with balls bouncing off of jutting roofs and into narrow galleries. Apparently the sport persists at Harvard for the sole purpose of extending, unbroken, a two-century-old rivalry between Harvard and Yale, the last remaining American colleges where the game is still played. All Stephanie has to do is keep up her grades, push up her SATs fifty points, and most of all, become a first class royal tennis player, and she will leapfrog over thousands of other applicants to Harvard. And Harvard, Dad says, is a pipeline to any damn thing Stephanie could ever want.

The problem is, Stephanie is not sure what she wants. She is pretty sure she would like to travel—to Europe, maybe to Asia and Africa. If she goes to these places, she believes she will have a better chance at understanding where she fits in the world. That plan is pretty vague, she knows, so vague that she would not dare mention it to her father or mother. But she wonders if going on a journey—it feels more like a 'journey' than a 'trip'—before even choosing a college might be the only way she will ever really find out what she wants to do with her life.

The only people she has talked to about this idea are Marta and Herb in the vigil group. As Stephanie expected, Marta said that it sounded like a good idea for something to do *after* college, when Stephanie would be more able to digest her experiences. Maybe Steph could learn Japanese or Urdu in college and *then* go to Asia. But Herb said it was a fabulous idea, that she would learn more about the world and herself in one year living in a foreign country than four years at any American college. Of course, that was typical of Herb; he calls himself an 'anti-professor' because he thinks most of what you learn in college is a load of crap. Weird how the people Stephanie felt she could be most honest with these days were Marta and Herb. Certainly more open than with her parents or teachers, but also more than with her school friends, including her boyfriend, Matt. She had told Matt about the Harvard business and he said she would be crazy not to take advantage of it.

But Stephanie does not see much of Marta and Herb anymore. Between her new workout program and her twice-a-week SAT prep tutorials, Stephanie had to cut back her vigil time to once a week, and often not even that. More than anything else, that is what makes her feel like a hypocrite—putting her personal ambition ahead of doing what little she can to stop the stupid war in Iraq. To stop kids her own age—kids like Bret Stephenson—from putting their lives at risk for no good reason. When she thinks about that, Stephanie is disgusted with herself.

At bottom, her dad's scheme does not make any sense anyhow. In many ways, her experience at regular tennis is more of a handicap than a help; she has to unlearn as much as she has to learn. Did Dad actually believe she could become a champion at it in a single year?

But her father is consumed with this plan. He calls it a once-in-a-lifetime opportunity that could change her entire life. A couple of Saturdays ago, instead of taking the Mass Pike all the way to the downtown Boston tennis club, he had turned off at the Cambridge exit. "No workout today, Hon, we're going to Harvard."

She had never seen him as ecstatic as when they toured Harvard Yard with a group of other kids and their parents. It was as if he was going to apply there himself, start his life over as a Harvard man instead of a Canisius College man. And the truth is, Stephanie had a better time with her dad on that day than in years. They had held hands as they walked along Massachusetts Avenue back to their car. He did not mention royal tennis that entire day—he did not have to. The reason Stephanie Cyzinski works out twenty-plus hours every week is she cannot bear to break her father's heart.

Starting as a knot in Stephanie's right buttock, the cramp creeps down to her hamstrings where it puts her lumbar nerves into a brutal vice. Utter weakness precedes the pain. Her leg buckles and she falls hard onto the wood floor, bouncing on her left hip, then rolling half a turn onto her front where the floor takes another hit at her, this time to her jaw. She blanks out for a second, but the excruciating spasm in her thigh hauls her back to consciousness. She is sobbing hard—from the pain, of course, but when she hears the awful words gushing from her mouth, she knows her agony runs deeper than tissue and nerve.

"You're . . . killing . . . me! Don't you see? . . . You're . . . killing . . . me!"

Lila deVries hears these words as she passes the gymnasium doors. She assumes that it is just sports talk—an outmaneuvered player giving her opponent a boisterous compliment—and continues on her regular, Friday after-school rounds, killing time before heading for the Nakota. But after a few steps, Lila stops. Nothing followed that burst—no scrambling feet or bouncing ball—and that silence is unsettling. She retraces her steps to the gym door, pushes it half-open, and peers inside. At first, she cannot see anyone in the gym, so she opens the door all the way and steps inside. Now she sees Stephanie Cyzinski in the nearest corner, rolling back and forth on her back, holding her left thigh in both hands. Stephanie's face is flushed and wet, her eyes closed. She is whimpering.

"Hello?" Lila calls.

Stephanie does not answer.

"Are you okay?"

"Yeh. I just fell."

"Sure?"

Again, no reply. Lila walks closer. She sees that some of the dampness on Stephanie Cyzinski's face comes from tears sliding out of her unopened eyes.

"Should I try to find somebody?" Lila says. "You know, like the nurse?"

"I'm okay."

Lila hesitates, then turns to leave. But at the door, she stops. "How about your father? Should I get your father?"

"No!" Stephanie cries vehemently.

"Whatever," Lila replies, half to herself. She pushes open the door.

"Lila?"

Lila turns back again. Stephanie is sitting up. Her eyes are open and she is staring at Lila. Lila is surprised that Stephanie called her by name—surprised that Stephanie even knows her name—and she immediately chides herself for finding this gratifying. Lila does not move; she says nothing.

"I . . . I'm feeling kinda . . . I don't know—crazy," Stephanie says.

"You're probably dizzy," Lila answers.

"No. It doesn't feel like that."

Lila takes a couple of steps toward Stephanie. She studies her face. Stephanie's pupils are dilated, her lips are trembling. She looks as if she is stoned, on a bad trip, but of course that could not be possible.

"Maybe some fresh air?" Lila asks.

"Yeh, some fresh air," Stephanie says, but she does not get up.

Lila glances up at that the wall clock. It is past four o'clock, time to leave for work. Stephanie follows her eyes.

"I'll be okay," Stephanie says. "Thanks for stopping, though."

Lila feels a rush of contempt for Stephanie and her brave face and good manners, but then she sees that Stephanie is weeping again.

"Need some help getting up?" Lila asks.

"Guess I do."

Lila goes to her, reaches out both her hands. Stephanie grasps them and Lila pulls her to her feet.

"Thanks, Lila," Stephanie whispers.

"Yeh."

Side by side, they walk silently to the gym door, then down the corridor to the exit. Outside, Stephanie takes a deep breath. "I feel better," she says.

"Do you still feel crazy?" Lila asks.

Stephanie manages a little laugh. "Just half," she says. "Half crazy."

"That's the way I feel all the time," Lila blurts out.

"Really?"

Lila shrugs. She certainly does not want to get into a discussion of her personal feelings with Stephanie Cyzinski and regrets that she seemed to open the door to one.

"Maybe half-crazy is normal," Stephanie says.

Lila studies Stephanie's eyes, trying to determine if the girl is making some kind of lame joke, but Stephanie looks dead earnest. She also looks shaky again.

"Actually, it's the other way around for me," Stephanie goes on. "Trying to be normal *makes* me crazy."

"How do you mean?"

Stephanie starts to answer, but stops. Her face clenches. She takes a deep breath. "I don't know. I don't even know what I'm talking about anymore."

They are silent for a moment. Then Lila says, "I'm late for my job."

"Hey, I'm fine now," Stephanie says. Then, before Lila realizes what is happening, Stephanie abruptly hugs her and whispers, "You're a good person."

A moment later, Lila is trotting down the school driveway toward the highway, her long blonde hair fluttering behind her. She cannot get away fast enough.

* * *

As Ralph, the FedEx guy, always does when carrying a package into the shop, he informs Franny she looks like a million dollars. But clearly Ralph is not looking carefully today, possibly because the carton of greeting cards he is lugging in front of him comes up to his eyes. The real worth of Franny's appearance today is way off the million dollar mark and she knows it.

She looks this way on purpose, starting with the baggy jeans and frumpy, floral blouse she has been wearing for the last two days. Her hair is pulled back severely, fastened at the nape of her neck with an orange scrunchy, and there is not a spot of makeup on her face. Franny has decided to never again impersonate anybody, glamorous or otherwise, or to symbolize any cause or stance. Instead, she has resolved to present herself to the world as she really is: a regular townie of a certain age. Truth in advertising.

Franny watches Ralph hop back into the driver's seat of his double-parked truck, check his rearview mirror, adjust his cap, and begin to back down Melville Street. She allows herself one quick glance up at the Phoenix—yesterday she spotted Babs and Gil Crespert striding into the theater, he with a sketchbook under his arm. *Tweak, tweak.* God knows what they had been doing in there—to the set or each other. Seeing no one there now, Franny heads for the shelf behind the counter where she keeps her carton cutter.

As promised, Gil had phoned a couple of times suggesting they get together before he returned to the city, but she had declined, politely the first time, sarcastically the next. "Come on, fella, it was just a one-nighter, a Halloween treat," she said in their final conversation. "We'd both be disappointed if we tried for an encore." She had been about to add an acknowledgement of what a sweet treat indeed it had been, but she desisted. The man already had enough vanity under his belt—and slightly below it—to carry him smugly back to New York. As for herself, she already had endured enough humiliation to keep her home and shop-bound for a month of Halloweens.

Franny presses the toggle on the cutter handle and slides out the blade. She cannot look at this instrument without thinking about the terrorists who crashed the plane into the Pentagon by threatening flight attendants with a box-cutter no bigger than this one. The idea that a tragedy of such massive proportions could be produced by something so small frightens her more than anything else about September 11th.

Franny kneels next to the carton and slices through the tape on top. Pulling up the carton flaps, she sighs. Inside, separated by strips of bubble wrap, are smart, paper-covered boxes containing greeting cards sorted by occasion—birthday, anniversary, Christmas, New Year, confirmation, bar mitzvah, sickness, bereavement. The elegant little boxes bespeak an earlier period of craftsmanship—classic proportions, sharp edges and corners, smooth, glossy paper casings in tasteful pastels. Years ago, after unpacking these boxes, she would bring them home to Lila who adored them. That was when Lila still took pleasure in meticulously organizing her possessions—her matchbook collection, pencils, pins, dried leaves, Christmas cards going back the length of her young life, and dozens of other treasures. She labeled each box in her neat handwriting and stacked them against the wall beside her bed. Whenever Franny brought home another bagful of them, Lila would shriek with delight and rush upstairs to start arranging her inventory all over again.

When had that stopped? Since then, nothing she gave her daughter pleased her as much; to be truthful, nothing she gave Lila after that pleased her at all.

Franny lifts out a birthday card box. Along with Christmas cards, these are her biggest sellers, but they have caused her the most exasperation, starting when she objected to the new, fixed-target cards: 'From Grandmother to Granddaughter,' 'For My Uncle,' 'For My Mother-in-law,' even, 'For my Stepfather.' It was obvious to Franny that by allegedly becoming more personal, these cards had crossed the line to utter impersonality. It was a cunning sales gimmick; a customer saw 'From Grandmother to Granddaughter' and she thought, 'Well, isn't that just the perfect one for me to give to little Nancy.' It cut short the tedium of scanning them all, row by row, while simultaneously congratulating the buyer on the fine focus of her thoughtfulness. Never mind that she was turning the object of her good wishes into a cookie-cutter category. Franny had asked her card and stationery distributor to eliminate such cards from her shipments, but he—a dyspeptic man in his seventies who had serviced Berkshire County for more than forty years—countered that *all* greeting cards were guilty of the same charge. "If you want 'em personal, you don't need a card—you write 'em yourself," he told Franny. He had a point, she had to agree, but nonetheless she considered it a small victory for personhood when the next shipment arrived minus the offending cards.

But lately, more and more cards for all occasions have begun to disturb Franny with their callousness. Mean-spirited jokes replace expressions of affection, even if those tender expressions had been composed by a stranger in Kansas City who was paid by the word. Now there were birthday greetings that said, '10,000 sperm and *you* were the fastest?' and 'If your IQ was two points higher, you'd be a rock!' For starters, they were not even funny, but beyond that, what was the significance of these sentiments on a day of personal celebration? Was civilization so far gone that words of fondness had evolved into insults?

Franny did not even bother to complain to the distributor about these cards. She let them pass in the name of free speech. She even accused herself of premature curmudgeonliness. Still, she detested those cards, hated selling them, judged harshly those customers who bought them, and filed them behind more genial cards in her display racks.

She picks up a box of bereavement cards, sets it on the floor beside her, and lifts off the cover. The topmost card pictures Jesus on the cross smiling beatifically. At least beatitude must have been the intent of the artist who rendered Him, but this artist was clearly of the same school of feel-good biblical imagery as the one who illustrated Lila's children's Bible, he who had inspired Franny's ironic set design for *How's Never?* In the card illustrator's hands, beatitude came out looking like a barely-suppressed smirk. Franny smirks back at Him. And then she reads the message printed at the Son of God's feet in Corsiva superscript:

> 'Life is Short,
> Death is Sure,
> Time the Thief,
> Love the Cure'

Jesus, what drivel! What simple-minded crap! Did they actually think their pathetic little rhyme would console some miserable, weeping widow who got this in the mail?

Franny's lips suddenly begin to quiver. Tears fill her eyes and drop onto the card. She does not know what is coming over her. She does not recognize the dread that is ambushing her, nor can she grasp why it is attacking her now. She starts crying full out, bawling helplessly. Her arms are shaking, too. She stares at her trembling right hand. Beside it lies the carton cutter, blade extended. It takes all the control left in her to shove the cutter away, beyond her reach. And then she waits for the terror to release her.

CHAPTER TWELVE

Herbert Blitzstein's most popular course—indeed, the most highly enrolled course at Grandville Community College—is titled, 'The Philosophy of Being Human.' In large part this popularity is due to the fact that in the five years Herb has taught it, he has not given a single student a grade lower than a 'C.' But the students also like the course because Professor Blitzstein is funny; they say his lectures are like Seinfeld routines with some Chris John vocal impressions thrown in. And every once in a while—well, in truth, just twice in these past five years—there is a student who prizes the course because she actually understands what Herb is getting at.

There are only four books on the syllabus: Plato's Republic; Freud's The Psychopathology of Everyday Life; Kierkegaard's Fear and Trembling, and The Analects of Confucius. And throughout the course only a single sentence remains written on the antique slate blackboard that was originally used for the shipping list of the building's former occupant, Foster's Printing Company. That sentence is from the Republic: 'The state is the soul writ large.'

'The Philosophy of Being Human' is the course Herbert Blitzstein wishes he could have taken as an undergraduate at Brooklyn College or as a graduate student at the New School for Social Research, but even the latter school, acclaimed as it was for its creative curriculum, was stuck in the notion that philosophy was basically about arcane puzzles and not about what makes life worth living. Herb started designing the course when he was twenty-four and has been refining it ever since. He has no illusions as to why only two of the seventy colleges and universities he applied to for teaching positions responded; his 'dream course' did not fit in their curricula. More than that, it undoubtedly suggested to some department heads that the young man from Brooklyn had a few screws loose.

Herb's sweeping idea is that if we could fully understand what it means to be human—everything about human consciousness that makes us unique in the animal kingdom—then we would live more fulfilling lives. And, incidentally, lives inspired by a generosity of spirit.

When Herb writes, 'The state is the soul writ large' on the board at the beginning of his first lecture, he always says, "Substitute 'Grandville' for 'state' and it means the same thing. Figure out what holds this ridiculous town together and we'll find out what keeps our souls from shattering like shot glasses thrown against the Railroad Car's wall on a Saturday night."

The line always gets a laugh.

* * *

Wendell is sitting in the last pew of the AME Zion Church on Pleasant Street. It is the first time he has attended a Sunday morning church service in over fifty years and the only time he has ever been inside an African-American church. Next to him is Esther, and next to her are her two children, Kaela, who is ten, and Johnny, five. Johnny has Esther's red hair and upturned nose, and Kaela is Chinese, a particular that Esther had never mentioned to Wendell. He met the children for the first time this morning and while the four of them walked from Board Street to Pleasant, Esther told the story of how she ended up going to Wuhan, China, to pick out and bring home her adopted daughter.

"Bob and I had been married for ten years and I just couldn't conceive," she said. "We went through the whole medical testing rigmarole but they couldn't find anything, so we decided to adopt. And then when Kaela was four, bingo! I got pregnant."

"I've heard of that one before—getting pregnant *after* you've adopted a child," Wendell said.

"Me too, hundreds of times by now. One theory is that loving a baby gets your juices flowing—some hormone that's needed for conception. So Kaela primed the pump for Johnny."

"Lovely theory."

"I like to think so. And so does Kaela."

It is no surprise to Wendell that Esther's daughter is in on all the biological details that account for her family's composition: Esther is an irrepressible truth-teller. In any event,

Kaela appears eminently well-adjusted, far more lighthearted than either Franny or Lila were at that age—or now, for that matter.

They took the back route to Pleasant Street, climbing onto the railroad embankment at the end of Board Street and walking from tie to tie along the tracks until they reached Methuan Road. Wendell had not walked these tracks since he was a teenager and it felt like an adventure. At one point Kaela, who was larking ahead, turned around and announced that they were all running away to join the circus. Wendell knew exactly what she was feeling.

At the end of Methuan, they turned back toward town, then turned again at the intersection with Pleasant. The clapboard church looked the same as it had when Wendell was a boy—a small, square structure that could easily be taken for an old one-room schoolhouse but for the sign in front: 'A.M.E. Zion Church, founded 1862. All welcome.'

Wendell had called on the church's pastor, Reverend Willa Jones, last Tuesday and told her what was on his mind. He asked if he could take a look at the church's membership books, especially those of the late nineteenth and early twentieth centuries. After Wendell entered her home, Jones—a large woman, as big around as Wendell though a head shorter—remained standing. Although her flat face struck him as plain and stolid, her eyes were spellbinding in both their warmth and intensity, as befitting a clergywoman.

"How do you spell your name?" Jones asked.

"D-e-V-r-i-e-s."

Jones had chuckled, then said, "Why don't you come by my church this Sunday?"

Wendell resisted asking why. Or why she was not producing the church records for him to inspect. Reverend Jones obviously had something else in mind for him. So in the intervening days, he contented himself with reading more about Grandville's blacks at the Historical Society—the first bunch who came as slaves and recent freemen, then the wave of escapees via the Underground Railroad, and finally, a few decades later, the small colony of Pullman Car porters, relatively well-off family men who collectively bought a parcel of land on Pleasant Street where they built identical, shingled, two-story domiciles on either side of the church. These were now run down and several were boarded up and empty, but a few still housed their descendants.

Reverend Jones slowly raises her upturned palms as if she is lifting open a window to let in a warm breeze, and the congregation stands to sing, "Wade In The Water."

> "Well, who are these children all dressed in red?
> God's a-gonna trouble the water
> Must be the children that Moses led
> God's a-gonna trouble the water . . ."

Wendell and Esther sing along from the start, and Kaela picks up the melody by the second chorus and joins them while Johnny peers around, doing some serious nose picking. There are no more than twenty other people in the congregation and most of the faces are familiar to Wendell from town—from the Soup and Sandwich, the Post Office, the theater—although he has never seen a black face inside the Railroad Car, a realization that only now comes to him. Seeing all these Grandville blacks together affects Wendell in a way he never would have anticipated. Alone or in pairs on Main Street, they register effortlessly as part of the town, but as a group, they appear a people apart. He detects that difference in their faces; here, they look much more comfortable in their selves, more animated, and certainly more genial than when he encounters them in town. Undoubtedly, they hold back who they are and what they are capable of on Main Street, just the way they did two generations ago in James Baldwin's book.

> Who's that young girl dressed in white?
> Wade in the Water
> Must be the Children of Israelites
> God's gonna trouble the Water.

Reverend Jones's sermon is abstract and puzzling—something about baptism, redemption, and keeping up hope—but it is thankfully short. She leads them in a final hymn that is unknown to Wendell, "Wrestling Jacob," and then announces the reception in the basement. Jones passes down the center aisle, shaking hands with every parishioner. When she comes to Wendell and his entourage, she shakes their hands too, then smiles at Wendell and says, "You all come down too."

In the church's fluorescent-lit basement, a long metal table is set with enough chicken legs, mashed potatoes, coleslaw, macaroni salad, collard greens, Jello, and sweet potato pie to feed the entire audience of the Phoenix on a Saturday night. Johnny instantly grabs himself a paper plate and gets in line, but Wendell, Esther, and Kaela hold back, feeling awkward— they did not know to bring food for the table.

Down here, Wendell nods to some of the parishioners he knows from town—Dan, from Guy's Auto Parts; Martha, the seamstress at Balmot's Cleaners; Winny, the groundskeeper at Sway Lodge. They all nod back and Winny even extends his hand for a quick shake, but it is obvious to Wendell that encountering him here causes a prompt, reflexive shift in their demeanor—a shift back to their Main Street persona. Wendell is unused to being an inhibiting presence—the last time he felt this way was at Sunday dinners at Sway Lodge when he was still married to Beatrice. It makes him want to leave as soon as possible.

"Here he is," Reverend Jones says cheerily, walking up to Wendell with a cup of coffee in her hand. Behind her stands a light-skinned black couple near Wendell's age. Both the man and the woman are white haired, and both are dressed in upscale Sunday clothes—at least, more upscale than anybody else's in the room. Wendell had not spotted them in the chapel; perhaps they had been sitting in the front pew.

"Wendell deVries, I'd like you to meet William and Sharon deVries. These good people come up all the way from Connecticut to pray with us every Sunday."

Wendell has to restrain himself from letting out a whoop of gladness—a 'Hallelujah!' would feel just right. He shakes William's hand first, then Sharon's.

"We appear to have something in common," William deVries says with a pleasant smile.

"We certainly do," Wendell says. Without thinking, he reaches out to shake William's hand again and William obliges him.

"My people are from here," William says. "My father, his father, and his father before him. And before that, Mr. Henk deVries, a white man from Holland."

"He was my great-great-grandfather's brother," Wendell says. Only two weeks ago he had ferreted out that piece of information from a family tree diagrammed on the inside cover of the deVries family Bible found on the top row of his bookshelf next to a 1918 atlas of the world.

"So that makes us cousins—far distant cousins, but cousins," William says.

"I've missed you," Wendell says. He has no idea what put these words in his mouth or quite what they mean, but he is not embarrassed by them, especially now that he sees William smile back at him.

"Do you have time to have lunch with us?" Esther asks.

Wendell realizes that he has not introduced her or Kaela—Johnny is off in the corner scarfing down sweet potato pie—so he does so now.

"We live nearby," Esther says.

William and Sharon confer for a moment, then Sharon says, "That's very kind of you. Are you sure it's not too much trouble?"

"Not at all," Wendell says, although he is as surprised by the invitation as they are.

They locate Reverend Jones again, make their goodbyes, mount the stairs, and exit the church onto Pleasant Street. Somewhere along the way, Wendell suggests to Esther that they go to his house because it is more roomy, and Esther says she will make a quick detour to the co-op to pick up food. Kaela and Johnny skip ahead, while the adults walk four-abreast, Wendell and Esther sandwiching their guests.

"Willa tells us you've been searching out your relatives," William says. "Are you working on your genealogy?"

"I guess I am," Wendell answers. "At least one part of it. My granddaughter learned in school that Grandville used to have some black deVrieses and it made quite an impression on us."

"I can imagine," William says. Unlike Professor Gnomes, William deVries does not appear to find anything wry or suspicious about either Wendell's or his granddaughter's curiosity.

"To tell you the truth, it makes me feel all kinds of things, Mr. deVries—"

"Bill," William interjects.

"Okay, Bill. Probably the biggest thing it makes me feel is relieved," Wendell goes on. "I've got a constitutional aversion to secrets. Been that way since I was a boy. So that's part of it."

"And the rest of it?" Sharon asks.

"I'm not sure," Wendell replies. "I'm getting up there, you know? Getting closer to seventy than sixty. And some things I've never paid much attention to suddenly seem consequential, like—well, I guess you'd call it connectedness. I've got this itch to feel connected to as many things as I can. I never left Grandville—that might have something to do with it."

"Well, Bill certainly did," Sharon says. "Left when he was fourteen."

"Closer to fifteen actually," Bill says. "After my father took off and my mother died."

"To go live with relatives?" Esther asks.

"No. Just to get a new start on my own."

"But you were here until you were fifteen. Funny I don't remember you from school," Wendell says.

"I didn't go to school here," Bill says. "I went in Pittsfield. My mother drove me both ways."

"Private school?"

"No, public. My mother made some kind of special arrangement. She didn't want me to be the only black kid in school and they had a few like me over in Pittsfield."

"Did you want to get out of Grandville? Is that why you left?" Esther asks.

"Yes," Bill says.

"Prejudice?" Esther asks.

Bill smiled. "I guess so, although not the way you might think of it. Nobody burned any crosses in front of our house. I don't even think I was called 'nigger' but once. It's a subtle thing, but you can't help but notice it. It just made it real hard for a boy to know who he was."

"Except at Zion," Sharon says.

Bill laughs softly. "That's the truth. Back then there were only about ten people in the congregation, some of them

~ 125 ~

coming from way out of the way, like Blandford and Montgomery. But it was the only time of the week when I felt like . . . well, you know, one of the gang."

"That's why he keeps coming back," Sharon says.

After a moment, Esther says quietly, "I worry about that with my daughter."

"She's adopted, I figure," Sharon says.

Esther nods. "From China. There aren't any Chinese kids in the schools here either."

Listening to all of this, Wendell feels both ignorant and inspired. And as the four of them follow the children onto Main Street, everything in town momentarily appears sharper to him than usual—the colors keener, the edges of things more treacherous. Congregants are flowing out of St. Peter's Church clogging the sidewalk, and Wendell sees familiar faces all around him, many of them people he has known his entire life. Automatically, Wendell smiles, nods his head, and says, "How you doing?" but he quickens his step, shepherding his little flock through the host of white Christians.

"Well, lookee here." It is Archie Morris, fresh from mass with his wife, Iris, and son, Flip. He is looking at Wendell and his group with his usual easy smile, yet this morning that smile makes Wendell feel less than easy. He ducks his head and walks on without greeting the Morrises.

A few steps later, Bill says, "Yup, it's a subtle thing."

Indeed, it is; Wendell nods silently. They are now passing the Onion Café where they can hear a jazz trio playing brunch background music and Bill comments on all the new restaurants in town since he was a kid.

"They're for second-homers and retirees mostly," Wendell says. "They get a country home with an authentic country kitchen and first thing they want to do is eat out."

At the corner of Melville Street, Esther takes her son's hand and heads down to the co-op, but Kaela insists on staying with the other adults. As they head up along the Melville Block, Bill says, "Did I say the Zion was the only place I felt at home here? Well, that's not the whole truth. Here's the other place." He points at the Phoenix's marquee.

"That's my theater!" Wendell says, sounding very much like his teenage self boasting to his classmates at Grandville High.

"I know that."

"You do?"

"Your father used to let my mother and me in free for the Saturday matinee."

"Well, that was sure good of him, but it doesn't sound much like my old man. That man counted every nickel."

"He said it was because of our name," Bill says, grinning. "Called it the deVries special discount."

Wendell stops in his tracks. So his father knew about this family—probably knew they were distantly related too—but he had never said a word about them to Wendell or anyone else at home.

"Oh, he knew, all right," Bill says, easily reading Wendell's thoughts.

"So you must've known too," Wendell says. There is some hurt in his voice that he did not anticipate and it is too late to disguise it.

"We certainly talked about looking you up, Wendell," Sharon says. "But we weren't sure that's something you'd've welcomed."

"That's why we were so pleased when Willa phoned us," Bill says.

Wendell feels so many things at once that all he can do is laugh. Bill joins in and as they pass by the window of Write Now, the two very distant cousins are lost together in giddy laughter. Inside, Franny is so busy handing out reserved copies of the Sunday Times and the Sunday Globe to her regular weekend customers that she does not see them.

"Mom says you have the key!" Kaela declares. She has skipped ahead and is now standing under the theater marquee, facing the adults with her hands on her hips.

"The keys to the kingdom!" Wendell says, fishing a ring of keys from his pants pocket and holding them up in front of him. "I think we'd better check it out, don't you?"

"Oh yes, please!" the girl says.

And so in they all go to the old Phoenix Theater. Wendell snaps on the house lights. For several minutes, none of them speak. They are gaping at the Nile green ceiling with its Greek revival frescos of wooly-haired godheads blowing winds from the four corners of the world which, in here, are the four corners of the Phoenix Theater's vaulted ceiling.

"My grandfather worked on that," Bill says.

"The paintings?"

"No, just the plastering. He was proud of it, even if he never got to see it finished."

"He died?"

"No," Bill laughs. "This wasn't a place a black man went to in those days."

"Looks like it could use some plastering now," Sharon says.

"That's for certain," Wendell says. "But it's been a movie theater for so long nobody really notices. Truth is, I barely notice myself."

"Mom says you live in a booth upstairs," Kaela says.

"Just about. Do you want to see it?" Wendell starts for the stairs.

"Don't you think your wife will be wondering where we are?" Sharon asks.

"Esther? Well, she's not my wife, but you're right. I'll show you another time, Kaela."

"Me too, I hope," Bill says. "It's every boy's fantasy, you know. The secret hideout of all secret hideouts. The great control booth in the sky."

Wendell laughs. "I'll tell you, Bill, up there is the closest I ever get to feeling like I've got control of anything," he says.

Lying on her side, a lank of blonde hair covering her eyes, her knees bent almost to her chest, Lila straddles the worlds of wakefulness and sleep—a labyrinthine, pot-scented sleep. Once again, she has had her 'flying nude' dream, sailing naked over rooftops, swooping down now and then to peer into windows where families sit silently in front of television sets. It is a thrilling dream that makes her feel buoyant and free.

With semi-consciousness come voices, strains of conversations overheard last night at Nakota's tables. Since Lila began toking up with Pato upon arrival for her shift, these conversations have become more interesting to her. She plays a game of scripting in her head what was said just before she arrives with a tray of food and what will be said after she has left.

At a table of five college boys, they were arguing about Red Sox pitchers when she swooped down their plates of *tempura*, but from their unmistakably tempered smiles, Lila knew they were playing a game too—they had been snickering as she approached, an obvious indication that they had been talking about sex, as they surely would again after she departed. And at a table of two New York couples, the conversation was about President Bush's latest public gaff: "It will take time to restore chaos in Iraq." The subject appeared to make them as giddy as sex did the college boys. She imagined that in moments their conversation would move on to weightier topics, like which private schools their children were applying to.

The Dowds's table was harder to read. They had reserved the large round table in the front window alcove where they played host to a group of eight men and women, every one of them as smart and confident-looking as Mr. and Mrs. Dowd. The Dowds had even placed the entire party's order ahead of time—shrimp *shirumono* and two supersized wooden platters of *sushi* and *sashimi*. Lila knows her mother thinks the Dowds are phonies and she, herself, finds them patronizing, but nonetheless she is intrigued by their self-assurance, Mr. Dowd's straying adolescent eyes notwithstanding. Lila wonders how people come to be so sure of themselves, so certain that everything they do is meaningful and correct. Were they born that way? God knows, no one in her own family had anything near that kind of confidence, not even Grandma Bea who always seems to Lila to be talking as fast as she can in order to deflect her self-doubts.

An entire squadron of waitresses was enlisted to serve the table their soup course and when Mrs. Dowd saw them coming, she instantly raised a single finger and the guests clammed up. If Dowd and company had any secrets, it could not be from Lila's Japanese cohorts, so they had to be keeping something from Lila's ears. Tantalizing. Even a bit thrilling to think that she could possibly pose any kind of threat to the Dowds. Instead of returning directly to the kitchen, Lila had lingered on the other side of the alcove partition trying to catch the conversation that resumed after the help was gone, but all she heard were undecipherable whispers and bursts of laughter. That laughter sounded remarkably like the giggling she had recently heard at the college boys' table, suggesting that sex was the Dowd table's keynote topic too. Wife swapping? It was all over town that Mrs. Dowd was giving 'private coaching' to her leading man, Ned Shields.

Now downstairs, the laughter gets louder, a great cascade of it, but it is more hearty than caustic. The loudest laugh indisputably belongs to Grandpa Wendell. Lila blinks her eyes, stretches her long limbs, and rolls onto her back. It sounds as though somewhere in the house there are as many partiers as there were last night at the Dowds's reserved table. She rolls again so she can reach the drawer of her bed table, opens it, and withdraws her cigarettes and lighter. She swings her legs over the side of her bed, lights up, goes to the window, and opens it. Sitting on the sill, she takes three deep drags in quick succession, exhaling the smoke through the screen. As usual, these first puffs fan the embers of last night's marijuana high.

"You're probably wondering what a fifteen-year-old black boy thought he was doing in Atlanta, Georgia." From below stairs, a robust, deep voice that Lila has not heard before in this house or anywhere else.

"Looking for black girls!" a second, unfamiliar woman's voice roars, and again howling laughter.

Lila finds herself grinning along with the laughter. Just the idea of a lively party going on downstairs is delighting. For years, their only guests have been Mother's drama group friends and lately they have not been around, either. In any event, Lila is positive these cannot be Grandville Players down there; this laughter is far too genuine.

She stomps out her cigarette in a piece of aluminum foil, wraps the butt, and drops it back in her drawer along with her cigarette pack and lighter. She pulls on her robe and steps out into the hallway. Fumes of coffee waft up to her.

"I'll tell you one thing, Wendell, after Grandville, there was something refreshing about men's rooms labeled 'colored.' I'm not kidding. It's kinda like truth in advertising. You didn't have to be taking a leak next to some white guy who's so nervous about you being beside him that he can't get his flow going."

"Bill, please! There are children here." The strange woman's voice again. She sounds as if it is difficult for her to keep a straight face while scolding the man named Bill.

Lila paces softly to the top of the stairs, starts down, then sits on the step just below the second story floor line. Through the banister rails, she looks down through the living room into the kitchen where only one half of the kitchen table is visible. The occupants of this end of the table are an old black man, a black woman, and a small Asian girl, Binx lying at her feet. For a fraction of a second, Lila quite literally wonders if she is still dreaming.

"Registering in a black high school down there was a piece of cake," the old man, Bill, is saying. "They don't expect any parents or guardians or whatever to accompany you. Parents are too busy working or have too many other kids to tend to. So I just signed myself up and started classes that day."

"Where did you live?" Another new voice—a woman's—from the blind end of the table.

"At the 'Y.' They had a separate one for blacks, full of drunks mostly, but I got a nice room for ten bucks a week. They had a cafeteria too. I worked there, washing dishes mostly, but that covered everything I needed. Sweet setup for a mother-less child."

"Did you graduate?" Wendell asks from the invisible end of the table.

"*Did he graduate?*" the black woman repeats rhetorically. "Bill was the valedictorian. Smartest boy to come out of Booker T. Washington High in decades."

"And the competition was tough, I'll tell you," Bill says. "I had to contend with Sharon here. And she got help on her homework from her daddy."

"Now that's a lie!" Sharon retorts, but just as Lila suspected, when the lady speaks she cannot suppress a wide smile, and soon the whole bunch of them are roaring again.

Lila wants to join them at the table, mostly because she is dying to know who these people are and what they are doing here, but also because she is dying for a cup of coffee. Yet she also wants to keep listening unseen. She has always felt more comfortable as a bystander, and as one, she has developed a talent for filling in the blanks in conversations, so she remains on the stair, watching and listening.

"That must have gotten you into college," the hidden woman says.

"Got me in, but didn't pay for it," Bill responds. "I had to work another two and half years before I could pay my way. But the time went by fast seeing as I'd gotten myself a girl. Fancy girl from a family that had a two-car garage."

"But only one car in it!" Sharon interjects, getting another laugh.

Lila is convinced this couple has told this entire story hundreds of times before and that it has developed into a routine with Bill as the straight man for Sharon's sassy comeuppances. But damn, it was one hilarious routine.

"A two-car garage—that's a sign of hope even if there's not a single car in it," Bill is saying. "I've always had a weakness for hope-filled people. Got that from my Grandaddy deVries."

DeVries?

Lila is on her feet, trotting down the stairs and through the living room. She arrives at the kitchen table where, clutching her robe to her neck, she leans her head down in front of Bill's. "Are you my uncle?"

A second of stunned silence is followed by boisterous cheers.

"What do I get if I am?" Bill says, looking up at the beautiful young woman.

Lila is smiling. She shrugs, "Well, a kiss, I guess."

"Then I'm definitely your uncle."

"Wait one minute there, child," Sharon says, all smiles herself. "That's my man. And he's only your cousin about ten times removed."

"Hell, that's close enough!" Bill says, proffering his wrinkled cheek.

Lila plants a big smooch on it and that elicits a bigger laugh than Sharon has roused all afternoon, a surprise among so many other surprises for Lila—she cannot remember any other time when she made a roomful of people laugh. Only now does she take in the other occupants of the kitchen table, a cute, forty-something red-haired woman on one side of Wendell and a small boy on the other. Lila is pretty sure she has seen the woman in town.

"My granddaughter, Lila," Wendell announces and she is introduced all around.

"I didn't mean to interrupt," Lila says, sitting down next to the boy. On the table are a basket of bagels, a ripped loaf of

French bread, a plate of cheeses and another of fresh fruit. Lila takes a pear and bites into it.

"You didn't interrupt much," Sharon says. "Bill, here, was just discoursing on the story of his life. The *long* version."

"Hell of a lot more interesting than mine," Wendell says. "But you know, we still haven't got around to the missing link—Mr. Henk deVries. I can't find more than a word or two about Henk in any book."

"Henk?" the little boy chirps, grinning. "Henk? What's a Henk?"

"He's the man who owned Bill's great-great-grandmother," Sharon replies, her tone abruptly cool, colorless. "Henk bought her from another white man."

For the first time that day, there is no quick, jocular response, no smiles, no laughs. No one even speaks or looks in another's eyes. Wendell is crestfallen. He wishes he had not brought the subject up—not now, not yet. He wonders if he should make an apology for his ancestors, like the kind the new generation of Germans make for the sins of their fathers, but he is afraid it would sound lame, trivial.

Lila sets her pear on the table and looks over at Bill deVries. "I'll tell you what I think," she says as earnestly as Wendell has ever heard her speak. "I think your great-great-grandmother was the love of his life."

"What makes you think that, child?" Sharon asks.

Lila quickly glances at her grandfather, a tacit acknowledgment that she has been examining the open history books and family Bible that he has been leaving open on virtually every surface of the living room.

"Because she and their children were the only family he ever had," Lila says.

"Then I think so too." The speaker of these words is the bright-faced, ten-year-old girl sitting to Bill deVries's right; and everyone at that table, with the probable exception of her brother, knows without a moment's thought that this child from Wuhan is speaking with unique authority. They all look at her in gratitude. Bill raises his coffee cup as if in a toast. The phone rings.

Wendell stands, goes to the hallway phone, and answers it. It is Franny.

"Dad? It's three-thirty! There's a line in front of the theater!"

"Geez, I lost track of time," Wendell says. Keeping his customers waiting does not disturb Wendell, but the tone in Franny's voice does. Lately, she always seems on the verge of panic. "I'll be right over," he says.

Wendell hangs up and returns to his guests. "Totally forgot about the Sunday matinee."

"Now that's a sin if there ever was one," Bill says.

"We need to get going anyhow," Sharon says, rising. "Tomorrow's a school day."

"You're teachers?"

"I am," Sharon replies. "Bill's the principal."

"Somebody's got to keep her in line," Bill says, laughing again. He shakes everyone's hand, including Johnny's. "See you in church," he says.

* * *

Wendell does not even try to read in the projection booth this afternoon; the day is too much with him. He reviews every moment of it in his mind as down below Harry Potter zooms around his school campus, a jet-propelled preppy. Of all the day's encounters and exchanges, the one Wendell keeps coming back to is the sudden eruption of laughter he shared with Bill deVries on Melville Street. It felt like grace, a wordless, riotous commingling of souls. He wonders if theologians ever turn their minds to the spiritual possibilities of laughter.

A knock at the booth door surprises him. Esther was not planning to come until late this evening. He takes a quick gander through the booth's tiny window. No problem down there: Potter zooms on.

"Who is it?"

"Lila."

He lets his granddaughter in, gestures for her to sit in his upholstered chair so they do not bump into each other. Lila has not been up here with him since she was thirteen.

"Those people were nice," she says.

"Very. I had a great day, kiddo. And I liked what you said a whole lot."

"I really meant it." Lila pulls up her legs so she can kneel on the chair seat and peer down at the screen. After a few moments, she says, "Do you get the whole Harry Potter thing?"

"Nope, but I didn't get Cinderella either."

"If I tell you something, can you keep it to yourself?" Lila keeps her eyes on the screen.

"Yup."

"Like not even tell Mom."

"Okay."

"Or your . . . whatever? Girlfriend?"

"I can keep a secret," Wendell says.

Lila keeps staring through the little window. "Potter is an incredible dork," she says.

"Okay, I promise not to tell a soul," Wendell replies, grinning.

"I'm serious about this!" Lila snaps.

"And I'm listening," Wendell snaps back. Uncharacteristically, he finds himself resenting his granddaughter. She has broken in on his perfect day, burglarized his sense of unlimited connectedness. But, of course, she is a teenager who undoubtedly feels connected to nothing.

"Somebody's doing a number on me," Lila says. "Somebody you know."

"How? In what way is he doing a number on you?"

"You know, following me around all the time. And acting stupid."

Wendell does not respond right away. He is not in a mood to talk around things. "Is he harassing you? Is it sexual?"

"I guess so."

"Can you tell me who it is?"

"No."

Wendell sighs. "Well, there's not much I can do then, is there?"

"It's Flip Morris."

Wendell's reverie of his happy day is all but gone, shoved aside by rancor. "What exactly does Flip do to you?"

"He follows my bus after school. Or sometimes he's just there when I get off it."

"In his police car?"

"Yes."

"Does he try to get you in the car with him?"

"Yeah."

"We have to report him, you know."

"No!"

"Yes, we do, Lila. That crosses the line."

"You don't understand, Wendell. That'd just make things worse."

"How?"

"It just would," Lila says. She has turned in her seat to face him as if to accommodate the about-face of her logic.

"Well, I can't let this go on," Wendell says.

"I shouldn't have told you."

Wendell says nothing. He and his parents never discussed his own problems. If there was ever anything he could not hold in, he went with it to his sister, Marie, but he was adept at holding things in so those occasions were rare. At Lila's age, Franny often unloaded to him on a single subject: her impossible mother. Wendell would listen sympathetically, but he always ended up counseling patience and forbearance. Franny lived most of the time with her mother—what else could he say to her?

In many ways, Wendell is more of a father to Lila than he had been to Franny, clearly because he lives with Lila fulltime and is a stand-in for her real father, but also because he feels more adequate to the role in his sixties than he did in his thirties. Yet right now, Wendell is feeling far less than adequate. Lila has always been an ambivalent child and has only become more so in her teens. It is singularly difficult to argue with ambivalence.

"What if I said something to Flip's dad?" Wendell says finally.

Lila thinks a moment, then shrugs. Wendell takes that as an ambivalent assent. He takes a step to the window and peers down at the screen. "Definitely a dork," he says.

Bridget Jones's Diary elicits howls of laughter from the evening audience, but the film makes Wendell feel melancholy— the plight of Ms. Jones, single and frustrated, reminds him too much of Franny. A few weeks back, he had returned home to find Franny in the darkest of her blue moods; if he had not been able to figure that out from the look in her eyes, he would have from the half-empty bottle of Zinfandel beside her on the kitchen table. It had taken a few more glasses of that saccharine stuff for her to name her torment—a man, of course, a set designer from New York she had met at the Dowds's. He was a theater snob with a lean body and a caustic wit, her favorite poison. Jean-Marc *redux*, Wendell surmised, although neither of them voiced the obvious comparison. For reasons Wendell could not completely follow—something to do with the Players' new production—she refused to see him again, punishing him and herself at the same time, her specialty. Sometimes Wendell wonders if Franny would be happier in New York or Boston, although judging from Bridget Jones's slapstick romances in London, city life for a thirty-something woman was not always a picnic on the Thames. But then again, who would have predicted that a sixty-five-year-old man who had forged a life of solitary contentment in his small hometown would, in a matter of months, become steeped with feelings of tenderness for a woman he met in a grocery store?

The film over, Wendell empties out the popcorn machine as he does every Sunday night. By week's end, the popcorn remaining in the glass-walled case is more gummy than crunchy and the denture crowd starts to complain. Binx knows that it is Sunday; he waits patiently on the lobby carpet for his weekend treat. Then Esther walks in the Phoenix's outer doors carrying a large, lavender candle, an item that recently went on remainder at the co-op.

"It's for atmosphere," she announces. She kisses Wendell's cheek.

"What kind of atmosphere does it do?"

"Romantic," Esther says. "I decided it's time we made love."

Wendell grins. He sets a family-size tub of popcorn in front of Binx. "We don't want to rush into anything," he says and laughs.

"But there are rules," Esther says, her tone balanced between sober and giddy. "Like, only candlelight."

"Good. I look like Spencer Tracy in candlelight."

"And I may not take my top off," Esther says.

"Fine. Does that mean I can keep my socks on? It keeps me from getting foot cramps."

"I'm serious, Wendell."

"So am I."

"I haven't done this since Bob left."

"I know."

"I don't think I'm particularly good at it, either."

Wendell laughs. "No fancy stuff, eh?"

Esther wraps her arms around Wendell, hiding her face against his chest. "This scares the shit out of me," she whispers.

Wendell strokes her hair, kisses the top of her head. "I love you," he whispers back.

Esther does not remove her blouse, nor Wendell his socks. In the flicker of the lavender, lilac-scented candle sitting by the bed on the dressing room floor, Wendell looks more like Steve Martin than Spencer Tracy. They make love slowly, carefully, tenderly, with their eyes and hearts perfectly open.

Later, her head resting on Wendell's chest, Esther sweetly weeps while outside the door, Binx, sated with popcorn, snoozes in the bassinet recently deposited on the Phoenix's stage for the upcoming production of *How's Never?*

CHAPTER THIRTEEN

It is 1921. The war to end all wars is over and America has gone back to work with a vengeance. Production rates soar, employment is nearly full, and new homes are being built at a breathtaking tempo. Yet the industry known as show business is in free fall, at least the live end of it. Performers scramble to adapt their talents to two-dimensional, black-and-white projection on a sparkling white screen; producers close up their offices on Broadway in New York and rent retired airplane hangars in New Jersey and California to launch new careers; and in Grandville, Emile deVries spends all of his waking hours trying to figure out how he can thwart their misbegotten enterprise.

It is not just the full-dimensioned vigor of live theater that compels Emile; it is the Phoenix itself. To him, the edifice is a monument of classic proportions, an homage to European grandeur, the Temple of La Ville Grande, all of which could vanish in deathly darkness. At his dinner table, he decries motion pictures as cheap facsimiles of peerless art—tawdry postcards of timeless masterpieces. He predicts that movies are a fad that will expire in two years' time, three at best. By then, even the dimmest audiences will find themselves hungering for voices and color and the tantalizing possibility of seeing one of the players dining on oysters and champagne at the Phoenix Café after the show. All Emile needs to do is hold out until then, to make do with the road shows still available to him.

Enter Aaron Fine, an octogenarian impresario who mentored with Florenz Ziegfeld himself. One of the last of the Broadway holdouts, Fine throws Emile a lifeline in the form of The New Ziegfeld Revue. It is Fine, himself, who takes the train to Hudson, New York, then a taxi to Grandville, carrying with him a sepia portfolio of his vaudeville extravaganza featuring operatic singers, dance artistes, magicians, prestidigitators, and a horse that can spell polysyllabic words in two languages. Fine's price is steep—higher for three consecutive nights than an entire week of High Country Fair *just five years earlier—but his competition is virtually nil and his results guaranteed. He* proffers the receipt ledger for his show at the Wurlitzer Theater in Buffalo, Reynold's Variety House in Fargo, and Proctor's in Troy—sold-out houses every night, every one of them. Emile signs up, feeling indomitable.

Emile launches an unprecedented, two hundred-dollar publicity campaign with two-color posters that he personally affixes to utility poles, grocery windows and, when permitted, Post Office bulletin boards in towns and cities as far away as Springfield to the east, Bennington to the north, Hillsdale to the west, and Winsted to the south. He runs a full-page advertisement in the Grandville Courier under the headline, 'The Show That Will Not Die!'—a line that his wife finds morbid and, for some reason, sacrilegious. But, indeed, Emile's diligence pays off: he sells out advance tickets for the first two nights.

The New Ziegfeld Revue comes to town in a single, modestly refurbished, Army troop truck. Emile stands just outside the Phoenix's doors as performers and stagehands debark from the truck's rear via a stepladder onto Melville Street. He draws deeply on his cigar, reflexively masking the fumes of whiskey that accompany the troupers. He ignores a paroxysm of foreboding that momentarily dizzies him, causing him to brace himself against the Phoenix's closest marble pilaster. He rereads a poster glued to the theater's door to reassure himself.

That night the curtains part to reveal Fine's finest dancer, Mlle. Culottes, direct from Paris. Accompanied by a pianist and a clarinetist playing a truncated version of M. Maurice Ravel's masterpiece, Scheherazade, the artiste Culottes performs 'The Dance of the Seven Veils.' Although her inspiration may be biblical, Mlle. Culottes execution is profane, especially the lascivious smirk on her crimson-painted lips as she dispatches the seventh and final veil into the first row and around the head of Mr. Ambroise Meechum, recently retired pastor of the Grandville Congregational Church and emeritus chairman of the Council of Clergy. Some cheers follow, particularly from the Phoenix's balcony, but these are quickly subdued by the overwhelming silence in the orchestra seats. Mlle. Culottes is swiftly replaced by Rupert, the orthographically-gifted equine.

"Rupert, how do you spell 'undergarments'?" the horse's master of ceremonies intones with exaggerated diction. Although this man is identified in the program as Professor

Abner Wigglesnorth of the Department of Animal Sciences at London University, Emile, watching from the wings, sees that he is also Sr. Rodolfo St. Ambrogio, first clarinetist of the Metropolitan Opera Orchestra and very recently of the Phoenix's orchestra pit, where he just performed Scheherazade. Emile's bout of foreboding stages a comeback.

In the meantime, Rupert, a knock-kneed mare, traipses over to a colorful placard sitting on an easel. On it is the alphabet in red uppercase letters. Rupert dips his nose to the placard, then abruptly snaps back his head with a pair of women's bloomers between his teeth. Even the boys in the balcony are unamused. One shouts down to the stage the single word, "Faker!" and is rewarded with applause.

"Rupert, we apparently have some skeptics here in Grandville," Wigglesnorth-St. Ambrogio responds indignantly. "Unwashed, undereducated skeptics who cannot comprehend that a single bloomer is worth a thousand words."

From the balcony, a chorus of 'boos.'

"A rowdy bunch, aren't they?" the clarinetist says to Rupert. "Let's show'em, Sweetheart. Spell 'bloomers'!"

Rupert lowers his head to the alphabet placard, taps at it with woodpecker speed, and straightens his head.

"Close," Wigglesnorth declares, "but there are two 'o's in bloomers."

Of course, no one—not even in the first row—could have possibly determined which letters Rupert tapped with his broad bridle. The animal might have just as conceivably spelled 'anthropomorphic' or 'vivisection,' and the Phoenix audience is not fooled. "Faker!" and "Cheat!" launch from the four corners of the theater in lieu of the tomatoes many now wish they had brought with them.

In The New Ziegfeld Revue's defense, it must be said that according to Aaron Fine, Rupert's act is a parody of sorts, a comic take on the German wonder horse, Clever Hans, who was subsequently proven not to be a prodigious arithmetician after all, but simply a middling-bright animal who could read his trainer's hand cues. St. Ambrogio's see-through flimflam gag may have charmed audiences in Buffalo, even in Fargo, but in Grandville, whose culture has been framed by Dutch colonial literalists and Puritan purists, and layered with Eastern

European suspiciousness and Mediterranean short-temperedness, it is an intolerable insult. Exit Rupert and company stage left amidst rumbles of indignation.

Emile deVries's heartbeat accelerates, his face flushes, and as he stares out from the wings, he sees whole clumps of the audience rise from their seats and head for the exits. Next to him, the stage manager, Reuben, Mr. Fine's youngest son, shouts over to a tall man in a tuxedo and top hat who sports a pencil-thin moustache, "Maestro, you're on! Now!"

'Maestro' is Michelangelo the Magnificent, listed in the program as Harry Houdini's internationally acknowledged heir. Emile is relieved on two counts: first, that Michelangelo is not the pit pianist; and second, that Reuben has skipped over the next scheduled act—the Can-Can as performed by a mélange of short-skirted women and identically-costumed, hairy-legged men—to put the magician on stage. Clearly, in Reuben's estimation The Magnificent One is just the act to quell an insurrection.

Michelangelo struts to center stage and bows, removing his hat with a flourish. Out of it flies a dove that immediately soars to the vaulted ceiling of the Phoenix, there flying from corner to corner as if gliding on the draft provided by the puffing Greek gods. Every eye follows the bird in its rounds. The audience is spellbound, as much by the magnificence of their theater as by the bird's graceful flight, although Michelangelo's trick itself means little to them—in fact, nothing at all to the old timers who remember Hilton Burke, a Grandville farmer who often kept a few chicken eggs under his felt cap as his patented method for accelerated incubation. The magician's next trick is straight from the front bin at Abracadabra Supplies in New York—a multicolored silk scarf that he pulls and pulls and pulls seemingly endlessly from his sleeve, a good twenty feet in final length— yet Michelangelo performs this less-than-surprising feat with surprising grace and a look of wide-eyed astonishment worthy of a French-trained mime. The audience responds with polite applause, as they do for his next bit of business, flipping a silver dollar into the air and catching it on his upturned forehead.

Back in the pit, St. Ambrogio lets loose with a ferocious drum roll. Michelangelo the Magnificent steps out to the stage's apron. His voice is stentorian; his accent vaguely Italian, if by way of Brooklyn.

"Let me be honest, ladies and gentlemen, what you have witnessed thus far are mere parlor tricks. Sleights of hand any dexterous teenager could execute after only a day's tutelage from yours truly. But prestidigitation is one thing. Magic—genuine magic—is quite another. I will now demonstrate the genuine article. Not a magic trick, dear friends—but pure magic!

"I will now spread a complete deck of cards on this stage, face up. Then I will request the assistance of one of Grandville's most trusted citizens—a man whose father and grandfather before him created this veritable cathedral, the most celebrated theater in all of New England. I am speaking, of course, of Mr. Emile deVries. Mr. deVries will blindfold me and lead me backstage where I shall remain until he selects a card, writes his name plus a word of his own choosing upon that card, rips it in half, and hands it to another of Grandville's estimable roster of esteemed citizens, Reverend Ambroise Meechum who, I trust, will immediately deposit it, sight unseen, into one of his estimable pockets. I will further ask Mr. deVries to dispose of the remaining cards by placing them in this leather sack"—here, Michelangelo produces said sack from his waistcoat pocket—"and cast the sack into your midst as far as he is able. Then, he will guide me back to you and remove my blindfold. At that moment, dear citizens, I will, quite frankly, astound you!"

The Magnificent's peroration is greeted with a roar of applause. All told, Grandvillians are a Christian people who appreciate nothing more than a man who can redeem himself in an act of virtue, preferably a dramatic act of virtue. Indeed, Emile feels redeemed as he paces slowly onto the stage at Michelangelo's beckoning. He, too, receives a small round of applause when he appears on the apron beside the magic man. The audience is clearly rooting for a happy ending.

Michelangelo spreads the playing cards on the stage floor and hands Emile a blindfold. Emile inspects the blindfold closely, holding it up against the spotlight for any possible breach. None found, he binds it tightly around the magician's eyes and leads him in halting steps to the wings. There, he guides Michelangelo to a stool where the magician slowly seats himself. As Emile starts to rise, Michelangelo grips his sleeve tightly, pulling Emile's head down to his. "Queen of diamonds," he whispers. "Word, 'giraffe.'" He releases Emile and folds his arms across his chest.

Emile is already back on stage in view of the audience before the meaning of Michelangelo's whispered instructions fully registers. He is to pick the queen of diamonds from the deck and inscribe it with the word 'giraffe' before signing it, tearing it in half, and handing it to Pastor Meechum. Indeed, there is art to Michelangelo's magic: He knows how desperately Emile wants to save this show and his theater. All Emile has to do is comply with this little artifice. No one need ever know about it. Furthermore, every piece of magic is a trick of deception anyhow—only a fool would doubt that—so what harm would be done?

Emile stoops over the cards, scans them. He begins to pick one up—the nine of clubs—then retrieves his hand, still studying the cards. He is acting—pretending to search for the most obscure card in the deck, whatever that possibly could be. He spots the queen of diamonds, quickly picks it up and stands straight. He pats the pockets of his blue serge suit jacket, locates his Parker pen, removes it, uncaps it, and writes his name and 'giraffe' onto the card. He rips the card in half. The audience silently watches his every move, studying Emile's face.

Emile starts for the edge of the apron. Reverend Meechum rises to meet him, his hand extended. Emile gazes out into his theater. He knows virtually every face he sees. He also knows without a scintilla of doubt that he cannot willfully deceive any one of them. He stands straight and clears his throat.

"Ladies and gentlemen," Emile says. "The price of your tickets will be refunded in full at the box office on your way out. Forgive me, please. The show is over."

As with Emile, himself, just moments ago, it takes a long moment for the audience to absorb these words. When they do, they rise from their seats, but remain in place. The applause begins in the front of the theater, but moves in a wave to the sides and back, then to the balcony. It is the loudest, most sustained ovation of the entire evening. Emile bows, tears in his eyes.

To the day, it was three weeks later when Wendell saw his father lug his newly purchased Vitascope up the balcony stairs of the re-christened Phoenix Motion Picture House.

* * *

~ 144 ~

Franny's four complementary tickets to the Grandville Players production of *How's Never?* were for center orchestra seats, but she exchanged them for balcony seats, telling Sally Rule, chairwoman of the ticket committee, that her father was a balcony man by habit. Franny is now sitting in the third-to-last row of the balcony next to her father who, in turn, is sitting next to Esther and her daughter, Kaela. For the occasion, Esther's son, Johnny, is spending the night with the family who lives below them in the house on Board Street; Johnny has been known to talk back to live performers.

Below, the orchestra is filling up quickly, a testament to Babs's super publicity campaign—she appeared four times on Bob Balducci's radio show in as many weeks—and to the fact that for the first time in the Players' history, their autumn production preempted the film scheduled for Thanksgiving weekend—in this case, the mega-hit, *Barbie in the Nutcracker.* Barbie's official cancellation to make way for the local theatrical came to Wendell via the London office, doubly astonishing considering that Thanksgiving weekend was one of the top grossing movie weekends of the year. Not that Wendell minded—he was spared the prospect of watching a vacuous doll with a gravity-defying bosom dance the Tchaikovsky classic. This fortuitous scheduling of *How's Never?* brings in second-homers and their families and holiday guests in addition to the Grandville Players' loyal hometown followers. It sold out its three-night run.

Franny had not wanted to come at all. She had managed to avoid the theater entirely the past few weeks, thus evading even a glimpse of the fully assembled and painted set. She had broached the idea of skipping the show to her father—casually she thought, just saying she needed to catch up on her sleep, which, God knows, was true; she has been unable to remain asleep for more than an hour at a stretch lately—but Wendell seemed unhappy with that idea. He did not come out and say so, but Franny is an expert at reading her father. Wendell was obviously worried about her lately and, God love him, he subscribed to the idea that any deviation from standard routine was bad for one's equilibrium; they *always* went to the Players' shows together. So Franny compromised with the balcony seats; at least she would have some distance on the spectacle.

It is Sunday, the final performance. The house lights fade, Sting's "If I Ever Lose Faith In You" issues from the loud-speakers, and the one-hundred-year-old, original asbestos curtains of the Phoenix Theater draw open. Before the actors utter their first lines, the set receives a lovely round of applause. Franny shrinks in her seat. Like an anxious child, she squints at the stage, only allowing herself to take it in one section at a time. Several seconds pass before her eyes are fully open and focused on the set. *How about that?* Gil Crespert had barely changed her design at all! Yes, he had added some concealed floodlights under the straw so that they threw long, ominous shadows against the rear wall, a touch that was too obvious by half, even if Saturday's review of the play in the *Berkshire Eagle* singled out Franny—and those shadows—as an example of the Players' New York-worthy production values. God knows, Gil knew how to wow them in the boonies. But in the end, it is a minor tweak. Franny pulls herself upright in her seat. Let the show go on.

"Did you pack my book?" Ned Shields, as President of the United States, intones earnestly to his wife (Sally Rule) on the stage below.

The audience snickers appreciatively.

"The Bible?" the First Lady responds.

"No, the other one," the President replies petulantly. *"You know,* Bicycle Repair for . . .'" Here, Ned cups a hand around his mouth and stage-whispers, "Dummies."

On this boffo line, the audience roars.

Franny has read the play several times and sat through many rehearsals, but this is the first time she has seen it per-formed before a live audience. She knows from experience that most Grandville audiences arrive at the theater aching to laugh and willing to do so at the puniest provocation. Jean-Marc used to call such audiences—say, an Ithaca College audience filled with visiting parents—'red hatters' meaning that all it would take for them to double over in hysterics is one character coming onstage in a red hat. Babs Dowd has a houseful of red hatters tonight. They are here to giggle and howl, especially at the president and company; for them, any-thing relating to the current administration is a red hat. That is what always bothered Franny about *How's Never?* She sees it as all goofy hats sitting upon empty heads, easy laughs without a single compelling revelation. And tonight she grits her teeth as laughter echoes inside the theater. The audience is not only complicit in Babs's bludgeoning polemic, they are applauding themselves on their political astuteness. When Ned-qua-George W. says, "Sometimes I think evil people have a real hard time doin' good things," the audience acts as if it is being swept away on a wave of high wit. Franny feels a rush of contempt for everyone inside the theater.

During the act break, Franny remains in her seat while the rest of her group goes downstairs to buy Kaela a soda. A few people she knows come over to praise her set and Franny accepts it uneasily. She would like to tell them about Gil Crespert's pretentious tweaks—she wants no credit for those over-the-top shadows—but she decides to let it pass. Eavesdropping on audience members discussing the first act, Franny's suspicions about their discrimination are confirmed: the author of *How's Never?* is being compared to Brecht. The world is loaded with idiots and most of them appear to have taken up residence—at least second-home residence—in Grandville.

Early in the second act when the fanciful bassinet descends to the bunker with the Clown/Angel aboard, the audience howls, then breaks into applause. But Franny observes one exception to this spirited response: two seats away from her, Kaela is hiding her eyes behind her hands. The ten-year-old is terrified. Esther puts her arm around her daughter and pulls her close. For a moment, Esther and Franny's eyes meet, both imagining what horror the image has awakened in this once-abandoned child. Franny finds herself thinking that for the first time this evening the play has had a profound impact on a member of the audience.

As the Clown/Angel flounces around the stage tossing off politically correct platitudes, a super spot follows him, making it look as if he is superimposed on the rest of the action. Franny shifts forward in her seat, studying the spot-lit set behind him. The set *is* different from the way she designed it and she can easily perceive that now. It is a difference in coloring. How had she missed that? Instead of the watery greens and browns she had appropriated from the children's Bible, Gil Crespert had shifted the palette to the Renaissance masters, rich earth tones with glistering highlights. Under the spotlight, any subtlety that the New York designer's alteration might have possessed in dimmer illumination totally vanishes. Gil knew what he was doing; he was giving Babs Dowd precisely what she craved—a patina of classiness. And in the process, of course, he had erased every trace of irony Franny had planted there.

Franny is furious. The son-of-a-bitch probably thought Franny was too dimwitted to discern the real effect of his sneaky tweaks. It was a fucking conspiracy—Babs, Gil, the whole bunch of them parading around on the moral high ground while there was nothing to which they would not stoop to inflate their infantile egos. Franny suddenly stands up in front of her seat. She needs to get the hell out of here before she shouts out something that will bring this stuporous audience to its senses. But before she can do either, Wendell grabs her hand.

"Are you okay, sweetheart?" he whispers.

Franny hesitates, then sits down again. "Okay," she whispers. She manages to sit still for the rest of the performance.

There are five curtain calls, Babs Dowd appearing with her actors for the fifth with a bouquet of roses in her arms. She is wearing a Vera Wang one-shoulder silk gown. She throws kisses like a prima ballerina. She bathes in the applause for several minutes, then raises her hand for quiet.

"I cannot tell you how happy you make me," Babs begins. "Thank you, thank you, thank you, from the bottom of my heart. It goes without saying that this production is the result of a synergy of talents—from Ned and Sally and Tom and Frank and Amy's superb acting to Franny deVries's magnificent set. My stage manager, Billy Foutier. Milly Desmond on lights. Danny Cohen's sound. This was a collaboration made in, well, a manger!"

The line gets a laugh, then more applause. Franny has no doubt that Babs rehearsed it for hours in front of her hallway mirror. When the audience quiets again, Babs hands off her flowers to Sally, then gestures to someone in the front row. It is her husband, Michael. He now shuffles with studied shyness to the steps at stage right. A moment later, he is standing next to his wife, his arm loosely around her waist.

"I'm not usually very good at keeping secrets," Babs goes on. "In fact, a week before Christmas everybody in my family knows exactly what I've gotten them." She pauses here for another trill of titters. "But this time, I've managed to keep my big mouth shut until right now."

For one heady moment, Franny is convinced Babs is going to announce that she and Michael are getting divorced. Considering all the rumors about Babs and Ned's backstage romance, that simply has to be it. God knows, for Babs Dowd everything is show biz—why not her sex life too?

"Michael and some of his old Harvard buddies have done something quite wonderful," Babs goes on. "They have put together a rescue team. A twelve-million-dollar rescue team."

Wendell again reaches for his daughter's hand, squeezes it tightly. He does not know precisely what is coming, but he knows instinctively it will collide with their lives. Franny's hand lies limply in his. She sits there numbly.

"Michael and his friends have purchased this magnificent theater and starting this winter, they will begin restoring it to its former glory," Babs says. "They will enlist the finest artisans and craftsmen in the world. And when they are done—with a little help from yours truly—live theater, dance, and opera will once again tread these hallowed boards all year round. *The Phoenix will rise again!*"

The applause is instant and thunderous. In a moment, it is joined by cheers of 'Bravo!' Virtually everyone inside the Phoenix is on his or her feet, including Franny, who releases her hand from her father's and steps alone into the aisle. She is both light-headed and frantic, floating free and sinking fast. She feels utterly weak yet she moves with keen determination. She makes her way to the stairway as the cheering goes on, now accompanied by stamping feet that make the balcony floor vibrate beneath her. Franny is barely cognizant of her transit to the stairs or of the pale yellow light of the sconces on the stairway walls. She feels as if she is being led by an exotic external force. If she is aware of anything about herself, it is that she is entirely on her own, utterly and irrevocably on her own.

Her head bowed, Franny pushes her way down the center orchestra aisle, brushing against the shoulders and hips of the exiting audience. Here and there her name is called in greeting, but she does not respond. In truth, it does not even register. The curtain is still open and many of the players still stand on the apron accepting the hands and good words of friends and relatives. Among them is Sally Rule who motions to Franny, beckoning her to join this receiving line of praise. As if following Sally's direction, Franny goes to the steps at stage right and ascends the stage, but instead of moving toward Sally, Franny steps behind the row of actors to the set for *How's Never?* There, she reaches into her jacket pocket for her cigarette lighter and ignites the manger straw.

II

~ Migrations ~

Chapter Fourteen

If, some one hundred and fifty thousand years ago when homo sapiens first appeared on the African contintent, we had resolved to stay put—to root ourselves forever after in the soil where we found ourselves—human history would be a far simpler affair. To be sure, the force of expanding population would have elbowed us out of the Original Cave or Hole in the Ground or Mountaintop Stump, bumping us out in concentric circles to new caves and holes and stumps where we would propagate anew and push ever outward. But over the millennia, however far we spanned from that First Place, we would be one contiguous tribe with one language and one culture. And despite variations in climes and topography, soil and wildlife, this world would be a single place.

But we made no such resolution. Rather, individually, in pairs, but most often in hordes, we gathered up our sharpened stones and desiccated skins and mewling infants, and traipsed to new worlds where life and survival might somehow be better—safer, easier, a more harmonious match of place and desire. In a trek that required untold generations to accomplish, we put entire mountain ranges and rivers and emerging continents between us and our forebears as we marched north to the Himalayas along what one day would be called the Silk Road, making our way to Eurasia and eastward to Oceania, or branching across the Straits of Gibraltar and, scores of millennia later, westward to the Americas.

Along the way, we awake one morning to see that an antelope is munching contentedly on a red orb that has dropped from a tree, so we take a bite too. Finding it sweet and nourishing, we gaze around and see that these red orb-bearing trees cover the hills on every side of us. Such is the provocation to abandon our millennia-old journey, to stop right here and make this newfound land our own. From this decision, a new people will grow as if we had been born here at the beginning of history. We evolve to match this place, with, say, eyes the color of its sky or perhaps of its soil, with lank hair or curly, pink skin or brown. A language is bred too, say, Aramaic or Latin, or at other times and places, Norse or Basque. An indigenous way of building a house, of styling a hat, of wooing a mate—all of these follow ineluctably from a bite of succulent fruit that promises a better life.

* * *

The only times Hector thinks of his birthplace are when he sings the songs he learned there from his father: "El Pilon," "En Una Tiniebla Oscura," "Zafra," and, of course, "Mis Flores Negras," the melancholy ballad that will forever resonate for him with the randomness of death—his father's murder in front of their farmhouse by a boyhood friend turned revolutionary guerilla, and Rico's murder in his Soacha hut by Hector's own hand. Singing "Mis Flores" with Mano and Sylvia in the alleyway alongside the Casa Medina, Hector can smell Puerto Alvira's sugarcane-scented mountain breezes while in his mind's eye he sees the stilled body of his father.

Because the income from Hector's street performances permits him to house his family in a fine, two-room apartment in La Sabana, he no longer needs to sell contraband cigarettes in the Sagrado. On his trio's expanded round of Bogotá tourist spots, he gives wide berth to that section of town lest any street hawkers from Soacha see him; the coincidence of Rico's murder and Hector and his family's sudden disappearance surely did not go unnoticed in the shantytown. Nonetheless, Hector is convinced there is no room for revenge in the feeble hearts of Rico's survivors. As it happens, Hector is mistaken about this.

Hector's trio has prospered. In the mornings, they perform in the outdoor cafés in the *Plaza de Toros de Santamaria,* at midday in front of the historic homes in *La Candelaria,* then to cafés in the *Parque de la Indepencia* before finishing the day at the *Casa Medina.* Hector designed the route himself after painstakingly translating a chapter entitled "A Fun Day Tour of Bogotá" from a copy of Fodor's English language guide to Colombia that he found discarded in the Medina's trash. In this way, the musicians shadow the day tourists, those visitors who want to pack their allotted twenty-four hours with as much authentic Bogotá experience as possible and who, grateful for any efficiency to this end, are big tippers. Each day, Hector, Mano, and Sylvia pocket more pesos than a dozen Bogotá factory workers.

The pinched nasality of Hector's voice notwithstanding, he has a natural gift for love songs. With his large mournful eyes and animated, long-fingered hands, he can sell the torment of a broken heart more convincingly than any number of balladeers with rounder timbres. He and Sylvia often conclude a set with a duet of "Amor Sin Medida" that brings tears to the eyes of women of all ages and pesos by the handful into Hector's upturned hat. Yet Hector's real heart is far more pragmatic than the romantic one with which he sings; he is, after all, a survivor.

It is a sweltering afternoon in December. Under a towering palm, the singers perform for the outdoor patrons of the Café Flora in the *Parque de la Indepencia*. The café is cited in Fodor's for its sweet crepes with ice cream, strawberries, and chunks of dark chocolate, so most of the patrons are foreigners—today, English and French, thus the trio's sprinkling of Beatles and Brel. The day has been long, hot, and already quite profitable, all of which takes its toll on the liveliness of their performance. Much as they usually enjoy making music, their singing this afternoon is merely a labor of habit. They sound like a cheap recording.

But when they segue from "Zafra" to Brel's "Ne Me Quitte Pas," Sylvia unexpectedly drops an octave at the line, '*Et le temps perdu, a savoir comment oublier ces heures qui tuaient parfois,*' adding a tremolo ache of longing to its stark depiction of a past that is forever lost. It takes a moment for her now-impassioned voice to rouse Hector from his listlessness, but once revived he shifts from picking at his *cuatro* to stroking it like a flamenco guitar, echoing Sylvia's lament. Thus following her lead, he now follows her eyes to see what it is that inspires her. It is a lanky American in a seersucker suit who has risen from his table at the Flora, espresso cup in hand, and is walking toward her.

It is hardly unusual for men to gaze at Sylvia with ardor or lust or, most often, a mixture of both. She is dramatically beautiful and, though regal in bearing, she projects the easy availability of all beguiling performers. But Hector is unconcerned. He has accompanied Sylvia so many times that he can comfort himself with his knowledge that however rapturous her performance, she is just teasing her audience. Yet at this moment he realizes he is witnessing an exception: Singer and song are one. Sylvia is singing of the absolute necessity to seize passion before it passes, and she is singing this imperative directly to the American.

The song finished, the man speaks to her. He introduces himself in perfect Spanish that is accented not by American English, but by Colombia's purer mother language from Spain. For a moment, Hector wonders if he was mistaken to assume from the man's boyish haircut and self-assured smile that he was American, but then he hears him inform Sylvia that he works at the American Embassy. They immediately begin to walk off together when Sylvia abruptly turns to Hector and Mano and sweetly asks their permission to call it a day. Permission granted. *A Dios.*

"God in heaven, now we have to drown our sorrows," Mano quips to Hector.

The two young musicians laugh. Both of them adore Sylvia. Late one night over tumblers of rum they had confessed this to one another, concluding that if one of them ever won her heart, the other was clearly entitled to plant a knife in the winner's heart.

Arm in arm, Hector and Mano start for the Café Andes just outside the park. It is early in the day for them to have time to spend just on pleasure, they have money to spare in their pockets, and the blazing winter sun that oppressed them only minutes earlier now invigorates them. Yes, the price of their delight is Sylvia's departure with a handsome foreigner, but so it goes in life as in song. Hector looks back over his shoulder for a final glimpse of Sylvia. And that is when he spots a boy in rags darting behind a cycas palm that now barely conceals him.

Hector recognizes the boy immediately—Diego from a Soacha mud hut just meters away from the one Hector's family formerly inhabited. The boy looks malnourished, his arms spindly and his belly distended, impetigo blisters on his lips and chin, but this hardly distinguishes him from other children from the 'city of the disposables.' What is distinguishing is the intensity of the contempt in Diego's eyes when he boldly steps out from behind the cycas and glares back at Hector.

"Did you think you could hide from me?" the boy cries. It is a familiar accusation.

"What do you want, Diego?" Hector responds, reaching into his pocket for money.

"Killer! *Murderer!* You'll pay for it in blood!" the boy shouts, and he runs away.

"My God, what was that?" Mano asks, amused.

"A ghost," Hector answers flippantly, but he is trembling. Diego has obviously been following him, although Hector has no way of knowing for how long or to how many places on the trio's daily rounds. In that moment, Hector realizes that it is not loyalty and certainly not affection that bound a boy like Diego to Rico. No, it was something far more basic: subsistence. Rico, the sadist and cheat, had kept the boy alive, and with Rico gone, Diego is now on the brink of joining his erstwhile benefactor in the grave. What greater reason could there be for contempt and its natural consequence, revenge? Diego probably does know every location where Hector sings with his group, perhaps even where he lives. And limp and weak as the boy is, he undoubtedly has many confederates in Soacha. Banded together, they would be capable of avenging their late savior's murder with one of their own. God knows, they had little to lose by trying.

Hector is a joyless companion to Mano in the Café Andes that afternoon. His eyes perpetually scan the streets and corners and alleyways, looking for Diego or any other boys from Soacha whom Diego has enlisted in his vendetta. When Hector parts from Mano after only a single glass of rum, he makes his way home by a roundabout route, his eyes relentlessly roaming, vigilant, frightened. By the time he is sitting with his mother in the kitchen of their magnificent La Sabana apartment, Hector knows that his time has arrived for another migration.

While Hector brought the folk songs of Puerto Alvira with him to Bogotá, his mother, Marcella, brought the village's folk wisdom in the form of its fables and epigrams. Many of the latter are enigmatic to the point of comic obscurity, like, "One hungry wolf is a menace, but ten hungry wolves are a circus." Many more are self-evident truths that provide nothing new of value, say, "The man who owns the land owns the man who tills it." But here and there are Puerto Alvira maxims that embody a kind of pragmatic mysticism that only a native can apply wisely. Such is the one that springs to Marcella's mind that late afternoon: "The way out of a storm lies in the breeze that preceded it."

Marcella asks her eldest son to repeat the day's events for her, not sparing a single detail. His third time through, she stops him at the moment when the tall stranger speaks to Sylvia.

"You say he works at the American Embassy?"

"Yes, Mamma. He said that to her."

"And what does he do there?"

"He did not say."

"Did he look important?"

"He looked American."

"He is the breeze," the mother announces.

Ideally, Hector would have waited to see if Sylvia's connection to the American was a one-day romance or an enduring affair before he asked her to intercede with the man on his behalf. But the threat to Hector is too serious and the possible cost to him and his family too great for him to delay. The next day when he meets up with Mano and Sylvia at the *Plaza de Toros*, Hector dispassionately recounts the circumstances that led him to kill Rico, although he omits the exact method of his murder. Neither of his comrades is shocked by his story; they have heard many like it. But when Hector describes his urgent need to flee Bogotá, Mano is instantly angered, not so much by Hector's predicament as by the prospect of losing the trio's handsome *cuatroista*. Yet Sylvia, may the Blessed Virgin anoint her, touches Hector's cheek and asks how she can help him. He tells her.

The fleeting look of misgiving in Sylvia's eyes when she says she will contact her American friend—a Mr. Arthur Jessel—makes her offer all the more generous and Hector all the more guilty. It is clear that Sylvia sees a risk to her relationship with the American by asking him a favor so soon in their affair. And to be sure, it is no small favor. Hector realizes he cannot let her go through with it.

"But don't talk to him yet," Hector blurts out. "I have other prospects to look into first."

"Like what?" Sylvia asks, raising her feathery eyebrows skeptically.

"Well, there is a boy I know in the Sagrado. He has a cousin who—"

"My dear friend, I will talk to Arthur this evening," Sylvia declares emphatically.

"He may not be pleased."

"But he is very pleased with me," Sylvia replies, smiling proudly. Even if this is the response Hector hoped for—the one that could save his life—it strikes a dagger in the love song singer's heart.

Mr. Arthur Jessel is a third generation diplomat, educated like his father and paternal grandfather at the prestigious American college, Yale, and at the Johns Hopkins School of Foreign Service. His gift for languages—he is fluent in five—surpasses that of all of his colleagues and serves him well in his profession as well as in his most passionate avocation, women. Indeed, for that pursuit he has expanded his linguistic repertoire to include such words as 'eyes' and 'hair' and 'breasts' and, of course, 'love,' in six additional tongues. None of this is to say that his infatuation with the exotic Bogotá street singer is tawdry or trivial; Arthur is one of those rare men who can defy the laws of logic by giving his heart totally to several lovers at the same time.

When, over a dinner of langouste ravioli at the terrace restaurant of the Hotel Andino, Sylvia tells Arthur about her singing partner's plight, Arthur is pleased to offer his help. Contrary to Sylvia's fears, Arthur is not in the least affronted by being asked a favor so early in their relationship. So rewarding are his experiences with women that Arthur never feels exploited by them. Before the couple retires to the suite at the Andino that Arthur rents by the month, he promises to meet with Sylvia's young friend, Hector, at the American Embassy the very next day.

As a successful diplomat, Arthur is adept at the *quid pro quo* of personal indulgences. Unlike banking with its assigned numerical values, trading in favors is more art than arithmetic. The worth of the door key for Arthur's hotel suite to his Deputy Chief of Mission cannot be calculated in terms of pesos or dollars because along with the loan of that key comes knowledge of incalculable value, namely that the Deputy Chief is cheating on his wife. This is easily worth a freshly minted tourist visa, one that dispenses with the mandatory six-month-long security-checking period. However, *like* banking, a favor granted begets favor debt and so, as a matter of principle, Arthur Jessel feels obligated to keep the favor economy cycling on. And that is one reason why, when he presents the visa to Hector, he asks the young man for a personal indulgence in return.

"There is a woman in Coral Gables to whom I need to convey a private message," Arthur says to Hector in his crisp continental Spanish. "Her name is Faith Moffet and her address is 754 Jeronimo Drive. You must remember this; you cannot write it down, just as I cannot mail a letter to this address. I want you to go there—it is not so far from Miami airport—and to ring the doorbell. A maid will answer and you will ask for Mrs. Moffet. If she is not there, leave immediately. If her husband is about, you must leave quickly also. But when you get to speak with her alone, tell her that I will be in Miami on the evening of January third. The Colony Hotel. Tell Mrs. Moffet that—well, simply say that I am counting the days until I see her. Do you understand?"

Hector understands. He repeats both the address and the message for Jessel's approval. Then they review Hector's preparations for his departure to Miami, Florida. He must obtain a passport, a round-trip ticket, and two thousand American dollars to show that he can support himself for his 'two-week vacation.'

Sylvia is waiting for Hector outside the embassy. When Hector shows her his American tourist visa, she grabs him by both hands and swings him around in a joyful dance in the middle of the sidewalk. Hector wonders if he should warn her that her American is a faithless lover who will break her heart. He also wonders if perhaps that is the *real* message Jessel wanted him to deliver—and to Sylvia, not Mrs. Moffet—a cowardly preparation for the rejection Jessel is already planning for his new young mistress. But, of course, Hector says nothing of any of this.

"I wish I could take you with me," is what he says to Sylvia.

There are easily twenty Colombian men Hector's age on the flight and he does his best to avoid contact with them— even the one seated next to him—in an effort to evade any suspicion by association. On Sylvia's advice, Hector purchased a second-hand linen suit at a stall in the Pasaje Rivas. Wearing it now with a white shirt and brown tie, his hair freshly cut and combed, he looks more like a student or perhaps even a genuine tourist than one more impoverished illegal with a questionable visa. Also at Sylvia's recommendation, Hector packed only a carry-on bag; it contains two changes of clothes, his 'Look-and-Learn' English lesson book, and his *cuatro,* its fingerboard jutting out from the top. In this way, his stop at the customs counter would be brief. It is well known in Bogotá that the distance from the landed airplane's doors to the Miami airport's exit is the longest expanse in America.

But none of these precautions prevents the first American immigration officer who inspects Hector's visa from promptly and expressionlessly dispatching him to a holding room ten feet behind him. Along the short passage to this room stand half a dozen men in slacks and short-sleeved shirts, attaché cases at their sides. As Hector passes by them, each mouths a single word: '*Abogado.*'

Hector stops at the last of these men and says, "I have a legitimate tourist visa from the American embassy. So why should I need a lawyer?"

"To avoid being sent home tonight," the lawyer replies dryly.

"This makes no sense," Hector says.

"That is something for you to think about on your way back to Bogotá."

"What is your fee?"

"Five hundred dollars."

Hector shrugs and begins to walk away.

"Four hundred," the lawyer calls after him, but Hector walks on into the room.

Inside is every young Colombian man Hector saw on the plane. About half of these, he sees, have acquired lawyers and Hector wonders if this places him among the most wise or most foolish of them. Over an hour passes before any of them are called to the small desk wedged in the corner of the windowless room.

The immigration magistrate makes short business of the first six boys she summons, all without lawyers. She simply holds their visas over a blue light and declares them forgeries in both English and Spanish. The rejected young men are then handcuffed by an officer and escorted out of the room—to a prison cell to await their flight back, Hector overhears one lawyer explain to his client. The seventh called is the boy who sat next to Hector on the plane. No linen suit or barbered hair for him; he looks like a typical specimen of Ciudad Bolivar poverty, yet clearly the boy arrived in America with enough cash to buy himself an *abogado*. And it is his *abogado* who does all the talking to the magistrate, holding the boy's passport and visa in front of her face with a peculiar grip that involves raising his forefinger and middle finger above it. Hector realizes immediately that this is a signal and an artless one at that; the lawyer is offering her two hundred dollars of his five-hundred-dollar fee for the boy's visa validation. Indeed, the validation is granted without a single pass of his visa in front of the blue light.

Hector panics. He is about to ask one of the lawyers in the room to represent him too when the magistrate calls his name. Hector inhales deeply, then strides to the desk and presents his documents.

"This is real thing," he declares resolutely in his 'Look-and-Learn' English. "I catch it myself at U.S.A. embassy in Bogotá. I am person they know."

The magistrate, a dark-skinned Cubana-American, offers him a sardonic smile. She considers him impudent for speaking at all, let alone with such self-assurance, but her eyes do linger on his fine-boned face.

"Why have you come to Miami?" she asks him in Spanish.

"For pleasure," Hector replies.

"Such as?"

"Dancing. Making new friends," Hector says with a shy smile. Without thinking, he is playing the coquette, the innocent pretty boy who charms the lady tourists.

The magistrate appears amused. "And do you have money for such pleasures?" she asks.

"Enough."

"Show me," the magistrate says.

Hector hesitates, then reaches into his pocket for the four one-hundred-dollar bills left over after buying his round-trip plane ticket. He holds the bills in front of the magistrate. She laughs.

"Do you really believe you can sleep and eat and drink and dance in Miami for two weeks with only four hundred dollars?"

Whatever slight interest she may have had in his face or his charm has already evaporated. She turns toward the officer beside her, the man with the cardboard box full of handcuffs.

"I am the guest of an American friend!" Hector exclaims. "An important American friend with much money." The gambit he is now playing is a treacherous one and he knows it. But he also knows how little stands between him and the night flight back to Bogotá.

The magistrate looks at Hector with disdain. She does not for a moment believe he knows a single American, let alone one with money. But what Hector has failed to accomplish with his charm, he has achieved with his audacity. There is nothing this bureaucrat relishes more than making a fool of a vain and pretentious young man. She will call his bluff.

"And what is this very important person's name?" she asks mockingly.

"Mrs. Faith Moffet. Of Coral Gables. With address of 754 Jeronimo Drive."

"Really? And what is her telephone number?"

"She told me to find it in the telephone directory when I am here. Do you have a directory, Madame?"

The magistrate appears both incensed and intrigued. She most certainly still mistrusts the handsome young man and further, he is wasting time she could be using to much greater profit, but she has a grudging admiration for the degree to which he is playing his hand. And it promises a more glorious humiliation than she usually provokes.

She orders the officer to bring her a telephone directory. Indeed, she does find a Paul and Faith Moffet listed at 754 Jeronimo Drive in the Gables, but she knows too well how easy it is to pick a name out of a directory and memorize it. That trick has been tried on her before. She removes a cell phone from her pocket and dials the number. It is answered on the second ring.

"Mrs. Moffet?" the magistrate asks. After the reply, she says, "May I speak with her, please?"

The magistrate watches Hector's face, waiting for the first signs of foreboding to register. Just how long will he let her go on with this charade before he concedes defeat? Hector smiles weakly back at her.

"Yes, Mrs. Moffet, I am calling from the United States Immigration Service where I have a young man who claims to be a personal friend of yours . . ." She looks down at Hector's passport. "His name is Hector Mondragon."

"Arthur Jessel's friend!" Hector interjects loudly in English, aiming his voice at the magistrate's phone. "From embassy in Bogotá."

The magistrate glares at Hector. She has had quite enough of his impudence. She moves her thumb to the Off button on the phone, but before pressing it she hears the party at the other end speaking sharply. The magistrate puts the phone back to her ear and listens a moment, then says in a subdued voice, "Yes . . . yes . . . Miami International. He will be waiting for you in my office."

Hector sits in the passenger seat of an open Jaguar convertible, his overnight bag between his knees. Driving is Faith Moffet, a silky haired blonde wearing wrap-around sunglasses and a one-piece garment that consists of shorts with a halter top. To Hector, this article of clothing looks like a child's playsuit—later he will learn that it is actually called a 'playsuit' by mature native women—except for the milky-white crescent of breast at the sides which the halter is built to reveal.

Even as his fate was being determined by Mrs. Moffet in the immigration office, Hector was comparing her to Sylvia and finding the wealthy American wanting in both beauty and grace. Although he is an uneducated, rural-born, street hustler of not yet twenty years, Hector has a sophisticate's eye for refinement. In fact, Hector's background makes him more discerning in this regard than, say, someone like Arthur Jessel, whose judgment is impaired by the money-bound prejudices of his social class. Of the two men, only Hector can see the royalty in a half-breed street singer and the vulgarity in a wealthy socialite.

But Mrs. Moffet's vulgarity notwithstanding, Hector was impressed by her confident manner when she strode into the magistrate's office, announced herself loudly, and then embraced Hector like a long-lost cousin. Or lover. And although the Cubana magistrate had lost her contest with Hector, she had to smile when she saw the rich *gringa* kiss his smooth cheek.

Hector and Mrs. Moffet are cruising along Lejeune Road heading for Coral Gables. So far their conversation amounts to no more than her inquiry of how his flight went and his reply, "Very excellent." Now Hector turns to her and relays Jessel's message, complete with the diplomat's exact words about counting the days until he sees her. The woman nods, pleased, and then says, "Where should I let you off?"

Hector looks out. He sees hotels and shops and restaurants on both sides of the road.

"Here is good," he says.

CHAPTER FIFTEEN

It took three generations for Grandville's first white settlers to make their way from Boston.

The first, the English-born Malcolm Wright family, trekked west by foot to Sturbridge Village, having heard that settlement was in need of a blacksmith to replace the one who had succumbed to bronchitis the previous winter. There, some ten years later, the Wright's eldest son, Robert, married a young woman by the name of Louise Button, the only child of Sturbridge's barber and blood-letter, Barnard Button.

Feeling hemmed in by the village's increasing density—there were already more than thirty houses, barns, and shops thickly settled at its center—the newlyweds saved up for a horse and wagon before taking up the second generational leg of the westward journey. But crossing the Connecticut River on the third day of their expedition, they lost both horse and wagon to a frenzied current that had begun as a squall in the White Mountains on the same day they departed Sturbridge. With literally no more than the sopping clothes on their shivering backs, Robert and Louise staked out a plot on the west bank of that great river. Here, in the course of two decades, they built a homestead and a subsistence farm, and bred eight children, five of whom survived to maturity. In that time, several other families settled nearby, forming the nucleus of what would later be Westfield.

Of Robert and Louise Wright's brood, it was their second son, James, who completed the odyssey to the Housatonic River valley at the foothills of the Berkshire Mountains, to the place that would, half a century later, be incorporated by the Massachusetts Settlement Council as Grandville. To understand why James Wright stopped at this particular spot and did not range on to Albany or points further west, or turn south to the fertile soil of what would become Connecticut to grow tobacco along with other enterprising colonial farmers, or even north, deep into mountains teeming with deer, rabbit, and bear whose pelts were prized on the other side of the Atlantic, we first need to fathom this young man's character and heart.

From the time he was a toddler, James was an eccentric boy—argumentative, dreamy, and given to fits of melancholy that his father saw as laziness and his mother as a sign of spirituality. Indeed, James grew to be an avid Bible reader, although this was fundamentally because the Bible was the only book in the house. The Good Book was both his primer when, at the age of ten, he taught himself to read, and his fodder when later on he discovered that the written word could nourish his dreams. He favored the Old Testament, in particular tales of flight. He could recite by heart long passages from Exodus.

As it happened, James was declaiming the story of the parting of the Red Sea in the family barn when he had his final clash with his father. Robert told his boy he was sick and tired of his malingering ways, that the cows needed to be milked, not preached to. James replied with a straight face that enlightened cows produced richer cream. This, of course, was a preposterous idea, and James knew that as he said it, but the impulse both to argue and to spin fantastic tales was second nature to him, so much so that when his father screamed back at him, James stood his ground, insisting that his enlightened cows principle was well-established fact. By the end of their skirmish, James had a blackened eye that hardened into the resolution to leave his family immediately even though it was the middle of winter. So it was that James Wright set off from Westfield—not to search for more fertile land or more open space or, a common motive for young men living on remote farms, to find a wife, but simply to escape. But this only accounts for James's flight, not for why he subsequently alighted in the future Grandville, never to leave.

It is February twelfth, 1685, the tenth day of James Wright's journey. Half of those days, the snowfall was so heavy and unrelenting that he tramped no more than four or five miles from sunrise to sunset, his eyes flicking from the faint outline of the sun to whatever visible patch of snow-covered ground lay west of him. At dusk, he crammed himself under an overhanging rock or into the well of a tree stump where he spent the night murmuring Bible verses to himself or falling into a half-sleep of delirious dreams.

On this tenth day, he awakens to a clear sky and brilliant sun. Instead of making himself a breakfast of flat bread and raspberry preserve from the bundle his mother packed for him, James sets off immediately to make up for lost time. He has only taken twenty steps when he asks himself what 'lost time' can possibly mean if he has no destination? Is there a faster or slower passage to nowhere in particular? It is just such paradoxes that always tickled James's imagination and, when expressed out loud, infuriated his father. At this moment, the thought makes James laugh. When the sound of his laughter echoes off the mountain to his right to the one on his left and then back again, back and forth, accelerating and dimming to a vanishing point that feels like Eternity itself, James Wright is in a state of bliss.

At noon, in the afterglow of this ecstatic moment, James begins to ascend the next fir-covered hill on his trek. The frigid air feels fresher in his nostrils and more vital in his lungs than any he can remember. Miniature prisms made of pebbles of ice suspended from the needles of blue spruce trees throw off tiny rainbows, dazzling James's vista and making it more exhila-rating. (Over two centuries later, this phenomenon will be mim-icked by pinpoint light bulbs strung on cut pines inside heated houses at Christmastime.) Near the top of the hill, the trees give way to a great mound of granite. It would be easy enough for James to skirt this boulder and pick up his westward path on its far side but, without thinking why, he climbs on to the hill's stone summit. It is here, looking down into the snowy valley, where James begins to cry.

If we saw him at this moment, we might assume that the tears falling on his cheeks were the result of his eyes smarting in the cold air. But as he weeps on, his shoulders trembling, we might be prone to admit that he is, indeed, overcome with emotion. Yet, given his fatigue, his hunger, his days of solitude, and his abrupt and acrimonious departure from his family, we would be likely to pin the cause of his outburst on these condi-tions rather than on its authentic source.

James is crying over the beauty he sees. The crisp shadows of pines in virgin snow, the crystal blue sky, the flock of pine sis-kins swooping across the open valley—this immaculate winter panorama, distinct from any he ever saw in the plains from whence he came, strikes James with awe. And for this reason alone—beauty—he decides to make this place his new home.

* * *

James Wright's impulse survives in the greeting Wendell deVries has already heard a dozen times this February morning. Folks walk in Write Now's front door saying, "It's a Grandville day, all right," the traditional acknowledgement of a clear blue sky and generous sunlight dazzling the snow-covered trees and rooftops of their town in mid-winter. For some locals, the greeting has acquired a defensive subtext—*We'd rather be right here than take off for Florida like some 'snowbird' rich folk and retirees we know.* But for most, it is a simple expression of appreciation and pride of place, especially for those who take the plowed path up to Wright Mountain's peak, there to gaze down at their snowy village as if sighting it for the first time.

In the past, Wendell joined the Historical Society's annual, February twelfth trek up Wright Mountain, listened patiently to Dr. Armbruster's monotone recitation about James Wright's epiphany, and even sang along with the others in 'A Living Prayer'—

> 'Through many dangers, toils, and snares,
> I have already come;
> 'Tis grace hath brought me safe thus far,
> And grace will lead me home.'

But this year, what with running the shop, visiting Franny in the sanitarium, and looking after Lila seven days a week, Wendell had to miss it.

Although Wendell has migrated little more than a hundred feet from projection booth to news shop, he has experienced something akin to culture shock in the process. He has gone from a sequestered life to a public one, from books and movies to a perpetual rotation of living, talkative people, from a sense of immunity to one of risky exposure. On Esther's advice, he hauled as much of his Phoenix memorabilia as he could from his booth to the store to serve as a cushion of familiarity, but he quickly realized Write Now's racks, shelves, and counter only left enough space to accommodate his old posters, calendars, and photographs—that is, if he still wanted his customers to be able to get through the door. So his cherished easy chair, footrest, and box of *Silver Screen* magazines—not to mention his mammoth Brenkert projector—had to be trucked home where they now made an obstacle course of the living room. Binx made the transition to shop life far more gracefully than his master; his first day there he discovered one of the Melville Block's original brass heating vents in the store's far corner, a divine sleeping spot for a connoisseur of sleeping spots.

During lulls in business, Wendell steps outside the shop and walks up to the Phoenix to investigate its overhaul. So far, it has been all egress and no ingress—workmen shouldering charred floorboards from the stage, long rolls of ripped-up carpeting, and entire rows of iron and velvet seats out the front doors and into trucks. Wendell feels neither saddened nor cheered by what he sees. From what he hears from his customers, he supposes that it represents progress, but mostly he has too much on his mind to think about it, even if he takes just about every opportunity he gets to watch the workmen.

Wendell has run into Babs Dowd several times there. On the work site she wears denim overalls topped with a hardhat, possibly because she thinks it puts her on equal footing with the workers—just one of the guys—but more likely because she sees it as a juicy role. Franny had her share of that same theatrical whimsy in her, often dressing for the day as if she was an imagined character, but Wendell doubts that is part of his daughter's life these days. When he visits Franny at the psychiatric center, she seems to have lost so much of herself that he cannot imagine she has anything left over to invest in the role of someone else.

Babs always asks about Franny, and Wendell replies, "She's coming along" or "She'll be back on her feet in no time." The situation is fraught, to say the least. From one perspective, it was Mrs. Dowd herself who drove Franny over the edge. But from another, more tangible perspective, it was Franny who set Mrs. Dowd's newly acquired real estate on fire. Little damage was done and no charges were pressed. Furthermore, Michael Dowd's investment syndicate gave Wendell what they called a 'golden parachute' in the form of a check for six months of his former salary as the Phoenix's manager. Accepting the money was rough for Wendell; it made him feel shabby and patronized. But he knew this was not a time to let pride determine his decisions. He had only one goal these days—to keep his little family intact.

One day, the Dowd woman told him she had an appointment to visit Franny at the sanitarium, that she wanted to tell Franny personally she bore her no grudge and wanted to remain friends. Wendell panicked. It sounded like a prescription for another breakdown. He rushed back to his store and, for the first time, phoned Franny's psychiatrist. Dr. Werner could not speak to him until the end of the day, and when he did, he told Wendell that he was completely aware of Mrs. Dowd's role in Franny's life and it was precisely for that reason he had approved the visit. "It will help us dig deeper," the psychiatrist said to Wendell, a response that made Wendell feel both angry and helpless. For Wendell, psychiatric treatment seems as arbitrary and opaque as mental illness itself.

Wendell is trying to train himself to be hopeful about his daughter's recovery. For a while, he spoke with Franny's mother on the phone almost every day—many times over the number of times he had spoken to her in the previous thirty years—and Beatrice's confidence in Franny's doctors helped Wendell considerably in his pursuit of optimism. But after a few weeks he discontinued these conversations because they had ceased to comfort him. Beatrice's cheery descriptions of the sanitarium she and her husband had chosen for Franny began to make it sound more like a finishing school than a treatment center—the finishing school Beatrice believes Franny should have attended years ago.

Still, on balance, Wendell has faith Franny will make it through this bad period. He is a deep believer in the body's resilience and the recuperative power of the passage of time, and since he has never sensed a disconnection between body and mind, he is confident time will heal his daughter's illness wherever it resides. But he does have to admit that being away from the shop and home will probably speed the process for her. She needs a break from Grandville. Watching the workmen shouldering burnt planks out of the Phoenix could not be good for her, and dealing with Lila on a daily basis would probably be worse. Lila has become even more withdrawn than usual, and on the subject of Franny she is relentlessly uncharitable: Lila maintains that her mother is a victim of herself. Even if Wendell doubts Lila fully believes this, he never disputes this position with his granddaughter, mostly because he does not want to quarrel with her about anything, not now, but also because the prospect of arguing that Franny's condition actually is out of her control is too painful for him to contemplate.

Wendell returns to the shop this morning to discover that a customer has entered during his brief look-see at the Phoenix. He is a retarded man, a resident of one of the town's so-called halfway houses, although as far as Wendell can determine, there is no other half to these people's lives—they remain in these houses into old age. The man standing at the counter is a familiar presence on Main Street, recognizable as much by the backpack crammed with books he always carries, as by his large head and mongoloid features. At this moment, Wendell sees the books as an affectation, the man's absurd pretense that he is not what people think he is, but actually quite the opposite, a scholar. If there was any blessing to being sub-normal, one would think that at least they would be spared pretentiousness.

The man comes into Write Now every morning at about this time and asks the same question, "Where's Franny?" Wendell tells him that she is away on vacation, then watches him shake his head back and forth before leaving. But after Wendell's reply this morning, the man lingers, fingering the packets of Altoid breath strips that sit on the counter between them.

"I talk to her sometimes," Wendell says. "Do you have a message for her?"

"No!" the man retorts loudly, still not moving.

"Maybe I can help you?" Wendell says.

Again, a loud, petulant, "No!"

Wendell is annoyed. If the man is self-conscious enough to try to pass himself off as bookish, he is capable of knowing he is behaving rudely.

"It's a small shop," Wendell says. "Got to make room for other customers."

"Who are you?" the man asks belligerently.

"Franny's father. And I'd like you to leave now, young man."

The retarded man looks stunned. Wendell sees tears spring to his eyes as he turns and scurries out of the store, his back-pack jiggling behind him.

Wendell sits down on his stool. He is shaken. Binx bounds off his grate, ambles over to his master, and lifts his front paws onto Wendell's lap. Wendell is massaging Binx's neck to soothe himself when Mrs. Carpolino stumbles in on her walker and asks for the latest issue of *Vogue*.

Every day at eleven-thirty, Esther brings lunch for them both from the co-op, usually a thick soup and salad plate from the co-op's salad bar. She slips behind Write Now's counter and the two eat standing up. Afterward, Esther tends to the shop's bills and orders, a job she volunteered to do after watching Wendell struggle for hours over candy bar inventory. Before she returns to her job in the co-op's produce depart-ment, they hug and, if no customers are around, kiss. Because of Wendell's lost access to the Phoenix's dressing rooms along with his job, plus his decision to stay home evenings with Lila, he and Esther have not made their way into bed together since Franny's breakdown.

Today, between their soup and salad courses, Esther touches Wendell's arm and says, "What's up with you today?"

Wendell shrugs. "Just tired," he says. He does not want to go into the Backpack Man incident. He still feels ashamed of his behavior, but he does not think the little episode is impor-tant enough to mention, certainly not in the current scheme of his life.

"And sad?"

"I don't know, Esther," Wendell answers, more firmly than he intended.

"Okay," Esther murmurs. She takes a couple of bites of her salad, then sets it aside and pulls out the order folder from under the counter.

Wendell watches her work. He does feel sad. He squeezes himself behind her, groin to buttocks, and wraps his arms around her waist. "Just one of those days," he says softly.

Esther does not respond. She does not in any way pull away from him, but Wendell can feel her taut discomfort. She keeps checking off columns of candy brands as if he was not there.

"It's just a matter of time," Wendell whispers.

"What? What's just a matter of time?" Esther asks over her shoulder.

"I don't know. Everything."

"Well, that's certainly true," Esther says, a suspicion of sarcasm in her voice. "Everything is a matter of time. Time is the stuff life's made of."

"Come on, Esther!" Wendell snaps. "I don't need any New Age wisdom right now, okay?"

"Actually, Benjamin Franklin said that," Esther replies.

Wendell disengages himself and walks out from behind the counter to the front window where he stares through the rectangle of glass at the still winter day. He longs for his projection booth; he wishes nothing had changed or ever would.

A moment later, Mel Gustal walks in saying, "Well, it sure is a Grandville day." Esther silently leaves while Mel dithers over the rack of birthday cards. Today is his mother's sixtieth.

That evening after closing up and shopping for steaks and spinach at the Grand Union—Lila has reverted to carnivore with the vengeance of a born-again sinner—Wendell is driving up Mahaiwe Street, Binx beside him. Turning into his driveway, his headlights again flash on the 'For Rent' sign in front of the house conjoined to his. Pressing clutch and brake, he lets the truck idle in front of the illuminated sign.

CHAPTER SIXTEEN

If, on a mid-winter's weekend, a family from Boston or New York or Darien were to take a long-planned trip to the Berkshire Mountains to go skiing at Jiminy Peak or Butternut Basin or Catamount, and wanting to take in all the renowned spots of the area, made reservations for lunch at the Red Lion Inn in the center of Stockbridge, they might pause on the long front porch of that picturesque landmark to take in the quaint shops and churches that line Main Street to their right, buildings that are already known to them because they have seen them on calendars and greeting cards in reproductions of paintings by the town's most celebrated resident, Norman Rockwell. Such is the cross-inspiration of life and art that the vine wreaths and velvet bows decorating the windows and doors of these buildings today perfectly match those in Rockwell's 1940s and '50s paintings, as if the town were a picture of its past self.

Looking now to their left, the visitors view the old colonial and Victorian mansions in the center of town, museum pieces too—grand, white, stately, yet at the same time cozy and snug-looking, storybook homes of contented New England families. One in particular catches their eyes, a vast neo-classical home cattycorner to the inn. It displays rows of columns along its first and second stories, open balconies, long-windowed sun porches, parapets, sloping dormers, side wings each the size of a twelve-room suburban house, and an annex that seems to ramble behind it without end. Even with snow on the ground, they see that the shrubs and gardens surrounding the mansion are masterfully designed in the French manner. One or two members of this out-of-town family are likely to indulge in a fleeting fantasy of living in this place as a serene lord or lady of the manor, and they smile secretly as they now enter the Red Lion Inn and luxuriate in the warmth of its blazing fireplace, unaware that the mansion of their fantasy is home to the troubled souls of the Austen Riggs Psychiatric Center.

* * *

Only after residing at Austen Riggs for close to a month did Franny deVries finally ask her psychiatrist exactly what her diagnosis was.

"The technical one?" Dr. Werner asked.

"Sure."

"You had what we call a Major Depressive Episode."

"How major?"

"I believe you are through the worst of it, don't you?"

Franny shrugged. "So what is the non-technical diagnosis?"

"You had a nervous breakdown."

"That sounds less ominous."

"If that is what you like, I can tell you what they used to call it—'a spell of the vapors.' Sounds almost ladylike, doesn't it?"

Franny shrugged again. "If the worst is over, I suppose I should go home," she said.

"Is that what you want to do?"

"I don't know."

"I think we can wait a bit longer, Franny," the doctor said. "We want to be sure you never have to suffer through something like that again."

"Like setting a fire, you mean."

"No, like the psychological state you were in *when* you set the fire."

"It's all about me, isn't it?"

"In here, yes," Dr. Werner said. "Out there, no. And that is one reason for you to stay here a while longer."

"To protect the people out there from me."

"No, to protect you from them."

"So they don't put me in jail for arson."

"You know that is not an issue. No one holds you responsible. We have gone over this before, Franny."

"The insanity defense."

"If you like."

"Me, me, me."

"Okay, you *are* guilty. Is that what you want? Endless guilt?"

"To tell you the truth, I don't feel that guilty, just tired. Very tired. I want to sleep my self away."

"You sleep too much, Franny."

"It's better than anything else you have to offer," Franny said. And that was all she had to say in this session. It was already much more than she had said in most of them.

Awakening in her room, Franny's first thoughts are how she can make the time pass quickly until she can sleep again. Certain daily events seem to take an eternity, particularly group therapy. In her estimation, those regular after-breakfast gatherings in the upstairs 'Round Room' have only one beneficial effect: For one hour she hates other people more than she hates herself. This, in its way, is a relief, although not one with any lasting benefits; leaving the Round Room, her rage lingers but instantly turns inward.

In every session, her fellow groupers relentlessly blame Mother or Father, Sister or Brother, the Government, Society, or the one that makes Franny cringe every time a group member venomously spits it out, 'The System.' The *System* is what has fucked them up, gotten in their way, tricked them up, conspired to make them stumble, tremble, whimper, and fail. *The System, for Christ's sake! Well, idiots, the name of that System is Life!* Not being an idiot herself, Franny is quick to realize that she is only blaming these poor souls in her group for her feeling of emptiness, and that this, her own form of pettiness, is ultimately no different from theirs.

Dance therapy passes the time more quickly, in part because Franny is not required to interact with anyone. She dances solo, rarely looking at the others as, at the therapist's instruction, they choreograph their inner demons. As a rule, these demons appear to be intent on making the people they possess look like spastics.

Franny, on the other hand, dedicates this hour to trying to recall what it once felt like to live in a state of expectancy. And what in the name of God that ever did for her. She dances dimly-remembered routines from as far back as Mrs. Hampton's dance class, but also from her college workshop in modern interpretive dance where their inspiration was presumed to be more celestial than demonic. Unlike those classes of yore, there are no mirrors on the walls of the Austen Riggs dance room, just as there are few in the facility at large; in general, the institution's residents are demoralized or, in some cases, bewildered by images of themselves. In any event, Franny is trying to recall what expectancy felt like, not how she looks seeking it. But it eludes her. Most often she ends up standing immobile in the center of the dance floor, unable to even conjure what it is she is searching for.

Lunch is easy enough to get through, considering that Franny picks at her food for only a few minutes before leaving the dining room. And the craft period that follows five days a week offers an occasional consolation when, say, cutting out a paper snowman, Franny is momentarily transported back to kindergarten in the Lenox-Stockbridge Montessori school that still occupies the basement of the Congregational Church just down the street from Riggs.

But on Tuesdays and Thursdays, lunchtime is filled with dread as the minutes tick away until Visiting Hour. Franny was spared this ordeal her first four weeks at the sanitarium, but then Dr. Werner authorized it as a much-needed strategy for putting his patient in touch with her emotions. Franny, he believed, had gone directly from feeling too much to feeling too little—to being utterly numb most of her waking hours. This, he explained, was a common compensatory reaction for people recovering from a Major Depressive Episode, and contact with significant people in her life could help her 're-animate.' But most importantly, it could give Franny and the psychiatrist something to work with in their thus-far unproductive therapy sessions. Werner's strategy, however, has had the opposite effect: Franny's visitors make her retreat even more into auto-anesthesia. The visits feel like punishments.

None more so than her mother's, starting with the fact that Beatrice dresses for the occasions in her Saks finery and comes through the glass-paneled, inner front door of Austen Riggs aflutter, as if arriving late for a tea party at the Lenox Garden Club. In case no one had mentioned it (Beatrice mentioned on her first visit), *she* was paying for Franny's stay at the pricey institution, and it was Beatrice's husband, Barclay, who had arranged for her swift entrance into it. 'Entrance' is the operative word here, as Beatrice considers getting into Austen Riggs, the *crème de la crème* of mental hospitals, equivalent to getting into an Ivy League college. She can recite Riggs's illustrious alumni, starting with that most gentlemanly of pop stars, James Taylor, and working through the sons and daughters of various eminent Harvard theologians and Yale bankers. To her, the neuroses and psychoses of Riggs patients are simply the thwarted artistic expressions of the elite.

It was not that long ago when Franny would have recoiled in despair at her mother's perspective on Riggs, reflexively feeling inadequate—that she was even unqualified for admission to this nut house. But in her current state, Franny just stares at her mother as if observing a stock character in an amateur production of a comedy of manners. The strongest emotion Franny feels is detached amusement, although after her mother departs she feels even more benumbed than usual.

Franny's reaction to Babs Dowd's single and mercifully brief visit was much the same. Babs began by looking into Franny's eyes with Stanislavski-esque intensity and announcing in what appeared to be a prepared statement that she bore Franny no resentment for the fire 'thing' because—her exact words—"I can feel your turmoil as if it was my own." From there Babs had rattled on about the progress being made in renovating the Phoenix and everybody's hope that Franny would be ready to jump right in when the Grandville Players mounted their first production in the refurbished theater.

Listening, Franny was struck by her realization that plays, theater, even the Phoenix itself, no longer meant a thing to her. She could not understand why they ever had. If life itself was so hollow, what possible value could there be in depicting it on a stage? It was as if in her unstable condition Franny was channeling her all-too-stable grandmother, Sally: *"Why in heaven's name does one need to dramatize life? Isn't life ridiculous enough just as it is?"*

For once, Franny had gained an insight worthy of discussion at her next session with Dr. Werner, but she quickly lost interest in it, bored with her perception that one more aspect of her former life bored her.

Her father's visits are the most awful for Franny. His first time at Riggs, the big man began to cry the moment he saw his daughter. Wendell reached for her, drew her to his barrel chest and bulging belly in a bear hug. Franny wanted to cry too. She longed to. But no tears came, nor that blend of sweet sadness and sanctuary that had always accompanied weeping in her father's arms. This is the most dreadful part of Franny's condition: wanting to feel an emotion, but the wanting itself being the only emotion she can feel.

Lila has come with Wendell a couple of times and these are torturous. Franny can plainly see her daughter's isolation and wants desperately to console her, but with what? Franny is bereft of reassurances. Yet these occasions do awaken some semblance of feeling in Franny: Isolated herself, Franny feels a paradoxical empathy with her isolated child.

The last time Lila visited, she sat blank-faced on the Visiting Room couch, tearing at her cuticles with her teeth. Franny summoned what strength she had to breach the barricade between them and said, "I know this must be hard for you, Lila."

Lila's expression did not alter in the least. "You don't seem that different to me," she replied, and Franny, more than ever, wanted to cry, but again all she could summon was the desire to be a person—a wounded mother—who *could* cry.

Dr. Werner deemed this a significant breakthrough. "Do you see yourself in Lila?" he asked.

"I guess so. The detached part."

"Do you think she got that from you?"

"Who knows? She pretty much came into the world that way."

"And you?"

"I used to be more, you know, outgoing. Social."

"You enjoyed other people."

"I thought so. Now, I don't really think I did. I was just acting that way. It's a distraction. People are a convenient distraction."

"From what?"

Franny shook her head back and forth. "Exactly. From *what*?"

Werner waited for her to go on, but Franny had nothing more to say.

Franny lies on her bed staring at the ceiling. She is hoping that if she falls asleep, the social worker will leave her alone instead of summoning her to the Visiting Room. No such luck.

Slowly making her way down the corridor to the Visiting Room, Franny realizes it is the day her mother comes. She stops and leans her head against the wall. She closes her eyes. She could sleep right here, on her feet.

"Hi, Franny." A man's voice.

She opens her eyes. Herbert Blitzstein's face pokes out from the Visiting Room door.

"I thought you were my mother," Franny says.

"People are always mistaking me for somebody else," Herb replies with a crooked smile. "I heard your mother cancelled, so I finally got in here."

Franny walks into the room and sits in the reclining chair that is usually reserved for elderly visitors. Looking at Herbert's face, she realizes she has not thought about the vigil group since her breakdown. Herbert is sitting on the couch, a pile of papers and a couple of books beside him, a Navy pea jacket thrown over the back of the couch.

"I've got some work to do if you don't mind," Herb says.

Franny stares at him quizzically.

"Correcting papers," Herb says. "One thousand words on irony. Socrates via Kierkegaard. Way too hard for them. Hell, it's way too hard for me." He dons a pair of reading glasses, picks up the topmost paper, and begins to read, the pen in his right hand poised in the air.

For the next hour, Herbert goes through the papers, here and there turning one sideways so he can write a comment in the margin. Once in a while he sighs or rolls his eyes or looks over at Franny and offers her an ironic, pained smile. He finishes just as visiting hour is over. He stands and pulls on his jacket.

"You look like you could use some sleep," he says. Then, before Franny can take in what he is up to, he comes over and kisses the top of her head. "Hang in there, Franny," he says and he leaves.

After he is gone, Franny finds herself almost, but not quite, smiling.

CHAPTER SEVENTEEN

Half-dozing in American history class on her first day back at Grandville High after Christmas vacation, Lila heard her name called on the PA system. She gathered up her books, stuffed them in her backpack, and left the classroom without a word to the teacher or a glance at her classmates, then sluggishly made her way to the guidance office. Mr. Cyzinski's secretary instructed her to take a seat until Cyzinski could see her, but Lila remained standing, idly wondering what brand of bullshit he had in store for her this time.

She glanced at a bulletin board covered with glossy fliers promoting colleges she never heard of—Barstow, Cedar Crest, Fullerton, Saddleback, Orange Coast. Each displayed vivid, full-color panoramas of sunny campuses that looked like botanical gardens. Smaller photographs showed the colleges' apparently deliriously happy students walking in twos and threes under arbor-ways. Invariably, one of these blissful scholars was non-white, Asian or Black, but at Orange Coast College in Southern California, Latino—a bit of niche advertising. The very thought of spending a single day at any one of these places—undoubtedly the only tier of institutions that would admit Lila other than Grandville Community College, which was required to admit anyone who graduated from Grandville High School—was utterly repulsive.

If high school was a lie, college was a massive hoax. Its only purpose was to bleed hard-earned money from families who actually bought the preposterous idea that courses in French and anthropology and macroeconomics prepared their children for success. Never mind that ninety-nine percent of their children ended up with insufferable jobs at insurance companies and retail chains and, God pity them, as teachers in public schools—the fix was in. And none conspired more industriously in the fix than high school guidance counselors like Mr. Cyzinski.

Cyzinski opened the door to his office with an expression of dramatic concern on his florid face, a sure sign that he had concocted another whopping lie for Lila's consumption. Lila considered simply turning around and walking down the hall and out of the school, but a scene would follow and Wendell would probably be phoned, so she marched into the office. If there was anything in her life that still had any significance to Lila, it was her grandfather.

After they both were seated, Cyzinski looked across his desk at Lila, that over-the-top expression of deep concern still on his brow.

"I know this must be a difficult time for you," he said, gravely.

Hanging on the wall behind Cyzinski's desk were his diplomas, a B.A. from Canisius College and an M.A. in Career Counseling from North Adams State, plus a half-dozen certificates proclaiming that Terrance R. Cyzinski had satisfactorily completed seminars or workshops in 'The College Application Process,' 'Vocational Guidance—Automobile Trades,' 'Student Motivation,' 'Visions and Values,' and, the one that Lila's eyes lit upon as Cyzinski waited for her reply, 'Empathetic Dialogue.'

Lila grinned back at him manically. She simply could not help herself. There was not a doubt in her mind that Mr. Cyzinski had practiced his current facial contortion in Empathetic Dialogue Workshop.

"Did I say something funny?" Cyzinski said, his empathy momentarily slipping.

"No, I'm just thinking of happier times," Lila said back, not having any idea what she meant by it. But it did steer the guidance counselor back to mellower ground.

"I had an idea for you, Lila," Cyzinski went on. "You have room on your schedule for an elective and I thought you might like to try 'Communications.' Mr. Allen teaches it and it's very popular, as I'm sure you know. But I've already talked to him and he promised me he could fit you in."

Lila did know about the course. It was a fairly free-form class of photography, videography, and computer stuff. About half the students were artsy types and nerds, the other half 'at risk' kids who somebody in the school administration— undoubtedly someone who had taken a workshop in student

motivation—believed could benefit from expressing themselves. Mr. Allen was known as a bit of a goof by Grandville
High faculty standards; he was also reputed to be liberal to the
point of not giving much of a shit what his students did in his
classroom.

But Lila was not interested. She had a different program
in mind for expressing her personality: Staying stoned 24/7.
During Christmas vacation when she worked ten consecutive days at Nakota waiting on second-homers and skiers, she
had had a taste of what it felt like to be high all the time, and
she had concluded that it overwhelmingly beat the alternative. Wendell, a connoisseur of the graffiti he used to scrub
off the walls of the Phoenix's bathrooms, said that the best
were inscribed in the '60s and '70s, his all-time favorite being,
'Reality is a Crutch.' That one said it all. Settling for the life
that Grandville had to offer would be an act of cowardice, so
Lila felt almost heroic committing herself to a life of unreality.
And Pato, the Colombian busboy, was more than happy to sell
her all the unreality she wanted.

"Thanks, but no thanks," Lila said to Mr. Cyzinski. "I'll stick
to study hall."

Cyzinski nodded slowly, clearly working on how to phrase
his next volley. Waiting, Lila felt an unexpected swell of sympathy for Stephanie Cyzinski. The accepted wisdom at school
was that Stephanie was lucky to have such a good-natured and
caring father, a regular guy who could relate to young people's
problems. But Lila had been privilege to a personal observation of Cyzinski, the dad. The man was a guidance counselor
to the core: a control freak.

"It's a little more complex than that, Lila," Cyzinski said
finally, opening a manila folder on his desk. "You have two
consecutive incompletes in gym. You need the credits or you
won't graduate."

The manic grin reappeared on Lila's face. *Not graduate?
Did he actually believe that was some kind of momentous
threat?* The open folder, Lila's school record, was obviously
meant to give weight to the threat, just as the words 'permanent record' had instilled terror in the hearts of Mrs. Paddick's
third-grade students at Grandville Elementary. *("You do that
one more time, Billy, and it goes on your permanent record!")*

In their precarious minds, the children—Lila included—saw their failures chiseled for all time in tablets that were readily available not only to future teachers and Scout leaders, but to the President of the United States and God. But seventeen and stoned, Lila did not give a flying fuck about either her record or graduating.

"I'll stick with study hall," she repeated.

"I'm afraid that's unacceptable," Cyzinski said.

"That sounds like your problem, Mr. Cyzinski," Lila sliced back with a sneer.

"Let me put it this way, Lila: if you have no intention of graduating, I see no reason for you to continue as a student at Grandville High School."

Before she realized it, the grin vanished from Lila's face. Had she been asked only one hour earlier what she thought of being permanently liberated from public school, Lila would have cheered and tossed her books in the air. But seated in Cyzinski's office, Lila once again found herself thinking about her grandfather and how he would take it. It was not as if Wendell was a stickler for the normal way of doing things; hell, he had barely gotten through high school himself and never given a thought to going to college. But Mom's breakdown had broken something in him too, and on top of that he had lost his beloved booth in the sky at the Phoenix. Even his relationship with Esther had changed, or at least they did not seem to see that much of one another any more. Sure, if Lila dropped out of school she could help him at Mom's shop, but she knew Wendell would feel as if one more part of his life had crumbled. Even as Lila dedicated herself to a universe of unreality, her flesh and blood grandfather pulled at her.

"Whatever," Lila said to Cyzinski. "Sign me up for Communications."

This, then, is how Lila ended up in Mr. Allen's hyperexpressive classroom sitting in front of an online computer.

Before enrolling in 'Communications,' Lila had little idea what a blog was, let alone that MySpace.com, the mother of all teenage blogs, existed. Mr. Allen assigned Jenny Winthrop, the nerdiest girl in the class, as Lila's mentor, and it was Jenny—she of the pungent armpits—who showed Lila her very own web page on MySpace. "It's like going to confession, but instead of a priest on the other side of the wall, it's Howard Stern," is the way Jenny described it.

Lila spent her first week and a half in Mr. Allen's class scrolling through web pages on MySpace. She could not believe how self-involved and full of crap her peers were. Honest to God, who gave a shit if Little-Girl-Blue, somewhere in the Pacific Northwest, had been dumped by her boyfriend, or if JumpinJack, whereabouts unknown, jerked off while doing his French homework, or if MPD, in New Jersey, was back stuttering again? Lila was convinced that instead of getting a life, these narcissists had gotten a blog, and they could not tell the difference. But on her eighth day of bouncing from one web log to another—it *did* keep Mr. Allen from bugging her about what her class project was going to be—Lila came to a blog called TheShitStopsHere:

> I am still hacking my way thru the lies. In case you haven't noticed, they're everywhere. EVERYWHERE! Holy shit, here comes another one now—I can tell it's a lie because Mr. K is moving his lips. That's always a dead giveaway. Get this: Mr. K is saying that Athens was the cradle of democracy. S.S.S. (Super Sly Shit) Like anybody really knows what passed for democracy back then, right? But The Big Lie is in that CRADLE shit Mr. K. slips in there. Athens was the CRADLE so, Children, what we must have now in the United States of Assholes is Grown-up Democracy. . . . BEEP! BEEP! BEEP! Big Lie Alert! Put on your Big Lie Detectors before another one slips onto the pile of bullshit they've already loaded into our brains . . .

Lila breaks out laughing, not that anyone notices in the boisterous classroom. She looks at the top of the web page. Pictured at the left-hand side is the eponymous 'ShitStopper'—a girl, and one who looks to be about Lila's age. She also appears to be nice looking, although it is hard to tell from her pose—she is looking at the camera upside down as, bent at the waist, she peers out from between her legs. Lila hits 'Comments':

> You make me laugh, girl. I'm swimming in bullshit myself (the backstroke mostly). I live in the place that invented it. We actually have a gift shop in town with embroidered pillows in the window

that say, "Sharing is Caring." Yeah, right. How about "Sharing is Getting Ripped Off by a Smiling Asshole"?

But here's the deal, SS: You gotta see the forest for the trees. (We've got trees all over the place here, maybe that's why nobody can see more than three feet in front of their dumb faces.) Like, your Mr. K is a typical asshole teacher, but he's just one tiny asshole in The Big Asshole called High School.

Here Lila sets down her theory about high school being no different from any other level of public school in that it is just a holding pen to keep kids under surveillance. She thinks of going on to her rap about The Big College Hoax, but stops. *Did anybody really read this stuff? Or was it just an excuse for masturbatory ramblings, the kind she used to address to 'Dear Diary,' as if 'Diary' was some kind of super-tolerant teen god?*

Lila feels like some brainless, heartsick girl in a Young Adult novel who mails intimate letters in a tree hollow. She decides to close the page without sending her response. She looks at the wall clock—still twelve minutes to go until lunch period, also known as quick-toke period. What the hell? She *will* send it. But when she presses the 'Send' button, a window pops up that says, 'Hey, how 'bout signing your letter, Shit4Brains?'

When Jenny had shown Lila her web page, she went into a long harangue about the significance of choosing the right blog name. "It's like more important than your real name, because you invent it, not your parents," said Jenny. Jenny had spent several days coming up with her own, 'Night Owl.' "Like I am this person who sees everything, even when it's dark, you know?" *Right, Jenny!* Mr. Allen had tacked a cartoon to the bulletin board that showed two dogs in front of a computer, one typing while talking to the other one; he is saying, 'On the web, nobody knows you're a dog.' Somebody had crossed out 'dog' and inserted 'nerd.'

The first name that pops into Lila's mind is 'Prisoner.' It has a certain authentic ring to it. She types it in the name space. The next space—'Where are you?'—is optional, but Lila is inspired. She types in 'Parolee in Halfway House' and laughs out loud. Why the hell not? Sure, it is a lie, but all this stuff is supposed to be made-up—a kind of truer-than-reality version of your inner self or would-be self or something like that. And anyway, Mr. Allen gave this whole speech about keeping your whereabouts secret because pedophiles trolled the Net for victims. The last space, also optional, says, 'What are you?' Lila writes, 'Black, and proud of it!' and pops the Send button. She has not had so much fun in a long time.

Only now does Lila sense that the classroom's usual din has dimmed. She looks up and sees that everyone is eyeing the open door where Mr. Allen is talking to Stephanie Cyzinski and a small, freckle-faced girl in a skirt and blouse, a combo that has not seen the inside of Grandville High's walls for a generation. Blousy Girl is gazing warily at Lila as the three at the door whisper back and forth, and now they are heading toward Lila in a phalanx, Mr. Allen as point man. Lila feels a pulse of panic. Obviously, this girl has accused her of something—probably of smoking weed across the street—although she is not any Grandville student Lila has ever seen before. Still, there is something familiar about her face, especially the apprehensive pucker of her faint eyebrows. Just as they arrive in front of her computer table, Lila remembers that she has seen the girl in Nakota with her parents, the Dowds.

"I guess you two know each other," Mr. Allen says.

"Not really," Lila answers. The Dowd girl winces.

"Daphne just transferred to Grandville and she's going to be in this class," Allen goes on. "Maybe you can help her get started."

Stephanie is trying to make eye contact with Lila. Since their after-school encounter a few months back, Stephanie acts as if the two of them have some kind of private understanding, but Lila suspects what is really on Stephanie's mind is the fear that Lila will blab around school about Stephanie's little calamity of tears in the gymnasium. Lila has no intention of blabbing about this or anything else to her schoolmates, so Stephanie's secret is safe, but Lila also has no intention of reassuring Stephanie of this.

"If it's . . . you know . . . awkward or anything . . ." Stephanie is saying, and Lila realizes that what Stephanie is concerned about is Lila's feelings about the Dowd family in general considering the role they played in her mother's breakdown. Actually, that connection had not even occurred to Lila until this moment, and obviously it had not occurred to Mr. Allen, Grandville High's expert on sensitive communication, either.

"No problem," Lila says, then adds mockingly, "I'll teach her everything I know."

Stephanie makes another vain attempt at eye contact before withdrawing behind Mr. Allen. Daphne remains standing next to Lila's table, fidgeting with her hands.

"You can probably find a chair somewhere," Lila says to her.

Daphne nods, but does not move. Despite her Rockwell-esque freckles and perky nose, there is something unwholesome about the girl's face that Lila finds appealing.

"Why the hell did you want to come here?" Lila asks, her eyes remaining on her computer screen.

"You mean 'Communications'?"

"No, Grandville High."

Daphne shrugs. "I didn't have a whole lot to say about it," she replies.

"Weren't you at some fancy private school?"

"Hotchkiss."

"Didn't you like it?"

"Not really. Anyway, I got thrown out."

Lila looks at the girl with tentative admiration. "Really?"

"Yeah, really."

Lila guesses that the girl failed calculus or Latin, maybe even skipped classes or did not do her homework, the kind of infraction that at Grandville High would, at worst, send you to summer school, but was grounds for dismissal at a posh private school.

"Inappropriate dress," Daphne says with the barest suspicion of a smile.

"You're kidding. They can throw you out for that?"

"In extreme cases." Daphne's smile is now beyond suspicion.

"Let me guess—dirty tennis whites?"

"Bikini underpants."

"How the hell did they know?" Lila has a fleeting recollection of her mother's account of Grandma Beatrice's regular morning inspections of her underwear when she was a child.

"That's *all* I was wearing," Daphne says. "On the front steps of my dorm in broad daylight."

"Jesus!" Lila laughs, amazed. "What'd you do that for?"

"Fashion statement," Daphne says deadpan, and both girls laugh. Before Lila can press her for details, Daphne gestures toward the computer screen and asks, "You got a blog?"

"No. I'm just killing time." Lila hits the Refresh button as Daphne leans down to eye level with the screen. TheShitStops-Here.com reappears with a new headline: "THE PRISONER SPEAKS!" Right underneath it is Lila's letter, and under that is ShitStopper's response:

> Okay, Prisoner, you got balls! But are they real or just gum drops? I'm talking about your 'forest for the trees' bit. Aren't all lies created equal? Mr. K's, the High School Lie, the President's, God's (you know the one I'm talking about)? Or lemme put it the opposite way, Isn't there always going to be a Bigger Lie out there?
>
> So, Prisoner, You tell Me the Biggest Baddest Lie in Amerika you can think of and I bet you I can top it. (That's a CHALLENGE, girl!)
>
> Shitstopper

Lila has just finished reading this when Daphne says, "You're 'Prisoner,' right?"

"How'd you know?"

"Just guessed. You skipped the letter and went straight to the answer, so I figure you wrote the letter yourself."

Lila is impressed, but she also feels embarrassed by her 'parolee' and 'black and proud' pose on the screen in front of them.

A moment later, Daphne says, "Well, I know the biggest lie of them all, if you want it."

"Yeah?"

"You know, the one they tell you about sex and love—that they always go together. Like sex and love have *anything* to do with each other, right?"

Lila looks at the Dowd girl, wondering if she is a liar herself with her intimation that she has vast sexual experience or even *any* sexual experience. But then again, Daphne did do some kind of strip show on her school campus, an act that certainly does not appear to have a whole lot to do with intimacy—unless she made up that whole story, too. It was hard to tell. But if Lila is so enthralled with honesty, how about her own? Does she really know anything about love *or* sex, let alone what they have to do with each other?

"There's got to be a bigger lie than that," Lila says, trying to sidestep the subject.

"Yeah, maybe," Daphne replies softly, suddenly sounding unsure of herself again. Lila senses that the girl is never very far from self-doubt even if she does make herself do some pretty outrageous stuff. "But the thing that makes this lie so big," Daphne goes on in almost a whisper, "is it makes people get married and then regret it for the rest of their lives."

Lila types Daphne's exact words in her response to Shit-Stopper's challenge.

* * *

Stephanie Cyzinski is angry with herself for letting Lila deVries get to her again. Lila always makes her feel so judged, as if the girl is some kind of spy who knows all her dirty secrets. Not that Stephanie has any worth knowing.

But there is more to Lila than just the contempt she puts out about everybody and everything. Stephanie can see it in Lila's eyes. She always seems as if she is searching for something—something that really counts. It takes a brave soul not to settle for the *status quo* and Stephanie wishes she had more of that kind of courage. Of course, they say Lila is stoned most of the time and that could account for that perpetual searching look in her eyes.

Or maybe what Stephanie feels has nothing at all to do with Lila. Maybe, Stephanie thinks, she is feeling judged by herself and is just trying to pin it on Lila.

In spite of herself, Stephanie is having the time of her life playing royal tennis. For one thing, she is getting better at it in leaps and bounds, and the main way she is getting better at it is by cultivating the art of sneakiness. With its wacky rules and tricky, off-the-tambour bounces, royal tennis has ten times the bluffs and feints, finesse, and outright subterfuge as modern tennis. Stephanie is fascinated by the rich vein of game cunning she has uncovered in herself; it makes her feel deliciously mischievous.

Stephanie also has come to adore the regular weekend trips to and from Boston with her dad. They chat and joke and make impromptu stops at homey, off-the-beaten-track restaurants, things they have never done together—just the two of them—before. There is something about being insulated in her father's Vega coupe that invokes a rare level of candor between them. It was inside that speeding capsule, between Worcester and Framingham, that her father told her how his boyhood dream of becoming a professional tennis player had been thwarted by a Buffalo tennis club that denied him admission based on the last three letters in his name. He had never confided a story as personal as that before.

But, not to put too fine a spin on it, the main reason Stephanie revels in her Saturdays at the Boston Tennis and Racquet Club is Mark Saunders, the Harvard sophomore with whom she is regularly paired in mixed doubles. He is droll, smart, a patient mentor, and terribly cute. Stephanie has a mad crush on him. Not that she knows much about Mark. The closest they have come to a real conversation was when he asked her how she came to play royal tennis and she lied that she had seen a documentary about the game and was instantly fascinated. Mark, in turn, said he learned the game from his father who had also played at Harvard. So Stephanie has done nothing more than play the game and joke around with Mark, but nonetheless she feels guilty about her feelings for him. And that is because she still goes out with Matt Maxwell every Friday night, with all its kissing and fondling, as if nothing in her world has changed. But more has already changed—and will continue to change—than Stephanie can imagine, and that change comes flying at her from the trickiest of angles even now as she and Mark stand at the gallery overlooking Court A, waiting for a match to finish so they can begin theirs.

Over her whites, Stephanie is wearing the loose-knit, V-neck cotton sweater her father bought in the club shop after she won her first match. From her reflection in the gallery window, she can see that the sweater makes her look taller and more shapely than she usually appears. In fact, she decides, she looks very much like other young women at the club, girls with names like Kip and PJ and Alexi. Next to her, Mark is grinning broadly as he watches the game below, another mixed-doubles match. When a long-legged young woman with a blonde pony tail chases down the ball and backhands it off the tambour for a point, Mark cheers and Stephanie feels a thrill of jealousy.

"She's good," Stephanie says.

"Bunny? Oh, she's good all right. Too good," Mark replies, not looking away from the court as the girl named Bunny prepares to serve.

"Did you ever play with her?" Stephanie asks, even as she wishes she would just shut up.

"Only my whole life," Mark says with laugh. "She's my sister."

Stephanie smiles softly, relieved. "I bet if they paired the two of you together, nobody would stand a chance."

"Could be," Mark says. He watches his sister take another point with a perfect bounce into the grille before he adds, "God knows that's what Harvard is counting on."

"Bunny's at Harvard too?"

"Not yet."

"She's still in high school?" Even as Stephanie asks this—as offhandedly as she can muster—she senses what is coming.

"Yes, well, at Andover. She still has a year and a half to go, so we'll only get to team up for one year. When I'm a senior."

The match on Court A suddenly comes to a standstill as all four players gaze up at the gallery windows in search of the source of shattering laughter showering down on them. But they cannot see Stephanie Cyzinski because she has sat down, dizzy to the point of faintness from the rush of her laughter and from the realization that set it off.

Stephanie's spot on Harvard's royal tennis team is already taken! Bunny Saunders is not only a Harvard legacy, but a royal tennis legacy. And on top of that, she is a champ at the game. It's a done deal, folks, signed and sealed. Bunny is the female player Harvard is signing up for the upcoming sole vacant spot on the team!

Poor, ridiculous, overreaching Dad was misinformed. Possibly even lied to, the way places like Harvard undoubtedly lie to guidance counselors at insignificant public high schools in an attempt to mask their elitist biases. God knows, Dad would be ripe for a lie like that.

It was hilarious, really. After all the time she and Dad had spent, this whole campaign was an utter bust. After all the money Dad had invested in his preposterous dream. After all the effort she had put in—the twenty hours a week in the gym working on her hip adductors because—Don't you see, Stephanie?—hip adductors are the ultimate key to getting into Harvard!

Oh yeah, it was hilarious, all right.

Returning from Boston, Terry Cyzinski always crosses the Charles River on the Longfellow Bridge so they can take Memorial Drive to the Turnpike. In this way, they cruise past Harvard College's red brick dorms that face the river— Dunster House, Leverett House, Winthrop House, Eliot House. They look so solid and majestic, even if their crowning bell towers remind Stephanie of the cupola that used to top the old Friendly's in town. Terry never says a word as they pass by Harvard. He does not need to; his look of consummate delight says it all.

As they glide by this evening, the last rays of winter sun make the buildings iridescent. The dorms throw off sharp-edged shadows as if they are spot-lit dioramas in an historical museum. It is here and now that Stephanie planned to tell her father what she learned that afternoon above Court A, but she gazes at the glowing Harvard houses in silence. This is not because she has suddenly decided to spare her father a terrible disappointment and the anger that would surely follow from it. In fact, at this moment Stephanie believes he deserves that and more. No, Stephanie says nothing because of her newfound pleasure in devious spins and cunning drop volleys. She is going to play this game out to the end.

* * *

As an experiment, Lila has decided to fuck Flip Morris. Although she hardly thinks of herself as an intellectual, she has a skeptical cast of mind along with just enough deVries Dutch pragmatism to appreciate that she cannot continue with her web debate about sex if she has no experience in the subject. *Ipso facto*, the experiment.

Like a methodical researcher, she has assembled all her motives and expectations in her mind, beginning with the concession that it is actually more than just her daily exchanges with ShitStopper that prompt her project, even if they are what tipped the balance. Lila has simply concluded that she is too old to be a virgin. Virginity smacks of immaturity, and immaturity, above all, is unacceptable to her. If that was not obvious to her before she met Daphne Dowd, it is now. The diminutive sixteen-year-old, with her quaint, silk hair bows and plaid pinafores concealing her skimpily-developed physique, keeps a list tucked in her backpack of what she calls her 'conquests.' They total six and include, she says, a Hotchkiss groundskeeper and a bartender at a Salisbury, Connecticut country inn. Even as Lila suspects there is something compulsive, even bitter, about Daphne's sexual adventures—not to mention her list-keeping—she finds the girl inspiring. Daphne Dowd definitely has balls.

Lila settled on Flip because, God knows, he would be a willing subject, not requiring any sloppy, extraneous preliminaries. Plus, he does not go to Grandville High, which means she would not have to deal with him afterwards in the school's hallways or classrooms. Finally, Lila has decided to go through with the experiment totally sober. She knows too well how Pato's pot can embroider experience with phantom feelings and she wants this one to be absolutely pure.

Lila's cool calculations fortify her. When she thinks about her mother—which is usually only when Wendell talks about her—Lila is repelled by Franny's fragility. Lila's prescription for survival is to be the very opposite of her mother, and for a teenager as tender and remote as Lila, personal survival is an ongoing struggle, one that does not promote charity. In Lila's view, her mother always put on a big show of her emotions as if her loud, girlish laughs and teary-eyed sulks made her bigger than life, when in the end they only made her more vulnerable. Lila is not even convinced that her mother actually suffered a nervous breakdown so much as got carried away by one of her over-the-top self-dramatizations.

Ever since Wendell asked Archie Morris to have a word with his son about Lila, Flip has been wilier in his pursuit of the girl. Instead of dogging Lila in his cruiser or waiting for her at her bus stop, Flip has taken to leaving mash notes in her locker, slipped through the grate in the locker door before school opens for business. As a town cop, he has keys to every public building in Grandville.

Flip's notes are pathetic, veering from what he must think of as poetry ("Your hair looks so slippery and nice") to natural, heartfelt smut ("A hottie like you needs a real man to make you scream.") She never answered them. But now the man's stupidity and juvenile vanity figure in Lila's experiment: He is so simple he can be depended upon to be a predictable constant. That way Lila can focus entirely on her own reactions.

On a Wednesday afternoon in late January after the last school bus has departed, Lila tapes a folded piece of paper to her locker door. On the outside, it says, "F.M."; inside it says, "Meet me at Wright Mt. path Thurs. 3PM. L." The next morning, the note inside her locker says, "I'll be there, babe. Flip."

For the occasion, in lieu of wearing her standard high school uniform—worn jeans and a sweatshirt—Lila opts for primness, her getup inspired by Daphne Dowd's straight-laced wardrobe. Lila does not, of course, own a pinafore and would not think of wearing a skirt, but she does put on the pressed black chinos and short-collared white blouse she wears as a waitress, and she pulls her blonde mane back under the pink headband Esther's daughter, Kaela, bought her for Christmas. Lila wants to personify innocence; making her inexperience an ironic pose helps her handle the fact that it is real. Honest as Lila tries to be with herself, she does not realize just how much this bit of theatrical self-mockery makes her similar to her mother.

But she cannot trick her nerves. As she crosses the highway to the access road that leads to the Wright Mountain path, a riot of fear erupts in her guts. The acrid taste of barely-checked vomit stings her throat. She feels drained, unstable. It strikes her for the first time that while she was convinced this entire enterprise was coolly conceived, it actually came to her under the influence of three-weeks-running daily doses of marijuana. And on this, her first pot-free day in that period, she plainly sees the peril in mixing heady fantasy with physical fact.

She could easily enough turn around and head back toward town. No one other than Flip knows about the rendezvous and even Flip does not know the scenario she has planned. He certainly would be angry if she failed to show up, but what could he do? He was already on notice for stalking her.

Lila stops. The granite peak of Wright Mountain looms above her, swirls of windswept snow circling it. For a moment, she takes in its celebrated beauty, but an instant later she once again feels its overbearingness, a stone sentry guarding against her escape. Lila continues on to where the path meets the road.

Flip is leaning against the driver's door of his cruiser, a cigarette dangling from his lower lip, a short-billed, black cap tilted back on his crew cut dome, one hand on his hip. Seeing him before he sees her, Lila has to stifle a laugh. So Flip, too, has assumed a role for their encounter and it is none other than Elvis. Lila even knows the poster photograph he is aping—it is in Wendell's collection: Elvis leaning against his Harley in black leather jacket and motorcycle cap, he, himself, aping Marlon Brando. Flip is a copy of a copy, and, thus diminished, he renews Lila's courage.

"Hey, girl," Flip says as Lila approaches.

"Flip," Lila replies dully, looking past him.

Flip ambles toward her with a rolling, Elvis-like gait. He places a fat, short-fingered hand on her shoulder and Lila reflexively steps back, causing it to slip off.

"You've been getting my notes, I guess," Flip says.

"Yeah."

"Yeah, well, that's good," Flip says.

This close, Lila sees drops of ice in Flip's blonde moustache. They are brown and shiny, reminding Lila of the frozen rabbit turds that dot the back steps of her house. For all her mental preparation, Lila has not reckoned on just how repulsive she finds Flip, even *before* he opens his mouth. God knows, there are more attractive men in town—even in school, for that matter—and it would not be that difficult to get them to participate in her experiment. Daphne says the one advantage of being a girl is all you have to do to get laid is make yourself available. But maybe, Lila thinks, her first instinct was right, maybe Flip's repulsiveness makes her investigation purer, untainted by any sense remotely connected to the heart.

"Cold, huh?" Flip says.

"Kind of."

"Car's warm."

Indeed, the police cruiser's exhaust pipe is throwing off puffs of steamy smoke. At Grandville's annual town meeting, there is invariably some citizen who cites a list of fiscal excesses by the town's public servants, including gas squandered by idling school buses and police cars. No citizen, however, has ever openly complained about their public servants' moral excesses.

Flip opens the passenger door, waits for Lila to slip inside, then slams the door hard as if the better to contain her. Once he gets in on the other side, he leans back, planting a hand on the steering wheel. Like many men, he draws a buzz of virility merely from sitting in the driver's seat. He reaches inside his jacket, pulls out a pint of Wild Turkey, unscrews the top, wipes the mouth of the bottle against his sleeve, and offers it to Lila. "Ice breaker," he says.

"No thanks," Lila replies. A rumble of dread again churns her stomach. She feels like she could very easily throw up right in Flip Morris's lap. She either has to get this thing over with fast or get the hell out of here right now. She draws in her breath. "Let's do it," she murmurs.

"Huh?"

"You want to fuck me, right? So let's do it." Saying the word 'fuck' out loud soothes Lila's nerves. It is the word she has always used in her mind for the experiment. She and Shit-Stopper share a disdain for euphemisms like 'having sex' and 'making love' and the latest and most coy, 'doing the nasty.' "That's like calling 'murder,' 'doing the dead thing,'" Shit-Stopper wrote.

"You bet," Flip responds a beat later than Lila expected. She realizes that her directness confounds him, that he has his own mentally-rehearsed scenario for the event and he is not, of course, talented at improvising. This only emboldens Lila more.

"Are you ready? Are you hard?" Lila says.

"Yeah, are you?" Clearly, Flip tries to make his retort sound like a tough counter-challenge, but it comes out much too defensively for that; he sounds petulant.

"As ready as I'll ever be," Lila says, and that is the truth.

Flip grabs both her shoulders and pulls her toward him. Lila turns her face away from his. "I didn't say I'd kiss you, for crissake!" she says. She feels Flip's grasp momentarily weaken and takes it as an opportunity to pull away from him and add, "Just fuck."

Lila quickly disengages the fastener on her pants, unzips the fly and, lifting her bottom off the seat, shimmies her slacks to her knees. She loops her thumbs under the elastic of her panties, then decides to wait before pulling them down too. Flip gapes at her, flush with excitement and stupefaction.

"Your turn," Lila says. In spite of herself, she smiles at the juvenile, 'I'll-show-you-mine-if-you-show-me-yours' sound of her words.

Flip unbuckles, unbuttons, and unzips, then pulls his pants down exactly as Lila has. He is indeed hard, his erection pushing through the slit in his boxers like a prize morel poking through the grass.

Until this moment, Lila deVries has only seen drawings and photographs of stiff penises. This flesh one is far less daunting than the pictures. With its pulsing vein and purple-pink helmet, it looks like a wounded soldier lost from its regiment. Lila reaches out her hand to touch it.

"Jesus! Jesus! *Jesus!*"

It abruptly oozes into her palm. Lila is fascinated by the impeccable whiteness of the fluid, its purity.

"Fuck! That never happened to me before!" Flip yowls. His face, just a moment ago wrenched in a dumb grimace, is now flushed and fuming. And Lila, just a moment ago drenched with wonder, even mercy, pulls away from him anxiously.

"It's okay," Lila murmurs. It is, in fact, more than okay—it is a relief. She has realized her experiment—at least, *sort of*—and without any damage to herself. She even felt something related—albeit distantly—to fondness for Flip: He was privy to her experiment's denoument. But suddenly Lila's experiment is not about what she intended; it is now a study in humiliation of the most venomous kind. Lila pulls up her slacks and reaches for the zipper, but Flip smacks her hand.

"Just wait, goddamit!" Flip roars. "Just give me a minute and we'll do this thing right!"

Lila pulls back against the car door. She is trembling. Flip looks like he could kill her. Craving sex, he was vulnerable; spent, he is villainous. Lila's experiment is producing counter-intuitive results.

"Wendell's expecting me," Lila manages to say.

"Just wait, you hear?" Flip barks. He raises his open hand threateningly.

Lila nods, terrified. She darts her eyes around the interior of the cruiser. She imagines grabbing the nightstick hooked to Flip's belt—now down at his knees—and slamming it against his skull. She imagines snatching up the microphone of the two-way radio and calling for help.

Flip is holding his fallen dick in one hand. He pulls on it.

"How long does it take, Flip?" Lila says. She does not know what put the question in her mouth or how she knew to ask it so demurely, but even as she asks it she senses the balance of power tilting back to her.

"Fuck it, I don't know," Flip answers.

"So why don't we do it another time?" Lila says, sounding very much like her grandmother, Beatrice. She smiles politely at Flip's penis. Lila knows, of course, that there will not be another time.

Flip gives one vain, final pull, and says, "Yeah, right."

CHAPTER EIGHTEEN

Long before Grandville Community College began offering evening courses in its continuing education program, townspeople could improve their minds and hone their skills in the Bible study groups at Grandville Congregational Church, the farming workshops conducted by faculty members of the University of Massachusetts Agricultural School and held in the barn and fields of the Harry Thatcher spread out on what is now the south end of Mahaiwe Street (the 1951 series on contour plowing was so oversubscribed it needed to be repeated the following year), the appliqué 'seminar' conducted by and in the parlor of Madeline La Monte in the 1930s, and the acting and elocution classes presided over by Françoise deVries on the Phoenix's stage way back in the early 1900s.

But in the late 1980s, the influx of retirees with time on their hands, fear of mental atrophy in their hearts, and most importantly, money in their bank accounts, provided the opening for an entirely new level of adult instruction, one that the financially-struggling community college was eager to fill. Using his own faculty—along with some members of that tribe of non-tenured professors who spend much of their time shuttling from one small college to another—GCC's dean, Norm Ruprecht, cobbled together a catalogue of continuing education courses that included, Estate Planning, World Religions, Local Geology, Italian Cooking, Case Studies in Constitutional Law, and Indoor Gardening. It was an immediate success. As a result of the substantial extra income it provided for teachers, it created an ongoing competition among them for 'saleable' courses. Associate Professor of Philosophy, Herbert Blitzstein, joined these sweepstakes two years ago.

Although Herb lives modestly in a two-room apartment over Digby's Music Shop, he has a weakness for expensive books and CDs that keeps him in constant debt to the MasterCard Corporation, so he readily admits that his motive is more pecuniary than pedagogical. Dean Ruprecht warned Herb there was no call for philosophy classes in the questionnaire he regularly circulates to adult students at the end of each term, but Herb had an inspired idea for a course he promised Ruprecht would knock the socks off white-haired exurbanites. It was called 'Philosophy in Film' and consisted of screenings of select feature films followed by classroom discussions of their philosophical content. After considerable coaxing, the dean included it in the next catalogue with the proviso that if fewer than six people signed up, he would cancel it. Twenty-two signed up and the course, now carried every term, has even acquired a popular nickname, 'Phil of Flicks.'

The job has not, in fact, pulled Herb out of debt, but it has substantially increased his library. And because Herb discovered he could attract repeat students if he changed his menu of films each term, he is constantly viewing and reviewing movies in search of philosophical hooks.

* * *

Beatrice is in Florida with her husband on an extended vacation. At her last visit before departing, she told Franny she was in terrible need of a break, but that she would keep in touch by mail. Franny, of course, was relieved even as she understood that the break her mother needed was from her daughter, or rather from the stain Franny's little catastrophe had spilled upon her. Austen Riggs's cachet notwithstanding, real Cosgroves did not do mental breakdowns. After her mother left, Franny's first impulse was to hope Herb Blitzstein would fill in Beatrice's spot at Visiting Hour. This, her first conscious wish in months, was granted.

Franny is already in the upstairs recreation room, seated in front of the TV, when Herb arrives for his fourth consecutive Thursday. At the other end of the room, a half-dozen other residents are playing cards or Scrabble. Another young man is playing table soccer against himself, cursing and cheering in rapid succession. Thankfully, none of Franny's comrades in turmoil has ever exhibited any interest in the videos Herb brings with him. Dr. Werner, for reasons unstated, allows Herb to stay beyond his allotted single hour of visiting time.

As usual, Herb kisses the top of Franny's head by way of a greeting, then immediately steps over to the VCR to insert the day's offering. Watching his stumbling gait, his oversized head bent forward, its kinky ponytail swishing against his neck, Franny wonders if her former self would have found him attractive. Lately, this cryptic entity—her former self—figures as a reference point in Franny's imagination. Although she senses she will never be the same again, Franny feels the need to stay on good terms with who she was. This is not merely to provide her with psychic continuity, it is to claim selfhood itself; if she is going to be a viable person again, she needs to start somewhere. She doubts that her former self would have found Herb attractive in the least.

"*Groundhog Day,*" Herb says, starting the film. He sits down beside Franny, opens his spiral notebook, and takes a ballpoint pen from his pants pocket.

While the credits run, Franny scans the open page of Herb's notebook. He has written, "Cause & Effect" at the top. Then, in parentheses, "see Hume on billiard balls." The rest of the page is occupied by either a goofy, Rube Goldbergesque doodle or a recondite diagram whose circles and arrows distill the very essence of causality, Franny cannot be sure which. Even though she and Herb have barely said a word to one another about the films they have viewed thus far—*It's a Wonderful Life* and *Back to the Future*—Franny had no trouble figuring out their common denominator: How changing a single event can change all the events that follow afterward. It strikes her as a whimsical notion at best, and at worst, repulsively sentimental. Her former self was always suspicious of *It's a Wonderful Life* for that very reason: It gave small acts of kindness way too much credit for big, happy effects. Franny always gravitated toward the no-good-deed-goes-unpunished school of thought.

She certainly likes Bill Murray's sarcastic, pock marked face a hell of a lot more than Jimmy Stewart's. Even as a child, viewing *It's a Wonderful Life* from the Phoenix's projection booth during the movie house's annual New Year's Eve showing, she detected a lode of superiority just beneath the surface of Stewart's average-American-guy face. She did not much like his signature bumbles and stutters either; not only were they self-indulgent, but Franny was sure any decent man who could not stop himself from stammering would be more embarrassed than bemused.

Murray, on the other hand, carries an expression of perpetually amused irony on his mug, and it appears to be indiscriminate: no subject is too grand to fit inside the quotation marks of his arched eyebrows. Franny can relate. Now watching Murray as Phil Connors, Pittsburgh weatherman, as he delivers a weather report on the local TV channel, she is intrigued by the self-mockery that bubbles beneath his smugness. She wonders if Herb's philosophical point has more to do with irony than cause and effect. She hopes so. She remembers he once gave a class assignment about irony.

But as *Groundhog Day* rolls past the third morning that Phil Connors again awakes to the very same day, February 2nd, Franny has no doubt they are back in familiar territory: life's little options that can alter fate. She is disappointed. She had hoped Herb was going to move on from that bit of hokum. She feels a cloud of fatigue settle over her; her eyes flutter shut.

Franny dozes so often her nervous system compensates by keeping her sleep shallow, consciousness always hovering nearby. In this soupy state, her mind blends half-heard dialogue with loopy dreams. Her current dream has her wandering aimlessly in the Phoenix's sub-basement when she hears Bill Murray say, "What would you do if every day was the same, and nothing you did ever mattered?" A beat, and another voice replies, "That about sums it up for me."

Franny's eyes snap open. Next to her, Herb is scribbling madly in his notebook.

"That about sums it up for me," Franny says softly.

"Fabulous line, huh?" Herb says.

"I mean it," Franny says. "Nothing I do matters really."

Herb hits the 'Pause' button and turns to her. "I kind of figured it was like that for you," he says. "Feels like shit, I bet."

"Actually, it doesn't feel like anything," Franny answers.

"So maybe it feels like meta-shit."

"Meta-shit?"

"You know, shit of a higher order. The shit that precedes the real stuff. You can't feel it yet, but you know it's just waiting to sop you one."

Franny cannot really grasp what Herb has said, but his words swerve around in her mind tantalizingly. The hint of a smile creeps onto her lips. Herb smiles back and starts

Groundhog Day going again. Franny watches to the end when Murray/Connors finally decides to take a crack at doing this same day—for the umpteenth time—with grace instead of bitterness, and as a result he gets the girl.

"Corny," Franny says.

"Hey, corny has its compensations," Herb replies, standing and ambling to the VCR to remove the video cassette. He pulls on his pea jacket and walks over to plant a goodbye kiss on top of Franny's head.

"What did Hume say about billiard balls?" Franny asks. She had not planned the question, and she does not realize the reason she asks it is to keep Herb with her a few moments longer.

Herb grins. He pulls his long frame up straight in professorial mode, but Franny catches something Bill Murray-ish in his demeanor, as if he is doing a stand-up comedian's impression of a stuffy professor.

"Hume said you can see Ball A strike Ball B, and then you can see Ball B roll away, but what you can't see is the *how* of it," Herb says. "You don't actually *see* the force Ball A passes on to Ball B, but you'd be crazy not to decide that is what's going on. So the idea of cause and effect is really just the way our minds make sense of the world. It certainly beats living in a world where you can't make head nor tail out of what's going to happen next."

"What *is* going to happen next?" Franny asks softly. Again, her not-quite-conscious intention is to delay Herb's departure, but hearing her own words, Franny is suddenly overcome with a pang of angst. *What* is *going to happen next?*

Herb hunkers down in front of Franny. He takes one of her hands in both of his. "Better times, Franny," he whispers. "Just keep your eye on Ball A."

* * *

Wendell is lying on his back on the floor of the Phoenix watching a man named Livio repaint the ceiling. Livio, a fifth generation restoration artist, was imported from Rome by the theater's new owners. His English is limited, but this does not keep him from giving Wendell a running commentary on his work, replete with anecdotes about other restorations he has done over the past thirty years all over Europe. Between Livio's musical accent and the fact that he, too, is lying on his back but on a scaffold some forty feet above the floor, Wendell understands little of Livio's narrative. Nonetheless he enjoys the connection it establishes between them. Livio obviously takes great pride in his work and is thrilled to have an audience for what usually must be a solitary occupation. Wendell, for his part, admires any man who is dedicated to his craft and proud of his skills, but above all, Wendell is spellbound by the gradual transformation of the Phoenix's vaulted ceiling. It feels magical, like time travel.

Livio is daubing ochre highlights on the woolly mane of the North Wind, the blustering Greek god head in the ceiling's north-most corner. The first flecks of orangey paint strike Wendell as garish, even though he knows this is his impression whenever Livio attacks a new portion of the fresco. It is an illusion produced by the contrast of fresh wet paint with the muted tones of the faded original. Livio, who spent an entire four-week vacation watching the masters of his art restore the Sistine Chapel, once told Wendell that civilian gawkers always had this same complaint, comparing the artisans to billboard painters.

Wendell's arms are folded tightly across his chest as insulation against the cold. As many times as Wendell has camped on the Phoenix's frigid floor this winter, he never brings his overcoat with him from the shop. This is because Livio always works in a sleeveless undershirt; never mind that it is twenty degrees warmer up there, wearing an overcoat would feel to Wendell like a breach of companionship. Binx, on the other hand, has given up on the trips to the Phoenix; whatever curiosity he might have about his former second home is eclipsed by the warm draft from Write Now's heating vent.

Watching Livio work, Wendell's mind again drifts to thoughts of his father. Wendell can feel Emile's pleasure in the renewal of the ceiling and the proscenium arch. Emile, like his own father before him, rejoiced as much in the theater itself as in any production mounted on its stage. "It's a palace of dreams," Emile used to say. "The dreams come and go, but the palace outlives them all." Wendell crooks his left arm above his eyes and looks at his watch. He has already been lying here for almost fifteen minutes. Although his customers are trained to take their newspapers and cigarettes themselves and leave their payment on the counter, they also come to chat with him. Wendell rolls over onto his belly and scrambles to his feet.

"I'm off!" he yells up to Livio.

As always, Livio calls back a goodbye in Italian that sounds something like, 'A dope, huh?'

A piercing wind is coursing down Melville Street as Wendell steps outside the Phoenix. Icicles suspended from the rain gutters of the fire station crack and fall, slicing perpendicularly into the snow to form a row of crystal pickets. Shivering, Wendell scurries back to the shop, but as he comes alongside the front window, he stops. Inside, Esther is leaning across the counter, apparently in conversation with the retarded man who wears the book-filled backpack. Wendell takes a step backward so he can spy on them unseen. The wind is too shrill and his ears too cold for him to hear a word that passes between them.

In the past few weeks, the retarded man has not entered Write Now, although Wendell has seen him walk by a few times, his big face floating moonlike past the window. In that same period, Esther's lunchtime visits have become briefer, their conversations crisper, their kisses more perfunctory, if at all. Wendell knows she is waiting for him to change things between them, to declare a new program, but he cannot get himself to focus on their situation. Whenever he tries, he is pulled away by the specter of selfishness, as if any happiness he added to his own life would automatically be subtracted from Franny's. Wendell's sole self-indulgence these days are his stolen minutes watching Livio work.

Wendell sees that Esther is writing in the shop account book as the retarded man speaks. The man is probably unaware of the fact that she is barely paying attention to his slow-coming words as she adds up bills.

A fresh gust of frigid air slams against Wendell's neck and back. He decides there is no reason for him to remain outside: The retarded man has had his due; if he has a problem with Wendell returning to his own shop, Wendell is not going to feel guilty about that. Wendell goes to the door, but as he is about to reach for the handle he sees that Esther is weeping, tears sliding down her cheeks, some dropping onto the open page of the account book. Again, Wendell abruptly withdraws, this time backing blindly off the curb into ankle-deep slush. He remains there until the man departs.

"What was that all about?" Wendell says when he comes inside.

Esther is wiping her face with a Kleenex. She shakes her head and says, "The world makes me dizzy."

Wendell, his feet wet and cold, his nose running, is annoyed by her response. In general, there is an inverse proportion between the frequency of their kisses and his annoyance with her metaphysical *non sequiturs*. He remains on the customer side of the counter. Esther turns back several pages in the account book, then spins it around so it is right side up in front of Wendell. Esther's penmanship is small and neat.

"Born: August, 1972, Washington, D.C. William Alan Forester III, son of WAF II, librarian (archivist?) at Smithsonian Inst. Mother deceased. One sib: Monroe F., four years younger—lives in Sarasota. (Find on Yahoo?) <u>This letter is for his brother</u>."

Wendell looks up at Esther. "That's the retarded guy? William Alan Forester?"

Esther nods.

"He wants you to write a letter for him?"

Esther nods again. Her eyes have filled up again. "Franny promised to do it for him."

"I get it. He's been waiting for her to come back," Wendell says.

"I told him I was Franny's mother."

"Good idea, I suppose. He corresponds with his brother?"

"No," Esther says. "This is the first. He's been thinking about writing him for a long time."

"How long?"

Esther shakes her head back and forth several times before replying. "Who knows? Twenty-five years? That's how long he's been gone. Monroe—the brother—was three when Billy was sent away. They haven't seen each other since."

"That's when he came up here?"

"No, first to a boarding school for children like him. In upstate New York somewhere. He was twenty when they put him in the halfway house on Hawthorne Street." Esther takes a deep breath, then nods at the account book. "It's all there. The story of Billy's life. He wants his brother to know the story of his life."

And so Wendell reads through Billy Forester's dictated letter that is squeezed beneath columns of payments due for candy and cigarettes and greeting cards: Billy had a friend at his school who could not talk. His name was Ronnie. Billy likes the chicken noodle soup they serve at Soup and Sandwich. He has a rash on his belly that never completely goes away. He likes his room at the halfway house. He has a picture on the wall of Monroe and himself when they were little. He sometimes has a dream at night in which he is a librarian like his father.

"My God," Wendell murmurs when he is finished. He, too, finds the world dizzying. He steps around the counter and gathers Esther into his arms. He holds her tightly, slowly rocking them both back and forth.

* * *

Stephanie lunges for a shot Bunny Saunders has dribbled off the tambour. She is able to reach the ball with the web of her racket, but it just dies there and drops to the court floor. Even after over two months of playing royal tennis, Stephanie is regularly surprised by the wood-cored ball's inertness. It strikes her that there is something quintessentially Anglo-Saxon about the ball's lack of response, as if it would be unseemly for it to have any real bounce to it.

Stephanie is her old self again. More canny, perhaps, and less eager to please, but liberated by her secret knowledge that the whole Harvard delusion was nothing more than that, she revels in her recovered reality. It is even consoling to be back to her old confusion about what to do after she graduates from high school. She finds Mark Saunders's uncritical acceptance of the roadmap handed to him at birth—Andover, Harvard College, Harvard Law School—dreary. She would take confusion over that any day of the week.

Since Mark's revelation about his sister's upcoming, rubber-stamp acceptance at Harvard and its royal tennis team, he has lost whatever attractiveness he once had. Stephanie honestly does not believe she resents him—or Bunny, for that matter—for their place in the non-egalitarian scheme of things. But Mark's total lack of curiosity about life outside his little world is another matter. Now that *is* unseemly. It is just that kind of insular-mindedness of privileged types that has put all those poor American kids in harm's way in Iraq. The war over there is very much on Stephanie's mind again. Despite her resolution to keep up with the Grandville vigil group, she has only joined it two evenings since beginning her royal tennis regime. That is going to change now.

Bunny is waiting for Stephanie to signal she is ready to receive the next serve. There is even more politesse in this game than in modern tennis. Players are forever saying, "Thank you" and "Ready now?" and "Well done." In a sport built on deception, these starched locutions sound uncommonly passive-aggressive. Stephanie nods, Bunny serves.

This is the first time the two young women have played one another. Both are seventeen and high school juniors (although Mark was quick to correct Stephanie for applying the term 'junior' to his sister; in Andover parlance, she is an 'upper-middler') and though Bunny is half a head taller than Stephanie, Stephanie can reach higher in a standing jump. The match was arranged by Mark, who hinted he had placed money on its outcome. He did not, of course, reveal on whom he bet or with whom. Stephanie can see him up there in the gallery next to her dad. *Is Dad the one Mark placed his bet with?*

Stephanie takes the ball low in the bounce and swats it back to Bunny's backhand. Bunny replies with a drop shot so loaded with backspin it bounces backward towards the net, but Stephanie is familiar with Bunny's spin game from watching her play doubles so she has anticipated the shot. She not only gets to the ball easily, but sends it sailing right into the dedans to make the point. That is something else Stephanie noticed watching Bunny play: The girl is lax about protecting her dedans. The set is now tied, three all.

Switching sides for Stephanie to take service end, she again glances up at the gallery. Her dad salutes her, smiling broadly. Mark's face, however, exudes strained nonchalance—*very* strained. No, there is not a particle of doubt about who the parties to the wager are and who is betting on whom.

Waiting for Bunny to announce she is ready to accept service, Stephanie is again struck by her opponent's genteel bearing, particularly the way her elongated neck sets up her perfectly oval head. From Advanced Placement Biology, Stephanie understands enough about Mendel's law of independent assortment to know that the Saunders genetic line has been class-selective for scores of generations; squat-neck genes—even *recessive* squat-neck genes—need not apply. Bunny nods and Stephanie whacks the ball off the penthouse into the far corner of the service box. Bunny stumbles trying to get behind it. Point, Cyzinski.

Only now does Stephanie realize she can take the match. Going in, she did not believe she stood a chance. In fact, going in she did not care. The charade was over, so what difference did it make? But now Stephanie can taste victory and the bittersweet irony that would come with it.

On the next serve, she catches the edge of the penthouse, sending the ball to a near corner of the service box, then skittering into the net before Bunny can reach it. Stephanie wins the game in straight serves. Different as royal tennis is from the game Stephanie grew up playing, the looseness and spontaneous inventiveness aroused by winning a string of straight points is the same. Stephanie is in the zone. On a roll. This is the way to end this whole episode, she thinks. Not with a whimper, but a bang.

Stephanie takes the first set, 6–4, the second—and the match—6–2. Coming to the net to shake Stephanie's hand, Bunny bows her regal head and says, "You're beautiful," and Stephanie thinks, 'No, *you* are beautiful, but I won.'

Her father had indeed bet on her and won. As they roll by the Harvard river houses, he proposes they use the winnings to splurge on a fancy dinner in Harvard Square. He even has a restaurant in mind, Chez Henri.

"No, thanks, Dad," Stephanie says. "I kinda want to get home. A hamburger on the Pike is fine."

"Hey, Steph, we're celebrating!" Terry Cyzinski says. He has been in an ecstatic mood ever since her win. He takes a right onto John F. Kennedy Street toward the Square.

"I'm not going to Harvard, Dad," Stephanie says in a flat, matter-of-fact voice. She had planned to tell him this today, but not until they were home.

"What are you talking about?" Terry says. He laughs.

"I'm just not. I'm not going to get in. The place on the team is already filled. It's a done deal, Dad. Somebody lied to you."

"Don't be ridiculous." Terry keeps driving, only slowing at intersections to read the street signs. "We're looking for Shepard Street. It should be on the left."

Stephanie watches her father's face bob up and down as he searches for the street that will lead them to Chez Henri. She has always admired his single-mindedness; it inspired her to do her best in school and sports since she was in grammar school. But in the last few months the mania that drives that single-mindedness has become impossible for her to ignore. Until this moment, that realization saddened Stephanie, but watching him now in a fit of dumb denial, she feels contempt crowding out her compassion.

"Bunny Saunders," she says. "Her father was on the Harvard team. And now her brother. She goes to Andover, same year as me. She's a legacy, you know? And she's New England girls junior champion."

"And you just beat her, kid!" Terry barks back at her.

"So what? That doesn't make any difference! Nobody gives a crap about that! *Don't you get it?*" Stephanie's tone is sharper than it has ever been with either of her parents, or with any other adult, for that matter. Yes, she just beat Bunny Saunders and the grit of that win is still with her.

"Harvard will hear about what happened today. You can bet on that," her father goes on, but his voice is already losing command. Both of them can hear that.

He turns onto Shepard Street. Chez Henri is right there. Terry halts the car in the middle of the road.

"Who told you about that open spot on the team?" Stephanie asks quietly.

Her father shrugs. "I'm a guidance counselor, for crissake. People talk to me."

"You talked to somebody at Harvard? The coach? You talked to him personally?"

Behind them, a car stops, unable to pass. It flashes its high beams. Terry looks in his rearview mirror, then back at his daughter. He is breathing hard and his face is flushed. "I have my sources," he murmurs.

The car behind them blasts its horn. Before Stephanie can take in what is happening, her father is out the car door stomping toward the horn-blaring car. "Shut the fuck up!" he is screaming. "Shut the fuck up or I'll wring your neck!"

* * *

This time, Flip's note is written in all capitals with a red Magic Marker:

"TOMORROW, 3 O'CLOCK, THE MT. I GOT US A MOTEL ROOM WITH A JACUZZI. BE READY, BABE."

Lila crumples up his daily missive and dumps it on the floor of her locker with the others.

CHAPTER NINETEEN

In the 1620s the deVries family of Rotterdam in what is now The Netherlands unknowingly participated in a social experiment that would resonate in Western civilization forever after. Jacob deVries, a retired ship captain turned shipping agent, presided over a household of relatives, servants, business associates and visiting clients, plus the occasional former shipmate in town between voyages, for a total of sometimes up to thirty occupants. At night, every room of the deVries dockside residence was slept in, including the chamber where Jacob conducted business by day, the laundry and cooking outbuilding behind the main structure, and the long ground floor quarter where the ten-meter board on which meals were served was transformed into a bed by covering it with a silk drape imported from Persia. This last was the boudoir of Jacob and his second wife, Marta, a woman twenty years his junior whom he had married one year after his first wife succumbed to tuberculosis. Up to seven others slept on the floor of this same chamber.

Marta, light-haired, blue-eyed, and well-proportioned, had lived and worked in the house since she was ten, the age when girls of her social class typically left their parents to earn their keep and a pittance more. At the end of each month Marta delivered her entire five stuiver salary to her parents' door. She began as a maid, moved on to become a kitchen helper, and was the household chef at the time of her mistress's illness and death. With Jacob's blessing, Marta retained this last responsibility after their marriage in spite of the fact that it was considered unbecoming for a woman of her new station to do any household work other than supervision. But Marta took great pleasure in planning meals, shopping in the market, and preparing food, and more significantly, Jacob, a gourmand by the standards of any era, loved the way she cooked. In permitting this small exception to the cultural mores of Rotterdam—in fact, of all of Western Europe—Jacob unwittingly contributed to the start of a social revolution. It began in the kitchen and climaxed in the bedroom.

Jacob deVries adored the way his new young wife prepared oysters: shucked, dipped in batter, fried in pig fat, and served in a sauce of her own invention whose ingredients included beaten eggs, minced onion, and a spice recently come upon in Constantinople and brought back to Rotterdam by a sailor in the family's employ—cumin. Jacob could eat the dish four and five times a week, but he was denied this indulgence because the cost of oysters was prohibitive—they had to be imported from France—and the supply of cumin limited. This, in itself, would not have prevented Jacob from enjoying this dish regularly, but the custom of the age was for the entire household to eat the same meal at the same time and, well off as Jacob was, he could not afford a steady diet of oysters for twenty to thirty people.

Marta had a brainstorm that resolved this predicament: She would prepare and serve her husband's and her own meal separately. From the perspective of a mere century later, Marta's proposal would hardly appear ingenious; and certainly from the vantage point of one of her New World descendents, Lila deVries, Marta's idea would seem like a total 'no-brainer.' But the conventions of a late-Renaissance household were as fixed a reality as, say, the conventions of a twenty-first century American high school where it would be unimaginable for pubescent boys and girls to sit at their desks stark naked, logical as that might seem on a ninety degree day.

Jacob was caught in a wrenching dilemma: Oysters or convention. Again, his appetite won.

This seemingly small change in the way things were done chez deVries set the stage for a series of other small changes, starting with the request by Jacob the Younger, Jacob deVries's eldest son and right-hand man in the family business, to sit at the same meal table with his father and stepmother. The younger Jacob made his entreaty more as a matter of pride than of a lust for oysters; indeed, in short order he tired of Oysters Marta, although the same pride that brought him to the table kept him there. The second son, Henrik, also in the family business, predictably became jealous of his elder brother's privilege and requested a place at the table too. It was only a matter of two years' time before all of Jacob the Elder's children shared their meals with him and Marta.

From this new order, there followed other readjustments. The cost of feeding oysters to a table of eight was straining the

~ 215 ~

family budget, so Marta prepared separate dishes for the rest of the family, most of which, to the children's unspoken relief, were heavy on potatoes and sausages. In time, much as Marta enjoyed preparing food, enough was enough, so she turned over the task of feeding the non-immediate family to the help.

It was about this same time when Marta, emboldened by the ease with which old routines could be revised, suggested a change in the household's sleeping arrangements or, more to the point, its accommodations for sexual activity. Although the word 'inhibited' did not exist in Middle Dutch, it perfectly describes how Marta felt about engaging in sexual congress with her husband in a heavily populated room. She was not, of course, so ahead of her time that she was concerned about her own pleasure in the act, but hearing the rustle of the room's other occupants while she lay on the table top as her oyster-invigorated husband energetically gratified his lust made her shrink with shame. And this, she believed, was the reason she had not conceived a child with Jacob in over three years of marriage. She told him so. Thus it was that Jacob and Marta decamped for a third floor chamber of their very own where, in a matter of months, the seed was planted for Lila's direct ancestor.

For Jacob and Marta deVries, these subtle shifts in house-hold arrangements stopped here. But generated by the same zeitgeist—if for different particular reasons—families like the deVrieses all over the Lowlands were making similar incre-mental changes in the way they ate and slept, emptied their bowels, and made love. Family diners became segregated from unrelated boarders, interior doors were installed and closed, squat pots were curtained off, and sex became a sequestered enterprise. The twin values of private space and personal com-fort had slipped almost unnoticed under their front doors, and with them came the concept of home—a place where families could thrive.

* * *

It is a Sunday morning in mid-February and Wendell, having left Lila sleeping in her bedroom, is taking Binx for a walk. It is an overcast day with the promise of snow and Wendell is swinging his arms and slapping his chest to keep his blood sprinting ahead of the penetrating cold air. Meanwhile Binx, dog to the bone, laps up street slush as if it is hot cocoa. They are heading for town.

Wendell's mind is frozen. Even reading poetry, a diversion that has always stirred his thoughts, leaves him cold. At home in his easy chair when he tries to recapture the once-dependable solace induced by reading old favorites, he is overcome with gloom. Last night, waiting to pick up Lila at her job, he opened his collection of William Blake poems to the "Songs of Innocence" and read the familiar lines,

> *The Sun descending in the west,*
> *The evening star does shine.*
> *The birds are silent in their nest,*
> *And I must seek for mine.*

But Blake's scene of a tranquil nightfall only deepened Wendell's melancholy. It provoked an image of Franny waiting interminably for the sun to rise. Wendell set the book on top of the living room's new centerpiece, his Brenkert projector, without reading on.

Binx trots down Mahaiwe Street making for Write Now, unaware that it is Sunday, the one day of the week Wendell takes off. A woman Franny recommended, Tiffany Korand, fills in for him, selling the Sunday newspapers. As Wendell and Binx approach the shop, Wendell sees Michael Dowd exiting, a two-pound paper under each arm. In addition to wanting to spend as much of his Sundays as he can with Lila, Wendell's reason for hiring Tiffany was to savor one idle chat-free day a week, so he stoops and scurries past Dowd without a word. Binx stops in front of the Phoenix.

Wendell automatically reaches into his pocket for his ring of keys and lets them in. He wonders if Livio works on Sundays; Livio's family did not come with him from Rome and Wendell doubts he has any friends in Grandville, so what else would there be for the man to do on a Sunday? But the theater is dark. Maybe Livio is catching mass over at St. Peter's, even if they no longer conduct it in Latin the way Livio must surely believe it is supposed to be done.

Wendell switches on the lights and Binx bounds up the stairs to the balcony. Wendell follows, master after mutt, and in a moment they are both inside the projection booth. This is the first time Wendell has been in here since he cleared out the booth months ago.

Empty, it feels twice the size Wendell remembered it. He steps over to the peep window that frames the stage below. Livio has completed repainting the proscenium, its now-dry Nile green embellishments far subtler to the eye than they must have appeared to the Phoenix's original audiences in that period before pigment chemists created a screaming palette of unnatural colors.

Gazing down, Wendell waits for nostalgic thoughts; this is, after all, the spot where he spent most of the waking hours of his life. But no such thoughts come. That, too, has come to an end. 'Too many endings,' Wendell muses, then smiles ruefully to himself—that was a criticism he had often heard about the films he showed.

Outdoors again, Wendell gulps in cold air. He feels unaccountably refreshed. Binx is trotting down the alley between the theater and the fire station. By the time Wendell catches up with him, the dog is prancing up the embankment to the railroad tracks. In unison, they strut from tie to tie. It reminds Wendell of an animal act in an old vaudeville variety show, and he laughs out loud. This time Wendell leads the way as he and Binx descend the embankment to Methuan Road and make their way to Pleasant Street.

Wendell and his dog are now standing in front of Zion church. The temperature has risen and snow begins to fall. Wendell hears the congregation singing inside.

> "Who's that young girl dressed in white?
> Wade in the Water
> Must be the Children of Israelites
> God's gonna trouble the Water."

Wendell senses a sweet synchronicity between the lilt of the hymn and the slowly falling snow, and the sweetness of the moment begins to melt his frozen heart.

Wendell and Binx are still there some ten minutes later when the church doors open and out steps Reverend Willa

Jones in her black robe. She looks to the sky, smiles at the falling snow, and whoops, "Hallelujah!" Esther and her children are the first to shake the minister's hand on their way out. And Kaela is the first to see Wendell. She skips up to him and wraps her arms around his waist. "Hi, Wendell!"

It is because of Kaela that Esther attends Zion. Esther has not been a churchgoer since she was a child and alternated Sundays between her mother's Eastern Orthodox and her father's Presbyterian church, but her daughter took to Zion from the first time they attended a service there last autumn. Esther thinks the attraction comes from Kaela being non-white too, but it may also be the music: Kaela sings the gospel hymns she learns in the church all week long. For Esther's son, Johnny, the after-service spread is enticement enough; he has become an authority on the differences between Martha Hodges's sweet potato pie and Sharon deVries's. Sharon's is significantly sweeter.

Esther has not urged Wendell to join her and her children at services, just as she has not urged him to make any changes in his routine since Franny's breakdown. Esther especially would not ask him to give up time on a Sunday, the day he devotes to Lila, even though the girl seems to sleep through most of that day's daylight hours. That is why Esther has not told Wendell about her regular, after-church brunches with Bill and Sharon deVries at the Soup and Sandwich; she does not want him to feel either left out or guilty.

Bill and Sharon are right behind Esther on the church steps. It only takes Wendell a moment to realize that the thirtyish woman standing next to the couple belongs with them. What gives that away is not her face—it is darker and more African-looking than either of theirs—but her clothing. Like Bill and Sharon, she is finely dressed, her tailored, camel-hair overcoat alone enough to set her apart from the local congregants. Bill sees Wendell and shouts, "Hey, Cuz!"

A moment later, they are standing in a circle in the falling snow—Wendell, Esther and her children, Bill, Sharon, and the young woman, Emmanuelle, their niece. Introducing her to Wendell, Bill says, "Strictly speaking, she's not a deVries, but she makes up for it by being a famous writer."

"If writing one book that about fifty people have read makes you famous," Emmanuelle says, shaking Wendell's hand. Then, more quietly, she says, "I'm sorry to hear about your daughter. I hope she gets well soon."

"Amen," Sharon says.

Wendell has to swallow hard before he can speak again. It is not simply Emmanuelle's good wishes that move him, it is the fact that she knew about his ordeal at all—he, a stranger to her. "Who can eat?" Wendell says.

"Church always makes me hungry," Bill replies.

"Oh yes, church and picking up the mail and watching television. *Everything* makes that man hungry," Sharon says.

"How about my place?" Wendell says. "Lila should be getting out of bed about now."

Wendell wants it to be a feast. Walking along Main Street with Esther beside him, he recites a list of items he wants her to pick up at the co-op: cheeses, cold cuts, jams, rye bread, bagels, tomatoes, avocados, onions, canned pineapple, bananas, coffee cake. He removes his wallet from his back pocket, pulls out all the money, and presses the bills into Esther's hand. He has not felt so excited about the prospect of a meal in a very long time.

The feast in Wendell's kitchen is glorious. If any of the group had already eaten in the Zion basement, it is not evident from their appetites. At one point, Sharon asks if there is any peanut butter in the house and when Wendell produces a jar for her, she proceeds to make her specialty for Johnny, a fried peanut butter and pineapple sandwich. But by the time the sandwich is passed and nibbled down the table to the boy, only a fraction of it is left. Sharon takes orders for five more.

Wendell asks Emmanuelle about the book she wrote and she tells him it is about life on a Gainesville, Georgia plantation in the early 1800s.

"It's actually about a single day in 1831," Emmanuelle says.

"Something special happen on that day?" Wendell asks.

"No, that's the beauty of it," Bill answers for his niece. "Just a regular day in their regular lives. I'll get you a copy, Wendell. It's as fine a book as I've read."

"I'd like that," Wendell says.

Emmanuelle laughs. "Uncle Billy owns twenty of the fifty copies they've sold, God love him."

"How did you pick the day?" Kaela asks.

"Good question," Emmanuelle tells her. "It went kind of backwards. I knew I wanted to write about only one day when I started my research. And March 18th, 1831, just turned out to be the day with the most documents and diary entries I could find."

"Like bills of sale," Sharon announces from the stove. "The master of the house bought two slaves on that day."

"How much did they cost?" Kaela asks. She has an instinct for quelling any potential disquiet with her earnestness.

"Three hundred and fifty dollars apiece," Emmanuelle answers. "They calculated it by the number of bags of rice a slave could produce in a year."

Kaela shakes her head back and forth. "I can't even imagine someone selling another person," she says.

"Neither can I," Emmanuelle tells the ten-year-old. "Not really."

Sharon's fifth and final peanut butter and pineapple sandwich comes off the griddle. She hands it to Wendell. "Emmanuelle's writing a new book about the Underground Railroad," she says. "From Georgia to Massachusetts."

"A single day again?" Wendell asks.

"No," Emmanuelle answers. "I'm covering fifteen days this time. Expanding my horizons."

"And one of those days is in Grandville," Esther says. "That's why she's coming to live here for a while. With us, actually."

"In your apartment?" Wendell asks. There is more incredulity in his voice than he would have liked, but he simply cannot picture another adult sharing Esther's two-room apartment on Board Street.

"We're putting a bed in the kitchen," Esther says.

"It's going to be cozy," Kaela says, grinning.

"They won't take no for an answer," Emmanuelle says.

It has been decades since Wendell has had what he would deem a *bona fide* inspiration. He can count his inspired impulses on the fingers of one hand, starting with the one in 1957 when he stepped out of his projection booth during a

Christmas week showing of *An Affair to Remember* and said to a lovely young woman he had not yet met, "It all works out in the end." Wendell simply does not consider spontaneous acts part of his nature and, the 1957 case in point, he has reason not to completely trust them anyhow. But the one that seizes him at this moment, lifting him out of his chair and propelling him to the hallway where he picks up the phone, is accompanied by an unprecedented clarity of purpose.

When Wendell returns to the kitchen a few minutes later, he says, "I just rented the house next door. You know, the other half of this house. You can all move in whenever you want to. Tomorrow, if you want."

The people at his kitchen table stare back at him, not one of them speaking. Wendell catches a look of apprehension in William deVries's eyes; the man is undoubtedly thinking that his distant cousin—a man he does not really know—has some loose screws in his head.

Sharon breaks the silence. "Is it the same size as this one?" she asks.

"Exactly," Wendell replies. "A mirror image."

"Sounds like a good idea to me," Sharon says. "About time, actually."

Esther's face is flushed. It is clear she wants to speak with Wendell in private, but it is also clear that Wendell wants to share every facet of his inspiration with everyone in his kitchen.

"I'm not sure I can afford it, Wendell," Esther says quietly.

"Oh, I'm paying for it," Wendell says. "They gave me a whole bunch of money for leaving the Phoenix without a fuss. It'll cover a year's rent and then some. I don't really think of it as my money anyhow."

"It's kind of a big step to take without—" Esther begins, but she is cut off by Sharon deVries who says to her, "Sometimes you just *do,* and you figure out what it *means* later."

Wendell laughs. "Hell, that sounds like something you'd say, Esther," he says.

"Of course, it does," Bill chimes in. "It's some kind of female code."

"Will I have my own room, just like Lila?" Kaela asks.

It is unclear to whom she is addressing her question, and it hangs in the air for a long while.

"I don't see why not," Esther replies finally.

A cheer goes up at the kitchen table that surely resonates in every empty room of the other half of the house. Upstairs in this half, Lila clamps a pillow over her head and waits for sleep to return.

CHAPTER TWENTY

William deVries's great-great-grandmother, Sarah, had an inborn talent for running that was already evident when she was a toddler. It is said that the first time Sarah put one foot in front of the other, she dashed from her mother's arms out the door of the women's quarters to a peach tree where the one-year-old jumped a foot and a half into the air to snag a piece of fruit. The story is undoubtedly an exaggeration—Sarah's mother, Abbi, was known to the other women as Matchuba, an Ashanti nickname that means, 'Pretender.' But Sarah's barefoot race against a horse-drawn wagon at a Gainesville slave auction on June 7th, 1855, is doubly documented—in a marginal note on her bill of sale to Mr. Hadley Jackson, Esq., and in the diary of her seller, Mr. Andrew Phipps. Sarah beat the horse by five feet. She was then twelve years old.

As a result of this spectacular demonstration of Sarah's gift, Phipps garnered the extraordinary price of $450 for the girl, a match to the $450 he won in side bets on the race. Jackson paid this premium for a reason. As owner of the largest Georgia plantation west of Atlanta and as a fastidious businessman, he kept a running inventory of his three money crops: cotton, tobacco, and peaches. With this information, plus his regular reports on the fluctuating prices for each of these crops at Port Savannah's produce auction house, Jackson calculated the most profitable days to go to market. He had already created the job of Tally Master and filled it with a quadroon house slave named Martin, but clever as Martin was with numbers and pen, his gait was slower than a mule's. And that is why, watching Sarah outpace the horse, Hadley Jackson, Esquire created a new position—Tally Runner.

Six days a week, Sarah ran from cotton field to tobacco field to peach orchard, and then around again and again, picking up tally sheets from the foremen, stuffing them in the cotton bag that hung around her neck, and bringing them to Martin at the Big House. She ran a good fifteen miles each working day and *is said to have done the same on Sundays when she ran through the fields just for the sheer exuberance of it.*

There is only one thing that ever slowed Sarah's pace or squelched her high spirits and that was Martin. Grandfathered and fathered by white men—a slave ship helmsman and Hadley Jackson's younger brother, Hugh, respectively—Martin enjoyed a lofty opinion of himself and his God-given entitlements. These last included the sexual submission of any slave on the plantation who caught his fancy. Indeed, inasmuch as Master Hadley conceded Martin this indulgence, it did amount to a personal entitlement. Sarah, though scrawny, small-breasted, and flat-hipped, caught Martin's fancy, possibly because of her sensational vitality. Almost every day after accepting Sarah's final tally sheets, Martin led the girl to the stable where he had his way with her in a vacant stall.

It was for this reason—and this reason alone—that Sarah crouched under a bed in the women's quarters on a moonless March night to listen to the whispers of Agatha May, a runaway slave from Maryland. Sarah had no argument with slavery itself; not only was it the only life she knew, but as a result of her much valued skill as a runner, she had never endured a single whip lash or worn a shackle, although she was well aware of both these abominations. Like the man who regularly raped her, Sarah had come to the conclusion that she was privileged, and she was too young and uneducated to understand that privilege was a relative concept. Still, instinct abetted by physical pain told her there was one crucial privilege she lacked.

Like Harriet Tubman, Agatha May's friend and colleague in the Underground Railroad, Agatha spent nearly a decade sneaking back to the provinces of her escape to inspire other slaves to run away too, and then to supply her converts with leaders (known as conductors), strategies, schedules, and maps dotted with safe houses called stations. Also like Tubman, May carried a substantial price on her head, a price that would be doubled if that head was delivered on the end of a rope. (Unlike Miss Tubman, Miss May was terrified of public speaking and therefore did not make her way into history books until Emmanuelle Jones wrote about her.)

Sarah almost did not sign on. The list of rules for passengers was far more lengthy and detailed than on the plantation itself where the single rule, 'Do as you are told,' sufficed. To join passage on the Underground Railroad, one not only had to pledge to always do as ordered by one's conductor, but to hide without complaint in bat-filled caves, hollowed-out dung heaps, and freezing root cellars, just to name a few locales mentioned by Miss May. Further, no matter what circumstances arose, one was required to remain with her group of deserters, and no matter how long one was forced to go without food, any risk taken to steal same was forbidden. The punishment for many infractions was execution. This was the invariable penalty for giving in to the all-too-understandable fear of getting caught by vigilantes and whipped to the bone, a fear that led escapees to 'escape' back to their masters to plead for mercy. The railroad's ultimate penalty was pragmatic: Returned runaways were repositories of critical information about the underground network. For the purpose of this penalty, all conductors carried pistols.

But on the same day as Agatha May's clandestine midnight visit to the women's slave quarters on the Jackson Plantation, Sarah had been victim to a particularly sadistic assault by Martin. As usual, he had bent her over a bale of hay and mounted her from behind, horse-like, but this time as he repeatedly thrust himself into her, he slapped her flank with his open hand. Sarah yelped, a sound that only excited the man to whack harder. She screamed. Two young coachmen, both white, came running. Upon beholding the savage spectacle, they cheered Martin on, then unbuttoned their trousers and commenced to masturbate. All that saved Sarah from being raped by them too was their revulsion at the idea of succeeding a black man in her body.

Sarah was left with a feeling she had never before fully recognized, one that pained her more deeply and lastingly than any blow to her thighs and buttocks: Humiliation. Certainly, she could not identify that feeling with any word in her vocabulary. The nature of language is that a term requires its opposite to have meaning; there can be no concept of hot without the concept of cold, so a slave, whose dawn-to-dusk existence consists of one act of subjugation after another, is at a disadvantage when it comes to identifying humiliation. Nonetheless, it was *that unspeakable feeling that compelled Sarah to enlist passage on the Underground Railroad.*

The landowners of Gainesville devoted their Sundays to church, mid-afternoon family dinners, visits to sickly friends and relatives, and drinking whiskey. Thus the Sunday of April 4th, 1858 was selected as an optimum day for Sarah to take off for freedom.

Of the three women who set off from the Jackson plantation on that day, only Sarah kept her nerve. The other two, both cotton pickers, began whispering between themselves less than fifteen minutes into the journey, and after only thirty minutes simply turned around and headed back to the safety of captivity. They had been gone for such a short time that it was highly doubtful their absence was noticed, so Sarah did not waste her breath trying to dissuade them. Better they returned now than later when they would be interrogated with a whip. And better yet, Sarah would not have to keep to their cotton picking pace any longer.

She ran. She loped invisibly between rows of six-foot-high tobacco bushes, breathing steadily through her broad, dilated nostrils. At the five mile mark, where the first tobacco wagon road intersected with the crop line, she stopped, rolled up the hem of her ankle-length skirt, tucked it into the waistband, and ran on, leaning so far forward that her pumping arms almost grazed the ground. With her long-muscled legs unfettered, she moved faster and even more effortlessly.

The sun is high and blistering hot by the time Sarah reaches the banks of the Chattahoochee River. It is the first natural body of water she has ever seen and she gazes across it with a mix of wonder and apprehension. She is to meet her conductor and other members of her group on a glittering outcropping of white feldspar on the far side of this river. She can make out that distant meeting point, but she cannot imagine how she will get there. She gazes to her right and to her left along the near riverbank, searching for a place where the water ends and the banks merge, but there is no such place in sight. For all Agatha Mays's detailed rules and instructions, she had not taken into account the fact that Sarah does not know how to swim, has not, in fact, ever seen anyone swim.

Sarah stands still, shading her eyes with one hand. She imagines flying across the river on the back of the osprey she sees gliding in the air above her. Then, on the back of the brown pelican she sees gliding on top of the water just below her. Swirls and bubbles follow that water bird. Sarah observes its water-churning web feet.

Sarah has a visceral understanding of propulsion. As naturally as she knows that bracing her hand over her eyes shades them from the sun's rays, she knows the soles of her feet drive her forward by pushing against the ground. Living inside her body informs her of the physics of the world. And so it is that an illiterate fifteen-year-old, one generation away from a landlocked mountain village in Africa, conceives of a way to propel herself in water. In effect, Sarah invents swimming.

But her invention lacks refinement—in particular, a method and rhythm for breathing. Also, she has not figured on the river's current that pulls her one foot downstream for every two feet she advances toward the opposite shore. Nonetheless, flailing and paddling, sputtering and choking, Sarah makes her way across the Chattahoochee River. Then she runs along the shore to the designated meeting point.

Her conductor, a mulatto named Isaiah, is waiting for her. His first words are to tell her she is a terrible swimmer, that all her splashing and splattering could have been spotted by any slave hunter within five miles. And that there were a hundred more rivers, lakes, and ponds between here and their final destination, Toronto. When Sarah explains that it was her first attempt at swimming, he rolls his eyes and, speaking to a phantom who apparently resides on his left shoulder, says, "Who chose this godforsaken child?"

It is sunset before the two of them are joined by another runaway, a rotund woman who had been nanny and wet nurse on the Cornelia Plantation in Absalom. She has no name other than Nanny. Like Sarah, she had taken off with another slave who changed her mind before reaching the boundary of their plantation, so instead of a party of six, they are a party of three. "But one can't swim and the other can't walk faster than an ox," Isaiah intones to his shoulder-top alter ego.

Isaiah leading, they make their way to Chattahoochee Ridge where they camp at the mouth of a cave that stinks of bat droppings. *They barely talk, which suits Sarah fine, but their torpid pace is already vexing her. Her muscles ache from braking back her natural sprint. This ain't runnin' away, it's strollin' away.*

In the ensuing six days, they zigzag north on Indian mountain trails, along riverbanks, across lakes and ponds, and today, traversing West Virginia, in the false bottom of an undercarriage of a farm wagon. Above the runaways is a load of cow manure, the cargo of choice of Underground Railroad voluntaries because of its natural resistance to inspection by slave hunters and militiamen alike.

Not only does the acid odor of the load stream into the passengers' hidden compartment, but yellow drops of its sweat dribble through the floorboards onto their faces. What is more, their heads are only inches away from where the wagon's axle connects to the wheel, and the relentless rasp of this imperfect connection drills into their ears. Sarah is resigned to all of these torments, but lying immobile on her side, unable to crook a joint or animate a muscle for hours on end, drains her spirit to the point where she can no longer remember the reason she fled the plantation, a place where she ran free all day.

This is Sarah's state of mind as she lies in the false bottom of the farm wagon driven by a Quaker farmer from Martinsburg, West Virginia. And this is the moment when Sarah first hears the humming sound. Her back is pressed against Nanny's bosom, just as Nanny's back is pressed against Isaiah's bony chest. For a long while, the sound had been of a piece with the grind of the axle and the thud of the wooden wheels against the stony roadbed, but now Sarah is aware that it comes from Nanny's throat. It has a melody, simple and sweet. Nanny is humming a lullaby.

Sarah's mother, Abbi, had never sung to her when she was an infant. In fact, Abbi had been permitted very little time to suckle her daughter or rock her in her arms. Instead, Sarah's feeding had been left to an old woman in the women's quarters whose milk was thin and disposition sour. No songs passed her lips. All of this may account for the depth of Sarah's reaction to Nanny's wordless song. Sarah's muscles, tensed with inactivity, relax; her mind, dulled by monotony, stirs. The bounces *of the wagon now comfort her with the reassurance of bass notes. Like a baby in swaddling, Sarah surrenders to the peace of immobility.*

On the eighth day of the journey, Sarah is awakened by the sound of a white man's shout.

The runaways have spent an unusually comfortable night in the storehouse of a Potomac River wood mill on the out-skirts of Cresaptown, Maryland. The night before, their hosts, a German-born, middle-aged brother and sister who own the mill, had served them a sumptuous supper of roasted venison and sauerkraut, both items they had never tasted before. The price of feast and lodging was to listen to an hour-long Bible reading in front of the couple's fireplace. Even if Sarah could have understood a word of the text, it would have been a small price to pay.

The white man is shouting, "Got me a fat nigra!"

Sarah is on her feet before she is fully conscious. She peers from her bed, a patch of straw between two stacks of planks, to Isaiah's, the rope hammock he carries in his pack, now slung between two beams twenty feet away from her. Isaiah signals Sarah to crouch down again, but she remains standing and puts one eye to a crack in the storehouse wall. She sees Nanny out-side. The woman is on her knees and there is a rope noosed around her neck. Sarah's peephole is too small for her to make out any more than this—no other person, not even where the loose end of the rope leads.

At the German couple's insistence, Nanny had slept in their house. They had been troubled by the sores on Nanny's neck and face, and by her hacking cough, so they made her a bed of pillows in front of their fireplace. Now Sarah can hear the German woman outside, pleading with Nanny's captors. Then she hears the German woman yelp and fall silent. Only seconds after this, Sarah hears the storehouse door rattle open.

Sarah knows the Underground Railroad's decree that hiding is always to be chosen over running in plain sight of slave hunters. In any event, there is no other door or window in the storehouse, so she and Isaiah are essentially trapped. But neither of these facts enters into Sarah's calculation because, in fact, she makes none: she acts on instinct, not deliberation. She runs.

Sarah runs through the storehouse door even as two men bearing Brunswick rifles are opening it. She brushes against one of them, her thin left shoulder against his solid right arm, without missing a step. She races to the river and dives in before either of the men can load and fire. This time, instead of fighting the current, she rides it downstream out of sight.

When the historian, Emmanuelle Jones, tried to establish the events of Days Eight through Fourteen of Sarah's journey, she could not find a single document, not even in the journal of Sarah's daughter, Edith deVries, a literary young woman who had appointed herself family chronicler. Not one of the Underground Railroad stations between Cresaptown, Maryland, and Hudson, New York, had records of a female, teenage, runaway slave traveling on her own during that period. But what was undeniable is that in those seven days Sarah covered close to four hundred miles. The only conclusion available to Jones was that Sarah ran the entire way, putting an astonishing sixty miles behind her each one of those days.

Also amazing is how Sarah found her way to the Hudson, New York station. It can be guessed that Isaiah told her about it, along with a description of other safe houses, at the beginning of their journey. But Sarah could only have had the crudest of maps in her possession if, indeed, she had any at all, and she had only the sun and stars to orient herself. Yet it is known with documented certainty that in the early evening of April 18th, 1858, Sarah arrived at the home of Dr. and Mrs. Timothy Wilson at the top of Prospect Street in Hudson. Dr. Wilson, an atypical combination of abolitionist and atheist, noted in his diary that the young Negress was thin to the point of emaciation, but when he listened to her heartbeat and lungs, and palpated her abdomen and back, he concluded that she was in excellent health. He also wrote that unlike most runaways who had stopped at his house, Sarah was vivacious, engaging, and in high spirits, her only complaint being that the evening chill "frustrated her blood." It was for this reason that the prospect of continuing further north into even colder climes distressed the young woman, and it is why Wilson and his wife encouraged her to make her way across the New York State border to western Massachusetts where the weather was more moderate than in Canada and where enforcement of the Fugitive Slave Act had become so lax it bordered on nonexistent.

It is the fifteenth day of Sarah's odyssey. With a white-capped mountaintop as her guidepost, she is loping eastward. Her pace is less hurried than it has been all week, in part because her stomach, unaccustomed to accommodating anything more than wild berries and fern shoots, is crammed with the previous night's dinner of lamb chops and potatoes, but also because she knows she is nearing her journey's end. This knowledge is both consoling and melancholy-making: she has almost run her course.

Reaching the crest of a muddy hill, she sees a farmhouse and barn. As she comes closer to it, she makes out a man just outside the barn who is shoeing a horse. He is tall and has a broad face with African features and a head of African hair, but his skin is light brown, fairer even than that of the quadroon tally master on the Jackson Plantation. In only a few minutes, Sarah will meet this man and learn his name, Hans Freeman deVries.

CHAPTER TWENTY-ONE

Hector could never forget the bone-chilling winter winds that blew through their house in Puerto Alvira. The family would huddle together under an alpaca blanket, their teeth chattering as they tried to assuage the gods by singing, "Con El Viento A Tu Favor." But the bite of those winds was nothing compared to the brain-numbing cold of the air conditioning in the Golden Glades Inn in North Miami, Florida. It is here where Hector works one hundred hours each week, ironing sheets and pillow cases in the hotel laundry by day, and sorting and carting garbage in the hotel's basement by night. Even as he works up a sweat at his tasks, the relentless refrigerated current deadens him. There are days when, stepping out onto the loading dock to grab a smoke and a can of beer, he reflexively shies away from the sunshine as if he is a petrified cave dweller.

For his labors, Hector is paid two hundred and thirty American dollars each week, well below the minimum wage for legal workers, but nonetheless equal to five hundred thousand Colombian pesos, enough to feed and house his family in Bogotá. For twenty of those two hundred and thirty dollars, Hector's supervisor in the laundry arranges for the money to be wired to Hector's mother.

Hector keeps only one hundred dollars a month for himself. Like many of the other boys, he scavenges his meals from the dumped leftovers of the Golden Glades's two restaurants—actually the leftovers left over after the bus boys upstairs have picked out the choicest bits, whole shrimp and scallops and chunks of swordfish that the *gringo* vacationers have forsaken in order to reserve room for the house specialty, key lime pie. Still, Hector dines quite grandly on *half-eaten* shrimp and scallops and chunks of swordfish that he first washes in a sieve under a spigot in the garbage room. Bite by bite, it is a richer diet than he has ever consumed, and as a result he has added more than five pounds to his thin frame in only a month. He sleeps in two three-hour shifts, wrapped in a blanket on the floor of the laundry where the overhead fluorescent lights are never turned off. The personal money he permits himself is spent on cigarettes and beer.

Hector aches with homesickness. Although he hears and speaks his native language all day long—albeit usually with Mexican, Chilean, and Argentine accents—it has begun to feel foreign to him. The Spanish words are the same, but the objects and feelings to which they are applied are different: the beverage they brew in the upstairs kitchen does not taste like *café,* even if that is what it is called; and the contempt he and his coworkers feel for the hotel guests is hardly captured by *'desprecio'*—that term ignores the bitterness that underlies their feeling. Even the Latin American music that blares non-stop from speakers in both the laundry and the basement alienates him. Although the CDs are the same ones he, Mano, and Sylvia listened to in Bogotá, here the singers sound mocking, as if their recorded voices were more alive than Hector's own as he listlessly sings along while he works.

Hector is alone among his fellow workers in grasping that their netherworld is the underside of the real world. Yes, his colleagues know *los otros* are always there, eating, dancing, swimming, and fucking above them. They even understand that their own sweat makes the *gringos'* revelries possible; that is the prime source of the contempt they feel for the *gringos.* But only Hector can see that the world above them is the real one. It is not simply sunshine and money that makes that world genuine, it is *los otros'* power to define what reality is.

Hector's awareness of this allows rays of North American consciousness to gradually penetrate his shadow world. Looking out the laundry window, he sees Americans romping and teasing one another by the pool. In the pockets of their soiled clothes, he finds their notes and letters. On the loading dock, he hears their chatter. From these clues, he pieces together their world. He perceives that autonomy has a different meaning here than in Colombia. He senses that personal identity is a fluid thing, not fixed the way it is at home. And he has even begun to lay hold of that quintessentially North American preoccupation: how one feels as compared to how one wants to feel. Hector wants to feel like a human being again.

Jesus, a Mexican in the garbage room, knows a way out of the Florida darkness. It is north. Over a thousand miles in that direction lies a place named Connecticut where an illegal can earn as much in two days as he can in a week in a Miami hotel. The work is hard, but it is outdoors, and the workers live in real houses with beds and doors and kitchens. Jesus even knows how to get there: in the back of a moving van driven by an American black man. The fare is three hundred dollars, but there is also a price for Jesus's arrangements—three hundred dollars more. Hector, of course, cannot put together that sum, not with ninety percent of his wages going straight to Colombia. Jesus says the truck is leaving in three days, with or without Hector.

Hector is no stranger to the urgency of deadlines, and when it comes to improvising ways to make money, he has an impressive record for a man his age. But here in North Miami, his imagination is tested. Even if he had the time, making music in the streets is a high-risk enterprise, especially for illegals—a city ordinance prohibits public solicitations and any illegal picked up for breaking this law is immediately turned over to the I.N.S. Also, handsome as Hector is, there is no shortage of more experienced and better-dressed Latin gigolos in the hotel's barroom. Through a process of elimination, Hector is left with burglary.

As it happens, the laundry room offers some fine opportunities for an intelligent thief. For starters, a cursory glance at the supervisor's clipboard informs him which rooms are occupied and for how many days. More tellingly, guests who use the laundry for their personal clothes are clearly richer than those who do not, and guests whose clothes include linen suits and silk blouses must surely have more money than those who send down acrylic blazers and rayon shorts. Most importantly, the chambermaids who exchange soiled bedclothes for those that are freshly laundered and pressed, possess passkeys. These maids make an appearance in the laundry room every morning between nine and eleven.

Unlike most of his coworkers in the laundry, Hector has not established a running flirtation with any of these women. Some of them have looked his way, of course—despite his pallor and spiritlessness, he is still an unusually attractive young man. But along with so many other parts of his constitution, the air conditioning has deadened his playfulness, possibly even his libido.

But now Hector has a motivation more compelling than sexual desire. He chooses his maid not by the sparkle in her eye or the turn of her calves, but by her obvious insecurity. Her name is Miriam, and she has pocked cheeks and a mountainous behind. When she enters the laundry, Hector rushes to hand her the stack of folded sheets he has just ironed. Addressing her by name, he tells her she looks happy this morning.

Hector's experience with middle-aged tourists in Bogotá has taught him that most plain women recoil at being told they are lovely or sexy—they are much more sensitive to bogus flattery than better-looking women. But to say they look happy even if they do not—indeed, *especially* if they do not—lifts their spirits and melts their hearts. They are thrilled and encouraged by the very possibility of being happy—and happy-looking. So it is with Miriam. Hector arranges to meet her on the loading dock at her eleven-thirty break.

In preparation for his assignation, Hector performs a simple, preliminary theft: He steals the key to the employees' shower off its hook on the wall. In size and general shape, this key is similar to the passkeys the maids carry in their apron pockets. He also unearths his *cuatro* from its hiding place under his locker.

On the dock, Hector serenades Miriam with "Amor Sin Medida." In his mind's ear, he can hear Sylvia's delightful descant dancing around the melody. It is for this reason he chose the song: his tender feelings for Sylvia show in the gaze he casts at Miriam. The girl is efficiently wooed. He has no sooner finished the chorus when he sets down his instrument and kisses her. For a moment, her warm lips excite him—his senses have been dormant for so long this little awakening feels sublime. But this is no time for sensuality. As he kisses her, he touches her blouse, then lets his hand slip from her breasts to her belly, and there, with the dexterity of an illusionist, he dips his fingers into her apron pocket where he exchanges the shower key for her passkey. He finishes the trick with an inspired flourish—pressing through the fabric of her apron into her crotch. Miriam bites his lip and pushes him away, flushed and happy. She says she has to go back to work. Hector says he will see her at the afternoon break.

As they saunter back inside, Hector hears a snicker behind them. He turns his head. About thirty feet away at the outdoor bar, two hotel guests in swimming suits grin back at him. The fatter of the two pumps his eyebrows and smacks his lips while the other mimes applause, a show of appreciation for Hector and Miriam's titillating sideshow. Whatever misgivings Hector may have harbored about stealing from innocent *gringos* instantly dissolve.

Taking the fire stairs, Hector goes straight to the hotel's fifth floor. He has chosen this floor because only six of its rooms are occupied, making it less likely that he will encounter any guests or hotel personnel in the corridor. Furthermore, three of those six rooms are occupied by owners of linen suits. Hector is carrying several freshly ironed pillowcases, the magician's diversion. He listens at the door of Room 505, hears voices whispering inside, and moves on. At Room 511, he listens again. Nothing. He raps lightly. No response. He inserts the passkey, lets himself in, and closes the door behind him.

The room has already been made up, a good sign—no maids will be barging in. He goes to the desk by the window where he opens and closes all the drawers. Nothing there other than the hotel directory and a copy of *Scuba Diving Magazine*. Same for the drawers of the bed tables. He goes to the closet. There are more sport coats, trousers, and evening dresses here than the couple could wear in several weeks. Hector pats every pocket. Not a thing. He is about to leave, but decides to scan the bathroom first.

On the shelf above the sink is a leather toiletry case. He probes inside it: several vials of pills; razor blades; Q-tips; a folded envelope. Hector lifts out this last item and opens it. It contains nine one-hundred dollar American Express checks. Hector slips the checks in his pocket. He almost laughs at the ease of it. At the door, he takes a deep breath and readjusts the expression on his face so that once again he is just another listless Latino.

He is almost at the door to the stairwell when the couple from 505 exit their room into the corridor. Hector stiffens; he fusses diligently with his load of pillowcases. The man glares at Hector while the woman stares anxiously at her feet. Once more, Hector's experiences with women tourists in Bogotá hotels inform him: The jittery woman obviously just had sex with someone other than her husband. No threat to Hector from them. He steps into the stairwell, smiling. It is his lucky day.

Hector is sitting in a La-Z-Boy recliner in the back of the van named, 'Mayflower.' There are seven other men in here, all of them brown-skinned and Spanish speaking, but not one of them is Jesus. That fellow makes more money flitting from one bottom-end Miami job to another, drumming up passengers for his human transport business, than he would make as a day worker in Connecticut, and with half the strain. Hector had intended to deposit a hundred dollars in his farewell note to Miriam, a gesture of appreciation and remorse, but Jesus quashed that plan. He took all nine hundred dollars worth of Hector's stolen traveler's checks, claiming a three hundred dollar fee for the risk involved in cashing them. So Hector just wrote to Miriam that he would think about her. He did not mention the passkey he lifted from her, the one that he hung on the wall hook outside the employee's shower just before he walked out of the Golden Glades Inn for the last time.

Although Hector has claimed the best seat in the van, the other passengers are comfortable enough. Whoever's household belongings are being carted northward is a person who prizes comfort; in addition to the La-Z-Boy, there are two easy chairs and two sofas. With a little rearranging of furniture, every man has a soft perch.

The constant darkness gets to some of them, but not Hector. After days and nights on end under flickering fluorescent tubes, the absence of light feels nurturing. It allows Hector to draw into himself in a way he has been unable to do in over a month. But the air in here does get to him. As the oxygen thins, the odor of sweat and excrement distills to a sickening gas that makes him gag. Jackson, the driver, only opens up the back of the truck for a half hour each day—always in the middle of the night, the vehicle parked on the shoulder of a desolate stretch of highway. This is the same time when Jackson sells them sandwiches and empties their slop pails. The men stand and swing their arms around, but they are not permitted outside. "Too risky," Jackson says, and Hector supposes he is right, but he also wonders how risky—and expensive—it would have been to take a public bus north. But Jesus, of course, was selling a destination as much as the means of getting there.

They arrive on the outskirts of Danbury, Connecticut, at dawn of their third morning. Jackson simply opens up the back door of the van and drawls, "This is it." The eight men are so relieved to be able to walk outside into the open air that they are not unsettled by the fact that there is no one here to greet them as Jesus promised there would be. Only after Jackson has returned to his cab and driven off, leaving them shivering in the middle of a barren road, do they realize that they have no idea where they are or where they should go.

While the other men are frightened and dumbfounded by their predicament, Hector is exhilarated. Unlike Florida, which felt like a refugee camp of fellow Latinos, this place already feels utterly foreign, and Hector senses the freedom that comes with being a total stranger. This new world, blank and brisk, seems charged with possibilities. For the first time, Hector feels like he has arrived in America.

Leading the way, Hector finds and follows signs pointing to downtown Danbury. Along the road, they pass a small illuminated building that looks like a railway car, a neon sign in front announcing, 'Hat City Diner.' Through its windows, Hector sees men drinking coffee. Most appear to be workmen and many have Hispanic faces. Hector tells his fellow travelers that he is going inside to make inquiries; all of them choose to wait for him outside rather than join him.

Hector goes directly to a stool at the low bar that runs the length of the Hat City Diner, placing himself next to a middle-aged Hispanic man in overalls. As Hector sits down, he is startled by his reflection in the mirror across from him: His drawn face, patchy beard, and red-rimmed, rheumy eyes make him look like a drug addict from Ciudad Bolivar. He sees the waitress eyeing him warily, so he immediately dips into his pocket and pulls out a five-dollar bill, one of the ten such bills that comprise his entire fortune, and places it on the counter. "One coffee and one cake," he announces in English.

"What kinda cake?" the waitress says, looking past him.

"Sweet," Hector says. He points to the Danish his stool neighbor is munching. "As so."

Leaving the money displayed on the counter, Hector finds his way to the men's toilet where he washes his face, shaves with a disposable American razor he lifted from a Golden Glades supply closet, and splashes and finger-combs his hair. When he returns, the waitress offers him an appreciative smile.

"Night shift?" she says.

Not having any idea what she is asking, Hector smiles and nods, then takes a sip of the coffee she sets in front of him. It tastes even less like *café* than the hotel's beverage of the same name. He smiles at the Latino next to him. "I've come a long way," he tells him in Spanish.

"So have we all," the man murmurs, only glancing at him for a second.

"They say there is work here. Day work in construction."

His neighbor nods. "Sometimes," he says.

"Where do I find it?"

The man does not answer.

"Let me buy you a coffee," Hector says to him.

"Listen, friend, there are too many of us already." With this, the man stands and heads for the door.

The waitress sets a Danish in front of Hector. "He's a grump," she says, gesturing with her chin toward the departing man.

"A grump," Hector repeats dumbly.

"What did you ask him?"

"Day work. Where find."

"Like it's a big secret," the woman says. "Kennedy Park." She points out the window in the direction of where the sun is just rising. Hector leaves the five-dollar bill on the counter when he walks out.

There are easily three hundred men assembled in the park. They range from smooth-faced teenagers to grizzled men in their forties—possibly older; all are Latinos. They are gathered in small groups where they talk and joke loudly with one another. Hector stands with his moving van comrades. The cold here is not dulling, like the chill from an air conditioner, but it seeps into his bones and makes him feel weak. Hector takes in long, deep breaths, his mother's prescription for countering any debilitating force.

"Play for me, boy!" This from a brawny man in the group next to Hector. The man has spied the fingerboard of Hector's *cuatro* jutting out from the pack slung over Hector's shoulder.

It would be impossible for Hector to hear those words from anyone and not immediately be brought back to Rico's Soacho hut, but to hear them delivered with *bravado* from a bully-faced man makes Hector's blood rise, ready for combat. Hector glares challengingly back at the man. The man repeats his demand, then steps away from his group and starts to strut toward Hector when a sudden hush descends on the entire population of Kennedy Park. The bully stops in his tracks. All that can be heard is the cough and rumble of combustion engines. Hector turns his eyes from the man's face. A caravan of brown and black trucks with canvas-covered flatbeds has begun circling the park. They look like military trucks, and for a second Hector imagines gun-bearing troops springing from their tailgates for a roundup of able-bodied men to join their ranks. His fantasy is close to the mark: the trucks have come to round up able-bodied laborers for back-breaking work. The confrontation between Hector and his taunter has been averted by a higher calling: cash.

Because of his height, Hector is among the first to be selected by the construction bosses. Tall men are rare in this ethnic pool and for certain tasks, like window hanging, they offer distinct advantages over five-foot-two Mexicans balanced unsteadily on stepladders. And so, within three hours of arriving in Danbury, Connecticut, Hector Mondragon becomes the 'top man' on a window-hanging crew at the building site of a new Wal-Mart store in Brookfield, Connecticut. Although he is tired and disoriented and has no idea where he will lay down his head at the end of day, Hector learns his trade quickly. At six o'clock, when a truck returns to pick up the workers,

Hector is presented with an envelope that contains a small fortune—eighty-five American dollars. That night, he sleeps on the couch in the apartment of a member of the window crew. The next morning, he arranges to make that couch his home in this new place.

In a matter of days, a rhythm is established: Up at five-thirty, genuine *café* in the kitchen he shares with the six other men in the apartment, to Kennedy Park, to a building site, back, dinner, bed. Even the work itself has a steady, predictable beat of lifting and pushing a prefabricated window into its designated frame, then balancing and bracing it as his teammates screw it in place, then lifting and pushing, balancing and bracing the next one. He sings in his mind.

The money is so good he holds on to a third of it, treats himself to dinners at the Hat City Diner twice a week, buys a radio and CD player, a bicycle, a padded overcoat, coveralls, boots; the rest of his personal allowance he stashes and locks in a tin box that he keeps in the pack he carries with him everywhere he goes. If the ache in his shoulders and the soreness in his neck pulse steadily with the beat of Hector's day, he does not think about it, and he certainly does not complain. In this regard, he has not become—nor will he ever become—thoroughly North American.

Hector is content not to think about the future. His family in Bogotá is healthy and well-supported by the money he sends home, his own life is easy and pleasant compared to the one he endured in North Miami, and the apartment he lives in is comfortable. He has companions, if not quite friends—men from Mexico, Bolivia, Chile, and even Colombia—whose lives are almost identical to his, although many have plans to bring their wives or girlfriends and children from home to live with them here. Once, on a mad impulse, Hector wrote a letter to Sylvia asking her to join him, promising her a new life in America, but she never answered. That was just as well, Hector decided in a cooler moment.

It is an early Monday morning in mid-March. Hector and his roommates are sauntering up Kennedy Boulevard on their way to the park. All have a steady gig with Boylston Contractors working on a new mall in Shelton, but they still go through the exercise of shaping up for the caravan of employers as a false gesture of equality with the other men who come out every morning. Before they can see the park, they hear people chanting in English: "Speak English!" and "Job Stealers!" and "Go home, Mexicocks!"

Hector and his fellows stop. They can now hear a counter chorus in Spanish: "*Bollo!*" and "*Asqueroso!*" and "*Foquin gringo!*"

"Protestors," one of Hector's colleagues says. "We skip work today, and they'll be gone tomorrow." He starts back toward their apartment house, and all but Hector follow him.

Hector is goaded by curiosity to stay and take a closer look. Even if he is content with the predictability of his life in Danbury, the way he has become a survivor is by always confronting the unexpected. This, in a sense, is his vocation. He continues up the hill that leads to Kennedy Park.

Wooden barricades run down the middle of the boulevard that fronts the park, uniformed policemen guarding both sides of it. The police wear helmets with clear plastic face guards, every one of them wielding a black nightstick, but to Hector the entire scene looks almost comically tame. Compared to the political riots he has witnessed in Bogotá where the police brandish—and fire—MP5s, this seems like a schoolyard feud. Indeed, its genuine peril is belied by the television cameramen who have planted themselves within feet of the putative combatants. Hector walks closer.

Just before he reaches the intersection, two white civilians in down hunting jackets advance toward him on his right. The taller of the two waves a hand-lettered picket that reads, 'INS—Where the FUCK are you?' The other glares at Hector and barks, "Fuckin' spic!"

Hector understands the man's words, but he is neither distressed nor frightened by them; their only meaning to him is that the man is crude and stupid. Hector keeps walking.

"You fuckin' deaf, Spic-head?" the man yells.

Hector stops, crooks his head toward the man, and says, "No." Then he nods genteelly and moves on.

"*Maricon!*" the man shouts at him. It is one of the four Spanish words in this man's vocabulary, all of them insults, his entire transcultural education.

In Miami, Hector had been patronized and exploited for the place of his birth and the color of his skin, but this is his first face-to-face encounter with brutal disgust based on nothing more than an abstraction of who he is. Hector has more experience than most young men as the object of personal hatred—it was a crucial part of his life in Bogotá—so perhaps that is why he can, in this moment, tolerate impersonal hatred.

"Fuckin' coward!" one of the men yells.

Reluctantly, Hector turns around to face the *gringos*. Although this last epithet is no more vicious than any of the others, it happens to increase their accumulated mass to the point that tips him to reaction. It is a matter of personal physics: Hector has simply reached his limit of passivity.

And he feels strong. He is sure he can land a blow on one of them that will be staggering enough to send them both running. But what he does not see is that there is a third man just behind the other two. This man, too, is carrying a picket but it is slung low at his side like a lance, and he suddenly comes barreling toward Hector, aiming its sharpened point at his chest. Hector spins away. The stick punctures the back of Hector's jacket, his shirt, his skin, and over an inch of tissue to where it creases his small intestine. He passes out onto the pavement. The men run. No one else sees Hector's fallen body until much later, well after the video cameramen have returned to their studios.

This, then, is how the next stage of Hector's journey begins.

He is brought in a police car to the emergency room of Danbury Hospital. Despite the fact that blood is still steadily oozing from his wound, he waits in this room for almost two hours before being seen by a doctor. Drifting in and out of consciousness while he waits, he hears the unmistakable cadences of Bogotá Spanish being spoken by two young men behind him. One of them is here because of chest pains, the other is his brother who is visiting him from a town north of Danbury where he works in the kitchen of a restaurant. Both of these men are still in the waiting room when Hector returns from being cauterized, stitched, and given a prescription for antibiotics along with the warning—translated into Spanish by a Puerto Rican nurse—to avoid heavy lifting for at least two months if he wants to keep his intestine from bursting. The name of the visiting brother from Bogotá is Pato and the name of the town he lives and works in is Grandville, Massachusetts.

CHAPTER TWENTY-TWO

From the middle of March to the middle of April is the 'fifth season' in Grandville—Mud Season. This is the time when the winter's snow begins to melt and to seep into the freshly-thawed soil faster than it can evaporate, the ubiquitous mountain springs revive and gurgle forth, and rain showers arrive almost daily. Great Pond Reservoir and Wright River overflow their banks, rivulets arise in gardens and cornfields, street gutters are ankle-deep with runoff, basement sump pumps chug away twenty-four hours a day, and virtually every home is surrounded by a mine field of puddles and muck.

Boots are general all over Grandville. Whitney Pierce, Jr., president of Grandville Savings and Loan, tucks his Brooks Brothers gray flannel trousers into an ancient pair of galoshes that he wears throughout the business day, Terrance Cyzinski, the guidance counselor at Grandville High School, laces up his water-resistant Power Foremans, Wendell deVries slips a pair of moccasin rubbers over his Clark's walkers (Wendell is the last person in town to wear rubbers), and even his former wife, Beatrice, freshly returned from Florida, dons a pair of Hunter Wellingtons to navigate from the portico of Little Sway Lodge to her Mercedes SUV. This is the sole season when complaining about the weather is not only condoned but encouraged, starting with such fifth season greetings as "Got your reservation on the Ark?" and, among the town's younger set, "Muck sucks." Most would argue that it is not the inconvenience of mud season that gets to them, it is its unsightliness. Like their founder, James Wright, today's Grandvillians are given to strong aesthetic judgments about their town.

The single ray of sunshine on all this slime comes from the lengthened days surrounding the equinox. As Herb Blitzstein's corroded Toyota slithers through the sludge of Austen Riggs's driveway at six-twenty on the last Friday in March, the setting sun shines in his eyes. He flips down the visor and a slip of notepaper flutters onto the dashboard. His passenger, Franny deVries, picks it up.

"It says, 'Check oil,'" she says.

"Shit. I bet that's been there a month."

Franny smiles, but she is not distracted from her anxiety.

Other than a half-dozen therapy group walks up and back the length of Stockbridge's Main Street, this is Franny's first expedition away from the sanitarium since she entered it over three months ago. In the week since Dr. Werner approved today's outing, Franny has changed her mind about it almost daily; chances are if it had been scheduled for tomorrow, she would be back to her position that she was not ready for it yet.

Franny cannot name what exactly it is out there that frightens her. As she gradually admitted to herself that it was nothing more dramatic than attending an amateur production of a simple-minded play that pushed her past reason into the depths of depression, she had to confront the possibility that absolutely anything could do it again. Of course, Dr. Werner insists that it was not Babs Dowd's play—or her takeover of the playhouse—that precipitated Franny's breakdown. No, the true cause of that can only be found in the more distant past—in Franny's childhood, to be precise. Franny finds Werner's line of reasoning about as compelling as the feel-good message underlying Herb's 'It's-the-little-things-that-change-the course-of-history' film series. But then again, there did seem to be *some* connection between Herb's movies and her precipitous announcement made during the roll of the end credits of *Sliding Doors* that she had been thinking about going to a Grandville war vigil again. That is where they are headed now.

"Did I tell you we've got some new people?" Herb says.

"Nope." Franny is staring out the passenger's window, both hands gripped to her seatbelt. The Christmas trimmings the Red Lion Inn still displays on its porch are mud-splattered and frayed, a timely reminder of the real season.

"There's Gloria, a friend of Tiffany's. Her daughter enlisted in the Navy. And a pair of geriatric Lefties from New York—gay, I think, and very funny. They sing."

Franny nods. They are on Route 7 approaching the Grandville town line. She can see Grandville High in the distance, the building lit up and the parking lot full. She tries to remember what sport is played in March. Still basketball? Volleyball?

"Does Stephanie Cyzinski still come?" Franny asks.

"Yup. She skipped for a while, but now she's back every night."

Climbing the foothill at the base of Wright Mountain, Herb's car sputters and backfires. He yanks it into first gear and pulls as far to the right as he can so the cars behind him can pass.

"The Little Engine That Couldn't," Herb says.

Franny looks at him. Whenever she asks herself what she feels about Herb, she comes up empty. God knows, she does not find him particularly exciting and she certainly does not find him sexy, although the truth is her libido seems to be sunk in the same deep sleep as most of her other feelings. She certainly feels gratitude toward him, but what else? Brotherhood? *Dependency?*

Nakota's much maligned spire appears at the crest of the hill and Franny shrinks back in her seat. One emotion has undeniably awakened inside her, and awakened with a vengeance: her guilt about Lila. She is now convinced she never gave enough to her daughter—enough time, enough understanding, enough love. Grudgingly, Franny has allowed this feeling to become Topic A in her thrice-weekly sessions with Werner, and inevitably the good doctor turns it around to Franny's experiences with her own mother. Was Franny unconsciously duplicating her mother's attitudes toward her with her own daughter? A repetition compulsion, perhaps? *Blah, blah, and more blah.*

Only once did Werner raise a question that resonated for Franny and that was when he asked about Lila's father, Jean-Marc. Just saying his name out loud elicited more bitterness in Franny than she thought she had left inside her. And despite the glint of 'gotcha' in Dr. Werner's eyes, she dug into that bitterness to try to find what it was made of.

It was not hard to recall how dazzled she had been by Jean-Marc Fournier when he arrived on the Ithaca College campus in the spring term of her junior year, a last-minute substitute for the Advanced Design instructor who had suddenly landed a production job in New York. Jean-Marc was Parisian, forty, long-haired, and slender. As a younger man, he had studied pantomime with Marcel Marceau. His specialties were opera sets and young women. Franny had been fully aware of his reputation as a womanizer when she took up with him, but the affair was so consuming, her connection to him and his wondrous world so intense, so unlike anything she had ever experienced with men her own age, that she did not doubt for a moment the affair was unique for Jean-Marc as well. She was terribly wrong about that, of course. By the time Franny realized she was pregnant, Jean-Marc had moved on to another young drama student.

"Did you consider terminating the pregnancy?" Werner had asked.

"No."

"You don't believe in abortion?"

"It just wasn't an option for me."

"Because you were in love with him?"

"I don't know."

"Because you thought abortion was bad?"

"What the hell does that mean, Doctor?"

"You sound angry."

"And you sound like a recorded message."

"Is it possible that some of the resentment you felt—you *feel*—for this man was unintentionally transferred to his child?"

Well, fuck yes, Doctor—Anything's possible. But what does any of this ancient history have to do with who I am now? Where the hell does it get me?

"I have no idea," Franny answered the psychiatrist.

They are cruising down Main Street in Grandville. Franny is struck anew by the lived-in authenticity of her hometown as compared to the period piece stage set that is downtown Stockbridge. It occurs to her that Austen Riggs, an institution dedicated to self-consciousness, is perfectly matched with its locale.

"Wow! Great turnout tonight," Herb says, pointing through the windshield.

Franny sees a good ten or twelve people in front of the town hall. More than half are holding up pickets that say,

'Support our Troops—Bring them home!' or 'Be patriotic! Stop the war!' or 'Peace now!' The death count—782 American soldiers and 2,300 Iraqis—is displayed in red chalk on a large wood-framed blackboard that is illuminated by a floodlight hung from a poplar tree. Virtually every protestor is splattered with mud thrown from the wheels of passing motorists. One of their number, an older man sporting a Russian fur hat, a red, white, and blue scarf around his neck, its long end thrown debonairly over his shoulder, is standing in the street, facing the others. He is waving his arms, conductor-like. Herb rolls down his window. The group is singing "Donna Nobis Pacem" in a round.

Franny never asked Herb if he told the others she was coming tonight, but as she and Herb walk across Melville Street toward them, she realizes that not only did he tell them, they all must have discussed how to behave around her and come to the decision to act as if nothing was out of the ordinary. They nod and smile, but keep singing, segueing smoothly from "Donna Nobis" to "Give Peace a Chance." Franny stands slightly behind the group under a tree. She feels a little dizzy.

Suddenly, Stephanie Cyzinski breaks away from the others. She just cannot do it the way they planned any longer. She comes running towards Franny, her arms spread wide. "God, it's good to see you!" Stephanie says, hugging her.

Franny stiffens in the girl's arms. She has not hugged or been hugged for so long it feels unnatural—not oppressive, simply confounding, as if it is a ritual of an alien clan. Stephanie lets go, backs away. "I'm sorry," she says. "I get excited."

"Please don't be sorry," Franny says. "I'm just out of it, I guess."

"I'm sorry," Stephanie says again.

"How have you been, Stephanie?" Franny asks. This, too—asking somebody other than a group therapy member how she is today—feels arcane to Franny. Yet she finds herself unaccountably eager to hear the young woman's reply.

"I'm okay," Stephanie says. She senses that Franny is asking the question in a more personal way than people usually do and adds, "Now, at least. I went through something kind of weird. Not awful, just strange. But I'm good now."

"I'm glad it worked out," Franny says. This little exchange, banal in the extreme by the standards of everyday discourse, feels more charged with humanity than any conversation Franny has had in the past three months.

Running a changing light signal, a milk truck comes barreling across the intersection of Main and Melville, and every one of its eight wheels flings a good shovelful of muck in the group's direction, one sailing so high it passes over the heads of the others and smacks Franny square in the chest. The singing halts. In spite of themselves, the singers turn and stare apprehensively at Franny.

"Baptized!" Franny cheers. Her smile comes from the same place whence smiles once came before her breakdown.

Franny is introduced around to the new 'vigil-istas': Tiffany's friend, Gloria, the two New York old timers, Gary and Tony (it is Gary who is the group's self-appointed music director, and yes, there is no doubt the pair is gay), and three members of Marta's Unitarian Universalist congregation, all middle-aged and thrilled to be out of their homes at dinnertime. Franny sings along in the next set, a medley of "Masters of War," "I Ain't Marching Anymore," and "Imagine." At one point in this last number, Tony takes a solo turn in which he mimics the stammers and inappropriate smiles of the Commander in Chief. Everyone roars. For a moment, Franny wonders if the vigil has lost its purpose: Everyone is having too much fun for it to be about death and injustice. But then she sees that Tiffany and Gloria, the mothers of beloved children who will soon be shipped off to battlefields, are laughing too. Franny had a drama professor in college who said the basic difference between tragedy and comedy is that the tragic hero is racked with despair while the comic hero cannot help but believe that salvation is right around the corner, and while he fumbles his way to that corner, he has a few laughs. When the next eight-wheeler brakes for a red light at the intersection, all the protestors scurry off the curb into the gutter. Some raise their signs, but most need both hands to shield their faces as the truck lurches off the mark and rumbles towards them, pitching mud as she goes. It is a game, its object to see who can take the biggest, juiciest hit of muck. One of the Unitarians wins this round.

At seven-thirty, they start breaking down their setup—removing the floodlight from the tree, stashing it and the blackboard and pickets into the back of Gary and Tony's pickup truck. Only now does Tiffany speak to Franny. "Thanks for the job," she says.

It takes Franny a moment to realize Tiffany is talking about filling in on Sundays at Write Now. "It's good for Wendell too," Franny says.

"I suppose . . . I mean, now that you're better, you won't be needing me anymore."

Franny studies Tiffany's face for signs of embarrassment, even mere uneasiness, but she sees neither. It is clear Tiffany's only concern is her once-a-week job and its income, not Franny's breakdown and her apparent recovery. Franny's old self would have been revolted by Tiffany's selfishness, but in the moment Franny sees Tiffany's priorities as no more and no less than what they need to be. "Nothing's going to change," Franny tells Tiffany, touching her shoulder.

"We'd better get back," Herb whispers in Franny's ear. Her curfew is eight o'clock.

"Okay," Franny says, but she does not move. For the first time, she is allowing herself to look up Melville Street. Write Now is closed, a bundle of unsold newspapers in front of its door. The Phoenix appears closed too, two dumpsters parked in front, both jammed to the brim. The marquee, however, is illuminated, black letters declaring *INTERMEZZO*. Apparently Babs Dowd's idea of wit had not changed. Franny feels mild amusement, nothing more. No anger, no contempt, no jealousy. And so it is that with a serene sense of certainty, Franny decides on the spot that she has finally and completely returned to strength and reason. "Let's just drop by my house first," she says to Herb.

"I don't think it's on the agenda this time, Fran," he answers.

"Oh, come on!"

"Really, I think this is supposed to be an incremental thing, you know?"

"Jesus, Herb, I can handle it. Stop treating me like some kind of nut case, would you?"

"I thought you *were* some kind of nut case," Herb replies, laughing. It is obvious he has already given in to Franny, just

~ 251 ~

as it would be obvious to any casual passerby that Herbert Blitzstein is very much in love with her.

Franny can hear voices and laughter coming from her house the moment she steps out of the car. As she starts toward the front door ahead of Herb, she tries to identify the voices; Wendell's seems easy enough to pick out and she thinks she hears Lila's too—although isn't this a work night for her? Mounting the front porch stairs, Franny realizes the cheery voices are not coming from her house, but from the one it is attached to, and she wonders why her father never mentioned it had been rented again. She is reaching for the knob of her front door when another round of laughter erupts in the neighbor's house and this time there is no doubt that she hears her father's laugh. She swings her legs over the low divide that cuts the porch in equal halves and steps to the neighbor's front window. Inside, she sees a table that runs most of the length of what, in her house, is the living room. A family is eating dinner there: Her father, Esther, Esther's children, Kaela and Johnny, and a black woman about Franny's age.

Herb is just behind Franny when she abruptly backs away from the window. Although he cannot see that the blood has drained from Franny's face, he senses her unsteadiness and reflexively grasps her around the waist. He braces her trembling body against his own all the way back to the car. Neither of them speak the entire ride back to Austen Riggs.

Of the people eating dinner at that table—it was Emmanuelle's turn to cook and she had again made her fabulous pot roast—only Kaela spotted Franny through the window. Kaela only glimpsed her for a moment, a fraction of which she doubted her eyes, thinking the face she saw must be a distorted reflection of someone—*her mother?*—inside the room. But in the remaining fraction, Kaela saw Franny's face turn from a look of wonder to one of utter desolation before it vanished from view. That look of desolation frightened the child, and the size of her fright was so overwhelming she decided not to tell anyone what she had seen.

CHAPTER TWENTY-THREE

Michael Dowd's instincts have always served him well. God knows, his success in the stock market is more a result of hunches than of calculations. He has a seer's sense of the fluctuations of supply and demand, a gift that permits him to move far faster than his peers who need to construct and consult elaborate charts on their computers before making a buy. His talent is not limited to stock picks either: He pretty much chose his wife on instinct, virtually making the decision to spend the rest of his life with her on the day he met her at a Young Democrats convention in Boston when he was a senior at Harvard. The same went for the town he chose to live in after the events of 9/11 persuaded him to leave Manhattan. And despite the fact that most people think it was Babs who made the decision to purchase, renovate, and manage the Phoenix Theater, it is Michael who instantly saw what a rare opportunity it was: He could turn a nice profit for himself and his friends *and* give his wife her heart's fondest desire in one sweet deal.

But lately Michael has been dithering. It is not that his stream of inspirations has dried up, but his trust in them is faltering. One morning last month after reading an article in the *Times*, he got right on the phone and bought six hundred thousand dollars' worth of stock in CounterPoint Body Armor, Incorporated. No need to pour over CounterPoint's books; the article stated that the new phase of the war in Iraq was ninety-percent close combat and Michael knew that CounterPoint was the Defense Department's pet supplier of bullet-proof vests. Michael was right, but wrong: indeed, CounterPoint landed a three million-dollar defense contract, but their product turned out to be flawed: bullets could penetrate it. The Marine Corps returned the goods after some thirty-five troops discovered this defect through personal experience. CounterPoint's stock tumbled and Michael's mutual fund suffered a half-million dollar loss. Michael's confidence took a hit too. Lately, he has been constructing labor-intensive charts of his own before he makes a buy, not that his results have improved significantly.

Also, Michael's gut decision following Daphne's little imbroglio at Hotchkiss—to have her live at home and attend the local public high school—has turned out to be less than satisfactory. Last week when Babs probed Daphne's backpack, she discovered two 'joints,' hand-rolled marijuana cigarettes, confirming one of Babs's worst fears about public schools. (Her absolute worst fear is that Daphne will end up at one of those third-rate colleges all the graduates of Grandville High seemed to attend.) Babs blames Michael for Daphne's 'drug habit,' as she calls it.

Even now Michael is dithering. He cannot make up his mind what footwear would be best for his evening jog: his New Balance night reflectors or his L.L.Bean work boots. The advantage of the latter is obvious in mud season, especially after today's afternoon shower. Even the extra weight of the boots could be considered a plus, aerobic-wise. But the running shoes are far more comfortable for one thing and for another they are, well, spiffier. Michael is well aware that spiffiness hardly qualifies as a consideration in most circumstances, and certainly not after dark on a desolate stretch of road. Yet how Michael looks to *himself* matters more to him lately, possibly because Babs is so preoccupied with her evening meetings dedicated to developing the theater's first season that she rarely spends any time with him anymore. Somehow, eyeing himself approvingly in the hallway mirror—his crimson Harvard sweatshirt definitely gives him a boyish air—compensates for his wife's inattention. He goes with New Balance.

It is this Terry Cyzinski business that has shaken Michael's faith the most, more in other people than in himself, although it was his own naïve trust in other people that contributed to making this molehill into a mammoth mud pile. At first, Michael assured Cyzinski that his daughter must be mistaken in her presumption that the upcoming vacant woman's spot on Harvard's royal tennis team was already spoken for, but one call to Assistant Dean of Admissions, Rupert Crawley III, confirmed that Stephanie was right, even if Crawley insisted that there are a hundred factors that go into selecting every 'admit,' right up until the end. But Crawley's oh-so-casual mention of Mark Saunders Sr.'s 'generous support' of Harvard's athletic program made it abundantly clear that some factors figure significantly more than the ninety-nine others.

Naturally, Michael wanted to know how this fuck-up had come to pass—it was Crawley himself who had told Michael just last fall about the forthcoming open position on the royal tennis team. But Michael did not challenge the assistant dean; that would have been ill-mannered. Although Michael Dowd never made any friends among the Harvard Brahmins when he was an undergraduate, he did pick up their rules of deportment. What is more, Michael's son, Mike Jr., will be applying to Harvard in just three years' time, so Michael certainly cannot risk antagonizing Crawley.

Michael called back Cyzinski in his office at Grandville High and reiterated the Crawley line: No decisions would be made until all the applications were in, so Stephanie was definitely still in the running. Cyzinski was not mollified. In fact, it was already in that phone call that the guidance counselor began using inappropriate language.

"In other words, you lied to me," Cyzinski said.

"I admit there was a mix-up, Terry," Michael replied calmly. "But I'm going to do everything I can to make sure they give Stephanie a real good look."

"A real good look," Cyzinski repeated mockingly.

And then Michael had another hapless brainstorm. "You know where we should be putting our efforts now, Terry? We should think about other ways we can make Stephanie stand out from the crowd, don't you think?"

"No, what I think is that you're full of crap. That's what stands out to me."

"I don't think that kind of talk is necessary, Terry."

"Fuck you, Dowd!"

Michael hung up. He decided to give Cyzinski some time to cool off and then to take him out for a drink and smooth things over. Cyzinski, however, keeps phoning almost every day, and Michael has taken to having his assistant tell Cyzinski he is not in.

"Going out for a run, Daph!" Michael calls up to his daughter before heading out the door. He does not wait for a reply because there never is one. Even though Daphne routinely breaks the house rule and locks her bedroom door, Michael is pretty certain she does not smoke marijuana up there; he surely would be able to smell it. What she does seem to do is listen to god-awful music for hours on end while sitting at her computer. Babs says Daphne has one of those teen blogs where kids share their gripes with other kids all around the country. No harm in that, Michael figures; it is probably a good way for her to get things off her chest.

The moon is high and almost full, casting sharp shadows off the plane trees that line the driveway and sparkling in the puddles that dot the lawn. As always, Michael draws in several deep breaths in quick succession as he sets off on his way, and as always he is thrilled by the freshness of the country air. No matter what little setbacks he has encountered lately, he knows he could never go back to city living.

Turning onto Pickwick Road, Michael's left foot slaps into mud and he skids an inch or two, but he immediately catches his balance and keeps loping along, smiling broadly. That little slip and his smooth recovery invigorate him; rather than slow his pace, he accelerates, almost hoping he hits another slick patch so his reflexes can snap on and make him right again. So it is that when he approaches his regular quarter-way point— where Hobb Hill branches off of Pickwick—and hears a car behind him, he does not break stride, but simply hops over to his right where he lands in a silty stream of runoff and slides a good six inches in the stuff, his other foot aloft as ballast as if he was a figure skater. And he keeps running. He feels terrific. Even as the oncoming car whizzes past him and wallops him head to foot with mud, the feeling stays with him. He is a glider, not a plodder.

At the old van Deusen farm, Michael makes a U-turn and heads back for home. Without really thinking about it—or much of anything else, for that matter—he has come to the conclusion that it is time to start trusting his instincts again. Sure, there will be a slipup here and there, but he still has the gift, no doubt about it. And when all is said and done, his instincts are what have brought him to where he is today. This is what Michael Dowd is thinking as he sees a pair of headlights come off Hobb Hill and head in his direction. Once again, he springs into the gutter ready to glide on one foot, but this time he slides sideways rather than forward, and as he tries to catch his balance, he flops onto his side on the road where the oncoming car swerves across the center line and makes for him. It bounces over Dowd, crushing the femurs of both his thighs. The car does not stop.

* * *

Lila was late getting to work this evening. Flip's cruiser had again been parked across the street from Grandville High at the end of the school day—the idiot simply cannot grasp the meaning of 'No'—so Lila took the school bus into town and then the Loop Bus back to the restaurant to avoid another stupid confrontation with him. As a result, no sooner had she changed into her work gear than she was sent onto the floor to wait on a table of early birds—a New York second-homer family that had obviously run out of daylight activities prematurely, it being mud season, and that, predictably, wanted to know if they could still order off the lower-priced lunch menu. No, they could not.

For this reason, Lila was unable to slip out the Nakota kitchen door for her regular startup toke with Pato until the New Yorkers were served. But now, standing outside that door, she finds she is in no hurry to get to Pato. She is listening to a voice that comes from the vicinity of the dumpster. It is softly singing a love song in Spanish—something about black flowers—accompanied by an instrument that sounds like a ukulele, only more resonant.

Unlike most young women her age, Lila has little attraction to music of any kind, and none to love songs. She is of the opinion that love songs are not about any real experience, but about an experience invented by love songs. Growing up in a house where for a good month of every year her mother and her little troupe of wannabe actors yodeled songs like "If Ever I Would Leave You" and "Hello, Young Lovers" and, the most nauseating of all, "Some Enchanted Evening," Lila is convinced that if any of them ever *really* fell in love, they certainly would find something more fulfilling to do than sing about it.

So it is that Lila surprises herself listening to the Spanish love song. She knows just enough of that language to understand that the love it sings of is a transient thing. The song is no zippy cheer or cloying whine; its intent is not to set feet tapping or elicit moans of saccharine sympathy. The song is stark and painfully sad. Even if she could not understand a single word of the lyric, Lila would know that the song's ultimate concern is time itself, and the futility of trying to hold it still. It is not simply the melody that conveys this to her, it is the voice itself.

She cannot guess the age of the singer. The voice has some of the squeaks and overtones of an adolescent, but it also contains a tremor of yearning that Lila associates with people who are much older. What Lila is hearing for the first time is a voice that expresses feelings she did not know she, herself, possessed. It is a revelation.

When the song is over, the audience of Spanish busboys responds with subdued applause, and Lila hears Pato ask for another. That is when she walks to the dumpster and sees the singer, a young man with high angled cheekbones and thick black hair who is taller than any South American Lila has seen before. He has large brown eyes that match the ache in his voice. He is beautiful. Pato offers Lila the joint smoldering in his hand, but she declines with a quick shake of her head.

"I'm Lila," she says, extending her hand to the young man.

"And I Hector." He slings his *cuatro* over his shoulder before taking her hand.

"You're new," she says.

"Every minute," Hector answers, and he smiles.

Lila laughs. "What about this minute?"

"Very new for me," Hector says.

Takaaki calls Lila from the kitchen door, telling her that Table Five is ready to order dessert, so that is it. Business is unusually brisk for a mud season Friday night, so Lila only sees Hector when she dashes in and out of the kitchen where he has been assigned the starters' job of stripping soy beans. They smile to one another, quickly and shyly. That is all.

But during a lull in customer traffic at a little past nine, Lila calls Wendell from the restaurant pay phone and tells him she has a ride home. In fact, she does not have one—she has no idea how she will get home—and she feels guilty lying to her grandfather. She also feels ridiculously childish, but that does not bother her.

At eleven-thirty, after helping with cleanup, Lila changes back into her regular clothes and puts on her leather jacket and Mucksters boots. She says goodnight to Takaaki who, unusually perceptive among her sister waitresses, touches Lila's cheek and says, "He is very pretty." When Lila exits the kitchen door, Hector is standing apart from the other Spanish boys. She steps up to him and says, "I can show you our town, if you want."

"I would like it."

Walking along the highway, their conversation jumps from one unfinished sentence to another so rapidly that Lila does not even try to keep straight the people and places of Hector's odyssey from his mountain village in Colombia to here in western Massachusetts, although the sheer distance of his journey electrifies her. In truth, even if Hector were speaking slowly and without an accent, Lila would have difficulty following his words; her ears cannot begin to compete with her eyes as they trace the delicate contours of Hector's face, drift to his long, tar-black hair, and then to his deep-set eyes that are at once mournful and full of life. From those eyes, Lila can discern what he has lived through more perfectly than from any words. The enchantment Lila feels looking at Hector is a totally new experience for her, and his beauty is only part of it. She senses a deep familiarity in his foreignness; he is the other world she has relentlessly dreamt about suddenly made flesh and blood. She reaches for his hand just as he reaches for hers. The lyric of "Mis Flores Negras" notwithstanding, time stands still.

When they reach the iron bridge that crosses Wright River, marking the point where Route 7, for a mile and a half, becomes Grandville's Main Street, a passing oil truck showers them with mud.

"Now you know why we call this mud season," Lila says, laughing.

Hector wipes his face, then holds his hand in front of his eyes. "They make houses of this in Bogotá."

"We could make hundreds of them with all the mud we've got in Grandville," Lila says.

"No, just one house. For us," Hector says. They have just crossed the river when he says this. Ahead of them, about a quarter of a mile into town, is the red neon sign hanging out-side Cohen's Hardware and Plumbing, and beyond that, the traffic light at the corner of Main and Melville. Lila puts her arms around Hector's neck and they press their mud-flecked lips together. It tastes to Lila like the sweet center of the Earth.

III

~ The Other World ~

CHAPTER TWENTY-FOUR

Among the retirees enrolled in the spring term session of 'Phil of Flicks' is an unusually supple-minded man in his seventies who made millions with a string of video rental shops on Long Island—Spiros Papacristo. Not only does Papacristo possess an encyclopedic knowledge of films—he once prided himself on his ability to make personal recommendations to each individual customer—but he has a philosophical turn of mind. As he had never read a philosophical tract nor taken a philosophy course before now—indeed, he had not attended college—this aptitude came as a surprise to both him and his teacher.

After screening It's a Wonderful Life, Back to the Future, Groundhog Day, and Sliding Doors in successive class sessions, Professor Blitzstein presented a thumbnail sketch of the concept of cause and effect in modern philosophy, starting with David Hume's billiard balls. No sooner had Herb finished when Spiros raised his hand.

"If everything has a cause, then every cause has a cause too, right?" he said.

Herb nodded enthusiastically.

"So the whole thing—you know, everything in the universe—is the effect of something else, going back and back forever."

Herb was so thrilled he could have walked right down the aisle of his classroom and hugged the man. He knew where Spiro was heading with his astonishing native reasoning—to the question of how it all began: What was the First Cause? And so Herb immediately began mentally rehearsing his reply, a comparison of the idea of creatio ex nihilo—that the First Cause came into the void out of nowhere—with the even more mind-boggling idea that cause and effect have simply always existed, so there is no First Cause, just causes reaching back infinitely. But as it turned out, Spiros Papacristo, a forward-looking man since he arrived in America as a teenager from Crete, had the future on his mind, not the past.

"So all these causes are still out there, right? Popping away every minute of the day, just the way they did starting on Day One, right, Professor?"

Herb was not only enraptured by Papacristo's snap induction, but thrilled to at last have an opportunity to talk about one of his all-time favorite philosophers, the little-remembered Pierre-Simon, Marquis de Laplace, and his imaginary wily demon. The Laplacian Demon is an all-knowing mega-mind that can comprehend every cause out there and therefore can predict with certainty the future down to the smallest detail.

"In other words," Herb said, addressing himself to the only student still listening, "everything that happens was predestined to happen, and it always will be. Kind of takes a load off, doesn't it?"

Spiros Papacristo burst out laughing.

As could be predicted, Spiros Papacristo wanted to hear more about this heady stuff and so, after class that night, he invited Herb to the Soup and Sandwich for tuna melts and coffee. There, they talked for hours on subjects that are usually reserved for bright and eager college students in their late teens and early twenties. Herb was even inspired to confide in his star student an idea for a new course that has been playing in his mind for years, the course he calls, 'The History of Now.'

"When does 'now' begin and when does it end?" Herb asked as Papacristo smiled delightedly. "Is the present so infinitesimal that we can never be fully conscious of it?"

At about the time Ted Sturget, Soup and Sandwich's night cook, was ready to close up, Spiro raised the question of how we decide to partition off time into specific periods. "It's like trying to divide up the water in a bathtub," Spiros said. "Who says the Golden Age of Greece started in this particular year and ended in some other one?" he asked, citing the one period of history that every modern Greek schoolboy learns about in first grade.

For Herb, the simple answer would be that people basically need to make neat portions of things to keep their minds focused so, along with everything else they think about, they divide history into neat portions too. But he senses that Mr. Papacristo is reaching for a different kind of answer, one that has preoccupied Herb, himself, since he was a kid. It is about Beginnings and Ends, and it is at the core of his incubating course:

In the narrative of a human life, what is the beginning and what is the end? Do 'birth' and 'death' do the trick? Or is that as arbitrary as saying the Golden Age of Greece began in 506 B.C. and ended in 404 B.C.? Do birth and death leave out too much of what makes a person who he is, all the causes that led up to his life, and all the effects that followed from it? But then again, wouldn't such a fully inclusive drama murmur on endlessly—an eternal Now?

* * *

To a musician, it would sound like utter dissonance or perhaps a newly-uncovered, cacophonous medley of American classics by Charles Ives, but to the people of Grandville the sound in the air is unmistakably and joyously the music of their annual Memorial Day parade, a salute not only to their fallen soldiers but to the unofficial conclusion of Mud Season. The symphony begins at the head of the parade with a fife and two drums played by members of the Grandville Chamber of Commerce, Syd Cohen, Whitney Pierce, Jr., and Mel Gustal, chosen more for their willingness to don Revolutionary War garb—and in Gustal's case, a *faux* head bandage—than their musicality. Pierce, the piccolo player, is interpreting "Yankee Doodle Dandy," but he can barely hear himself over the blaring trumpets and trombones of Grandville High's marching band just behind him. The high school band is playing a pasticcio of Sousa, Humperdinck, and the Beatles, as arranged by its music director, Mrs. Hammond who, remarkably, is conducting while marching backwards. As always, the band's volume is formidable, possibly in compensation for its intonation. Only a buffer of solemn-faced, uniformed veterans separates them from the next wellspring of music, the speakers mounted on the hood of a vintage Buick convertible. From these issue the recorded strains of the Mormon Tabernacle Choir which, having just completed, "When Johnny Comes Marching Home Again," is belting out "I'm Looking Over a Four-Leaf Clover." Bill Lakspur, the chairman of the Grandville Board of Selectman, is driving the open convertible, one hand on the steering wheel, the other waving to the folks lining Main Street. Some of the Boy and Girl Scouts, Cub Scouts and Brownies, plus a representative of the local constabulary, Flip Morris, all strolling behind the automobile, appear to be singing along with the Mormons. Bringing up the rear of the parade is the final lyrical touch, Stephanie Cyzinski's recently dumped boyfriend, Matt Maxwell, and his garage band, The Tombstones. All four boys are playing electric guitars, a rat's nest of wires and electronic gadgets snaking around their torsos and leading to a car battery and a pair of TDK Outloud speakers that ride behind them in a Gemini hand truck pushed by Matt's younger brother, Paul. The Tombstones are playing and singing Matt's latest composition, "Sick and Tired," a protest song of sorts, one he wrote with the hope of impressing Stephanie; however the lyrics, even when audible, are unintelligible.

"No doubt about it, we were right to vote down Gary," Herb says. He is standing with Franny at the open window of his apartment over Digby's Music Shop on Main Street. They can see—and hear—the entire sweep of the parade from their commanding perch.

Franny nods in the affirmative. Gary had proposed to the vigil group that they march in the parade, carrying their placards whilst singing "I'm Not Marching Anymore." Both Tiffany and Gloria had objected on the grounds that it would be disrespectful to the veterans and their fallen brothers, and that put an end to the idea. Not only because Tiffany and Gloria are mothers of new recruits, but because they enjoy a special 'grassroots' status as a result of their social background, they are the group's arbiters of Grandville good taste. What Herb meant, however, was that even if they had sung the antiwar anthem in the parade no one would have heard them.

"Holy shit!" Herb says. He is pointing toward the gaggle of veterans—a little under thirty in all—that is now passing under the window. From their uniforms, faces, and gaits, the men and women appear to be grouped by the wars in which they fought: in the lead, three World War Two army veterans, two with canes, one with an aluminum walker; next, about a dozen men and women from the Korean conflict; next, a dozen from the Vietnam War; and finally, two veterans of the Persian Gulf War, both of them women. Herb is pointing at the Vietnam contingent. He grabs up a pair of binoculars, stares intently through them, then hands them to Franny. "Fantastic!" he says.

Franny immediately makes out Herb's target: Gary and Tony in military uniforms. Tony's jacket is emblazoned with more ribbons and medals than any of his marching fellows. As far as Franny knows, neither of them had ever mentioned to the vigil group that they had served in the military.

"Their hands," Herb whispers urgently.

And now Franny sees that the two septuagenarian men are very discreetly, yet not entirely out of view, holding hands as they parade by.

"Good for them," Franny murmurs.

With the binoculars still to her eyes, she has started methodically inspecting every face on Main Street. She is looking for Lila. Franny knows that Lila stopped attending these parades years ago, but she searches on the chance that Lila made an exception this year so she could show her South American boyfriend another highlight of Grandville life. According to Wendell, among Lila's myriad personality changes since taking up with Hector is, amazingly, a newly adopted pride in her hometown. Apparently Hector, who has lived in many places, considers Grandville far and away the most civilized of them all. A paradise, he says, and Lila, learning about the wider world from her lover in a way she never could at Grandville High, has evidently quickly come to see her town from his perspective.

Franny cannot find her daughter out there. Since she was released from Austen Riggs four weeks ago and taken up residence in an apartment over Cohen's Hardware, Franny has only seen Lila twice, both times in the company of Wendell and Esther. Lila's transformation was obvious the moment Franny laid eyes on her. Lila's face was animated, her complexion luminous, her laughter easy and frequent. She even hugged Franny and whispered, "I'm glad you're better," the first time they saw one another. But they have not met alone or talked on the phone, and Franny still has not met Hector. Franny cannot help but think the reason for this is that Lila is afraid her mother could somehow ruin her wonderful new life.

Franny can easily understand why Lila might feel that way. Franny may now be safe from the specter of a major depressive episode and the irrational behavior that goes with it, but she remains dull and hesitant. She is not good company. In Lila's parlance, she is a 'downer' and Franny knows it. Lately, Franny has considered the possibility that mothers and daughters are ineluctably locked in a zero-sum game of happiness, that ultimately it took her breakdown for Lila to become her own person. By this calculus, Franny is hopelessly stuck between her own mindlessly chipper mother and her newly exhilarated daughter.

But Franny's greatest anxiety is that Lila is afraid she will not approve of Hector. Franny can understand that all too well, too. Because the truth of the matter is the very idea of a handsome young man from an exotic country sweeping her daughter off her feet fills Franny with anxiety, and one need not be a graduate of Austen Riggs to understand why.

Scanning the parade watchers, Franny now sees Stephanie Cyzinski next to a short, red-haired girl wearing an old-fashioned pinafore, the two of them standing behind a man in a wheelchair. The man's legs are enclosed in casts surrounded by metal braces. It is Michael Dowd and he, remarkably, appears to be enjoying the festivities. Franny knows about his accident from Wendell—an early evening hit-and-run out near Dowd's house. Apparently there was not much of a police investigation, but then there was not much for them to go on anyhow. Franny feels a fleeting quiver of distaste for Stephanie and her solicitous stance in this little tableau: the girl seems to glom to wounded people like Tiffany Korand and her son, Bret. Franny moves her binoculars on.

Wendell, Esther, Kaela, and Johnny are standing at the corner of Main and Melville in the spot where the vigil group usually gathers. Wendell has one arm around Esther's waist, the other over Kaela's shoulder. Johnny, standing in front of them, is waving an American flag on the end of a dowel stick with one hand, while eating a hot dog held in the other. They are the picture perfect all-American family of the twenty-first century—multicultural, with a white-haired *pater familias* and a sexy-looking, baby boomer mamma. Franny wishes to God she could feel happier for them. That will come in time, Dr. Werner has assured her.

The evening Franny saw Wendell and his new extended family through the porch window, her world changed irrevocably. And when she told Dr. Werner what she had seen and how it made her feel, the psychiatrist—for the moment, at least—changed also. "They were so alive," Franny told him. "Bigger than life, really. And they made it look so easy—you know, just enjoying each other, all of them. So effortlessly. But it was—I don't know—not completely real. Not connected to anything outside their little world. Like they only existed for themselves."

Listening, Werner found himself gazing through that window with her. For once and finally, Dr. Werner was able to enter the place where Franny lived, not through the pre-fabricated doors of psychoanalytic theory, but through the fundamental passageway to understanding another human being: imagination. Without thinking, he pushed aside the ever-ready Electra complex with its sexual sparks of father love, and simply imagined being Franny deVries. What Rolf Werner understood in that moment might seem banal to many people, to, say, someone like the historian, Emmanuelle Jones, who spends almost every waking hour imaginatively inhabiting the skin of other human beings. What Werner grasped is that every person, no matter how wounded, is the final arbiter of the meaning of everything in her own life.

"It's incredible how quickly people get on with their lives," the doctor said to Franny in his office at the sanitarium. "They just do. They get on without you."

Franny nodded, holding back her tears.

"I mean, I'm sure if you just went over and knocked on the door, they'd welcome you with open arms. But you'd probably feel like an intruder. An outsider."

Franny remained silent.

"I don't know what you can do," Werner said finally. And then the psychiatrist offered his patient the simplest, yet truest counsel: "Except—when it is possible—to get on with life. On your own. You know, the best you can."

Franny hands the binoculars back to Herb and goes to the couch in Herb's living room where she stretches out on her back and listens, trying to distinguish a single melody from the musical muddle.

Watching the contingent of Grandville veterans' parade in front of him, Wendell is bewildered. As always, he is profoundly moved by these men and women who risked their lives for the honor of their country, but his qualms and suspicions about his country's current military adventure are twisting his respect for these people into shame. Or, at least, pity. For the first time he can remember, Wendell is confused by the idea of patriotism.

Heaven knows, he had more reason to be confused back in the sixties when he drew a high number in the draft lottery for the Vietnam War. He did not think much of that war either, although more because it did not seem to have anything to do with America than because he believed it was immoral. But he never considered registering for conscientious objector status or moving with his wife and daughter to Canada. Basically he just held his breath, and when President Johnson declared that young married men with children were exempt from the draft, he simply shrugged with relief and got on with his life, fairly oblivious to the fact that a good dozen of his Grandville High classmates were shipped off to Asia, one of them never to return. Maybe it was easier to be passive back then when he rarely felt ambivalent about anything and, on the occasions when he did, neither of ambivalence's tines dug very deep. In those days, passivity felt to him like inner strength.

One reason he feels strongly about the war in Iraq is because Esther and Emmanuelle talk about it and its horrors almost every evening. It is clearly a terrible and wrong-headed thing. Still, it was Esther who wanted to bring the kids to the parade; she sees no inconsistency in honoring our soldiers but reviling their current Commander in Chief. Recently, she attached a bumper sticker to the rear of Wendell's truck that said: **"I LOVE MY COUNTRY—but I think we should start seeing other people."** She manages to be both more earnest and more light-hearted than Wendell.

It is just such juxtapositions in Esther's character that delight him. She constantly surprises him, and those surprises invariably cheer him, make him feel more alive. But on the subject of Franny, Wendell does not want any surprises; the situation is baffling and disturbing enough as it is. For this reason, he rarely talks about Franny with Esther, and Esther respects this. She rarely mentions Franny herself.

Just before Franny was released from Austen Riggs, Dr. Werner asked for individual meetings with Beatrice and

Wendell. It was Dr. Werner who informed Wendell that his daughter would not be returning to the house on Mahaiwe Street, that for the indefinite future it would be better for her to live apart from her father and daughter.

"She needs to define herself as an individual," the psychiatrist explained, but for the life of him Wendell could not fathom what that verdict meant. Wendell believed—indeed, he continues to believe—that Franny needs love, not definition. He wants to cradle her in security and unconditional acceptance. He wants her to wallow in the sanctuary of their home. But Wendell could not argue with Werner because he still did not understand what happened to his daughter and why he did not see it coming. Further, at the conclusion of his session with Werner, the doctor said, "It's better this way, Mr. deVries. She wouldn't be coming back to the same home anyway."

Those words devastated Wendell to the brink of tears— tears that he only managed to hold back until he was out the front door of the sanitarium. At that moment, he resolved to ask Esther, Kaela, Johnny, and Emmanuelle to move out so that Franny could come back to the home she knew. It was a sacrifice they all had to make, that they all could *afford* to make because, unlike Franny, they were stable and happy people. But Wendell could only maintain this resolution up to the Grandville town line. It was not that he changed his mind after carefully weighing the alternatives; he simply was overwhelmed by the magnetism of his present contentment.

Wendell lives with this act of selfishness daily. It is with him now as Matt Maxwell's band rolls by, guitars clanging, and Johnny salutes them with his hot dog, and giggles.

The ersatz music wafting up the hill and through Emmanuelle Jones's open, third-floor window serves a practical purpose: it almost blocks out the tumultuous hubbub on the other side of her bedroom wall. God knows, Emmanuelle does not begrudge Lila and her apparently indefatigable young man a single cry or groan of pleasure. They are joyful noises. But Emmanuelle's attempt to write clear, lyrical prose that captures the rhythm of Sarah deVries's nineteenth century trek from Georgia to Massachusetts is hampered, to say the least, by the young couple's relentlessly pounding counterpoint. The parade music is soothing by comparison.

Emmanuelle loves living in this house on Mahaiwe Street. She cannot remember a happier period in her adult life. Several weeks ago when she finally admitted to herself that there was not one more relevant document to be found in the Grandville Historical Society's or Zion Church's archives, or in the African-American collection at the University of Massachusetts, or in Wendell's personal trove of family journals, correspondence, and inscribed Bibles, she also admitted to herself that she did not want to return to her apartment in Atlanta, there to begin writing her book.

This change of heart began with the missing days—Days Eight through Fourteen of Sarah deVries's escape from slavery. Before coming to Grandville, Emmanuelle had convinced herself that all would be revealed in the journals kept by Sarah's daughter, Edith; surely the family chronicler would have an account of those missing days. But Emmanuelle uncovered nothing of the sort. In fact, Edith wrote, "[Sarah] will not speak of how she came to be here, neither of why—although the latter is self-evident. It is not my prerogative to insist she do so. Thus, it is left to the province of imagination."

Upon reading this, Emmanuelle despaired of continuing with her project. It would be more fruitful—and certainly more professional—to simply abandon Sarah deVries and start over with a fully-documented traveler on the Underground Railroad. She confessed to herself that she had too quickly been seduced by Uncle Billy's enthusiasm for a book about his great-great-grandmother and his promise of comprehensive resources about her here in Grandville. But such was the historian's lot. For every history written, millions go unwritten for lack of surviving evidence; a life unrecorded essentially does not exist. Still, that was hardly the case here. Eight days were unrecorded, but the days that framed the missing days were exhaustively documented. There was a vivid beginning and end.

Such was the private debate that babbled in Emmanuelle's mind for the better part of a week. Her housemates surely knew she was in some kind of turmoil, but they did not press her to reveal what it was—not even the hypersensitive and curious

Kaela. Emmanuelle took to long solitary walks down the hill, through town, across the bridge, and then almost to the town line before turning back. On one of these walks, she found herself repeating Edith's journal entry in her mind: 'Thus, it is left to the province of imagination.' Could not Emmanuelle imagine those missing days? Not out of whole cloth, of course. Indeed, with the bookend days of Beginning and End, the distance traveled from Point A to Point B, the geography and topography of the space between, even dependable accounts of the townships, flora, and fauna that dotted the way, could not Emmanuelle fashion a credible account of the missing days for her readers? Did perfect accuracy always trump a methodically inferred and richly imagined story? Some years ago, a colleague of Emmanuelle's had participated in a lecture series on memoir writing at the New York Public Library; the series was called, 'Inventing the Truth.' Emmanuel concluded that she, too, could invent the truth; she could conjure the missing days one at a time, even hour by hour, re-experiencing the passing landscape as Sarah deVries raced northward—the air she breathed, the shoots she ate, the spirit that drove her.

But no sooner had Emmanuelle reached this decision when she realized she dreaded the idea of writing such a speculative history among her friends and university colleagues in Atlanta. Even if they knew nothing of her *modus operandi*, she would sense their judgment of it every time she encountered them. Inexperienced as Emmanuelle was in this way of thinking and working, she appreciated that imagination did not flourish in a climate of doubt. Better to write where hardly a person knew her.

So, very tentatively, she broached the subject of remaining here with Esther. "You've got to be honest with me, Esther," she said. "This is your family and I don't want to intrude any more than I have already, so if—"

"What are you talking about?" Esther had said. "We always assumed you were going to write the book here. It's just part of—you know—the whole *gestalt*."

The whole gestalt! Emmanuelle has to laugh whenever she thinks about Esther's pronouncement. The heartfelt goofiness with which Esther expresses herself, her hodgepodge of Eastern philosophy and Western self-seriousness, never fails to charm Emmanuelle. It infects her with an optimism that goes a long way in quelling her personal doubts—not only doubts about her book project, but about why she feels so comfortable living here in an overwhelmingly white community. Why she, a scholar who has devoted her entire professional life to studying and interpreting the lives of African-Americans, feels so at home in this place. Is it some kind of escapism? In the end, is her fascination with her own tribe an inverse reaction to latent shame for belonging to it? Or more to the point, has she—as her ex-husband often said—become so white in her intellect that it has finally subjugated her black soul?

But then a compelling thought came to Emmanuelle: Maybe she was—for this little while—escaping her identity as a representative African-American, but in the process wasn't she regaining an identity of her own? In this small town, she finally could indulge her long-ignored desire to be a representative of no one except herself. No shame in that, no self-hate. Sure, she knew what Uncle Billy meant when he said that prejudice in Grandville was a subtle thing. She saw the puzzlement in townspeople's eyes when she walked down Main Street or waited in line at the Grand Union. She sensed their flashes of nervousness and wonderment. She was even aware of the self-congratulatory enthusiasm behind the vociferous, 'Hello's' and 'Hi there's' that some Grandvillians launched in her direction when she walked among them. But it was only *she* they were responding to—*her* strangeness, and there was something oddly reassuring about that.

Lila's ecstatic shriek eclipses the whole musical extravaganza down in town. Emmanuelle wonders if Lila could be heard in downtown Grandville. *God love young people who are discovering sex for the first time, and God keep them from realizing that it will never be the same again.*

Lila is laughing in Hector's arms.

"Oh God, I'm so loud!" she says to her lover.

"But it is beautiful," Hector replies. "The most beautiful love song I have ever heard." He nuzzles into a spray of golden hair that covers her right breast and kisses it. Everything about this girl tastes sweet to him. Here, in this bedroom, in this town in America, Hector has discovered a contentment he never could have imagined. This feeling is with him from when he wakes in the morning until he falls asleep at night in the apartment behind the Wright Mountain Motel that he shares with the other restaurant workers.

Hector loves Lila deVries. The truth is, he never in his life thought about love, not this kind, entirely different from the love he saw between his mother and father, or from whatever it was he felt for Sylvia. The love between his parents was gentle and honest, but it was not passionate; in Puerto Alvira, the business of day-to-day survival eliminated the very concept of passionate love. And as to Sylvia, she was a dream of passion, which is altogether different from tasting it on the naked body lying next to him. Even making love is as new to Hector as it is to Lila. Yes, he has performed this act with many women; it would even be false to deny that he had learned to perform it pleasingly under their tutelage. But what he feels with Lila, this union of souls, is as astonishing as if he had been a virgin too.

"We should probably get dressed," Lila is saying. "They'll be coming home soon."

"But first I must say goodbye to *all* of you." Hector slithers down to the foot of the bed. He kisses the soles of her feet and says, "*Mas tardes.*" Lila wiggles her toes and trills back in a TV cartoon voice, "*Mas tardes,* Hector." He repeats the game at her knees, her thighs, her mound of Venus, her navel, her breasts, her neck, her lips.

There is only one part of Lila that baffles Hector, and that is her insistence that before she met him, there was no tenderness in her at all. In fact, she says, she hated this town and everyone in it. But Hector does not believe this could be true; he believes her sweetness was always there, if only waiting for him to taste it.

"*Mas tardes.*"

"*Mas tardes,* Hector."

"*Sodomy, Fellatio, Cunnilingus, Pederasty*
Father, why do these words sound so nasty?"

Babs Dowd cuts off the singer, Ned Shields, and the rehearsal pianist in mid-song. The racket outside the theater is simply too deafening to get through "Sodomy" with any finesse. She calls for a ten-minute break.

Staging *Hair* for the Phoenix's grand re-opening was a brilliant inspiration—Babs's own, actually—and securing a name TV actor, Brad Doleman, to play Berger was one hell of a coup, but so far the rehearsals have been one little fiasco after another. For starters, there are electricians, carpenters, carpet layers, and plumbers all over the theater day and night. Even that imported, two-hundred-dollar-a-day Italian still lurks around the place, brushes and palette in hand, slapping on what he calls, "touches *brilliante.*" Never mind that the workers are a good month behind in the completion schedule; they simply cannot get it through their heads that Babs and her cast need some semblance of order if they are ever going to get this show up for opening night. Add to that the fact that some of the Grandville Players in the production are simply out of their depth, God love them. Like Sally Rule. The only age-appropriate role for Sally was the Tourist from Ohio—*Ohio*, for godssake, not London. *You cannot play Lady Britomart in every damn show we put on, old girl.* Even sweet Ned is lost. Miscast, to put it generously. He begged to play Woof and Babs gave in, convincing herself that a wooly wig and some heavy foundation would cut the requisite twenty years off his on-stage appearance, but there was nothing the makeup artist could fashion to disguise Ned's forty-something body and its forty-something ungainliness. If Babs had not been completely convinced of this in their private run-throughs, it was painfully obvious the first time Brad Doleman showed up for a rehearsal. Shuffling alongside twenty-two-year-old Brad in the 'Hashish' production number, Ned looked positively geriatric, more stone than stoned. But what could Babs do? She could not hire an *entire* out-of-town cast. Not for this show, at least. For that matter, not *ever* if every New York and Hollywood actor turned out to be as precious as young Mr. Doleman. The kid had missed three out of the first five rehearsals for reasons on the order of 'my dog ate my homework.' Damn it, if he thinks he is too good for Grandville, he should bow out now. Heaven knows, he would regret it later after the Phoenix was right up there with the Long Wharf Theater and the Louisville Playhouse in the pantheon of great American regional theaters.

Babs walks up the aisle and out the Phoenix's front door, offering a stoic face to the workers and technicians she passes along the way. Outside, she lights up a Virginia Slim, her renewed old vice. As usual, the actors gathered out here in groups of twos and threes give her wide berth. The first few times they did this, Babs assumed it was a gesture of professional courtesy, giving the producer/director some personal space to think creative thoughts. But a few overheard conversations set her straight on that: The actors, along with just about everyone else in this town, feel sorry for her, the brave wife of poor, broken Michael Dowd. They are leaving her alone in her despair.

Well, they are right about that—she does feel awful about poor Michael—but nonetheless she resents their solicitousness. If there is one thing she will never be able to tolerate about this little town, it is its sticky sweetness. Pity comes too quickly to Grandvillians. It is not exactly that Babs suspects them of reveling in their compassion, but the people here do take an unseemly amount of pride in their picturesque American virtues. It is supremely cloying.

Right there is one reason Babs chose *Hair* for her opener—as a little wake-up call for the town. Those old time values are sweet, but they are totally out of sync with the gritty realities of today's world. Show compassion to that Bush-Cheney bunch and all those Washington megalomaniacs see is another opportunity to pull a fast one. Babs's mission is to inspire her audience with the rapture of rebellion, to remind them what it feels like to be contrary and proud of it. Of course, she never mentioned this rationale for *Hair* to the Phoenix's board of directors. She was more than happy to let the seat counters embrace the American Tribal Love-Rock Musical for their own purposes, namely that it would pull in the baby boomer second-homers and retirees by the SUV-load—those folks were perfectly ripe for some '60s nostalgia about long hair, free love, and pot. *Whatever,* as Daphne would say.

Down the Melville Block on Main Street, the Memorial Day paraders are closing ranks in front of the Shays' Rebellion Monument. Even right on top of one another, each contingent persists in blaring its individual anthem, but suddenly—for just one second—the randomness of the universe conspires to put Whitney Pierce, Jr.'s piccolo, the horn section of the Grandville High School marching band, the Mormon Tabernacle Choir, and The Tombstones, on a single note—D sharp. Without quite being conscious why, the surrounding people smile in unison. Babs cannot help but smile too. There is hope for these people yet.

Pushing her father across the intersection, Daphne Dowd glimpses her mother smoking a cigarette under the Phoenix's marquee. She reflexively turns the wheelchair sharply to the left so her dad will not see her. At least once a day Michael says he is glad Babs has a project to keep her busy during this difficult period in their lives, and Daphne is inclined to believe he really means it—the accident has turned him into a regular pussycat—but Daphne despises her mother's selfishness and wishes her father did too. Not to mention her mother's hypocrisy; the woman actually thinks putting on some old-fashioned, feel-good musical about hippies is going to start a revolution. *Yeah, right—the old farts will charge out of the Phoenix and head for the barricades, humming those stupid ditties as they go.*

Both her parents are so out of it they do not have a clue the whole town is talking about them. One thing about going to public school is it plugs you in to the town where you live. The kids at Hotchkiss do not really have a hometown; when they slog to their parents' homes for vacations, it is like visiting some foreign realm, one that happens to be peopled by substandard human beings. Daphne hears every Grandville rumor the moment she clambers on to the school bus in the morning. And so she knows that her parents are the last two people in town who actually believe the person who ran over her dad was just some random motorist who did not stop because he was afraid it would jack up his insurance premiums.

The kids on the school bus do not attempt to shield Daphne from the gossip about the accident. Actually, her willingness to engage in the gossip with them has elevated her status considerably. She knows there is something seriously perverse about the source of her sudden popularity, but she cannot help but enjoy it. Anyway, she would give anything to know who the hell ran over her father, and that had nothing to do with gossip or popularity.

The first suspect Daphne heard mentioned was Lila's mother. Everybody knew the Dowds had stolen the Phoenix from Franny deVries and her father, and everybody knew Franny was a crazy who had tried to burn down the theater. It took Daphne to point out that Lila's mother was still in the mental hospital that night. One kid then suggested it was Lila herself who did it, an act of payback for her poor mother. There was no way in hell Daphne could believe that; she knew Lila well enough to know how she felt about her mother, and it definitely was not a feeling that inspired revenge on her mother's behalf. Sure, Lila had changed since she took up with that Spanish pretty boy—and dropped blogging, smoking pot, and their incipient friendship in the process—but that was after the accident anyhow.

The next candidate was Ned Shields, the drama teacher at the community college and an actor in the Grandville Players. The kids were a bit more circumspect about bringing up Shields's name in front of Daphne, never quite saying straight out that Daphne's mother was obviously having an affair with him, and that jealous Ned wanted her all to his own so he tried to kill her husband. People are weird that way: They have no problem talking in front of you about who had a good reason to try to kill your father, but they get all shy and giggly on the subject of your mother's sex life. Daphne truly does not give a damn if her mother screws the entire male population of Grandville, but she does not believe for a minute that her mother has a lover. The only thing Mother fucks with is people's minds—*that* is her sex life.

One morning, the cop, Flip Morris, was the suspect *du jour*. Any student of popular culture could have seen that one coming; it followed the predictable American pattern of trashing yesterday's hero. Flip is the one who found her father in the road that night, then lifted him into his cruiser and sped all the way to Baystate Hospital in Springfield. He may have saved Dad from bleeding to death, and he surely is the main reason Dad stands a good chance of completely recovering the use of his legs. Flip's face was on the front page of the *Eagle* the next day and the weekly *Chronicle* the day after. It is undoubt-edly why he landed that solo turn in today's parade along with the Girl Scouts—just his speed, according to Lila's appraisal of him. The revised story goes that Flip was drunk, ran over her father by accident, and then took him to the hospital so nobody would suspect him. It was his cover-up that gave him away. *Yeah, right.* That theory did not play any longer than fif-teen minutes in the yellow bus.

Last week, a new candidate emerged from the back of the bus. A senior from Stockbridge, who hardly ever said anything to anyone, declared with absolute authority that a hit man did it, hired by an irate New York investor who had lost money in Dowd's mutual fund. The senior allowed that his own father, an investment banker, knew this as a fact. This scenario had a lot going for it, starting with the fact that a senior proclaimed it, but closely followed by its artful mix of a TV crime drama's staple plot line with a villain based in the very city that—every local knew—was bent on destroying everything that was sacred in Grandville. At school, Daphne had tried the theory out on her new friend, Stephanie, but Stephanie dismissed it the way she dismissed all the others, saying it was just gossip with no way to prove it. "Let's just think about your dad get-ting better," Stephanie said.

Daphne positions her father's chair as close to the front as she can so he can have an unobstructed view of the goings on. The music draws to a ragged, unceremonious conclusion as Dr. Armbruster, president of the Grandville Historical Society, steps to the microphone set in front of the Shays Mon-ument. He holds an old, hardboard, loose-leaf binder in his hands and within a minute after he opens it, all the onlookers are silent.

"Abraham Hart," Armbruster reads. "Isaiah Pickens and Samuel Troy." He turns the page and continues, "Anthony Woodruff, Philip North, Thomas Elkins, Winfred Porter, Taylor Cookson, Robert Nation, Theodore Timmerman, Blake Forester, and Clive Filks." Again, Armbruster turns a leaf. "Arthur Finnegan, Arthur Murdock, William Ashman, Daniel Flowers, and Ralph Mapes." A new page, "David Love, Antony

Armbruster, Paul O'Mara, Mark O'Mara, and Philip Wigglesworth." A new page. "Michael Simmons, Hans van Ardsdale, Meredith Locke—"

Franny deVries swings her feet onto the floor and stands in front of Herb's couch as she listens to old Dr. Armbruster recite the names of the war dead from Grandville, Massachusetts, starting with the three who fell in King Phillip's War, and moving on to the Revolution, Shays' Rebellion, the Barbary wars, the War of 1812. As always, Armbruster's tone is a dull drone.

"Lyman Hicks, Peter Gladwell, Lincoln Redmonds, Archer Keith, Simon Heath—"

Herb is at the open window, his hands braced on the sill as he leans out, cocking his head in the direction of the reader of names who has now turned the page from the Civil War to the Spanish-American War.

"Elliot Pierce, Adrian ten Hooven, Brian Nowak—"

Walking soundlessly in stockinged feet, Franny comes up behind Herb. His face, generally boyish and innocent looking, appears even more so just now. To Franny, it looks like the face of a rapt schoolboy straining to understand the meaning of words that are just beyond his grasp. Indeed, the words Armbruster speaks are beyond her grasp too—names without faces, deaths without mercy. One after another after another.

Franny wraps her arms tightly around Herbert Blitzstein's waist.

CHAPTER TWENTY-FIVE

In autumn, winter, or spring, it is not surprising to hear a native Grandvillian say, "Meet you in front of Vanderwinkle's," by which she means Vanderwinkle's Five & Dime, a Main Street shop that has not existed for fifteen years. Since that time, Vanderwinkle's address has been occupied by a high-priced French restaurant named Le Bistro; yet during the off seasons Le Bistro is open only on weekends and so, despite its snappy red and blue Art Deco sign, it remains 'Vanderwinkle's' to those of us who walk Main Street daily. But come the middle of June, the bistro opens seven days a week for both lunch and dinner and, taking advantage of a new town ordinance, places chairs and tablecloth-covered tables on the sidewalk in front of it. For the summer, Vanderwinkle's withers into history.

At that same time, grand nineteenth-century houses as near to town as the bottom of Mahaiwe Street are suddenly unshuttered and come to life with entire young families who look to the unknowing eye like quaint villagers in their pastoral skirts and blouses, faded, threadbare denim shirts, straw hats, and long-billed farmer caps. But to us, of course, they are easily recognizable as second-homers from large cities east and south of Grandville, come to the countryside for the summer to indulge in alternate lives of rusticity, their annual emotional realignment. Quaint is new, then is now.

But it is the upcoming reopening of the Phoenix Theater that tricks past with present most delightfully. No one is alive to remember that first grand opening in 1899, yet it remains an indelible event in Grandville consciousness along with the misty figure of the anonymous arsonist who made it possible. And gazing up at the restored and repainted marquee on Melville Street, it is easy to mingle the enthusiasm incited by the debut of the comic opera, *Happyland*, with the buzz of anticipation surrounding the opening of *Hair* this very night.

Posters and newspaper advertisements for *Hair* have turned up as far off as Keene, Boston, New Haven, Albany, and even New York City, where a two column-inch ad was spotted in the 'Escapes' section of the *New York Times*. "Good Morning Phoenix!" is the ad's headline. Before the curtain goes up tonight, Babs Dowd, the theater's artistic director, plans to preside over a dedication ceremony that includes the reading of a proclamation issued by the Governor of the Commonwealth of Massachusetts declaring this 'Phoenix Theater Day.' Tonight's performance was sold out ten days ago.

This also happens to be the day Lila deVries begins working both the lunch and dinner shifts at Nakota for the summer season. This in itself is hardly remarkable, but what is extraordinary is that Lila and Hector are leaving for work this morning *together*, having spent the night together in Lila's bed—with everybody else at home! This new arrangement was not Lila's idea and certainly not Wendell's; it was Esther and Emmanuelle's. The two women brought their plan to Wendell with a well-rehearsed argument that began with the premise that Lila and Hector were already sleeping together, so the question was not *what* they were doing, but *where* and *when* and—most critically—*how* they were doing it. From here they assembled a catalogue of reasons why allowing Hector to take up residence in Lila's bedroom made infinitely better sense than any alternative, including the utterly ridiculous charade they were all engaged in now.

Under the influence of Esther, Wendell deVries may have waded onto the shoals of modernity, but the idea of giving his blessing to his seventeen-year-old granddaughter's carnal relationship made him feel irresponsible bordering on degenerate. Even when Esther and Emmanuelle threw down their trump card, their stipulation that the young people would have to promise to practice birth control (the two women would personally take Lila to a gynecologist in anonymous Albany to be prescribed birth control pills), Wendell reserved his consent. He said he would have to think about it. But two days later, upon returning home from the shop, Wendell surprised everyone by announcing that he gave the plan his full approval.

Lila is giddy about the new setup. It instantly inspired in her a heretofore invisible streak of domesticity: She cannot stop thinking about ways to decorate *their* room. It should reflect both of them—his world and hers—tying them together poetically. As for Hector, he has very earnestly and ecstatically decided that this turn of events means the two of them are married.

Watching the long-limbed beauty sail down Melville Street on the crossbar of a bicycle, her blonde hair fluttering behind her and flapping against the narrow chest of the handsome, angular young man who is peddling the bike, we might think for a moment we had slipped back to an earlier Grandville, say, of the 1950s, when young people on Schwinns and Raleighs could be seen on virtually every street of town on a day like today. Often as not, a young woman such as this one would be riding sidesaddle on the crossbar, one hand pressing down her skirt lest it fly up. Or, rolling right down Main Street, a pair of cyclists in tandem, each steering with one hand while holding hands between them, the driver of the Nash Rambler jammed behind them rolling his eyes. Over there, a pack of eighth grade boys rambling up Board Street on Triumphs, shouting and joking and jostling to take the lead. And the inevitable tricksters, one high school boy peddling madly while his buddy balances precariously on the handlebars, his arms and legs stuck straight out like Da Vinci's Vitruvian Man. Bikes then were as much a part of Grandville's landscape as convertible cars and dogs romping free of leashes on the sidewalks in the middle of town.

Of course, we still see bicycles here now, maybe even as many as half a century ago, but today's pedal pushers are generally beyond school age and are distinguished by their garishly colored spandex shorts and jerseys, helmets, goggles, and grimaces of grim resolve. Or, alternatively, they are distinguished by their brown skin. The latter cyclists are undocumented workers who, even if they could afford an automobile, do not qualify for driver's licenses.

Hector is singing Lila's favorite bicycle ride song, "Amor Sin Medida," piping it straight into her ear as they whiz across the Wright River Bridge to where the road widens to officially become the highway. Lila takes up the chorus with him, her pronunciation perfect if her pitch less so. The traffic is denser here, mostly with out-of-town cars freshly off the Turnpike, so Hector pulls onto the shoulder for a safer if bumpier drive. Lila, who carries Hector's *cuatro* while they ride, cushions the instrument against her bosom.

Behind the restaurant, Hector leans his bike against the dumpster. He is still astonished by the fact that he does not need to lock it or remove its front wheel, an act of trust as unheard of in Danbury, Connecticut as it was in Bogotá. Lila lifts the *cuatro* strap over her head and hands the instrument to Hector. The young lovers embrace and bid one another a tender farewell even though they will see each other frequently over the next few hours. Over the course of a day, these two can pack in more sizzling 'hello's' and 'goodbye's' than a ship-load of sailors and a wharf-load of wives and lovers.

In Nakota's kitchen, the radio is tuned to WGVS, which is dedicating the entire day to celebrating the Phoenix's reopening. Earlier in the day, they aired some vintage 78s of operettas from the golden age of the Phoenix—"Long Live the Hungarians" from *The Gypsy Baron*, "He's Gone and Married Yum-Yum" from *The Mikado*, and "Vilya, O Vilya" from *The Merry Widow*. But now, as an overture to Bob Balducci's live interview with Babs Dowd from the stage of the theater, they are playing selections from the original cast recording of *Hair*, starting with "Aquarius" and "Donna," but discreetly skipping over "Hashish" and "Sodomy" to "Air" and "I Got Life." Both the Japanese and the Latin American staff appear about as roused by *Hair* as they were by *The Merry Widow*.

The lunch crowd—the biggest so far this summer—is loud and happy. Lila overhears many of them talking about tonight's show. The big question seems to be whether or not the cast will appear naked for the grand finale—in particular, whether or not Brad Doleman will bare all—as the original cast did on Broadway over thirty years ago. The general excitement pro-motes tips that average close to twenty percent.

At the break between the end of lunch and the beginning of dinner, Ichiro selects Hector to scale, clean, and precut the fresh shipment of fish from Boston. Hector's dexterity and quick intelligence have propelled him to the top of the heap in the Nakota kitchen. Lila keeps him company on a stool beside him.

At the eight o'clock curtain time, theatergoers are still meandering into the Phoenix, reluctant to leave the late evening sunshine. Some are looking down the Melville Block to Main Street where the vigil group is staging a specially planned and rehearsed pre-theater performance.

Franny is just now locking up Write Now where she has taken inventory and made out order sheets. These tasks are her way of easing herself back into her job without yet having to deal with customers. Nonetheless, these past two weeks Franny has begun appearing at the shop a half-hour or so before closing time while her father is still there. At these times, Franny and Wendell stand together behind the counter listening to *All Things Considered* and chatting a bit, mostly commenting on the news they hear, but here and there talking about goings-on in the town, and even, gradually and delicately, mentioning subjects closer to home, like Esther and her children.

And last week for the first time, Wendell brought up Lila. He was unpacking a carton of magazines when over his shoulder he said, "I need your permission for something, Monkey."

Franny was so startled and warmed by her father's use of her old home nickname that his message did not immediately register. Wendell simply went on unpacking as he described Esther and Emmanuelle's proposal for Lila and Hector's new living arrangement. "I needed to run it by you first, of course," he concluded.

Franny closed her eyes for several seconds, overcome with a feeling she had not experienced so profoundly in years— certainly since long before her breakdown. That feeling was pure sweet gratitude. Her father had just made her feel more worthy and human and sane than had four months of psychotherapy.

"Sure, I'm okay with that, Dad," she replied.

Franny catches the eye of many of the dawdling theatergoers—especially the men—as she scampers down Melville Street to join the vigil group. She is wearing her tie-dye peace symbol T-shirt, her breasts bounding, her loose hair and the colorful ribbons tied to her neck flying behind her. This is the first time she has donned a striking costume for almost a year and she finds herself feeling as liberated and buoyant as doing so made her feel back then.

Taking their cue from *Hair*, Tony and Gary have put together a program of songs, posters, and *tableaux vivantes* that flaunt the parallels between the Vietnam War and the war in Iraq. They have just concluded singing, "The Ballad of Ho Chi Minh," and move directly to "Kill For Peace." Fluttering above the group is a fifteen-foot-long banner with an outline map of Vietnam on one end and of Iraq at the other, the words 'Wrong Then, Wrong Again' in between. Tony and Gary, in their army uniforms, are holding up the Vietnam end of the banner, Tiffany and Gloria the Iraq end. Like Franny, most of the other 'vigil-istas' are wearing vaguely hippie-ish garb. Herb Blitzstein is sporting an oversized bowler that captures a certain '60s spirit, but also happens to suggest the spirit of an Old World *schtetel*—the hat once belonged to his Polish Jewish grandfather. As Franny joins the group, she tenderly clasps Herb's hand.

Stephanie Cyzinksi is a sartorial exception; she is wearing a modest, J. Crew blouse and khaki slacks, her hair pulled back in a pin-through comb. As she is most often seen in public these days, Stephanie stands at the 'push' end of Michael Dowd's wheelchair, although this evening without the company of Dowd's daughter, Daphne, who is skipping tonight's activities to take advantage of her empty house and the opportunity to get stoned in any room she desires.

Stephanie's devotion to Mr. Dowd—she has resigned from every one of her Grandville High School extra-curricular activities to accommodate her new career—is puzzling to everyone who knows her. To the few people who have asked her about it, Stephanie has offered a quasi-spiritual answer that includes the words 'fulfillment' and 'dedication' which, in turn, has given rise to the popular notion that Stephanie has undergone some kind of religious awakening. But what has awakened in Stephanie is hardly spiritual—it is her agonizing conviction that she knows exactly who was behind the wheel of the car that shattered Michael Dowd's thighs.

From the stage left wing, Babs gazes out at the audience. The aisles are still crowded and a good fifty or more seats remain unoccupied. It is already ten minutes past the hour and Babs is beginning to feel irritated with their dawdling, even if their laid-back attitude is reminiscent of that of New York audiences. Actually, most of them *are* New Yorkers—second homers; Babs can tell by their haircuts and jewelry and Barney's wardrobe. Also by their ease—going to an evening of live theater is hardly an extraordinary event for this group. But what is rare is going to live theater in the countryside, and this juxtaposition generates some giddiness in them; many wear the ironic smiles of people who relish an evening of low expectations. *Well,* Babs thinks, *they are in for a surprise.*

Babs has resigned herself to the fact that very few in the opening night audience are local—she had already surmised that from the reservation list. Of the complimentary tickets she sent out to the Grandville selectmen, various members of the town clergy, and both Wendell and Franny deVries, only Selectmen Bill Lakspur and Frank Delmolino, and Reverend Moody accepted. But she is sure the rest of the town will come around before the run is over.

There is some kind of disturbance at the back of the theater. Babs squints. She now makes out Michael's shoes and his brace and plaster-encased legs propped up in his wheelchair at the top of the main aisle. Whatever other effect her husband's arrival may have had, it does get the rest of the crowd to take their seats so the show can finally begin.

Because Grandville is ringed with mountains, the longest days of the year are shorter by twenty minutes than in the plains only ten miles east of here. The sun starts to dip behind Wright Mountain at eight-thirty, throwing off refracted ochre light that illuminates the tops of trees and steeples and, out on the highway, the pagoda tower on top of the Nakota. The pre-theater crowd is gone from that restaurant and the usual lull before the arrival of older, child-free diners has begun. Lila has only one table left to deal with before she can take a break. It is occupied by a Connecticut family with two teenagers who are disappointed by the absence of ginger ice cream on the desert list and grouse about it before settling for green tea sorbet. Bringing their order back to the kitchen, Lila sees that Hector, Pato, and Alarico are already on their break, so she asks Takaaki to cover the Connecticut family for her. She goes to her locker, removes a cigarette and her lighter from her jeans pocket, and heads for the kitchen door. There, she stops for a moment, listening for Hector's voice in song, but she does not hear it. When she steps outside, a hand clamps over her mouth from behind. Another hand seizes her arm.

"Be good," Flip Morris hisses in Lila's ear.

Lila responds with a backward kick at Flip's shin. She wrenches her head back and forth, trying to free her mouth so she can scream. But Flip twists her arm behind her, pushing it straight up until the pain is so great she thinks she will pass out. In the instant, Lila wonders if losing consciousness might be her best option—that crazed as Flip is, he would take no satisfaction from raping her limp body.

"Bitch!" Flip seethes.

Suddenly Lila spots the beam of a flashlight out by the dumpster. Then the gleam of reflective stripes—no, not stripes, letters. White capital letters, 'STATE POLICE' and 'K-9.' The letters are on the backs of dark jackets worn by ghostly figures. Half a dozen policemen. It is a drug raid. Lila's eyes dart from one man to the other, from the corner of the dumpster to the black car idling behind it. She is searching for Hector.

Lila's jaw goes slack. Then, with a surge of extraordinary strength, she snaps her teeth into Flip's hand. He howls.

"Hector!" Lila screams, twisting away from Flip.

"Lila!" Hector cries back from inside the car.

Two of the men in lettered jackets intercept Lila as she races toward her lover. One of them, following procedure, tackles and handcuffs her.

The Phoenix Theater audience is on its feet, applauding and cheering as the curtain parts for a fifth and final time and the cast of *Hair* breaks into an impromptu reprise of "Good Morning Starshine," this time adding overtones of irony to the 'gliddy glub gloopies' and 'nibby nabby noopies' of the baby-talk lyric. Babs Dowd sashays in from the wings with a basket of daisies and proceeds to hand them to her players one at a time. The actors, dutiful Flower Children, tuck the blossoms in their hair and laugh.

As the theater's board of directors had hoped and predicted, the spectators are enthralled by the backward look
to the psychedelic '60s. But also, as Daphne Dowd predicted,
it has not inspired any one of them to tune in or drop out or
commit themselves to a life of rebellion. The sole noncon-
formist in the crowd is Selectman Frank Delmolino who found
the show to be in extreme bad taste but, per his wife's whispered instructions, he says nothing as they file out of the theater on to Melville Street.

On the porch of their house, Wendell and Esther hear the
cheery hubbub of the crowd leaving the theater below them in
town. Wendell groans. "That settles it," he says. "All politics is
entertainment."

Inside, the phone is ringing. Suddenly, Emmanuelle appears
at the door trembling.

"Lila's at the police station!" she cries. "And Hector's in
jail!"

CHAPTER TWENTY-SIX

We shall hasten ahead here as Herb finds an attorney to represent Hector. His name is Roland Axelrod and he is a Boston criminal lawyer who specializes in drug cases. Axelrod has a second home only ten miles from Grandville in the town of Becket—his wife is a modern dance aficionada and serves on the board of the summer dance festival in that town—so he generously invites the deVries group to his country bungalow for a face-to-face meeting.

Mrs. Axelrod serves lemonade to the guests—Lila, Franny, Herb, and Wendell—on her back patio before Attorney Axelrod commences business by placing a manila file folder on the wrought-iron table at which they are all seated. Then in a soothing, if somewhat mechanical voice, he lists what he calls "Mr. Mondragon's practicable options."

He starts by saying that regardless of the fact that the State Police found no drugs on Hector, Officer Flip Morris's testimony that he personally witnessed the Colombian smoking marijuana with a minor, Ms. Lila deVries, was sufficient to indict the young man.

"He's lying!" Lila shouts. She looks both haggard and wired, the result of an entire week of sleeplessness and fury. No one in her home has been able to calm her; indeed, she has barely spoken to any of them.

Axelrod nods evenly. "I have no doubt that he is," he says. "But a police officer's testimony is more or less inviolable in a case such as this one."

"But he's lying!" Lila repeats loudly.

"In any event," Axelrod continues, unfazed, "even if Mr. Mondragon were able to beat the drug charge, this would have no bearing on the finding of the Immigration and Naturalization Service that he was in the United States illegally, not only having overstayed his two-week tourist visa by almost a year, but by knowingly and willfully contravening its provision not to engage in gainful employment in this country. In most cases this means his best option is immediate repatriation with the proviso that he will never, under any circumstances, be allowed to re-enter this country. This is the option his two colleagues have taken."

"You mean they'd send him back to Colombia?" Wendell asks.

"Yes."

"I'll go with him!" Lila cries. There is not a doubt in her mind that she would be content to live anywhere in the world as long as she was with Hector, even as she knows that Hector never wants to see his homeland again.

"But fortunately there is another alternative that has just opened up," Axelrod goes on, barely acknowledging Lila's outburst. "In fact, I have already spoken with Mr. Mondragon about it and he has fully endorsed it. In this option, the drug charges will be dropped and the immigration offense suspended—in fact, in due time he will be granted citizenship in this country."

Of the group gathered around the patio table, only Herbert Blitzstein anticipates what is coming next and his craggy face involuntarily breaks into an agonized grimace.

"The compensation for this option," Axelrod says, "is two years' service in the United States Army."

* * *

Mr. Axelrod manages to arrange a five-hour window of freedom between Hector's Pittsfield cell and his troop bus to Fort Jackson, South Carolina. For three of those hours, Hector and his beloved Lila make love in their upstairs room in the house on Mahaiwe Street. Down below, Esther, Franny, and Emmanuelle play the stereo at top volume—a CD of Stravinsky's Greatest Hits that could mask the screams of a stadium full of Ricky Martin fans—while they concoct the Colombian yucca soup Emmanuelle found described on the web.

It would be impossible for the three women to hear one another if they spoke, so they make do with hand gestures and facial expressions, Emmanuelle pointing from the oxtail on the counter to the just-boiled pot of water as a signal for Esther to drop the former into the latter, Franny smiling through tears to show her co-cooks that she is all right, that her tears are only caused by the fumes of the onion she is shredding. Each of the women is thankful for this absence of words; there is nothing new they could possibly say. Nonetheless, there is a fervent message that passes between them which has nothing to do with the soup, although it could be said that it is embodied in its making: *Do not forget for an instant that this is a celebration. Of love and hope, and of the moment.*

Wendell returns from Write Now with Kaela and Johnny in tow. The children have skipped day camp so as not to miss a moment of Hector's going-away dinner. Instead, Kaela helped Wendell around the store while Johnny worked on his newly-developed reading skills by reading aloud every word on every candy wrapper. All three heard "The Rite of Spring" emanating from their house as they started up Mahaiwe Street, but as they mount the porch the music abruptly stops.

Inside, Lila and Hector are descending the stairs. Soup is on.

If that evening we were to mount the porch of the home on Mahaiwe Street much the way Franny deVries did over a month ago and, as she did, secretly peer through the front picture window on our right at the nine diners gathered around the long table as they ladle lumpy soup from a clay tureen at the table's center and pour red wine from a bottle into juice glasses, most of them chatting vivaciously, smiling, laughing, and looking into one another's eyes, we would probably be struck by the singular coherence of this motley assembly of young and old, brown and black, white and tawny people. And if, like members of an audience at the beginning of a new play or perhaps a film, we knew nothing about the characters arrayed in front of us, we undoubtedly would start making guesses about their relationships to one another and how they came to be together in this place on this particular evening.

We might be drawn first to the heavenly smile of the Asian girl who is seated between a handsome Hispanic young man and a middle-aged woman with frizzy red hair whose own smile—particularly its impish asymmetry—bears a remarkable resemblance to the girl's. This child's sparkling eyes dart from one face to another, never settling for longer than a split second. It is obvious that she is not merely observing with her flashing eyes; she is, in a sense, conducting with them, quickening the tempo of this little band's interplay, brightening its tone. It strikes us that she, more than anyone else at the table, is conscious of the unrepeatable significance of this gathering.

Next, we observe the dark complected young man to her right who, even as we watch him, becomes increasingly animated. He has just taken his first spoonful of the soup and every eye is upon him. He cocks his head back, causing a hank of black hair to fall across his forehead, and he looks toward the ceiling as if in deep solitary thought. He is impersonating a connoisseur, say a wealthy Frenchman in a four-star Bogotá restaurant who is evaluating the local Cabernet. Suddenly he stands, reaches for his wine glass and raises it high. He is toasting the soup. Everyone applauds, including the very young, red headed boy sitting on the other side of the red haired woman. Before we move on, we note that this little kid clearly was not in need of anyone else's appraisal of the soup—he is already reaching for seconds.

Next, we observe the oldest and quietest occupant of the table, a beefy, white haired man with rosy cheeks that appear even redder than they are in contrast to his white stubble. He, too, is looking from face to face, but his gaze always returns to the blonde, thirtyish woman directly across from him. Watching him for a moment, we gradually realize that every time he diverts his eyes from this woman they have just begun to dampen. Something about seeing her moves him deeply, so he has to look away to regain control of himself before he looks at her again. We cannot know what prompts this older fellow's reaction, but if it includes some sadness, it also contains contentment.

We cannot help but wonder what it is about this blonde woman that so disturbs the older man. She is classically beautiful; indeed, there is something regal about her bearing, her head fully upright on her slender neck. Even her eyes bespeak good breeding—deep mineral blue, a rarefied earthiness. Only by inspecting them closely do we detect the bewilderment they reveal. It is as if this young woman cannot know for certain where to look or what to feel, as if she cannot connect completely with either the world around her or the self within her.

As with any group this large, a minority of its members speak more and more loudly and animatedly than all the others combined. Among those here is a pony-tailed and bearded, Semitic-looking man whose voice is the only one to carry through the double-glazed window, not that we can make much sense of the words that penetrate the glass—'biconditional' and 'recursive' and 'ontological.' Surprisingly, the off-the-beat cadence of his speech and the goofball expression on his face seem more like those of a late night TV comedian than of a grown man given to using words like 'recursive' around a dining table. It is clear this man has met his match in the two other members of this vocal minority, the red haired woman and the attractive black woman seated to his right, both of whom cut him off regularly in mid-declamation.

There is an unusually pretty teenage girl at the table too, sandwiched between the handsome young soup connoisseur and the blonde woman who so deeply affects the white haired man across from her. The girl is blonde also; in fact, her eyes and mouth and long waist so closely resemble that of the woman next to her we have no doubt they are closely related, probably mother and daughter. There is so much emotion in this teenager's face, feelings that appear simultaneously to span hopefulness and despair, lovingness and fear, that it is difficult for us to look upon her face for long. In our uneasiness we drop our gaze, and in so doing we see one of this girl's hands resting on the thigh of the dark-complected young man and her other tightly clasping the hand of the woman on her right, the woman who most certainly is her mother.

Now would seem the apposite moment for us to step away from the deVries family's porch window, to gather up our jackets and bags and depart the theater into the cool evening with a sense of quiet fulfillment.

Now.

The world is a den of thieves and night is falling. Evil breaks its chains and runs through the world like a mad dog. The poison affects us all. No one escapes. Therefore let us be happy while we are happy. Let us be kind, generous, affectionate and good. It is necessary and not at all shameful to take pleasure in the little world.